ASPHODEL

The Second Volume of the Muse Chronicles

David P. Jacobs

To Van + Lisa —

Always remember — you can, and will, inspire anyone!

— David P. Jacobs

ASPHODEL
The Second Volume of the
Muse Chronicles
Copyright © David P. Jacobs
Published 14 February 2014
ISBN 978-1495433917

The right of David P. Jacobs to be identified as author of this Work has been asserted by him in accordance with sections 77 and 78 of the Copyright, Designs and Patents Act 1988.

All rights reserved. No part of this publication may be reproduced, stored in retrieval system, copied in any form or by any means, electronic, mechanical, photocopying, recording or otherwise transmitted without written permission from the publisher.

This is a work of fiction. Names, characters, businesses, places, events and incidents are either the products of the author's imagination or used in a fictitious manner. Any resemblance to actual persons, living or dead, or actual events is purely coincidental.

Cover design by Anelia Savova
https://www.crowdspring.com/user/Ann_RS/

For my dear friend Susan Summers
who, after hearing of my first volume, inquired,
"What happens next?"

*"Some people put walls up, not to keep people out,
but to see who cares enough to knock them down."*

Socrates

*"History is a cyclic poem written by time
upon the memories of man."*

Percy Bysshe Shelley

CHAPTER 1: CAULIFLOWER

History is inundated with haunting mysteries and long-forgotten secrets. It is twisted with darkened, shadow-riddled stairwells, catacombs of heroes, villains, unrequited love stories, ancient texts of wicked parables and disillusioned dreams. It is overgrown with the wastelands of wars, of unrealized desires, of precarious first steps and breathtaking quests of character. All one has to do is find the right stray string to tug in order to divulge the grander, more revealing thread which weaves itself deep under the surface like a persistent weed. But if there were ever a more inflexible twine to unknot, it would be that of the afterlife. There, in the outskirts of the waking world, lies even more complicated brambles. It is in these long discarded remnants where we find the commonality between the incongruous turns of the living. It is where we find the glue that ties the stories together. We find the true backbone of the tales, the spine to a fantastically crafted narrative which could only make sense in the make-shift world of midnight imaginings.

It was in the afterlife that our story began, on a day that such an inviting string presented itself, much to the chagrin of its owner. It quickly began to unravel, and would continue to, until all the surreptitious moments of his past would be displayed in their startling entirety. To fully comprehend how the lives of the man named

Nathaniel J. Cauliflower had been disentangled, one would have to review the day when, and how, the initial extrication took place. And it happened firstly with these simple instructions:

"'*Musing and You*' brought to you by Management. Narrated by Nathaniel J. Cauliflower," declared a male's voice. The instructional video could still be heard despite the sound of falling colored Lite-Brite pegs and distant roaring thunder. "Since the beginning of time, muses have been inspiring the world around them - painters, writers, sculptors, dreamers and lovers: you name it, they have done it. According to Greek mythology, there were nine. Born of Zeus and Mnemosyne, they each had their own private field of expertise: Terpsichore was the muse of dance; Urania, muse of Astronomy; Thalia, muse of Comedy; Melpomene, muse of tragedy; Clio, muse of history; and the four muse poets: Polyhymnia for sacred poetry; Euterpe for music and lyric poetry; Calliope of epic poetry; and Erato of love poetry.

"Each worked tirelessly, for centuries, criss-crossing backwards and forwards throughout time until, one day, they hired replacements and retired. These replacements were randomly chosen, given offices after their deaths, and trained by the very first muses in the universe's history. As time progressed, these 'First Generation Muses' filled their quotas and hired the next generation of replacements, and the Second Generation progressed to the Third. The Third passed it on to the Fourth, and then they passed it on to the Fifth, and so on . . . which means if you are watching this training video, you are now one of the elite. You, dear muse, are one of the Tenth Generation. Now we know what a muse is, so let's talk about what a muse does and, more specifically, how they do it.

"First introduced in the year 1967 by Hasbro, the Lite-Brite board was devised to allow artists to create pictures by the use of translucent colored pegs when inserted into a grid covered by opaque black paper. A light bulb inside the device, once activated, caused the peg colors to illuminate. A muse in training," the narrator preached, "is given an empty Lite-Brite board, but for a slightly different purpose. You see, dear muse, envelopes are delivered to a muse's post box, and inside each envelope is a colored peg. Whether it's blue, green, yellow, purple, pink, red, white, orange, or cream with bright red polka-dots, the peg is then taken from the envelope and placed into the Lite-Brite board. That's when things for the muse becomes quite complex. The office folds and unfolds like an elaborate pop-up book. The colored peg transports you into the corresponding life of a specific person, place and time. Once there, it's up to the muse to decide how to proceed. Your job, as the muse, is to inspire the person in that specific page of his or her very own story. Once the inspiration job is done in the allotted time, the book is closed, and the muse is returned to the office to await the next peg. This process repeats itself until the entire Lite-Brite board is full. Then, and only then, will the muse retire, with a replacement starting a . . ." the message grew obscured by static, finally returning to normal by the word "board."

The narration sustained in a battle of dialogue between its important memorandum and the rumbling that surrounded it.

"There are several things to think about before venturing forth, dear muse: the first is the water cooler. Water is a conduit, a necessity for traveling from place to place. Drinking the water lubricates the transition of traveling through these passages. Without it, the journey would be excruciating. Second," the narrator marshaled, "time for the muse is circular, which means that you can travel both forwards and backwards through time. Remember that past, present and future exist both harmoniously and simultaneously. Therefore, don't be surprised if you're inspiring a person suffering from vertigo to bungee jump with his friends one moment and then, inspiring the painting of the Sistine Chapel the next.

"Third and most importantly: do not, under any circumstances, leave an envelope unattended. The window of time, or the page of the person's pop-up book, is only open for a limited interval and can only be opened by you."

The instructional video skipped on itself, repeating the words "by you" three times before continuing on.

". . . Butterfly wings and earthquakes, dear muse! Finish one job before moving onto the next. You now play a vital part in humanity, dear muse. No one you inspire is too great or too small. No task is ever out of your control. You, by yourself, hold the reins to inspiration. You can and will inspi-"

The voice was then silenced completely as the ceiling of the conference room, which held the projector that had been playing the video, collapsed under the weight of the storm's onslaught. All that remained was the overlapping crashes of thunder along with the cacophony of raining colored pegs. The owner of the voice, and the narrator of the instructional video, Nathaniel J. Cauliflower, was currently standing in the Musing Department at the time that his pre-recorded words were forcefully muted. He wore a crisp white dress shirt, pressed corduroy pants, brown suspenders and matching circular glasses. His head was bald, his face was clean-shaven. Though Nathaniel looked to be in his mid-thirties, his brown eyes clearly gave away an age that was far older.

He stood in an office space adjacent, and three doors from, the conference room. The specific workplace had been constructed with dark stained wood and nine distinctly different porches. There were four on each side and a ninth vestibule in the far back of the room. Each opened up to dissimilar, but equally impressive, thunderstorms, forever stuck on their approach but never quite making it. The office had recently played host to a Tenth Generation muse who had allowed an individual to go uninspired, causing a chain reaction of colored pegs to fall. It had also, many envelopes prior, been home to a Second Generation Muse, a woman named Evangeline, who had done the same.

Evangeline's initial neglectfulness had become a renowned account throughout the decades. It told of a muse who had been assigned to put a misdirected letter into the wrong mailbox and, in so doing, further the life of a client. It also told of how Evangeline had failed and of the disaster that unfolded. It warned of how the individuals who had been destined to be inspired by the client never got inspired and, as a catastrophic chain reaction, the resulting client's pegs had begun to fall. It had been a convoluted web that Nathaniel had worked determinedly for years to regulate. The original story had become so remote, each muse who inspired afterwards merely thought of it as a cautionary tale. But now, because the Tenth Generation muse had intentionally followed in Evangeline's footsteps, the colored pegs were falling from the ceiling again. The once dormant legend of Evangeline was reawakened. Its astounding reality, and consequently the state of the living world by translation of the outpouring of colored pegs, was nothing short of staggering.

But to Nathaniel, the falling colored pegs did not cause his heart to race. Instead it was the presence of a cabinet at the far end of the "thunderstorm hall" which caused a single tear to trace down his cheek. The cabinet's top half was constructed by glass, which had been flung open before his arrival. There were several overturned framed photographs of muses past. The only two still standing upright, and staring back at him across the distance, was his own face along with the visage of a centennial-aged Evangeline. Upon looking on her pale remembrance, Nathaniel couldn't help but to recall how much he loved her, and how his love had inadvertently been her downfall.

He would never forget, after all these years, the last words Evangeline had spoken to him while they both stood before the mailbox in what would have been her final official inspiration.

"I'm sorry," Evangeline had told him on that day. "I love you, but I'm sorry."

He still heard those words, daring not to look away from the open cabinet for fear that, in doing so, it might forsake his affections.

The bottom half of the cabinet, which was once secured by a ten-lettered combination lock, also lay open. Atop a desk, beside a Lite-Brite board, sat the exposed contents: a sealed jar with twenty-one dead dandelions, another jar with a single page ripped from an ancient ledger and an opened hand-carved wooden box. The box was decorated with engraved dandelions along the surface and was once secured by a dandelion-shaped lock. Inside the box was a document entitled *The Lives and Times of Nathaniel J. Cauliflower*; loose-leaf pages that were now scattered in fistfuls by the gales of forthcoming thunderstorms. How Nathaniel hated to see his past displayed like this. Having it occupy his mind was one thing; physically seeing it before him, and mixed with the flood of colored pegs, was another.

There came a comforting hand on his left shoulder. Nathaniel turned to find Fiona, his Head Muse, a seemingly forty year-old woman who wore a baby blue pants suit, matching heels and pearl earrings. Fiona's hair waved luxuriously in the breeze. Both stood for several seconds respectfully staring into the office and toward the cabinet as the last few colored pegs tumbled down. Though the tinted falls had run dry, the work ahead of them would no doubt be a fatiguing movement.

"We've been through this before, Mr. Cauliflower," Fiona told Nathaniel. "You know what has to be done." The more words Fiona spoke the more Nathaniel could detect a subtle British accent.

"Yes, I know," said Nathaniel. He pulled out nine violet envelopes from his left pants pocket and handed them to her. Each envelope was firmly fastened with dried amber-colored wax emblazoned with a dandelion seal. "You'll find all nine of them there, including the invitation for Annette Slocum." Nathaniel's look was full of concern.

"You know what it could mean by bringing Mrs. Slocum back here, yes?" Fiona inquired. "What it could cost us?"

"Even so . . ." Nathaniel responded, deep in thought.

"I can stay and organize the colored pegs if you would like to fetch our muses," which was Fiona's way of telling Nathaniel she would secure his personal history within the cabinet for him.

Nathaniel, taking Fiona's hint, said "No. It's my mess now just as it was my mess then. I'll attend to the colored pegs and regain a sense of organization. Gather the others. Tell them a warm meal will be here to greet them."

"Don't go to too much trouble, Mr. Cauliflower," Fiona told her dear friend.

"I prepared it shortly before the colored pegs descended," Nathaniel reassured Fiona. "It would be a shame to have it go to waste."

Nathaniel had worn many hats over the past generations: colored-peg aficionado, post-master and chef, nevertheless all of those roles seemed quite insignificant now due to the conditions.

"I'm sure they will look forward to sharing a meal together, after all this time." Before leaving, she asked him "Will you be all right here on your own, Mr. Cauliflower? Honestly and truly?"

He turned to Fiona and said "Aren't I always?"

Fiona smiled and nodded but hesitated all the same. Eventually she turned and exited the office to the hallway. Nathaniel faced his personal reliquaries with careful courage as he had quietly managed to do throughout the preceding centuries.

*

In the interim between Fiona's departure and when the Nine Greatest Muses arrived, Nathaniel's obsessive mind worked industriously. The heart of the department was a long, plain rectangular hallway which connected the other rooms to the agency: a conference room to the north, a door leading to a waiting room to the south, five doorless offices to the west, and four doorless offices to the east along with a fifth bathroom door. The corridor, like the offices that surrounded it, was coated in a thick film of excess colored pegs. Nathaniel took a broom to the entire passage, exposing the tiled floors underneath. He buffed and waxed the ground until it sparkled under the newly installed energy-efficient bulbs of the ceiling. Even the post boxes, which varied in shape and size depending on which country it had come from, were now repositioned by the doorless offices awaiting envelopes. Nathaniel gave himself personal accolades for his work but knew there was still much more to do before the guests arrived.

Nathaniel swept each associated workplace of the colored pegs. He draped offices with their own brilliant displays in the same fashion that a designer would consult layers of multi-patterned upholstery fabric for a proper color scheme. He started with the office of thunderstorms. When he first entered the office it was a grievous pit with a flood of colored pegs almost waist high, but after locking the fragments of his histories back into the cabinet, taking a horizontal sweeping broom to the layer of colored pegs and taking wood polish to the banisters and floors, he left the office in the same pristine condition it had been. He decorated one office as a living Grecian beach with waves rolling upon rocky, sandy shores during a sunny mid-afternoon. In another office Nathaniel supplied a Russian cityscape and an expansive ballet studio complete with a barre, a wall of elegant mirrors and hardwood floors. Another office was decorated as the Titanic in its gleaming majesty days before the iceberg. He even took it upon himself to decorate an office with impressively sculpted ribbed vaults, elaborately constructed columns in clusters and statues of humbled priests, benevolent saints and winged angels that looked like as if they were about to take flight. Office after office, the department was revitalized and heightened from its former glory.

Nathaniel stood in the conference room looking at the mural of the nine naked beautifully dancing muses with laurel leaves on their heads. He allowed himself to remember the outlying details of Evangeline's soul, the sound of her voice, her soft touch, and the smell of her lavender perfume. An additional memory of her had then crossed his mind.

"That's it," Nathaniel told her in the memory. "That's right. Inside the mailbox."

In his mind's eye, Evangeline looked into the darkness of the space of the open mailbox. Raindrops chased the wrinkles of her face, cascading down the contours of her chin. And as she stood there, she considered what was to follow once the envelope was delivered. Eventually Evangeline, with envelope still in hand, closed the lid. She turned to Nathaniel.

"I'm sorry," Evangeline told him. "I love you, but I'm sorry." She surrendered the envelope, dropping it to the wet ground.

He stopped remembering her there for the time being. The memories of her were beautiful, yes, but the underlying, poisoned current of tragedy and intrigue ran too deep for him to remember further.

Nathaniel bowed his eyes to the rest of the conference room. The table in the middle was perfectly round with a diameter of polished cedar. Its center was topped by a glass vase of freshly picked lavender and hyacinth, nine kerosene lamps glowing humbly and a lone, empty Lite-Brite. Nathaniel took time to set out the finest china, polished silver and sparkling goblets for the occasion. He put the finishing touches on an antipasto of fried fava beans drenched in olive oil, covered with flakes of mouthwatering Pecorino Romano cheese. He set out soup bowls filled with steaming minestrone speckled with chopped vegetables, potatoes, beans and flavorful spices. Each setting was adorned with unique and various pasta dishes: some mixed with salty veal, others of tender pork, some of sumptuous lamb, coated in ground tomato, basil and dots of parmesan. Nathaniel even positioned loaves of crunchy artisan bread, which sprang out ornamentally from various white fabric draped baskets.

The door to the waiting room at the end of the hall opened. Nathaniel turned to the conference room doorway to find Fiona as she stepped through. She was followed by seven other faces of the predetermined exemplary muses.

Fiona smiled warmly at the sight of her department. She said to Nathaniel: "You have certainly outdone yourself, Mr. Cauliflower. The place looks superlative!"

Nathaniel couldn't help but to blush. Feeling proud of his work, pleased to no end that his efforts did not go unnoticed, he shook hands with each muse, offering a warm smile and a hearty greeting as they filed in the hall. The last muse he came in contact with was a woman at the back of the crowd. She wore a strapless Chiffon wedding dress around her slender figure. Her flowing locks of red hair glowed effervescently under the lights. Her green eyes sparkled. Her tan face and shoulders were spotted with freckles.

The bride, a woman named Annette Redmond, looked at Nathaniel and, not knowing quite why, said "Hello. My name is Annette."

"Hello, my name is Nathaniel J. Cauliflower."

Annette's face looked askance. "Cauliflower? As in the vegetable?"

Nathaniel's natural fondness for Annette quickly dissolved. "Better that than Broccoli," he responded with a hint of derision. If only Annette knew how he was given the name Cauliflower, she wouldn't be so quick to judge! But that was another memory for another time, and there were many more things to worry about in the present than genealogy lessons.

"Dinner is served in the conference room." He gestured to the conference room where the inviting feast's aroma was waiting for them. "After supper, Management has gifts for each of you which you'll hopefully find helpful and enlightening. We have a lot to accomplish before we send you back on your ways."

The guests followed Fiona through the hallway to the conference room with Annette Redmond close behind. Nathaniel watched her as she went, remembering the days when she lived a different life as a housewife named Annette Slocum. Upon seeing her again, Nathaniel's memories of her ruined library books resurfaced. He recalled the resounding echo of having rescuing young Annette's library books in her prior life. But those memories were from a concluded timeline, from a different history overall.

Annette turned to Nathaniel. She nodded for him to follow her as if to say "are you coming?"

For a brief second, Nathaniel was almost shaken. The look that Annette gave him was once the same kind of look that twenty-year-old Evangeline had given him so long ago. He frowned, trying to stuff the thoughts of Evangeline away, keeping the story from unpicking itself further. Little did Nathaniel know that the effort in keeping his story hidden would be in vain! It was Annette Redmond's second arrival, along with her unending inquisitiveness in pulling loose threads, which would trigger the vicious unsnarling of Nathaniel's private woes.

CHAPTER 2: NEFARIOUS NOISES AND OTHER NUISANCES

Nathaniel suffered from an affliction known as Misophonia: a hatred or sensitivity toward certain sounds. It developed in his many lives as an annoyance to the following: creaking floorboards, women's and men's heels of their dress shoes clipping the pavement, the scraping of silverware against plates while attempting to collect the remaining morsels, the timbre of some human voices, cawing of ravens, the flickering flame on a candle in a quiet space, pages turning in a book while in a reading room, celery snapping, chair legs grating against the floor, even to the sound of the brittle current of air as it whistled in his ears on chilly winter mornings. It was a wonder that he was able to enjoy any day of his seven lives with the intense anxiety, but survived each day Nathaniel did, and for one specific reason (whether he had been acutely aware of it or not): to find Evangeline again.

It was a hardship that he brought with him even into the afterlife and currently endured as he listened to Annette scour her plate of its lingering noodles. The others had politely finished their meals in respective silence, tucking their cloth napkins beside their plates. Annette, though, was determined to savor her meal to its last miniscule bite. Nathaniel raised an eyebrow, wondering if she had eaten anything prior to her wedding. She still sat in her wedding dress, which she seemed overly protective of, stuffing one of the corners of her cloth napkin into the cleavage, and with good reason. As Nathaniel stood listening to her efforts, he spotted several dots of olive oil that speckled the napkin's fabric.

Annette set her empty plate and fork on the table, took one final swig of her wine and wrested the napkin, wiping her mouth. Her eyes then caught sight of the guests. Clearly she was so invested in her meal she did not realize that the others were waiting for her to finish.

At last, Nathaniel spoke, taking Annette's plate: "If you are done . . . ?"

"I'm sorry," Annette said to Nathaniel with a smile of satisfaction of a full belly. "The only thing I managed to eat before the wedding was a bit of granola."

"Well, thankfully you've had your fill," Nathaniel said as he collected Annette's remaining cutlery and moved to another guest's setting. "I hope everyone else had the same luxury. Somehow you managed to clean out every bread basket and pasta bowl from around the table."

Annette, though aware of his snide remark, raised her glass as a toast anyway. "Thank you for the meal, Mr. Cauliflower. My compliments to the chef, as we can all agree."

The muses raised a glass in honor of Nathaniel's delicacy. Nathaniel was slightly stunned as he stood holding their plates. He had cooked for the muses before, but he swept out of the room strictly to avoid moments like these. Humbly, but begrudgingly giving in to the salute, Nathaniel gave a slight bow. He sat the dishes on a brass serving cart and headed for the conference room door.

"I hope you've saved room for dessert," he said over his shoulder. "I've prepared homemade Chocolate Ganache cakes with fresh-picked strawberries. While I fetch them, Fiona will begin orientation."

"Thank you again, Mr. Cauliflower," Fiona said, standing managerially from her swivel chair. "Now, I'm sure all of you are anxious to hear why we've summoned you and, most importantly, how we intend to get you back to where, and when, you need to be."

With Fiona's opening words, Nathaniel was out the door. Behind him he could hear Fiona handing out the party favors.

"Each of you sitting here - except for Harriet, myself and Mr. Cauliflower - have retired. As is customary at the time of every muse's departure from our department, the soul's memories are cleared from the mind. But memories, even as they are in life, are never truly discarded. Sometimes memories find themselves in attendance around bedtime; others dance about as wolves, disguised as sheep-clad daydreams; and then there are those memories which are handed back to us from the original source that took them. In each of these ivory Greek boxes, you will each find an object that will re-gift the old memories of your previous lives – more specifically the knowledge gained from the colored pegs and clients you inspired."

Nathaniel knew this orientation well. Fiona offered it to him directly each time he died in his seven lives and brought here to the department. Nathaniel recollected on the many times he held his own Grecian box and how his fingers stroked the engraved message on the stone which read "γνῶθι σεαυτόν."

Fiona patiently told him the meaning on each visit: "It means 'Know Thyself' in Greek."

He recalled opening his own stone box each time and finding the same mason jar of dandelions. On Nathaniel's arrival to the office after his first life, there were only three dandelions inside, but steadily the numbers grew so that, by the end of his seventh life, he found twenty-one in total. It was not the jar itself that brought back his memories. No, instead it was the dandelions themselves which held the most significance. The unscrewing of the glass jar's lid, as he opened it each time, became another sound that grew to disturb him.

No doubt the other muses were opening their boxes, holding their own personal artifacts and taking the time to remember the little things that had been erased.

Nathaniel found the entrance to his own office two doors down and to the right of the conference room. The door to his office was constructed of red oak and a plate of frosted glass which showed the words:

Nathaniel J. Cauliflower
Postmaster, Gourmet Chef
Envelope Auditor, Colored Peg Aficionado

He opened the door, wheeled the cart inside, and quickly closed himself into his silent, classified retreat. The "retreat" was an immense white marble-floored rotunda, supported by ten towering Corinthian columns which were topped with a dome. A perfectly centered oculus ushered in a ray of pure white sunlight, which shone directly down to the center of his empire. There were deep alcoves with shelves between each column. Every niche held unique facets of Nathaniel's seven lives: his greatest obsessions, all hidden at this time by formidable shadows. There were eight tiered display tables, acting as improvised gates to the alcoves, which circled the ground floor. On the tables, hoisted breathtakingly high, were thousands of kerosene lamps aglow with a humble orange-colored blaze. There were four of these tables to Nathaniel's right and four to his left, allowing a direct path to the room's epicenter. It was here that his simple office desk, swivel chair and water cooler sat. On the desk were three Lite-Brite boards sitting side by side, facing inward.

Nathaniel wheeled the cart counter-clockwise around the desk down the same path until he reached the columns at the far end. Between them was a tall, heavy violet velvet drape which he motioned aside to allow access to his kitchen. Nathaniel flipped a switch. Lights flickered on as if invisible apparitions raced through, fiercely yanking open shutters as they went. The kitchen was lit up by energy efficient bulbs which reflected off the elegant black marble countertops and gleaming white cabinetry. The cabinets themselves were adorned with glass windows showing hundreds of varying china patterns, an assortment of glass wine goblets, along with coffee mugs and drinking glasses of nearly every shape, size and texture. The cabinets and countertops stretched a ridiculously fifty yards wide, allowing for plenty of storage and room for preparation. There were countless meticulously sterilized stainless steel ovens, refrigerators, exhaust fans, fryers and stove tops.

    Nathaniel pushed his cart to the nearest sink and turned the knob. As the water cascaded from the faucet, Nathaniel found a bottle of dish soap and, turning it upside down, poured the soap into the water. Frothy yellow swirls gathered in the water. As they did, Nathaniel couldn't help but to let his mind wander astray from the present activity.

*

    The year was 1807. Nathaniel was twenty-three years into his first life. His brown, curly hair fell in abundant wisps around his shoulders, which he combed behind his ears. His eyes were blue; his face was as smooth as a cherub. He was a lanky lad who wore hand-me-down clothes too big for him, and the clothing was always spotted with various colors of paint. It was on that evening when a kindly puff of air passed through the window of his attic flat. He was a young apprentice to a painter who had given him lodging.

    The painter, while in a drunken state, had fallen asleep long before. Nathaniel was all alone. In the candlelight, Nathaniel set up a blank canvas and an easel. He carried with him a glass jar filled with water, which he utilized while dipping his paint-coated brush into the water, creating yellow swirls.

It was during the night when he had painted by himself, when his inexplicable craft proved most prevalent. After his painter collapsed in bed, Nathaniel felt a tingling sensation in his fingertips. It was a feeling he could not comprehend until he felt compelled to pick up a brush. Only then did the secret expose itself: during the day his technique was faulty at best, but during the late night hours it was oddly transformed, for he painted portraits so flawless they would be considered better than that of his master. He painted faces of ghosts, eerie eyes that seemed to stare at him after he later hid the works of art in the rafters. He dared not tell his painter of these incidences, firstly because he wasn't able to understand them himself and, secondly, because young Nathaniel had thought of himself as possessed during the creations. Thirdly, he kept it secret as he had been previously warned.

On this night, Nathaniel painted the face of a forty year old woman with luxuriously flowing hair. The woman staring back at him wore pearl earrings and a cream-colored pants suit. Nathaniel named the stranger "Fiona."

As the candle wick burned low and the flickering flame threatened to extinguish, Nathaniel climbed to the rafters of his loft, bidding goodnight to yet another painting. There were many phantom faces he had said goodnight to over the past few months. As he found footing on the French oak wood of his roof space, he questioned to himself how many he would construct before the painter discovered his secret.

Nathaniel sat at the open windows of his loft surveying the billowing embers of Paris' night life. A beautiful young woman, in her late teens, appeared and walked down the street in the company of her elderly female chaperone. She wore a flowing blue Victorian petticoat with opera gloves. Nathaniel could not help but to stare at her as she passed. The young woman, though bathed in shimmering candlelight, was the most beautiful woman he had ever seen. As the young woman passed by his window, she happened to look up and smile at him. And Nathaniel, having been instantly and uncontrollably taken by her, smiled back. He did not discover until the following day the young woman's name: Evangeline.

*

"Mr. Cauliflower?" The now muse Nathaniel was suddenly torn from the memory that he had allowed himself to be engrossed in. He turned to find Annette standing in his kitchen, holding a plate. "You missed one. I thought that I'd bring it to you, see if you needed any help."

Nathaniel took the dish from Annette and placed it in the sink. During his memory he had emptied the cart, save for a single fork, which he promptly added to the mix.

Annette went on. "It's such a shame that we got to enjoy the meal and you didn't eat any of it yourself."

Nathaniel told her, very matter-of-factly "I don't need to eat the meals to know how good they taste."

"But you do eat, don't you? Surely you nibble during the preparation to test it."

"I don't eat, Miss Redmond."

"Why not?"

"I lost the desire to eat a long time ago. It happens when you've been dead for as long as I have. But you wouldn't know anything about that, you being alive. I utilize the culinary gifts that Management bestowed on me and share it with others." Nathaniel frowned, changing the subject. "One should not burst into other people's offices uninvited, Miss Redmond," Nathaniel spat. "I'm a very private person and I like to keep it that way."

Annette was too busy staring over Nathaniel's right shoulder to the kitchen's breadth to pay any attention.

"Wow. So this is where all the magic happens. Adam, he's my fiancé, and I live in a studio apartment downtown. Oh, we're not married yet. When we moved and saw the kitchen there I said to myself, 'now *this* is a kitchen!' but now, looking at yours, I feel a bit humbled. I've never seen a kitchen so spacious. How many meals can you comfortably make in here at one time?"

"On the days the kitchen is really hopping, up to twenty meals. Miss Redmond, if you please . . ."

Annette stated plainly "You don't like me very much."

"I like you just fine," Nathaniel lied, holding the velvet drape open to the rest of his office.

"It's because of what I said about your last name, isn't it?"

Nathaniel said nothing, continuing to hold open the drape.

"Well, what can I say? It's an unusual last name. I've personally met some people with some pretty odd last names, but in all of my years I've never met a 'Cauliflower.' Where does a last name like that originate from?"

"From produce," Cauliflower replied dryly.

"Oh, I see. Of course."

"It actually derives from the Latin word 'Caulis,' which means 'cabbage' and 'flower.' It's a species of vegetable from 'Brassica Oleracea' which includes Brussels, cabbage, broccoli, kale, collard greens and sprouts."

Annette nodded as if understanding him, but in the end all she wanted to know was "and how does one get the last name of 'Cauliflower'? From your father or mother's side?"

"Why the interest?" he asked.

Annette shrugged. "Just making conversation. Anyone who names themselves Cauliflower seems like an interesting person to get to know."

Annette was once again distracted by the platters of Chocolate Ganache cake with fresh-picked strawberries, which had yet to be transferred to Nathaniel's cart.

"I am in awe of you, Mr. Cauliflower. Absolute awe. I feel like I'm standing in the kitchen with the world's most celebrated cook. And yet here you are, hiding away, as if you're almost ashamed of the talent."

"Really, Miss Redmond, it's a simple recipe with a few strawberries as garnish." He abandoned the curtain letting it close. Nathaniel began putting the dessert plates neatly on the tray. Annette reached out to help him, but Nathaniel swatted at her hand. "What *you* should be doing is opening your Grecian box and rediscovering your old memories of being Annette Slocum."

"Oh," Annette shrugged her shoulders. "I was given a box alright; a really neat ivory box that had this odd phrase on the side in another language." Annette reached for a plate again, but Nathaniel insisted he had it.

"The message on the box reads 'know thyself' in Greek, which is what should have happened when you opened it to find your object."

"Yes, that's what *should* have happened. There was this guy next to me that found a guitar pick. Mr. Richardson, was it? His eyes were overflowing with recognition. Another woman, some famous Russian ballerina from back in the day, found ballet shoes, and her eyes swam with memories. There was even this young eighteen year-old kid named Icarus who found a feather! Even *his* eyes lit up as if finally remembering the lyrics to an old, taunting melody. . . but not me."

Nathaniel stopped stacking the plates and shifted his eyes to Annette. "'Not you' what, Miss Redmond?"

"I opened the box and found a bundle of violet envelopes, maybe sixty or so in total."

"Yes?"

"But when I held them in my hands, I didn't feel, or remember, anything."

"That's impossible," he told her.

"Well, that's what happened, impossible or no. No memories awaiting *this* gal."

"There must be some kind of mistake," Nathaniel sat the last plate back on the counter instead of the tray and was lost in thought. "No. It can't be. I gave Fiona the invitations. They were supposed to lead her directly to the others, including you! Or maybe not to *you* but to the *real* reincarnation of Mrs. Slocum! But then why would everyone else's memories resurface except for yours?"

As Nathaniel pondered such things, Annette took it upon herself to hoist the remaining dessert plate from the counter in order to transport it to the cart. She lifted it up to her eyes to further inspect his craftsmanship.

"And you're certain you don't remember being here? You don't remember living a tragically boring, unfulfilled life as a housewife named Annette Slocum, or being struck by a Cadillac in front of your local library, or becoming a muse, or inspiring your clients? Anything?"

"Not a thing," Annette told him. In the short distance from the countertop to the cart, Annette suddenly lost her grasp on the plate. Within less than a second, the dessert landed at her feet sending the plate to shatter.

The splintering plate was an added sound that caused Nathaniel's blood pressure to boil.

"Oops!" Annette blushed, looking for a broom and a wet rag. "I'm so sorry."

As she did, Nathaniel stared at the mess and seethed. The whole arrangement of bringing the Nine Greatest Muses aboard and now his pristine kitchen floor were both polluted.

"Just leave it," he told Annette, who was making even more racket in search of the tools to clean the mess. He brought his right hand up and massaged the bridge of his nose with the middle finger and thumb. "*Please*, just leave it. I'll clean it up after orientation."

Annette found a cleaning cabinet with a mop. "Are you sure?" Unearthing the mop brought about even more of a raucous as the broom, and dust pan beside it, bumped and collided over onto the tiled floor, triggering a series of other handles of various brooms, also inside the closet, to fall as well. Annette stood still, mop in hand, looking guilty of her unintended actions.

Nathaniel held open the drape.

Annette, setting the mop up against the countertop, exited through the flap with Nathaniel close behind. Before leaving with the dessert tray, Nathaniel switched off the lights to the kitchen, turning his back on his work and the memories. For a brief second, as the light flickered out at the very end of the expansive kitchen, Nathaniel swore he saw Evangeline standing there, looking not a day older than when he met her in 1807. But such moments were not to stay. The kitchen was engulfed in darkness, and the memory of her once again receded into the dark pit of his subconscious from where it had initially fled.

As he and Annette crossed through the rotunda's atrium, Annette's eyes were suddenly drawn to one of the alcoves to the right of the front door. On display were portraits of painted faces. Nathaniel, who was too concerned with the dessert cart and also finding their way through the path to the door, turned to discover that Annette had strayed from his side. He found that she was looking at the portraits that made up Nathaniel's secret hoard enclosed in elegant frames and hanging perfectly in line upon the wall.

"I recognize some of these people," she told him.

Nathaniel took a shallow breath and said "Do you?"

"See here?" Annette pointed to the portrait of Fiona. "This was the woman who handed me the invitation moments before my wedding; she's the one that brought me here. And this one . . . the man in the argyle sweater-vest, he was given the guitar pick . . ." as she stood there, studying the painted faces of the muses, Annette brought a hand to her mouth in wonderment. Nathaniel took a step forward.

It was then that Annette had discovered another larger canvas which was a bigger dimension than its predecessors and had its own private easel. It was the unfinished representation of a man in his mid-thirties, whose hair had turned white. Wrinkles had been painted around the subject's eyes. The man in the portrait wore a black suit and tie and possessed piercing grey eyes that seemed to sputter in icy fury in the pale illumination of the surrounding kerosene lamps. Seeing this face seemed to stir something within Annette, Nathaniel could deduce as much, as she gave a slight gasp.

"Mr. Cauliflower . . ." Annette whispered with her eyes on the canvas "who are these people? And who is this man?"

Nathaniel took another step and cleared his throat to get her attention.

Annette turned to him.

"His name is Jonas Rothchild. He was a Tenth Generation muse. He's also the reason that you've all been invited back here." He held the office door open. "With that being said, Miss Redmond, it's time to continue orientation."

Annette exited the office through the red oak door and Nathaniel once again found himself alone. He turned to survey the rotunda and, as he did, Nathaniel let out a sigh. He brandished the handle of the dessert cart, leaving the office himself.

One of the most disheartening sounds that often anguished Nathaniel was the reverberation of his loneliness. Though it was not so easily recognizable, it still resided. It was a heavy quiet, which heightened his awareness to other grating miscellaneous intonations. So profound was the stillness of his lonesomeness that it often crept up on him during the most inopportune times, like a foreboding midwinter cloud-covered sunset. It grew to be such an occurring theme that he almost seemed overly calloused by it. Imaginary black rats, slick with sewer grime, pointed claws and menacing red eyes, perched on the mental barbed-wires surrounding this silence. Chattering to one another, the rats would repeatedly screech a common name: "Evangeline . . . Evangeline . . . Evangeline . . ."

CHAPTER 3: AN ORIGIN MYTH OF A TENTH GENERATION MUSE

The specifics of Tenth Generation muse Jonas Rothchild and his employment were scribed with these facts: the illusions of Ninth Generation muse Annette Slocum's retirement, which included rustling, sun-kissed cherry blossoms, passing meteor showers and the visages of planets from the known solar system, receded back into their own private, bleak corners of space. Plain egg-shell colored walls and energy efficient light bulbs of the department returned. Though all, yet again, became what it once had been, the muses who remained held Mrs. Slocum in their hearts. The muses, though each mourning their friend's departure, were given more envelopes containing colored pegs and they rightfully inspired their preordained clients. They thought of Mrs. Slocum from time to time. When they did, each muse gave a little smile in honor of her memory.

Nathaniel was one muse who externally didn't show emotion upon Mrs. Slocum's retirement. He dispassionately went about his work as usual, assigning envelopes and delivering them to his muses. Out of all the coworkers, he took it upon himself to console only one muse through her heartache. Though Fiona put on a good show, Nathaniel knew what true deep-seated emotions ran through the Head Muse's veins. On a particularly snowy Christmas Eve, Nathaniel took Fiona to Mrs. Slocum's grave.

"Why is it so difficult?" Fiona inquired that night. "You would think that after almost ninety retirement parties, I would learn not to take their departures so personally. I remind myself it's all a process, I put on a brave face, but . . ."

"I know, Fiona," Nathaniel said to her comfortingly.

"Out of all the muses, I miss her the most."

To which, Nathaniel said nothing. There was an unfamiliar feeling within the cavernous void of his heart; a sentiment he couldn't quite place. As quickly as the sensation occurred, it speedily fluttered away.

"Do you think Mrs. Slocum's happy, wherever Management sent her?" Fiona asked.

"I'm sure she's right where she needs to be."

As Fiona looked at the gravestone, Nathaniel's eyes turned up to find Annette Redmond, Mrs. Slocum's reincarnation, standing several graves away. Nathaniel wasn't sure how Annette found them amidst the wintery landscape, but she found them nonetheless. Annette raised her hand and waved. Nathaniel waved back. He knew that Mrs. Slocum found the happiness she had so desperately sought in her employment as a muse, even if it was in a new body, wiped clean of her memories. As a replacement for introducing himself that night, Nathaniel guided Fiona from the grave and back through the falling snow, allowing Annette to live her new life blissfully unaware of all the trials she had faced before.

Returning from their visit to her former muse's graveside, Fiona opened the waiting room door to discover Mrs. Slocum's replacement – Jonas Rothchild.

On the occasions that Nathaniel visited the musing offices to deliver the envelopes or to display various dinners, he felt the atmosphere of the department change. It was almost as if an unseen mold scaled the walls with invisible indifference. Men hurried by Jonas' office door without making eye-contact. Women purposefully wore extra layers of clothing. Even the light bulbs in the hallway appeared dimmer. From what Nathaniel gathered, Jonas was not a team player and he often stared out the door to his own office with his cold, impassive grey eyes.

Nathaniel's fingertips tingled after one visit to the department, as they had upon arrival of every muse who had been hired by Management. Nathaniel lit a kerosene lamp in his office and adjusted the flame, bringing it to a gentle glow. He swept his glasses up the bridge of his nose and sat down in the swivel chair behind his desk. Nathaniel produced a carved wooden box from within a drawer of his desk. From inside the box, he removed five tubes of acrylic paint: the three primary colors, white and black. Nathaniel then removed a set of brushes: round, flat, bright, filbert, angle, mop, fan and rigger bristles, each in various sizes. The tools were set on the surface of his desk, placed perfectly side by side. On a square palette, Nathaniel squirted a spots of red, blue and yellow. He added dabs of white and black. He started to mix. The canvas before him was blank, but would be no longer.

With his lips pursed, Nathaniel picked up a flat-bristled 30mm brush and commenced his work. His brushstrokes were careful, confident and precise. After a few moments, he picked up a round-bristled 20mm. With the background solidified, the true figure emerged. A chin appeared on the canvas, and sunken cheeks, followed by the curvature of ears. The neck was next, followed by the shoulders and then the chest. Nathaniel's head moved as if he were listening to a phantom orchestration that only he, himself, could hear. Brush after brush, bristle after bristle, the portrait came into strict detail. Nathaniel had painted portraits for the department before, but this one filled him with unquestionable discomfort.

The eyes that Nathaniel painted, Jonas' eyes, watched every brush stroke. When Nathaniel cleansed a brush into a glass jar filled with tap-water, Jonas studied Nathaniel's forehead. His eyes seemed to challenge Nathaniel, daring him to paint. *"Perhaps the eyes should have been painted last,"* Nathaniel thought to himself, but he then figured it would be foolish to discard this painting and start another. *"It is only a painting, after all,"* Nathaniel thought to himself. But he should have considered it to be an omen.

The work of a modern muse was quite involved, but that was not Nathaniel's job. That's not to say that his work didn't affect theirs. Indeed, Nathaniel and the muses were indelibly linked. Nathaniel was given an office, desk, Lite-Brite board, water-cooler, and an inbox like his fellow muses, but their occupations diverged from there. Colored pegs descended from the oculus of Nathaniel's office dome, landing in his inbox, awaiting his judgment. When he touched the little piece of colored plastic to his ear, he listened to them the way some might listen to the ocean inside shells. The pegs would whisper names to him. With the information given, Nathaniel turned to the proper volume of his encyclopedia corresponding to the last name. The volumes of encyclopedias were housed in two expansive alcoves that flanked the fifty yard stretch of his kitchen. The encyclopedias were labeled and alphabetized with the first letters of a client's last name. The letters A through J were housed in the bays to the left of his kitchen, and the letters J through Z were housed in the bays to the right. The volumes were his pride, joy and the obsession that he had collected from his third life lived. If the leather-bound volumes weren't spectacular enough, the messages scribed on the pages inside by calligraphy pen were as equally miraculous. Displayed had been an individual's destiny.

Once the destiny was discovered, he would fit the peg into the face of the Light-Brite, rotating the peg clock-wise and counter-clockwise. His office didn't fold or unfold into an elaborate pop-up book. Nathaniel remained at his desk as if adjusting from one radio station to another for a clear signal. Nathaniel then rotated the peg to the exact moment of inspiration, where the muse would provide the catalyst for change. Nathaniel then placed the colored peg into the corresponding envelope.

There were two stacks of recycled envelopes. One stack consisted of white envelopes to the right of his desk; the other, to the left, was violet. Color variations in the envelopes had been implemented by Management to warn a muse of the generalities of the upcoming inspiration. Pegs inside white envelopes delivered a muse to a specific person, place and time. Pegs within the violet envelopes delivered muses to more difficult situations, usually considered the "toughest of cases."

Nathaniel delivered the envelopes to the corresponding mailboxes of his modern day muses, returning to his office to await more pegs. At any given moment, depending on how creative Management had needed him to be, Nathaniel was able to work on forty to fifty inspirations at a time under his fanatical, perfectionistic eye. Envelope after envelope, client after client, the department's figurative gears were well-oiled.

That was, of course, until Jonas' twenty-second envelope.

Returning from his twenty-second envelope, Jonas told Fiona "There I was, in my violet envelope inspiration, when it suddenly occurred to me just how much I shouldn't be inspiring the client at all." He was in the hallway wearing a black suit and tie. He stank of singed fabric.

The faces of the other muses poked out from their respective offices to witness the altercation.

"Mr. Rothchild," Fiona told him then, "when we're given envelopes, we don't neglect our clients."

"Ah yes, I'm afraid I've sinned."

"Well, there's no harm done. Hand over the violet envelope; we will get everything squared away with Mr. Cauliflower."

"Yes, I suppose that would fix it all, wouldn't it?" Jonas' face grew grim. "Unfortunately, I can't hand it over to you."

"I'm not sure I follow," Fiona's demeanor did not falter in the slightest.

"I'm taking the violet envelope with me."

"Taking it . . . ?"

"With me. My exit is a bit dramatic but there's just no other way. After twenty-two envelopes, I've heard and seen enough. The operation that you run here is worse than I ever anticipated. A world of disease, pestilence, plagues, starvation, rot, disappointments, war, famine, terrorist attacks – man is a beast, and a ravenous one at that. And this grand evolution of the species that you so often promote is nothing more than a hoax."

"What are you saying, Mr. Rothchild?"

"For years before my death I prayed to Management for answers. Why does Management put us through turmoil? We are all Job from the Bible, and the world is getting worse by the minute! Now I know it's all due to Management! Because presumably *they* know what's best!"

"Mr. Rothchild, I want you to take a breath and think about what you're doing."

"I *have* taken a breath, Fiona, and because of Management's world, I had the wind knocked out of me." His bitter eyes were even more frozen as he ran his fingers along the door to the waiting room. "How it taunts me, Fiona, this door. How is it that only Nathaniel J. Cauliflower enters and exits from this door on a normal basis while the rest of us are trapped in here like rats? Even the walls of Babel had to eventually crumble . . ."

"Mr. Rothchild, please hand over the colored peg and violet envelope," Fiona asked of him, stepping forward. From inside his black jacket pocket he produced the violet envelope as if actually considering surrender. From inside the envelope a small blue peg toppled into the palm of his hand. Jonas licked his lips, hungry for destruction. "There are moments that we go through, Mr. Rothchild, where we question the motivations of Management. All will be forgiven."

"No," he pocketed the blue peg and the violet envelope.

"There's no reason to be ornery, Mr. Rothchild."

"No," he smiled like a petulant pyromaniac poised with a metaphorical match. The time came for Jonas to make his great escape.

"What's gotten in to you, Mr. Rothchild?" Fiona wanted to know.

"What's gotten in to me?" He turned to the Head Muse. "The world, Fiona. Everything about it sickens me, and knowing that Annette Slocum is out there somewhere unprotected . . . I'll no longer placate Management and all the manipulation as if I were a marionette with strings." He reached for the doorknob, which turned, but the door seemed stuck. *"Every . . . little . . . moment,"* his words were punctuated by his attempts to open it. *"Will need . . . to be . . . rectified!"*

The door swung open. A blinding white light erupted from the waiting room which accented his wrinkles. His gray hair caused him to look all the more malicious. Fiona raced toward him but the hostile stare in his eyes caused her to pause.

"How do you know what's on the other side, Mr. Rothchild? What makes you so confident?" Fiona asked. When he turned back to them, Fiona saw something around his neck – an old key with a dandelion insignia dangling from a chain.

"The Dandelion Sisters have shown me everything, Fiona. There is so much work to be done. Or undone, rather." He faced the light with the violet envelope in his jacket pocket.

"Mr. Rothchild, I beg of you . . . at least tell us a time period of where it sent you? A name! Anything!"

None of which he supplied. Offering one final kiss into the hallway's air, he stepped through the hallway door. He kicked the

31

waiting room chairs aside. His lasting silhouette disappeared into the swirling brightness ahead.

*

This story was told by Fiona to the Nine Greatest Muses as they sat around the conference room table.

The Chocolate Ganache cake with strawberries had long since been eaten and the plates were empty, save for a few brown crumbs. As the story was being told, Nathaniel sat and let his mind wander. He knew of how Jonas had let an inspiration go uninspired and he did not have to hear it again to refresh himself of the calamity that ensued.

It astonished him to think how Management had placed such blind faith on the individuals that had been brought to the office after their deaths. Thinking this, Nathaniel studied each of his Greatest Muses, marveling at Management's choices in the select few.

There was a young man named Icarus who had been no older than eighteen when he died. He sported a chiseled jaw line and flawless supple, tanned skin. His lips were a deep pink shade. His eyes were as sparkling blue as the waters of ancient Greece where he had originated. His brown hair was full of wispy curls which extended around his sculpted ears and neck, down to his toned and muscular shoulders. He wore dark stone-washed jeans with sandals and a black dress shirt with the sleeves rolled up. The collar was casually opened to reveal a defined Adam's apple. Icarus derived from the Greek myth of a young boy who had flown too close to the sun with makeshift wings, ultimately plummeting to his death. But there was more to Icarus' tale that had never been collected in any anthologies; Nathaniel alone knew of the horrors that Icarus faced between the time of his death and being indoctrinated as a Third Generation muse.

Seventh Generation muse Lucas Richardson was a man in his late twenties. He was a rather skinny fellow who wore a blue argyle sweater with a striped white and gray dress shirt underneath. The cuffs of the shirt were curled around the sleeves of the sweater and pushed up on both elbows in a relaxed, informal way. He wore tight-fitting jeans with black converse tennis shoes. His hair was a maintained crew cut with highlights and his eyes were hazel-green. He took a certain amount of pride in Lucas considering that Nathaniel had been the muse who inspired him. But Nathaniel knew that even Lucas harbored his own regrets, which centered mostly on Lucas' lover, Gabriel, and his partner's death during the assaults on the World Trade Center on September 11th.

Harriet, a strict looking, middle-aged muse with her hair tightly bound in a bun securely fastened with safety pins, was of the Eighth Generation. She was one of the few who had been around since the new wave of colored pegs had fallen. There were a select number of individuals who knew of Harriet's perils of an abusive ex-husband and, as Harriet liked to keep it that way, Nathaniel respected her wishes and spoke not a word about it.

An assortment other muses sat at the table listening to Fiona speak. There was Anna Pavlova, of the Fourth Generation; a Russian ballerina eternally stuck at age fifty, forever stunningly attractive and poised in an off-white gown and soft feather boa, like a well-groomed swan. African American poet Paul Lawrence Dunbar sat looking not a day older than thirty-four, as perpetually young as Nathaniel had remembered him from Mr. Dunbar's days as a Fifth Generation muse. He wore a gray pants suit with a white dress shirt with a buttoned collar. Mr. Dunbar looked refined and serious, immersed in his own indiscernible thoughts. Then there was Mr. Andrews, from the Sixth Generation, who had been the architect of the Titanic. Though he looked dapper in his tuxedo, Mr. Andrews was predominantly discouraged by everything.

"Building a stable Ship of Dreams only to have it buckle after hitting an iceberg at sea will do that to a man," Nathaniel thought to himself.

These were only eight of the department's finest.

Since the original muses had retired, Management had chosen seventy individuals total to carry on the legacy. Any one of them had their own dark sides, as all humans share. It could have been any of them that had caused this kind of series of events. Instead Management had given the inauspicious undertaking to Evangeline, and then to Jonas many generations after.

Nathaniel looked at Annette, pondering what was happening in her mind. Here she was without any memory of who she had been, and yet the look in her eyes read something singularly dissimilar. Annette stared with complete recognition of Jonas as if she had personally met him. It was a look that offered a sense of bafflement that the perpetrator's face was even been displayed by the projector! The only way Annette would have known him would be as if she had remembered her past life, which she claimed not to recall. This realization led Nathaniel to believe that Annette was lying to him.

"Mr. Cauliflower, do you have anything to add?" Fiona asked him after she had finished telling of Jonas' exit.

Annette, while studying the continual scowl of their enemy, raised her hand and, interrupting Nathaniel, said "Do we know anything about him? Where he came from, or what may have led to him wanting to neglect an inspiration? From what you mentioned," Annette went on, without realizing Fiona was in the process of giving an answer, "it seems that his personal life itself was troubled. Someone doesn't wake up one morning and think poorly of the world. There has to be extenuating circumstances that led to that kind of hatred."

As Annette said this, Nathaniel rolled his eyes due to Annette's audacity to interrupt his Fiona.

Fiona discretely shook her head to Nathaniel as if to say "it's no bother." When Annette became silent, Fiona answered the question.

"We know quite a bit about him," Fiona answered. "Mr. Rothchild, whom I'll reference as Jonas for the sake of the story, was born an only child to Thomas and Kathleen Rothchild on a frost-bitingly cold January day in 1979. His father was a prestigious prosecuting attorney; his mother was a housewife who, before conceiving her son, tried to enter the workforce herself. But Kathleen would not be employed by anyone after giving birth, as she died that same birth month. Thomas was heartbroken and buried himself in court cases and paperwork to console his grief. He hired a full-time nanny, a frail, middle-aged woman named Bethany, who raised Jonas from his infancy to the period leading up to his formative years. Jonas grew accustomed to the behaviors of his estranged father and, over time, called Bethany 'mother.' Bethany told Jonas not to use that word. It was the only word, save for Kathleen's name, which Thomas forbade in his house. Jonas' reliance on Bethany eventually ended as father and son had moved to another town that proved to have growth in Thomas' career. Bethany did not follow them as Thomas swore it had been time for Jonas to fend for himself. 'He's a man now, by God,' Jonas heard his father tell Bethany on her tear-filled last day of employment.

"The separation between Jonas and yet another important female figure was distressing; it was the allegorical trailhead to an imminent petrification of his heart. After moving several states away, Jonas found himself isolated. He grew to despise his surroundings until . . ."

Fiona paused for a moment. She looked around the room at the muses, thinking twice about what she was about to say.

". . . Until he climbed an apple tree to escape his bleak surroundings. He met a young girl, later our Ninth Generation muse

Mrs. Slocum, who was sitting in the shade reading a library book. Jonas made it his mission to 'fix' Mrs. Slocum. No one knows for sure what he saw in her. Perhaps Jonas believed that if he had to grow up, he would make that journey alone. He made it his personal objective to rid anti-social Mrs. Slocum of the library books that kept her separated from the talkative world. Little did Jonas know that someone else was out there who also made it a personal charge to rescue those very same books."

Fiona turned her eyes to Nathaniel as she said it. All muses, including Annette, turned their eyes to Nathaniel.

Nathaniel's gaze was glued to the conference room table, wishing Fiona would divert the attention back to the story. The rescuing of the library books was a sappy thing between him and Annette Slocum exclusively, acting as a critical puzzle piece to the tale.

Fiona, as the storyteller, explained to her muses "Jonas, in his adulthood, later married a woman named Roberta and together they had two children: Ajax and Josiah. Jonas was hired as one of the local meteorologists in town. Roberta worked for the state in agricultural resources. Together, husband and wife provided a decent life for their children. For several years they lived life as a perfect family. But Roberta was not a fool. She knew that Jonas still harbored a fascination for Mrs. Slocum. It was as if Mrs. Slocum was living with them; an invisible second wife regarded in such high standards that Roberta, no matter how hard she tried, could not live up to. When Jonas heard of Mrs. Slocum's death in 2009, he fell into grief-stricken despondency. Roberta decided her husband needed to be on his own to sort out his priorities. Jonas agreed it had been for the best that they separate, and asked for the boys to stay with their mother until he regained a sense of stability.

"But after three years, Jonas did not seem able to shake his feelings. Divorce papers were finalized and Jonas was caught in a nasty custody battle for his two children. The courts gave sole custody to Roberta. Jonas, feeling terribly apathetic by the tragedy, carelessly walked out into a thunderstorm one afternoon. It was during that thunderstorm that he was struck by lightning and killed. He woke up here in the waiting room. He was introduced as a Tenth Generation muse, and was given an office, Lite-Brite and envelopes."

Fiona concluded the story with these words: "One thing is for certain: if Mr. Rothchild had not met Mrs. Slocum underneath that apple tree in their childhood, we wouldn't be sitting here today. But Management has reasons for doing things, yes? Who are we to question 'why' when we should trust that things will work out in the end?"

Silence pervaded the conference room. Nathaniel looked to his muses and, eventually, to Annette who mentally sorted the details. She didn't appear to remember any of this from her former life but, from the look in her eyes, she sat pondering it thoroughly regardless.

Lucas raised his hand. "How is it that we know all of that about Jonas, but we don't know who he was destined to inspire on his twenty-second envelope? Or where he went after leaving through the waiting room door?"

Fiona shrugged her shoulders. "Perhaps the more inspirations we work, the answers will be revealed. For now, we don't know anything helpful."

It was true they didn't know anything about the client. In the process of looking up the client's name and destiny in question, Nathaniel had carelessly been distracted by thoughts of Evangeline.

"And what of the Dandelion Sisters who Jonas mentioned?" Annette asked. "Who are they and where do they fit in?"

"That and where are the fallen colored pegs?" Lucas asked in conjunction with Annette's question. "This place looks like it did when I worked here last."

"They're in your offices," Nathaniel spoke. Attention shifted to Nathaniel, who faced his muses with authority. "Each muse has a corresponding peg color. I'll fetch a bin from each of you shortly, and reassign specific pegs back to you. Some envelopes will be white, others violet. Once the envelopes are delivered to your post boxes, we can clean up this mess and send you on your way. I've seen the reverse of the falling colored pegs. You'll find that inspirations are connected. If we inspire one peg, it may cause a string of inspirations to right themselves automatically. When that happens, some colored pegs may rise and re-write themselves. Our goal is to fix as many timelines as possible by way of fixing others. I don't know how many Lite-Brite boards will need to be filled and emptied before we're done, but I can assure you that, eventually, all will become normal again. When that time comes, you'll each receive a retirement party the likes of which you've never before imagined in Heaven or Earth. Meteor showers, approaching planets, cherry-blossoms are just the beginning to the rewards that await you at the end."

"That's wonderful that you've answered Mr. Richardson's question, but you never answered mine," Annette said to Nathaniel.

"Staff meeting adjourned," Nathaniel said to his muses, shaking off Annette's comment as if he hadn't even heard it. When Annette stated once again that he had not answered her question, Nathaniel was out of the conference room, thusly ignoring Annette's inquiry.

*

"I wouldn't trust her as much as I can throw her," Nathaniel told Fiona. They were in his office with the door closed. He had nine large waist high bins in front of his desk holding separate peg colors.

"And you say she doesn't remember being here?" Fiona asked Nathaniel.

"Well, that's what she says, but something tells me that she remembers. You should have seen the way she was studying Jonas' face on that screen."

"They were all looking at his face like that, Mr. Cauliflower."

"Yes, but she was the only one who swears not to have any memory of him. Don't you find that strange?"

Fiona smiled and placed a hand on Nathaniel's shoulder. "Give her a chance, Mr. Cauliflower. She surprised us in her personal growth as Annette Slocum. Chances are she'll surprise us as Miss Redmond."

Nathaniel was left alone in his office to begin the adjustments of the clients' pegs and envelopes but before touching the colored pegs in the bins, he crossed to one of the alcoves to the immediate left of his office door. This is where Nathaniel kept the obsession from his seventh life: every single copy of Annette Slocum's library books he had carefully repaired. There were many titles he had collected over the years including Bram Stoker's *Dracula*, Ayn Rand's *Atlas Shrugged*, Oscar Wilde's *The Picture of Dorian Gray*, Victor Hugo's *Les Misérables* along with other rescued books that had not belonged to Annette. He opened the glass door to the cabinet and hoisted high a copy of J.R.R. Tolkien's *The Hobbit* to the dim light of a nearby kerosene lamp. He looked over his shoulder to check that he wasn't being observed and flipped open the cover page of the book. Inside, he found three unopened violet envelopes. He took out one of them, leaving the other two. Nathaniel set the book back on its shelf and closed the glass.

Moments later, he stood in the doorway of Annette's workplace. She was placed in the office of several stitched-together cathedrals. Rays of white sunlight poured through the stained glass windows, causing the space to look like a living kaleidoscope. Annette's back was to him. Though about to say something, perhaps warn her he was there, he paused. Annette, unaware she was being watched by Nathaniel, lifted the right side of her wedding dress where he noticed a leg holster. Annette unhooked a .45 pistol and held it for a moment. The fabric of her dress flowed back down. She studied the pistol, opened a drawer in her desk and placed it, with the safety on, inside. She closed the drawer and, looking at the desk, spotted a large rectangular clothing box with a fluffed orange ribbon.

Annette opened the package and found a yellow ankle-length cotton house dress. She gave a faint smile while holding it in her hands. Annette then proceeded to set the house dress across her swivel chair and reached for the zipper of the wedding gown.

Nathaniel turned his back to Annette. Even though he didn't care for her very much, and his trust for her was thin, he was still a gentleman. He heard the rustling of fabric as Annette switched from one dress to another. As she did, Nathaniel thought of Evangeline. He recalled the sound of Evangeline's dress as he had removed it from her on their last evening together in 1808. He remembered how it had fallen around Evangeline's ankles like a discarded clam shell, revealing the unique pearl underneath. Oh, how Nathaniel missed Evangeline. How he wished he could turn around and see her instead of Annette Redmond. Such wishes, sadly, were not to be granted.

"Mr. Cauliflower?" Annette's voice sounded. "Did you need something?"

Nathaniel found Annette standing in her yellow house dress. *"Perhaps there's still a hint of 'Slocum' in her after all,"* he had thought to himself. He handed her the violet envelope and said "It's time for the first inspiration. And, as you claim not to remember being here prior, I'm taking it upon myself to accompany you."

They gathered by her Lite-Brite peering at the initial violet envelope. A moment of hesitation from Annette brought Nathaniel to lie. "Go on, Miss Redmond, this envelope has been specifically designed for you."

"But how can I open the envelope if I don't remember being that Slocum woman? What if I really am Annette Redmond and not the muse you want me to be?"

"We'll never know for sure who you really are until we open the envelope. Now please, be so kind as to, at the very least, try?" There was a hint of doubt that passed across his eyes; it was a look that did not go unnoticed by Annette.

Annette nervously bit her lower lip, turned her back to him and brought her index finger to the flap of the envelope. Nathaniel couldn't help but to look over her shoulder. Annette looked to him. Nathaniel nonchalantly looked away, crossing to the other side of her desk to give her space. As he did make his way around her desk, Nathaniel heard a rip in the paper. He closed his eyes and gave a barely audible, indiscernible sigh.

"I opened it," Annette stated. "Even though I don't remember being Annette Slocum, I was able to open it."

"Well don't just stand there, Miss Redmond," Nathaniel spun and ordered. "Now that the envelope has been opened, you take a sip of water from the water cooler."

Annette took a sip of water from the water cooler as she was instructed.

"And then you fit the colored-peg into the grid of the Lite-Brite board."

"It's blue," Annette told him.

Nathaniel said "I'm sorry?"

Annette, who was still standing with the peg in hand, said "This peg is blue."

"So it is, Miss Redmond."

"But the colored pegs assigned to me are orange."

Nathaniel massaged the top crook of his nose with his right middle finger and thumb. "Would you please put the colored-peg inside the Lite-Brite?"

"You really should eat something every once in a while, Mr. Cauliflower," Annette retorted. "Check your blood sugar level with a temper like that. You might be hypoglycemic."

"Peg," said Nathaniel. "Lite-Brite." He finished massaging his eyes, showing a look that could only be described as severe indignation.

Annette then fit the blue-colored peg into the Lite-Brite. For a brief second, nothing happened. They both uncomfortably faced forward awaiting the great transition from the department to a client's life.

"So . . ." Annette said. "You never answered my question." She looked over to Nathaniel on her left who, in his own way, kept staring forward. "Who are the Dandelion Sisters and how do they fit into Mr. Rothchild's story?"

Nathaniel, figuring full well she wouldn't look away, shot his eyes to his right with a stoic expression but said nothing. The office then folded and unfolded with vehement black rage which barely matched the irritability Nathaniel kept within.

CHAPTER 4: THE FIRST OF THREE EXHAUSTING ENVELOPES

Nathaniel had been through enough inspirations to know how violent an erupting violet envelope could be. There were violet envelopes he personally worked where it felt as if ten tumbling avalanches simultaneously crunched down steep, snow-capped ridges. He endured several violet envelopes where the initial unfolding pop-up resembled overturned countless tubs of Lincoln Logs. Nathaniel was even tripped up by violet envelopes brushing through with the colossal, collective force of multiple monumental tsunamis.

In the particular case of Annette's initial violet envelope, the client's life folded and unfolded like various glass ornaments plummeting, clashing and shattering into tiny, fractured elements. These rudiments hastily settled themselves into the differentiating details of her dependent's days, depositing Nathaniel and Annette amidst an unfamiliar, yet imposingly fixed, timeline.

It was an indoor craft fair with folding tables and chairs strategically placed to display the following: shiny holiday baubles, hand-made ornaments, whittled Christmas figurines of both notable characters from the North Pole and the Nativity, booths selling icing-topped cookies, handsomely prepared gingerbread houses and steaming Styrofoam cups of hot chocolate, bubbling black coffee and assorted flavors of warm tea. Soft white Christmas lights, accompanied by red and green colored fabric, masked the speakers overhead which blasted the carol "God Rest Ye Merry Gentlemen." The crowds of shoppers were filled with bustling cheer, toddlers crying from tempered exhaustion, cranky slow-paced in-laws navigating with the aid of canes and walkers, proprietors utilizing dinging cash registers and, naturally, the joyous, deep bellowing laughter of a lively, plump imposter Santa Claus.

As Annette stood gasping for air in attempts to compose a normal breathing pattern, Nathaniel took an intrepid stance beside her, tackling the inspiration like a seasoned professional.

"Now see here, Miss Redmond," Nathaniel told her, coolly beginning the process of interpreting the details. "An inspiration is more than inspiring a specific person in a specific place and time. An inspiration is decoding the meticulous details that Management has laid in front of us to allow for a seamless, effective catalyst. Take this particular inspiration, for example. Here we are inside a craft fair filled to the brim with decorations, sweets and festive music. You may be thinking to yourself that your client might be one of the local harried shoppers, or perhaps one of the miserable-looking part-time employed elves with the green slippers and candy-cane patterned pantyhose. Or perhaps it's the big guy himself!" Nathaniel gestured to all of these potential individuals to drive home a point: "Amidst these probable patrons are the clues that will eventually lead us to the *only one* that Management has set us out to inspire."

"All right, then," Annette told herself, taking a few steps to her right. "Clues it is then."

Nathaniel was quick to stop her. "No, no, no. You can't go wandering about aimlessly in search of the clues. There are three reasons to stay exactly where Management has placed you in a violet envelope. The first is the time-clock." There came a distant roll of thunder which shook the ground and lights on the ceiling. Only the present muses detected it. "A moment in someone's life is opened for a limited time before it refolds. You don't have all the time in the world to go hunting for something that may, or may not be, in plain sight. You stay exactly where you are intended to be. Which for us is right here with our feet firmly planted . . ." the thunder came again, this time a little louder, ". . . on this Astro Turf covered floor."

Nathaniel went on distributing directions.

"The second reason is because of a muse's impulse which usually presents itself as an inherent tug on the heartstrings. This is one of the main reasons we've given back the memories. As you don't have the previous memories of being Annette Slocum, you won't have the luxury of using such a . . ."

As Nathaniel was talking, Annette intuitively turned round facing the opposite direction. Nathaniel pursed his lips. He faced her same direction. Before them was a perky white haired, female sales associate clad in an ugly holiday sweater that resembled a disfigured Christmas tree. Between them and the salesperson was a table topped with Christmas ornaments constructed of smashed soda cans strung with red ribbon. Likenesses of Santa's face had been painted on the exposed aluminum base of each.

"Hmm . . ." Nathaniel said out loud, trying not to sound too impressed by Annette's hunch, "very good." Nathaniel still felt he needed to have a helping hand. He said, as an aside to Annette, "As we've discussed before, even though we've turned and found a lady selling Christmas ornaments doesn't necessarily mean that we're here to change her life."

"Of course we're not here to change her life," Annette said.

"That's right, Miss Redmond, we're not," Nathaniel conferred. "What then do your muse heartstrings tell you we should do?"

"Why to pick out an ornament, of course," said Annette matter-of-fact with self-reliance.

Nathaniel frowned, not pleased with Annette's noticeable smugness. "Well, go on then."

"Hello," Annette said to the sales associate finally.

"Good evening," said the sales associate, gleaming with merriment.

"Did you make these yourself?" Annette asked. "They're lovely."

"Well thank you! And, yes, I do dabble in these kinds of things from time to time. I suppose you could say that I live in Christmas all year long, creating crafts for the holidays, while the rest of the world just goes on with the other seasons."

There came another rumble of thunder, this one so loud it was almost deafening.

"Get on with it," Nathaniel whispered to Annette.

"You'll have to excuse my husband," Annette told the burgeoning aluminum artist.

Nathaniel's eyes grew wide. His face went flush.

"I mean honestly, honey," Annette went on. "Here we are after three hours in this hallowed holiday haven and we haven't found a single ornament that best suits our living room tree. Nate here *hates* when all the ornaments are the same shape and color, don't you darling? So we go to these things every year to find the perfect mismatched trinkets to add to our chaotically ruffled hodgepodge!"

By now, Nathaniel was beside himself, boiling. Annette was acting the idiot, dramatically telling a ridiculous yarn and for what? All she had to do was find the proper ornament out of the one-hundred and twenty similarly festooned knick-knacks exhibited. Then it hit him. Annette, in flaunting her rusty heartstring deployment, had no idea *which* ornament to pick and was, most likely, babbling to distract him, and the sales associate, from her obvious lack of foresight.

"*Darling*," Nathaniel offered a smile through gritted teeth, trying hard to play the role he had been given so as not to confuse the sales associate further which, as a result, may ultimately spoil the inspiration. "It's the one on the left."

"Oh, how silly of me," Annette said with a lilting laugh. "He's a bit temperamental as you can see. We've been shopping for three hours and his blood sugar is getting a tad low. I keep insisting that he carry a piece of cheese with him, or perhaps a hardboiled egg." She reached for the nearest one on the left but Nathaniel stopped her.

"No, not that one. Two more up and one more over."

The thunder rumbled even more, vibrating the table's ornaments. The engineer of the ornaments didn't notice this. Both Nathaniel and Annette knew that the time for fun and games was over. The inspiration was about to refold bringing the craft fair and gaiety down with it.

Annette picked up the ornament that Nathaniel mentioned.

"We'll take this one," she said.

The sales associate smiled, opened her cash box and brought out a thin layer of tissue paper. As she did, a final clap sounded, signaling the turn of a page.

The crinkling, crashing and crumbling of glass ornaments returned, just as it had rushed over them at the beginning. Annette, knowing what to expect, seemed impartial by its uproar. The world around them settled into another time and place. The muses stood waiting for what would happen with the ornament hooked on her index finger fixedly dangling between them.

"The third reason why we stay exactly where we are in an inspiration," Nathaniel told Annette, "is because if we were meant to move around, Management would do so for us. You'll find that any specific location changes are controlled by our employers. Just because an inspiration starts in one place doesn't mean that it won't end in another."

"With a stolen ornament," Annette held up the painted face of Santa on the crushed cola can to her eye level and frowned.

Nathaniel put his hand on Annette's wrist and lowered it so that her eyes were focused on his. "We don't steal. It's not that kind of operation."

"And yet here we are with a Christmas ornament that isn't ours that we didn't pay for." Annette turned her head quizzically to the side. "Explain to me again how this isn't stealing?"

"It isn't stealing. Every item that we borrow is eventually brought back to the moment that it was taken. Case in point: the violin that you took from the violinist on your first inspiration as Annette Slocum. It was given to a musically desperate client named Jonathan in a derelict motel room. When the violin served its purpose in issuing his life's catalyst, that violin was returned to the same initial violinist it had been stolen from as if it had never been taken. You would've remembered this if you had regained your old memories of being a Ninth Generation muse!"

"You're not making a lick of sense, Mr. Cauliflower," Annette told him.

"I knew it was a mistake giving you this inspiration," Nathaniel barked. "Fiona told me to give you a chance and I had to listen to her! Since you've been here, you've questioned my knowledge, thoroughly humiliated me by making that sales woman think that I was your husband and, to mortify me further, you're accusing me of stealing!"

Annette opened her mouth for what would have been a witty and insulting retort but her words were cut short. In the small amount of time that she and Nathaniel bickered, they almost forgot their mission's second act. A menacing roll of thunder upset their argument, instantaneously settling them. Together she and Nathaniel gathered stock of their surroundings and grew equally horror-struck at the dwindling seconds that remained for them to complete the task.

"We're in a bowling alley," Annette stated the obvious.

"We are," Nathaniel confirmed.

The bowling alley in which they occupied was no different than any other bowling alley one might encounter on any nightly excursion. The fusty carpet beneath their feet was an appalling mixture of Technicolor patterns that had gone out of style back in the late eighties. The establishment held a mixture of scents: sour Lysol shoe disinfectant, the ancient combined chemicals in bowling alley wax, odorous bowling ball polisher, the stomach-churning stench of stale beer and greasy fried foods, and the lingering unpleasant smell of vaporous cigarette smoke, collected from years past that no amount of fumigation could eradicate. The rolling of bowling balls, cracking of pins and cheers of achievement were almost muted against the backdrop of the booming, thunderously ticking pop-up book countdown. Unlike other bowling alleys, which seemed to stand fortified against the trials of many years, this one was splintering apart, and at an alarming rate. Annette and Nathaniel watched as the walls burst forth with over-spilling out-of-place ornaments. The ground beneath them had, in its own right, begun to putrefy into thin strips of silver tinsel.

"I see her!" Annette shouted to Nathaniel over the din of the thunder.

Nathaniel looked in the same direction as Annette to find, only three yards away, a miserable looking middle-aged woman with the name tag that had read "Luanne." Their client wore wrinkled cargo pants and a frumpy black polo shirt complete with the bowling alley insignia. Luanne's slightly graying brown hair was tied in a pony-tail fastened with a barrette made of tarnished silver. Luanne's eyes drooped with heavy bags of disappointment. The look of unhappy concentration as she sprayed a pair of bowling shoes further detailed her dissatisfaction.

"Well then, Miss Redmond, what's keeping you?" Nathaniel told her sternly.

Annette, with ornament in hand, took several steps forward. The ground beneath her became unstable causing her to lose footing. She turned to Nathaniel who tossed his hands forward saying "never mind that, go!" Annette stood upright. With as much agility as she was able, Annette continued the short trek to the check-in counter.

Thunder signaled the end, circling them like an unbalanced spinning lighthouse beacon in a raging storm at sea. The walls crumbled uncontrollably into a dank abyss caked with rubble. The lights flickered until a handful remained. Nathaniel braced himself as the bowling alley, and floor around them, also gave way. A small circumference of space from the edge of Nathaniel's heels on one end to the distance it took Annette to sprint to their client was what remained. Beyond that, there was no indication that the world existed; only the rumbling of thunder and the small patch of silver tinseled land in which they fought to stay upon. In the darkness there was the sound of fluttering pages in a book, as if a giant-sized reader was maddeningly flipping the pages to find the passage where they left off.

Luanne, unaware of her muse's plight, faced her back to Annette to stuff the shoes into a cubby. The deteriorating floor beneath their feet dipped into a steep forty-five degree angle. Annette lost her balance but grasped on tight to the counter with her free hand letting the hand with the ornament dangle downwards to the growing darkness. She spun to check on Nathaniel.

He, himself, tumbled and was clawing for a good grasp on the remaining exposed torn strands of carpet fabric, like a neurotic cat about to be dropped into a bathtub filled with water. When secure, his eyes turned to Annette.

"What are you doing?" he screamed. "The inspiration is about to end! Don't worry about me! Put the bloody ornament on that counter and let's be done with this!"

Annette nodded, pulling herself back up to the counter. Nathaniel watched as Annette swung the ornament by the red ribbon until it landed upon the counter. Annette shouted victoriously, confirming the finished assignment.

The carpet was not strong enough to hold his weight, and the ground slipped away above him. Nathaniel had been in this situation once before, looking at someone's face while falling to his death in 1808. The memory that it invoked was extremely repulsive. Consumed by his miserable memory, Nathaniel let go of the carpet and allowed himself to plunge into the subterranean, page-flipping darkness.

He didn't have far to fall. Within no time he was returned to the safety of the department, landing harshly into one of Annette's office swivel chairs. Nathaniel was joined by Annette who landed in her own opposite swivel chair. She looked exhilarated, pumped with adrenaline.

"We did it!" She told him, exultantly bouncing from her swivel chair.

Nathaniel did not rejoice. He wasn't in the mood to congratulate her or to carry on conversation. Being around her exhausted him. Feeling numb, he headed out of her office and sought the solace of his own sanctuary. He needed to be alone. He needed to find a way to smash his memories back inside the cages of his mind. The only way he could do that was to work on his envelopes and immerse himself in that work.

"Well," Annette called after him "say something Mr. Cauliflower! How did I do? I'm sure you must have copious notes."

He stopped at her office door and, with his back still turned to her, said "one down, couple million more to reassign to your postbox."

With that, he was out the door crossing past the other postboxes and open doorless offices. Each muse was housed in their respective rooms and eagerly awaited their envelopes. With the first envelope out of the way, it was time to divvy the rest. Nathaniel swore to himself that it would be a while before he would give Annette her second one. He didn't have the energy to handle another with her so soon. There were two violet envelopes left to administer to her before their effects would begin to take hold. The Dandelion Sisters had promised Nathaniel, when he had visited them in his seventh life, that the three separate unopened violet envelopes would undoubtedly conjure her stubborn memories. It was a matter of time before Annette would remember being the Ninth Generation muse. Then, and only then, would the real work for her be galvanized.

CHAPTER 5: TWO SPECIAL STORIES BENEATH A BLUSHING BULB

There were no ready cures when it came to Nathaniel's numbness. Through the years, and throughout the Generations, Nathaniel had encountered heartache; his loss of Evangeline being the forerunner plus other character-corrupting regrets, pitiful personal insecurities and unforeseen unfriendly occurrences. He lugged these feelings around him like bronze medallions won in an imprisoning tournament for so long that, over time, Nathaniel gradually adapted to the deadness they presented. He polished the figurative "bronze" with a mixture of two things: keeping to himself while submissively assigning envelopes to postboxes and abetting his seclusion by cooking in his concealed kitchen. Nathaniel grew so accustomed to distancing himself from the world, and keeping himself out of menial interactions with people, that it was almost impossible to pierce his impenetrable exterior.

*

One of the last times Nathaniel felt any kind of emotion was in his seventh life after he repaired the Annette Slocum's borrowed copy of Victor Hugo's *Les Misérables*. He recalled spying on Annette from the tall, unkempt bushes of her front porch. He watched as the nineteen-year-old girl carried a metal bucket out to the road and, under the moonlit May evening in 1999, began the process of preparing the novel for execution. It was a warm evening with a slight breeze threading through the humid air.

Nathaniel heard a conversation between Annette's parents through an open window that night. It was Annette's father who spoke, in which he said to his wife "Just because she won't talk to you as she does to me doesn't mean she won't open up eventually. She's a remarkable girl, honey. I just wish you could see the potential that I see."

During this conversation, Annette stuffed a few leaves and broken pieces of tree bark in the bucket and lit a match.

"She's an enigma to me," said Annette's mother. "And I fear that, even though she has potential, she'll never reach it due to her shyness."

The words of Annette's parents were drowned out by the sound of crackling wood. Nathaniel was too invested in Annette's moments to further listen to the parent's conversation. Annette seemed completely focused on the fire, so he crept closer to her finding the coarse bark of a hardwood tree to hide behind.

Nathaniel was eighteen years old on this night, a year shy of Annette. He was a skinny, short fellow of 5'5". His hair was blonde and parted on the right in a bowl cut. He wore round silver spectacles, a buttoned light-blue dress shirt, brown corduroy dress pants which hugged his slender mid-section and a hand-me-down pair of stuffed loafers.

He watched Annette for several more moments. Annette held the novel to her heart and made an unspoken wish, tossing the book into the fire. She then abandoned the burning book, returning to the house where the conversation between her parents ended and most of the lights were turned off.

Nathaniel spotted a small rectangle of orange light shining on the side lawn from Annette's bedroom window that faced the woods in the opposite direction, which proved that Annette was still stirring. With the front porch sheltered in shadows, Nathaniel crept to the edge of the driveway. He stood listening to the sound of popping wood. As a fine glow emerged from the bucket's rim, Nathaniel felt the same way about her as Annette's father had. If Nathaniel had spoken to her that night, he wondered how his life, and Annette's, would change. Nathaniel knew that the only way to properly announce himself was to personally hand her the newly repaired library book. And so, as young Nathaniel stood there, peering into the bucket while the wilting, flame-licked white pages turned brown, he felt his hopes rise.

*

While in front of the glass case with the library book *The Hobbit* in hand at present, Nathaniel flipped open the first page to find the two remaining unopened violet envelopes that the Dandelion Sisters had given to him. Though he vowed that it would be a considerable time before he would inspire with her again, the time had come nevertheless. With the second envelope in hand, Nathaniel closed the glass. His attention caught sight of Hugo's *Les Misérables*. He shook his head, shut his eyes and turned from the collection of library books.

He found Annette in her office of composed stone cathedrals. The few times he had empty-handedly passed by her door, Nathaniel noticed Annette staring up at the winsome vaults. As he stood in her office doorway with the second violet envelope in hand, Nathaniel caught her looking at something else: the glass cabinet with the ten digit combination lock that had previously resided in the Hall of Thunderstorms.

"I see you've done a bit of redecorating," Nathaniel said as he crossed to her desk. He noticed that several accompanying flourishes had been added: a blank, unmarked wheeled dry-erase board was positioned with an assortment of colored markers. One of Annette's desk drawers was open, exposing the .45 pistol. Beneath the firearm was a manila folder fastened with a steel foldback clip.

Annette stood from her crouched position and turned from the combination lock to Nathaniel. As she did, he looked away from the open drawer towards Annette. The wrinkles in her yellow house dress smoothed themselves out naturally.

"I'd thought you'd forgotten about me," she told him, spying the second violet envelope. She brushed a stray lock of loose red hair back into place behind her left ear. "Out of curiosity, Mr. Cauliflower, and not to sound ungrateful," Annette took the envelope and studied Nathaniel, "but only one violet envelope? The other employees have already filled maybe twenty or thirty Lite-Brite boards by now. Yet here I am on my second envelope."

"It's true that I've been busy with the other muses, leaving you without your own inspirations to delve into," Nathaniel told her. "You must know that, until you remember who you are, or more specifically who you've been, I can't, in good conscience, give you the same amount of envelopes that I give the others."

"Why not?" Annette asked.

"What I need is one of the Nine Greatest Muses in history working these envelopes," Nathaniel told her. "What I *don't* need is a muse in training."

"For the reason that the Nine Greatest Muses are more in touch with their inner-heartstrings," Annette thought out loud.

"Precisely."

"And, correct me if I'm wrong, but didn't I already show you that I have that instinct?"

Nathaniel, evading her question, ordered to "Please open the violet envelope."

Annette opened the flap of the violet envelope and tipped it over an open palm. A red-colored peg tumbled out. Annette held up the peg, inspecting it in the rays of sunlight that poured through the glass openings of her office. She shook her head disapprovingly. To Nathaniel, she said "Where are you getting these colored pegs from, Mr. Cauliflower?" To the many bins filled with orange pegs that had taken up residence in her office, she asked "When am I actually going to start working on the orange ones?"

"When you finally remember being Annette Slocum," he responded.

"And what if I never remember being Annette Slocum?" she asked. "What happens then?"

He filled a cup from her water cooler and handed it to her. "Forgive me for prying," Nathaniel said to her "but the last I heard from Management about your whereabouts, you were living the life of a humble pie maker in a self-owned bakery. What's with the handgun?"

"Wouldn't you like to know," Annette told him, bringing the cup to her lips. "It seems as if we both have questions we want the other to answer but we both leave the other person's questions unanswered."

The peg was inserted. She drank the contents of the cup. Nathaniel also took a drink from the water cooler. Together they waited the few brief seconds before the office folded and unfolded. There came a disheveled discordance of falling nails, screws and the dropping of aged planks of wood which diversified with an explosive descant of giant, iridescent stars erupting amidst a placid nighttime sky. Proudly expanding Supernovas and spinning vortexes of a woodcrafter's worst daydream converged onto a single landscape: an attic smothered in fatalistic blackness where stars twinkled meekly outside of a tiny, half-frosted window.

A memory brushed over Nathaniel in the darkness. He took a few deep intakes of breath hoping that, by doing so, he could stop the memory from resurfacing. For a moment he was successful but then came Annette's words:

"There has to be a light switch or chain somewhere. Ah! Here we are!"

When she grabbed a nearby chain and said these words, Nathaniel's pulse quickened. He could no longer feel his legs beneath him. The light came on, ushering forth the memory he tried so urgently to conceal.

*

The yellow artificial light of the stone root cellar was switched on with the click of the chain. Eighteen-year-old Nathaniel, in his seventh life, entered the musty room by way of a heavy wooden door, which he quietly latched. His shoes sounded heavily on the stone steps as he hurriedly descended to the ground floor with the metal bucket of ashes in hand. There were jars on shelves that contained olives, green beans, corn, tomatoes and other stored vegetables. There was also a small wooden table and a single chair stationed in the center of his workshop.

Nathaniel set the bucket down on the table with as much care as setting down a wet, freshly-glued model airplane. He swept his silver glasses back up to the bridge of his nose and sat in the chair. With his eyes level to the table, Nathaniel slowly tilted the bucket until the ashes, little by little, formed a temporary mountain on his desk. He then set the empty bucket onto the floor by his feet. With vigilant eyes and cautious hands, Nathaniel began the process of repairing Annette's library copy of *Les Misérables*.

To anyone else, the task may seem unworkable. To Nathaniel, he had been told at age eight by an unknown stranger whom he had called his "muse," that he was capable of such unattainable goals. As he began the initial work, he acutely remembered the conversation with his muse:

"How do you do it?" His muse had asked of him when he had been a younger lad.

"Do what?" Eight-year-old Nathaniel had asked.

"Repair the books," the muse had clarified. From Nathaniel's height, the plain-looking, thirty-something woman in the yellow house dress had towered over him. His eyesight had not been the best, but he could tell she had a slender build.

"Oh, that . . ." he had told her, dismissively shrugging his shoulders. "I dunno. Just sort of happens, I guess."

"What sort of tools do you use?" she had then asked.

"Tools?"

"You . . . don't use tools?"

Nathaniel had shaken his head.

"Then how does it happen? How do you take a library book that looks like this . . . and turn it into something else?"

Again, young Nathaniel had shrugged his shoulders.

"Look," had said his muse, "there isn't much time, so I need to make this quick." The muse had paused here, and then announced: "Management sent me here to inspire you . . ."

"Inspire me?" Nathaniel had been confused. "Management?"

"If I inspire you, will you show me how you do it?"

"I don't know if I can. It's only happened once before."

"Once before?"

Nathaniel had nodded his head.

"How?" his muse had asked, coming down to his level. "What happened?"

"Well, there I was…"

"Yes?"

"Setting a small sailboat out to sea in the pond by our house," Nathaniel had continued, stroking the pages of young Annette's copy of Tolkien's *The Hobbit*. Nathaniel had gone on to explain that, a ways down the current he had found a single leather-bound volume from an encyclopedia. Damaged by the water, the ink on its pages had turned blotchy. The pages had the weight of water-logged rags. Where it had come from, Nathaniel hadn't been sure, but as he sat there watching the small sailboat drift along the water's surface, he flipped through the pages of the book. Nathaniel had fallen quiet, fearing that he said too much to his muse.

"What happened then?" his muse had asked him.

"And that's when they arrived."

"Who?"

"The Sisters."

"Come again?"

"They had this tent, you see. And it floated on the water like it was on its own little island. But it wasn't on any island. The tent sat on the water. And there was this sign that said 'Admittance: three dandelions.'"

Nathaniel had been almost certain that his muse's face, as she had stood upright now, went pale.

"There was a small patch of dandelions where I was standing. I swear they weren't there before."

"And what did 'the Sisters' do for you? What did you pay them for?"

"They told me I had the ability to repair things, especially things like the book I found in the water. And I was instructed to bring it home and repair it. So I did. I brought it back here," young Nathaniel had said with a sigh, thinking that he'd gone round the bend, "set it down on the table and stroked the pages of it. Like trying to bring back to life a dead frog."

"A dead frog," his muse had repeated, trying to understand.

"And that's when it happened," Nathaniel had said.

"What happened?"

"My fingers, they began working all by themselves, it seems, like they had the Devil in them. They worked for hours, piecing it all back together . . . until finally, there it was."

"There it was?"

Nathaniel had knelt to the floor where, from underneath the shelf with the jars of vegetables, an object wrapped in cloth had emerged. He had held the wrapped object to his muse, who had touched the fabric with her fingers. The single leather-bound volume from the backwoods pond had been meticulously stitched together. The letters "Sl-Sm" had been neatly scrawled on the cover and spine, labeled by a calligraphy pen. He had felt odd giving the book to her, for it had been a part of a secret that he kept to himself. By having handed it to her, it made him feel vulnerable.

His muse had then covered it with the fabric, handing it back to Nathaniel. He had stashed it back underneath the shelves.

"I've tried several times," Nathaniel had explained. "I've brought back several damaged books, but it's like the first time never happened. Trying to repair a book that's that bad off is impossible." Young Nathaniel had slumped in the chair, defeated. "When I saw Jonas toss the girl's book into the street, and saw her face as it was ripped apart, I thought I'd at least try. So when the girl left the library book in her room during dinner, I opened her bedroom window and brought it back here."

"So here it is."

"Yes Ma'am . . ." Nathaniel had looked ashamedly down at the library book. For a moment he had said nothing. Then, having needed to hear a voice of reason against all this insanity, he raised his eyes up to his muse. "It's impossible, isn't it?"

"Some people would like to think so, yes." His muse had smiled. "But some would say that time travel is impossible too, and they are wrong, aren't they? I've seen time travel. I've seen the books you repaired in my past. This library book, Tolkien's *The Hobbit*, was mine. You did it . . . honestly. It was miraculous, truly miraculous. And maybe I was meant to come here to inspire you and to encourage you to believe that even things that may seem impossible can happen."

"Do you really think so?" he had asked her. Nathaniel had felt excitement of promising adventures suddenly swirl within him.

His muse had nodded.

"I'm Nathaniel, by the way. Nathaniel J." she had then disappeared from the root cellar, leaving him alone with his work.

Eighteen-year-old Nathaniel, in 1999, thought of her as he repaired her copy of Jean Valjean's adventures. For many months, as summer turned into fall, and fall crept onto the cusp of winter, Nathaniel snuck to this specific root cellar, where he originally met his muse ten years prior. The hard work in rescuing Hugo's tome came to fruition. It was regularly reconstructed until, on one very cold evening in November, the novel looked as perfect as it had been before Annette had tossed it into the fire. He smiled at himself, knowing that the next day he would present it to her personally. On that next day, in Nathaniel's mind, he and his muse would be reunited at last.

He latched the root cellar door as he did every night, and faced the chilly night air. Though the stars were aplenty, there was a distinctly pure, wintery perfume in the air that warned of snow.

A second pair of hands unlatched the root cellar door that night while Nathaniel was away. Those hands belonged to a second pair of eyes, which belonged to a person designed to thwart Nathaniel's hopes of presenting such a newly fabricated treasure to its eagerly awaiting owner.

*

"Mr. Cauliflower?" Annette's voice was distant, like a voice in the winter wind of that long ago November night in 1999. "Mr. Cauliflower . . ." Her voice wasn't in the wind. It existed in the stark real time of Annette's second inspiration in a stuffy, dry attic which smelled of cedar and mothballs. The buttery shine of the single light bulb displayed a typical garret with its accoutrements: a female bust on a high stand, an ancient dust-coated black sewing machine with a cast iron breakfront and foot petal, gutted ornately-made frames stacked along the spider-webbed walls and timeworn trunks affixed with rusty, calcified locks that had not seen working keys in decades.

Nathaniel wasn't sure how long he was lost in his memory. He deduced it was a discernible amount of time as the attic around them was on the verge of refolding. A roll of thunder signaled the turning of the pop-up page, unsettling the dust on the sewing machine, rattling the frames, and forcing the trunks to move half a centimeter from their original locations. Even the stars outside of the window were monetarily diagnosed as schizophrenic, skipping about like fairies in a child's fantasy world.

"Mr. Cauliflower," Annette addressed him again. "You're sitting on the trunk that my muse-in-training heartstrings are telling me to take with us to the second act of this production."

He jumped up from the trunk to allow her access. The green trunk, which he had fallen upon for support at the time of his prodigious recollections, possessed a hard piece of old masking tape on the top. On it was a single name written in youthful scribble, "Phillip."

"There isn't a second part to this inspiration, Miss Redmond. We're already out of time."

Annette's eyes went wide.

"There's no reason to panic," he told her, adding the word "yet" as he grabbed one handle of the trunk. Annette grabbed the other handle. They moved it to the center of the room. The wooden rafters beneath their feet quivered under the pressure of the pop-up book's eminent end. "What puzzle piece follows?" he asked.

"It's not the trunk itself," Annette told him with indication of insecurity. "It's the items in the trunk that will provide the catalyst."

"Well then," Nathaniel told her. "Let's get this trunk open." But, much to their disappointment, the trunk was locked without a key in sight. Nathaniel took a deep breath and patiently asked Annette, who looked on the cusp of distress, if her heartstrings had any suggestions. "Miss Redmond, are you with me?" It was obvious from the shell-shocked look in her eyes that she was not.

"I . . . I can't . . ." Annette stammered. She was focusing more on the moving floorboards than her own instincts "I can't concentrate with things shaking so much."

"Miss Redmond!" Clearly, Nathaniel addressing her was making very little impact. "Miss Redmond, I need you to take a breath."

Annette started to take a few deep breaths. With each breath she took, the dismantling of the attic around her progressively worsened. Annette's eyes were not on Nathaniel. They were on the single light bulb and chain hanging from the ceiling moving like a pendulum gone certifiable.

"Look at me, Miss Redmond."

"I can't do this," she told him.

"Yes, you can," he challenged her.

Annette shook her head. "No, I can't. I'm not this 'Annette Slocum' woman, Mr. Cauliflower. I don't have muse-in-training heartstrings. Everything that I've done up to this point has been a hunch; maybe it was beginner's luck but, at this exact moment, I don't feel anything. All I feel is a sense of dread that the inspiration is going to end and the contents of our trunk aren't going to be seen by our client, causing yet *another* chain reaction. I'm supposed to be getting married to my fiancé in a sanctuary covered in yellow tulips! I'm not supposed to be here, in this attic, feeling this way! I just - " Annette's words were cut short by one simple word:

"Muse!" Nathaniel had clasped both of his hands on Annette's shoulders. His eyes caught hers and, as they did, Annette was entranced by Nathaniel's sagacity.

He was suddenly at a loss for words to say to her. The last muse he had officially inspired had been in his Second Generation, many Lite-Brite boards and thousands of colored pegs ago! He told Annette, "The ceiling and walls are standing, are they not? The floor may be vibrating but it's still beneath our feet! The setting around us *may* be on the brink of conclusion, but there is still time. There is *always* more time." Nathaniel had more to say. "I've seen what you can do. I've seen you tackle sixty-eight of these violet envelopes, back to back before you retired. You survived. You did it! Honestly! It was miraculous . . ." As he said this, Nathaniel knew these words had once been spoken to him, and were genuinely being replayed. He added as an aside to Annette, ". . . truly miraculous! Please, believe that even things that may seem impossible *can* happen!"

"Do you really think so?" Annette asked.

To which, Nathaniel nodded. "Take another breath."

Annette took a breath.

Yes, the walls were still standing and, yes, the ceiling was also resolute above their heads; Nathaniel had to wonder for how much longer.

"All right," Annette said. "How do you open a lock without a key?"

"That's my Muse," Nathaniel encouraged. "How do you open a lock without a key?"

Annette rushed over to the female bust. There she found a thick sewing needle poking through the right shoulder, which faced the wall. She took the sewing needle and raced along the gradually rupturing floorboards. She sat cross-legged at the trunk fitting the needle into the lock, muttering a prayer. After a few seconds, the lock gave way. She looked at Nathaniel and nodded.

Nathaniel nodded to Annette. The trunk lid was then opened and they looked inside. There were books with awe-inspiring pictures of the cosmos, star charts wrapped in frail hardened rubber-bands, a baby mobile made to look like the solar system and nine packages of unopened glow-in-the-dark stars.

"Well . . ." said Nathaniel.

"Well," said Annette. She grabbed four packages of glow-in-the-dark stars and handed them to Nathaniel. "You take the ceiling; I'll take the books and the star charts."

"What about the rest of the glow-in-the-dark stars?" Nathaniel asked.

"We're saving them for something special," Annette replied, standing up and taking a handful of the empty frames. "It's a last-second project you and I can work on together."

Nathaniel nodded, tore open the plastic, and went straight to work affixing the four packages of glow-in-the-dark stars to the easily accessible ceiling. There was a mixture of sizes ranging from small to large, which he scattered about the ceiling in attempt to emulate the night sky. His hands were steady, but the ceiling itself was shaking so badly he had to attach, and reattach the stars with the supplied putty until they remained put.

As he did this, Annette worked with the empty frames and star charts. She ripped open a packet of stars using the smallest ones as make-shift cornerstones for the backside. She stretched the star charts along the edges of the frames and set them on display, propping them against the walls. She lavishly organized the cosmos books around the frames with covers facing out so, in a short time, the collected images resembled a ring of deep space encircling the perimeter.

She looked at Nathaniel who affixed the last star to the ceiling. He also hung the child's mobile from a protruding nail head. The frames, books, stars and mobile were instantly unaffected by the trembling atmosphere when placed.

He joined her at the exposed back wall of the attic with the remaining packages of stars.

"What's the plan?" he asked.

Annette told him the phrase they were to put on the wall. Only the wall remained as the attic was eaten away by the same page-flitting darkness that had devoured the bowling alley. While the inspiration came to an end, Nathaniel watched Annette take one final look at the message they had left for her client: "Phillip, Don't Forget." (Complete with even the punctuation!)

With that, the ground gave way beneath them, extracting both Nathaniel and Annette out of the inspiration and returning them to Annette's cathedral office.

They stood in a comforting blade of sunlight, basking in its warmth. Nathaniel looked at Annette.

Annette looked at Nathaniel. "I appreciate what you did for me," was all Annette could say.

These words struck a chord inside of Nathaniel. He wished he had heard these words from Annette on that snowy November day when he was eighteen.

*

There was a great snowfall on the November morning when eighteen-year-old Nathaniel shuffled to the root cellar to collect the copy of *Les Misérables*. What troubled Nathaniel was when he discovered that someone was already there, at his table and chair, waiting. The individual was Jonas, Annette's childhood bully, who was actively responsible for destroying her previous library books.

"I don't know how you do it," nineteen-year-old Jonas told Nathaniel. "But I *do* know that you have plans to give this book to her." He held the novel in front of Nathaniel's eyes. "So you want to be her friend, is that it? Share with her your secrets about how you repair the books? What do you think she'll do? What do you think she'll say? Did you think she'd fall wistfully into your arms? Is that it? Did you think you could *fix* her the same way you fixed the books?"

Nathaniel knew better than to answer Jonas' questions. Answering them would only give Jonas more power. Nathaniel saw Jonas' involvement with the library books more of an annoyance and, perhaps on some level, a test Nathaniel was meant to overcome. Nathaniel fathomed, from Annette's perspective, Jonas was tormenting her.

"Well, regardless of what you thought would happen," Jonas went on, "things have drastically changed in the months that you've been working down here. Her father died from heart complications. And also, Annette is married to a detestable car salesman named Lyle."

During that afternoon, Nathaniel was shown the Slocum household where Annette had taken the role of housewife. The tumble-weed type bush beside the mailbox at the side of the road was partially caked with heavy snow. Nathaniel's shoes crunched in the snow as he made his way up the front drive. It was a different driveway, a different life, all together. Nathaniel found his way to the front living room window. He looked behind him to witness the uninhabited winter wasteland that was her new neighborhood before pressing his face against the glass, peering inside. Nathaniel noticed a wedding photo of Annette and Lyle on an end table. Nathaniel felt hopelessness creep within him, which caused his heart to slowly fracture.

Nathaniel walked up to the doorstep of the house. From out of the folds of his winter coat, he removed a parcel wrapped with wedding paper. Nathaniel turned the parcel over. There was a taped hand handwritten note that read the following message:

Annette,

**Sorry I couldn't get this to you any
sooner. Hope this gives you peace
in the present situation.**

Nathaniel then turned the package right-side up, placing it on the porch by the door. As the snow continued to fall, erasing his footsteps, Nathaniel began the long trek home feeling frostbitten both inside and out. That was the day that Nathaniel stopped feeling; it was a numbness that he felt until his murder many years later and, even now, in the afterlife.

*

"You're welcome, Miss Redmond," Nathaniel told Annette, coming out of his memory. He turned and left Annette alone in her office.

Yes, Nathaniel had an exterior to himself that was almost impenetrable since his eighteenth year in his last life. However, even the slightest change in breaking down that barrier could eventually cause his personal ramparts to collapse for good. Nathaniel felt in his pocket for a single, tiny glow-in-the-dark star which he had taken as a keepsake of Annette's latest inspiration; from when he considered feelings that he had not allowed experience in a very long time.

CHAPTER 6: INSIDE THE CANVAS' PAINTED CIRCUS TENT

While the living world trusted innumerable categories of clocks and wristwatches, which heartlessly ticked away trivial seconds, minutes, hours, days and even years, the afterlife participated in its own inimitable method of gauging the time. During a routine Generation, a muse's time was calculated by the amount of pegs that filled a single Lite-Brite grid. In the case of the current Nine Greatest Muses, time was measured by the amount of pegs that disappeared from the deep bins in each of their offices. Judging by the dwindling numbers, it could be ascertained that the muses worked attentively on each assignment. Envelopes were delivered to their postboxes, and those inspirations were administered, one right after the other, without pause. Seeing a project to its conclusion gave Nathaniel a suitable substitute for the unfinished love story involving him and Evangeline. Nathaniel was so thorough in reassigning those inspirations that, save for Annette who was waiting on her third violet envelope, no one had a moment to unwind.

It came as no surprise when they were given a slight respite from their trials. The recompense for their labors came in the form of Nathaniel's second fastidiously organized feast in the conference room. Nathaniel was assiduous in preparing the table for his guests; so much, in fact, that he measured the distances between the formal plates, elegant silverware and sparkling glasses to such precision as to be militantly sophisticated. The tines on the forks, and the slanted table spoons, were pointed down. Knives were pointed in toward the plates; spoons were also placed face-down. Even the dessert-ware had their proper place above the plate. There was an abundance of empty crystal plates purposefully located around the table. White cloth napkins were flawlessly folded into erect triangles and positioned to the left of the dinner plates.

Nathaniel's three hors d'oeuvres consisted of the subsequent menu: a Caprese salad with fresh basil, sliced tomatoes and mozzarella on their own separate dishes, including a watercress soup in individual bowls decorated elegantly with swirls of cream and a side of goat cheese. Thirdly, a notable Tapendale with finely pureed chopped olives, capers, anchovies and olive oil which acted as a spread for the brittle crackers lining the perimeter around it. Comprised main courses were primed on brass charger plates: a steamy roast duck in orange sauce, succulent braised beef and veal rolls with cooked barley marinated in vegetable stock, speckled with peas and sweet corn and, lastly, Lobster Thermidor drenched in a thick layer of melted butter. For dessert he produced poached pears in a port wine topped with caramel spice, a moist chocolate truffle cake, and pastries steadily piled to the conference room ceiling. Nathaniel supplied bubbling pots of coffee, chilled ice water in glass pitchers and even went so far as to flaunt diverse unopened bottles dated their best years: Chablis, Cabernet, Malbec and a wider selection of other red and dry white wines.

"Oh how I've missed these meals," Lucas said as the hors d'oeuvres were set in front of him. He said as an aside to Icarus, who sat to his right "It's about the only thing I've really missed about this place to be honest."

"Is that so, Mr. Richardson?" Icarus asked him. Icarus' voice had a heavy Greek accent, which coaxed a question from Lucas as to the Third Generation Muse's origins. As Nathaniel sat a helping of the hors d'oeuvres soup in front of him, Icarus explained: "I come from a Greek island known as Crete, where the palace of Knossos resided. The ruins, I hear, still exist today."

"Do they really?" Lucas asked, hoping for clarification. "When did you live there?"

"During the Bronze Age, dating back to almost 1600 B.C.," Icarus told him.

"You look young for having been alive back then," Lucas offered. "Also, the name Icarus. I've heard that before. Part of Greek Mythology?"

"Ovid," Fiona smiled. "He was one of my favorite clients."

"You inspired Ovid?" Harriet asked Fiona.

Fiona said humbly, "among other poets. But yes, Mr. Richardson, Icarus is the very same figure from the Greek myth, forever immortalized as one of mythology's most epic escapes."

"And yet there are some that would say that I never quite left Crete," Icarus said, hinting to his demise shortly after having taken flight from his homeland. Icarus took a sip of his soup, politely indicating that he didn't have anything more to say on the matter. He then asked Lucas: "And you? Where and when do you come from, Mr. Richardson?"

"Please, call me Lucas!" Lucas said, glowing, "I was born in the Midwest, in America, in a more modern day than you. I dreamed of someday visiting other states, perhaps exploring the world. *Anyway,* I finally ended up in Portland, Oregon where I became a music teacher." There was a shadow of misery that passed over Lucas' face as he remembered his heartache. "After I lost my best friend in the terrorist attacks on the World Trade Center on 9/11, I was visited by a stranger while in my classroom sorting music."

Nathaniel indifferently circled the table offering the hors d'oeuvres to his guests, setting food before Mr. Andrews, Mr. Dunbar and Harriet. He didn't look at Lucas, nor did he acknowledge that he had been an imperative part of the story.

"The visitor didn't say much," Lucas went on. "But I suppose, in retrospect, it wasn't really anything that he said, you know? It was the violet envelope that he handed to me that provided the catalyst."

Nathaniel stopped at Ms. Pavlova's setting, carefully laying the hors d'oeuvres. There was a moment of silence that passed over the room. He had been too intent on keeping his attention from Lucas to notice that his long ago client was steadily staring in Nathaniel's direction. He timidly accepted the awareness and looked at Lucas.

"Inside the violet envelope," Lucas verbally reenacted the events, "was a single guitar pick. An object which, when placed in my hands, helped cultivate my survival. Right after giving it to me he was gone. To this day I've never had the opportunity to thank my muse. When I was a Seventh Generation muse, I wondered who it was that inspired me, and considered that perhaps it hadn't been a muse at all; maybe it was a complete stranger unaffiliated with these offices. How could I have known that the muse who inspired me was the chef who made such mouth-watering meals between inspirations?"

The question sounded hypothetical so Nathaniel was tentative to answer. It was true that Nathaniel had inspired Lucas, and he was fully aware of how the catalyst had changed Lucas' life. But he had a reason for not introducing himself to his client, and a very good reason at that. It had been a reason that he kept to himself even during this awkward moment.

Lucas raised a glass of Malbec. "To Mr. Cauliflower, who saved me and, furthermore, who sets us all out to save others!"

The other glasses were raised. This was the second time the glasses were raised for him. Unlike the first time, which had been strictly due to his meal, this salute was because of his moral character!

It was Nathaniel's turn to speak. He felt ridiculous standing with the final bowl of watercress soup in hand. His stillness lasted only a second longer before he took a breath and changed the subject. "Where is Miss Redmond?"

The muses, taking their sips, looked about themselves and conceded that Annette was not at the table.

Harriet answered "I told all of them about the staff meeting like you requested. She must not have heard me. Go figure."

"I'll find her," Fiona stood.

Harriet stood with Fiona, impersonating a sense of authority.

"No, I'll go," Nathaniel told them, setting the bowl at Annette's empty setting. "Please, enjoy. Help yourselves to the rest of the hors d'oeuvres. I'll be along with her shortly." Before anyone could object, he was headed toward the door.

As Nathaniel left the room for the hallway, he could hear Icarus' comment to the room "there are nine place settings, yet only eight of us are being served. Do you think Mr. Cauliflower will be dining with us during this meal?"

"Mr. Cauliflower doesn't eat," Fiona could be heard. "At least not that I've seen. I assume he takes his meals in private once the plates are cleared."

"What about you, Icarus?" Lucas's voice chimed. "Who was your muse?"

"I didn't have the privilege of being granted a muse," Icarus told him. "However, if I were to give a word of thanks to someone who attempted to save my life, my individual would have to have been my father, Deadalus, who crafted my wings. He was the closest thing to a 'muse' for me."

"Mrs. Slocum once said that a muse doesn't need to have a Lite-Brite board and colored pegs to inspire," Fiona said to him. "Not a truer statement was ever spoken."

Nathaniel stopped paying attention to the discussion. Giving a slight knock on the wood frame, he entered Annette's office.

Annette was preoccupied in her own affairs. Since he had seen her last, Annette had solved the ten-digit combination lock on the glass cabinet. The contents were exposed, lying on her desk. She held up the mason jar of twenty-one dead dandelions, studying them from within the glass. Annette wore a pair of latex gloves as if handling a piece of important evidence.

Hatred seethed within Nathaniel as he watched her fondle the specific instrument of his past. The examination did not stop there. Nathaniel watched as Annette abandoned one container for another. Annette, with her fingertips, held up the jar that contained the piece of parchment ripped from a ledger. Some of the words were exposed to the sunlight. Annette squinted, bringing the jar closer to her face to inspect it more in depth.

He took a step forward but felt himself stymied by his fury. "Find anything interesting?" he asked, eventually finding his voice.

Unaware she was being watched, Annette jumped. The jar carelessly left her fingers and flew into the air. She scrambled to catch it but gravity was far more devious. The glass jar, like the dessert plate in his kitchen, collided with the floor and shattered onto a pool of sunlight.

"I'm . . . I'm sorry," she said.

"Leave it."

"I couldn't help myself," Annette tried to explain. "The cabinet was sitting there in my office with the combination staring at me, almost as if begging to be solved. After a while, the word came to me. Almost as if . . ."

"As if what, Miss Redmond?" Nathaniel wanted to know.

"Almost as if it were a memory," she told him defensively with hands on her hips.

Nathaniel's focus was elsewhere; not on Annette's words or the broken jar, but on Annette's eyes, trying to deduce the irregularity. It then occurred to him: Annette's eyes, which had noticeably been a shining green were, at present, undoubtedly blue. The Dandelion Sisters, upon having handed him the three violet envelopes in his seventh life, predicted this would happen.

"Ever since you arrived here you've been digging for information on me," he told her. "I'm equally curious about you. So I'll make a deal. I tell you a secret about me, and you tell me a secret about you."

Annette said without thinking twice "Deal."

There was a pause before they both said, at the same time, "You go first." To which Annette gave a sly smile.

Nathaniel frowned. He didn't know who Annette Redmond was, but he presumed she was far more dangerous than he had remembered her to be all those Christmas Eves ago.

"I'll start," he said. "But I'll need a pair of those latex gloves."

Annette nodded, turned to the desk and opened a drawer. Nathaniel spied her pistol, the file and an exposed box of latex gloves he had not seen before. Annette did not keep any of this hidden from Nathaniel. They were locked in a delicate, and conceivably intimate, game of truth sans the dare.

Nathaniel took two gloves from the box, fitting them over his hands. He bent down. Brushing away pieces of glass, he picked up the freed parchment. The page was held to the light, though not in the ray's direct path, so they could both view it accurately. The document listed the name Nathaniel J. Cauliflower seven times each with different, nonconsecutive ages and years throughout history; a cost of three dandelions was scribed by each entry. It had been since 1807 when he initially signed it, yet the day unfolded upon him like a gaping flap of circus tent.

*

The Paris of 1807 in Nathaniel's memory was ruled over by Napoleon Bonaparte, who had crowned himself emperor on May 18th, 1804. The ceremony of Napoleon's self-appointed inauguration had taken place in Notre Dame and was the precursor of many Roman buildings to appear in the landscape of the ever-growing metropolis. Nathaniel's painter practiced techniques in both Romanticism and also Neo-Classicism. In the year 1807, his master decorated many houses with tour de force and worked with well-to-do Parisians until he came into good graces with Napoleon's entourage.

Nathaniel was a faithful and quiet apprentice who assured that his painter's brushes and canvases were well cared for. Even though Nathaniel also enthusiastically learned techniques from his master, his amateur fingers were not motivated with such a skilled heart. Where perfection came naturally to his painter, Nathaniel worked conscientiously to improve on his own strokes. Day after day, the subjects sat in pre-calculated positions. Nathaniel sat and watched his painter work, studying the muscles in the painter's hands. Nathaniel moved his own hand in the same way hoping to emulate his genius. However, when it came time for him to practice on his own canvases, Nathaniel tried too hard and was ultimately dissatisfied with his inexperienced portraits.

"You have raw talent," said his painter one evening as they shared a meal. The painter was forty-nine and bore a clean shaven face with a jutting chin and well-defined cheek bones. His shoulder length hair was parted to the side. He wore fresh, high-collared linens with a cravat, tight breeches and silk stockings.

"The issue is harnessing it, boy," the painter told Nathaniel. "Control your brush. Be confident."

"But I do control my brush," said Nathaniel.

"Ah, but you control your brush the way I do." The painter lifted a single brush to Nathaniel's eyes. "You must have your own way of working a brush. Don't you see that each brush is as unique as a woman?"

The painter's apprentice shook his head.

"See here. The handle is like the bones and tendons, the bristles are as fine as a woman's hair. But it's the soul of the brush, boy. Within this brush, within all of them, is energy that the artist must control. You must immerse yourself within the soul of the brush and, to do that, you must paint uninhibited."

"Uninhibited?" Nathaniel had asked. "But the rules…?"

"What I've taught you is technique," said the painter. "What you must teach yourself is assurance and passion. A painting can be just a painting, but it's the relationship with the artist and his brush that gives the art its soul. It's the affair, the embrace."

But the painter's words were lost on Nathaniel.

"Have you never been with a woman, boy?"

Nathaniel had shaken his head.

"Well, there's the problem." The painter sat the brush on the table and took a sip of wine. "Today, I was commissioned by a wealthy family to paint their daughter. In three days time, you will go without me and paint her."

Nathaniel had choked on a piece of bread. "Me?"

"Yes, boy. You will find that the only way to experience true passion with a woman for the first time is to paint her. There is nothing more intimate than understanding their form, their shape. Painting a woman is far more erotic than simply having your way with her." Standing from his chair, the painter patted Nathaniel's shoulder, swigged a final sip of his wine and retired to bed.

Nathaniel sat at the table with his fearful eyes staring into the darkness beyond the candlelight. Starlight glowed gently through the open window. Though outside it was an early autumn evening fresh with the scents of gardens abloom with petals, the flowers barely masked the stench of Paris' sprawling city. There was a smell of fresh paint and thinner inside the studio which heightened the atmosphere around them. The room was cast in an orange, shifting hue of candlelight. Nathaniel climbed to his attic loft where he pulled out another blank canvas. He lit a thick yellow candle, setting it close to his work so that he could see.

He took a paint brush and held it in his hands. He tried to adhere to the master's words, attempting to paint with the soul of the brush. After half an hour, Nathaniel grew more and more disgusted with the painting. He poured his wishes of wanting to become the perfect painter into his work, but all he managed to create was the likeness of a withered old circus tent amid a field of motionless dandelions. How could he possibly be able to paint the young woman when all that he made was rubbish?

In a tempered fit, he grabbed the wet canvas by both paint-spotted hands and tossed it across the floorboards into the shadows. Nathaniel crouched down to gather up the paints and brushes he had used, fuming over his lack of talent.

There came a sound in his attic. Weight pressed on his floorboards beneath him causing them to rasp and cry out in objection. Nathaniel turned his eyes toward the shadows. Taking the candle he had painted by to the darkness, he revealed the miracles that had arisen. Nathaniel found a lawn of fresh grass dotted with real dandelions! Standing on the turf, housed below his rafters, was the tent that Nathaniel had painted, constructed out of real leather and multi-colored aged rugs. To make matters more unsettling, the tent's front flap opened invitingly, with pitch-darkness beyond.

Nathaniel pinched himself, thinking this to be an affect from too much wine at supper. The vision stayed. He slowly walked to the open tent. As he did, Nathaniel noticed a wooden sign had been shoved into the earth which read:

Dandelion Sisters
Admission: Three Dandelions

Nathaniel picked three dandelions and brought them with him as he approached the otherworldly tent, with candle in hand. He stopped outside of the tent's opening. Nathaniel thought it foolish to walk into a tent that had sprung from his own canvas, but there was a sense of adventure that kissed him on both cheeks, ushering affectionately.

*

Nathaniel, who retold the recollection's description to Annette, stopped. He held the ledger in his hands, feeling the heaviness of the paper and tracing the indentations of the quill as it had been used to document his visits. He wasn't quite sure why his hands began to shake while holding the parchment. Holding this ledger was a token of the decisions he had made which led him to be here in Annette's office. It was as if revisiting an old house with tumbledown wings and brittle, bare-branched winter gardens; a gallery of words said and actions taken.

He heard Evangeline's voice in his head again repeating the words she had spoken to him in front of the mailbox: "I can't . . . I'm sorry." Nathaniel wondered if he had never stumbled inside the tent on that fateful autumn evening in 1807, would the disaster with Evangeline have been avoided?

"There are seven appointments listed on this ledger," Annette prodded, "varying in years and ages. The only thing consistent is the name 'Nathaniel J. Cauliflower.' Surely you weren't named the same in all seven timelines?"

"No," Nathaniel confirmed. "I was only named Nathaniel in two of the seven lives that I've led: the first and the last. In one of my lives was I officially surnamed Cauliflower. But the Dandelion Sisters, and the cost of admission, have remained the same."

"And yet in every instance where you encountered the Sisters, you always signed as Cauliflower."

"Only because," Nathaniel went on to explain, "every time I stepped through the circus tent's opening, I was instructed to."

*

In point of fact, Nathaniel was instructed to scribe the name 'Cauliflower' on the pages in 1807. It took place in a tent, accompanied by the unkempt leather and mildewed rugs that made up the establishment's shell, which smelled of damp, ancient rot. Had it not sprung from his attic floor moments before, he would have turned his back on such a sad abandoned plot. Conversely, as it had entered his life in the most auspicious way, Nathaniel ignored the obvious blemishes of the dilapidated pavilion and went on to explore its contents.

His candle's meek glow uncovered an object: an ornate wooden lectern sat dead-center of the tent, positioned in a rigid stature the way some unlucky trolls become stone when exposed to the garish light of morning. The lectern, constructed of walnut wood, was richly carved into a substantial echelon overgrown with timeless dandelions. On the slightly slanted surface of the lectern's writing desk was a leather-bound ledger opened to a fresh page. To the right of the lectern were a quill and a bottle of black ink. He waved his candle to his right and left where he found nothing but the inside of the nearby putrid parapets.

He placed the three dandelions and candle on the lectern to inspect the quill further. As Nathaniel reached for the quill, the drops of melting wax slid down the side of his candle, spreading along the surface of the writing desk. The plume was light on his right hand. In a way almost childish, he brought the feather to his nose, tickling himself by brushing the wispy barbs against his face.

He unscrewed the bottle's lid and dabbed the end of the hollow shaft into the ink. Nathaniel was, by no means, an author and possessed limited skills in perfecting his penmanship. The action seemed almost reflexive, as if the quill knew what needed to be done, with Nathaniel as its vessel. The quill, having taken control of Nathaniel's motor skills, guided his hand to the page.

No sooner than he and the quill scrawled anything on the ledger's page, there came a horrendous screeching that besieged the encamping silence. The sound was an awful rattling of tiny, piercing bells repeating itself, over and over in a pattern: a two second ring followed by two seconds of silence in which the shooting bell's echo had extinguished, followed by the same distastefully obtrusive clamor.

Nathaniel, with the ink-stained quill in hand, lifted the candle from the desk, waving the flickering wick through the room to distinguish the noise's origin. It was after a few seconds of enduring even more persistently dreadful ringing, that he spotted the source: an antique wall phone mounted on the far wall opposite the tent's entrance. The wall phone was foreign to him but he examined it anyway.

The body of it was made of oak. There was a black ivory mouthpiece that jutted out from its front. Below the mouthpiece rested a small writing desk that curved downward. Above the mouthpiece were two silver bells that vibrated with deafening reverberation. To the left of the phone's body was another piece of black ivory, which dangled from a hook, connected to the phone by a thin black wire.

Nathaniel knew that the sound came from this device, but he didn't have the slightest clue how to tame it. It was then that the receiver jumped from the side cradle on its own, swinging down below. The ringing stopped. But with this comforting silence there came another far quieter sound.

The noise sang from the receiver as it had suspended below the phone. Nathaniel placed the quill on the phone's desk, picking up the receiver and placing it to his ear to hear the message. He hoped that the faint sound on the other end would explain everything to him. As Nathaniel would soon discover, the call proved informative, starting off with a single word queried by a young female child: "Cauliflower?"

"Bonjour?" Nathaniel asked into the receiver. Considering that the useful invention of Alexander Graham Bell would not yet be invented until many years following this exchange, Nathaniel had no idea how the voice managed to come from such a tiny box to his ear. He pictured himself stumbling farther and farther into a dream, embarking ever more as the voice then replied.

"I see that you have brought us three dandelions," said the child's voice.

Nathaniel turned his eyes back to the lectern. "How do you know I've placed them there? I'm the only one here."

"Into the mouthpiece, please," the child instructed.

Nathaniel turned to the wall phone and said "The mouthpiece?" He placed his lips an inch from the apparatus between the desk and two bells. "Is this what you are referring to?" He had inquired while keeping the receiver to his ear.

"Oh yes," said the child. Her voice had a decidedly neutral accent, which aided very little in attempting to calculate her current location. "That is lovely. Now, we must have you sign the ledger, Mr. Cauliflower. Once you have done so, we can begin."

"Mr. Cauliflower?"

"Why yes, you *are* Nathaniel J. Cauliflower, I presume?"

"I'm afraid you must have me mistaken for someone else. My first name is Nathaniel but I don't go by 'Cauliflower.'"

"I do believe we have the correct gentleman. Were you not, only moments ago, painting this tent on a canvas?"

"Well, yes."

"And were you not wishing that you had the talent of your master so that you can, in three days time, successfully paint the daughter of one of the Parisian aristocrats?"

"How do you know this?"

"We know about you, Nathaniel J. Cauliflower. We know that you were born on September 9th, 1784 into a farming family's care. We know that, due to a terrible harvest in 1788, your parents could not provide for an extra mouth. You were left in your master's care at the age of four and have been under his tutelage since. We were with you at the window of his house, listening to the screams during the storming of Bastille in 1789. We were with you at the beheading of Marie Antoinette and Louis XVI in 1793. We were with you when Napoleon Bonaparte crowned himself emperor in 1804! We also know that, if you don't put that candle down soon, it may burn your very important, very talented fingers."

By now, the candle in Nathaniel's hand had melted forcing hot wax to burn his left hand's skin. He grimaced. The time had come to set the candle down. He could not set it upon the fierce slant of the phone's small desk. Only the lectern's tabletop was a suitable surface. "Please place the receiver on the phone's desk, Nathaniel J. Cauliflower. We will wait patiently."

Nathaniel looked questioningly at the receiver. In retrospect, Nathaniel should have put the receiver back on the cradle, ending the call. But history had not been written in that way. Nathaniel placed the receiver on the phone's desk and approached the lectern with the dripping candle. Before he took a step, he heard the child's voice on the other end as she said "Please, don't forget the quill!" He reached for the receiver for more instructions. "Please scribe the following: Nathaniel J. Cauliflower, age 23, 1807, cost of admission: three dandelions."

Nathaniel turned to the desk where the quill had been set. He hesitated but grasped the quill anyway. When he approached the lectern, he spotted a ring of dried wax where his candle had been situated beforehand. Nathaniel rested the candle in the same location. He dipped the quill into the ink and timidly wrote what the girl had asked of him. It took him considerable time to form the letters. His schooling had not been sufficient, but the quill was patient.

The candle's burning light filled the room. He left the candle on the lectern and crossed to the wall phone, picking up the receiver.

It was not the young child's voice on the phone. The voice belonged to a melodious middle-aged woman. "We thank you, Nathaniel J. Cauliflower, for your contribution. We have not had customers in many years and we are delighted to share with you what we can about the days, years and lifetimes to come. We are not genies who grant wishes. Instead, we simply stir the dormant sediment within. You wish to have the talent of your painter do you not?"

"Yes," Nathaniel said.

"Whether you are aware or not, you already have the talent of your painter. You just don't have the confidence within yourself to produce what he can. What we can offer is to speed the process along. When you leave this tent, you will feel a prickling in your fingertips. And when that prickling occurs, you will find that, instead of bending to the brush's will, the brush will bend to yours. You will paint the most remarkable portraits, far exceeding the talents of your master. In three days, you will have the confidence to paint the portrait of a young woman of a wealthy Parisian family. And her name . . ."

The voice grew older, filled with moldering age. "Her name will be Evangeline."

"Evangeline?"

"Once you paint her, Nathaniel J. Cauliflower, you will find that there will be no turning back. The love story will erupt like a rampant wildfire in a dry wheat field." The voice had become raspier as if a strong wind wound itself through a decaying, hollow tree. "With this prickling of your fingers comes a dire price. You must keep these paintings of yours a secret or your master will find them. And if he finds them, you will find that your love story with Evangeline will become not a . . . saccharine tale . . . but a dreadful mania lasting seven lifetimes. You will find yourself chasing her, obsessively clutching to her memory, only to have it slip through your fingers. It will ultimately lead to your murder! And not one murder, oh no! It will be seven! Seven murders keep the continuum circling for decades and decades to come!"

"I will not listen to you anymore!" Nathaniel shouted.

"You *will* listen! We have been waiting for you! You paid your three dandelions. You signed our ledger! It shall be that you will have your talents immediately expedited!"

Nathaniel, with trembling fingers, slammed the receiver back on the cradle and the voices were silenced. He ran the short distance from the phone to the lectern and tripped. The lectern, and the items it held, collided with the floor. The candle's flame was snuffed out. He picked himself from the floor and ran to the circus tent's entrance, reentering the safety of his attic loft. He heard the rolling of his candle as it travelled out through the tent toward his feet. He bent down and picked up his candle, turning back to where he exited.

The tent was no longer there, nor was the field of dandelions. All that remained was the attic loft that he had lived in since 1784.

He walked along the creaking floorboards and found the painting that he had chucked to the shadows. He held the painting up with his left hand while clutching the candle in his right. He brought the painting to the starlight and studied it. Three illustrated female children stared knowingly back at him from the wide blackness of the painted tent. Nathaniel was certain he had not painted them.

He then felt a prickling in his fingers of his right hand. He looked down at the candle, dropping it. With each passing second, the prickling became almost painful! Nathaniel soon discovered that the prickling would only subside if he painted the portraits that the Dandelion Sisters had spoken. It was his secret, his curse, his duality. Nathaniel painted faces of strangers he had never before met all through the night. By the time the painter and Nathaniel sat down for breakfast, Nathaniel was back to his usual unsure self. At the end of the day, as the stars once again appeared in the sky, Nathaniel's gift returned. As he painted, Nathaniel knew that it had been foolish of him to enter the tent. On the evening of the second day, as Nathaniel finished Fiona's portrait, and after he hid it away in his rafters, he sat at his window looking out onto the city of Paris. How he dreaded what the third day would bring: when he would finally meet the young woman named Evangeline.

It was on that night that he spotted a beautiful young woman, who he would later recognize to be the subject whom he was assigned. She wore a billowing petticoat and opera gloves while being escorted by her elderly chaperone, passing by Nathaniel's open loft window. It was on the night, before he set out to paint her, when Evangeline looked up at Nathaniel and smiled.

*

Nathaniel finished his story.

Annette, who had listened to the tale, was silent for a few moments. She had then said: "It must have been terrifying inside that tent, Mr. Cauliflower."

Nathaniel sighed and explained evenly: "The seven past occurrences that I've shared with the Dandelion Sisters were nothing in comparison to the tragedies that quickly befell." He exhaled and stood from the swivel chair. "But, that's a different story for another time."

There came a knock on Annette's office door. Fiona stood in the frame with her hands casually resting at her sides. "Mr. Cauliflower, Miss Redmond, the others are wondering if you'll be joining us for the meal in the conference room?"

Nathaniel and Annette looked at one another. Annette took the single ledger artifact from Nathaniel, placing it in her desk drawer for safe-keeping. Nathaniel didn't object of her touching the paper. They then walked out of Annette's office, joining Fiona, leaving behind the memories that had recently been shared.

After the meal ended and the muses visited their offices for a long rest, Nathaniel cleared the plate settings. As the brass cart was piled high, he exited the conference room and disappeared into his private office. He found himself in his kitchen emptying the dishes into a sink bubbling with soap and water. There was enough food for a single setting. He considered the remaining portion.

In a short time afterward, Nathaniel emptied his office desk of the three Lite-Brite boards. He situated a table cloth on the surface, setting out his own last helping of hors d'oeuvres and main dishes. He poured himself some wine. He then opened his desk drawer, taking out a single candle; the very candle he had held in his hands back in 1807. It had been decades since he lit the wick. Considering that he had revealed the secret events leading to him meeting Evangeline, he thought it appropriate.

He sat in his swivel chair and consulted the food. With the fork, he procured a piece of the lobster. He held the lobster to his lips. After a quiet prayer to Management, Nathaniel took his meal. For the first time since he had been murdered in his seventh life, Nathaniel was able and allowed himself to taste it.

CHAPTER 7: SCREAMS IN THE SNOW

The sun had already taken its rightful noon-time stance as the horse-drawn carriage pulled up to the impressive French chateau. The horse hooves, that had once been filled with pride as they traipsed the Parisian countryside, were quieted. The carriage driver descended from his seat and footboard, promptly opening the door. It was then that the carriage's occupant, twenty-three-year-old Nathaniel, stepped from the transport, setting foot on the folding step, then to the washed stones of the front walk.

He wore polished shoes a size too big for him, well-fitting, perfectly tailored trousers, a waist length single-breasted coat with long tails, and a high-collared white lace shirt. He carried a strapped leather satchel that held his brushes and paints. The house attendants transported the easel and canvas he had brought with him. Though he appeared professional and collected, Nathaniel shuddered on the inside. The Dandelion Sisters had given him all of the tools that he needed to successfully complete this painting, but he still heeded their warnings while crossing the manor's threshold.

The chateau itself had been constructed in the Baroque period. Colonnades lined the exterior of the bold white massing of the façade. The gray roof was capped with constructed domes and dramatically slanted rooftops spotted with chimneys. If it were not for the glass in the numerous windows, which reflected the skies, the manor would have been comparable to a gray monochromatic canvas.

From the front door through the atrium, venturing through great sitting rooms, Nathaniel noticed rich tapestries, lavishly imagined staircases and paneled rooms with hand-painted murals of faces from Evangeline's family history. The entire house seemed to sparkle with as much vivacity as a giant's hoard of multi-colored jewels.

Nathaniel was led to the solarium: a room with black porcelain floor tiles, a flowing three-tiered stone fountain and a garden of mismatched foliage. The beveled Baroque windows of the conservatory stretched to the soaring glass-domed ceiling.

The easel and canvas were faced toward the fountain. A sitting chair was positioned by his media. He was left to his own devices and, with trembling fingers, unfastened his satchel, removing his paints. He removed a glass from his master's studio, dipping it under the fountain's trickling waters until it three-quarters filled.

The door to the conservatory opened to reveal his subject and her chaperone.

He recognized Evangeline immediately as the young woman who had smiled at him from the street. The fabric of her dress was a pale cream. Layers of petticoats flowed eloquently to the ground. Nathaniel stood motionless, staring at the locks of her hair that had been positioned around her fabric-covered neck. Her face appeared soft and innocent with white powder. Constricted by a corset, Evangeline barely took a breath. It was apparent that Nathaniel and Evangeline were unbearably uncomfortable in their clothing. Nathaniel understood the unease of wearing a compressing costume. He felt perspiration under his coated arms, and could no doubt imagine that Evangeline felt similar sufferings.

"I'll be quick about this, Mademoiselle." Nathaniel's voice was beleaguered by nerves.

Evangeline said nothing. She raised her chin a centimeter in recognition of his words.

He instructed Evangeline into the pose that he wished to paint her in and frowned, shifting his eyes from the subject to the canvas. Nathaniel sat in his chair and started to paint. At first, Nathaniel felt as he always had, succumbing to the routine of emulating the painter's technique. But the more that he concentrated on Evangeline and the way that the sun struck the fabric of her petticoat, or the way that her nostrils carefully flexed as she breathed, the more Nathaniel's work improved.

He imagined himself standing from his chair abandoning his paints. In his mind, his young fingers untied the strings of her corset, granting his subject the ability to breathe. In his mind he stood behind her, listening to her intake of breath, his eyes catching a single drop of sweat tracing her earlobe. Nathaniel imagined walking his fingers around her waist, where he would place his hand on her stomach. In mentally feeling her body expand and contract, Nathaniel imagined the sensation of her freedom from constriction.

His portrait was finished as the mid-morning sun dipped below the evening's horizon. When he packed up his paints, Evangeline relaxed as best she could in her corset.

"May I see it, Monsieur?" she asked him. Her voice was like the euphonious chirping of an elated nightingale.

Nathaniel was suddenly protective of his work. He fretted that, if Evangeline saw his painting, it may trigger the Sisters' predicted havoc. But the world didn't crumble around them as Evangeline crossed behind the canvas. Conversely, the world seemed to finally converge for him like a shadow merging into light.

Evangeline asked "May I visit your studio one afternoon? I would like to see more."

"More, Mademoiselle?"

"Surely you've painted others?"

The stunned look on Nathaniel's face could not hide the fact that he had, indeed, painted more. Nathaniel closed his satchel. Without suitably answering her request, Nathaniel bid her farewell.

"Monsieur," Evangeline called to him as he passed her chaperone. "May I at least have the pleasure of your name?"

Nathaniel turned and said, after a moment's hesitation, "Cauliflower."

"It was nice spending the day with you, Monsieur Cauliflower. My name is Evangeline."

To which Nathaniel bowed his head slightly to her, then to the chaperone, showing himself out. As he climbed into the horse-drawn carriage and as stars sprinkled the horizon, he noticed three random dandelions that had grown beside the stone porch. He wasn't sure if it was a fluttering of his heart for Evangeline, or if it was a twinge of fear from the significant dandelions but, either way, he hurriedly closed the carriage door. All through the carriage ride home, even into the night hours, his thoughts were consumed of her and of the events of that day.

*

Nathaniel startled awake. Somehow, in the short time after he had eaten his meal until now, he had fallen asleep, dreaming of Evangeline. It didn't surprise him that his dreams had been of his beloved. What surprised him was that he had fallen asleep and dreamed in the first place! Being a respected afterlife representative, Nathaniel slept and dreamed very little. Most of his memories of Evangeline were presented to him in perceptually reconstructed phantasms. When the thought of death approaches, it is often immediately equated with the idea of a final Judgment. In the afterlife, Judgment did not personify itself in the form of a divine being with scales who outweighed transgressions. The real sentencing occurred within the scope of one's self.

All muses, in their brief stay in the department, shared the same blank stare as they remembered the details of their lives. They were swept up by memories while in mid-step, or perhaps mid-chew, or perhaps mid-inspiration. At this moment, the department was tranquil as each muse had collapsed on soft couch settees, four poster beds with fluffy pillows, cushiony recliners and even tautly fastened windblown hammocks that Management provided. Much work had transpired thus far and the muses deserved their rest.

As Nathaniel parentally checked on his slumbering muses he wished that their dreams were not filled with the same vivid recollections that his had been.

He opened the common bathroom door at the end of the hall where a black hoodie hung on the inside hook. He took the hoodie with him as he made his way to Annette's office doorway. Nathaniel prepared to knock, finding that Annette was fast asleep in her house dress, cradled by a three-cushion leather couch blanketed with a hand-woven quilt. The sunlight from the cathedral windows dimmed slightly by a passing white cloud, which aided in casting the room in a soft, blue light apt for napping. As Nathaniel watched Annette sleep, he deduced that her dreams were pleasant.

The placid nature of Annette's face hinted to a memory of which she was fond. Perhaps she was dreaming of her upcoming wedding day. Perhaps she was dreaming of being in a safe place around friends of whom she was particularly enjoyed. Regardless of what she was dreaming, Annette's face scrunched. Her brow furrowed as she sneered a single word in her sleep: "Cauliflower," which was followed by her unconsciously adjusting on the couch with her back to him.

Nathaniel's liking to her in this state was quickly abated. With the black hoodie in hand, he turned to Annette's desk. There he found the closed drawer that held the pistol. The dry erase board had been etched with a few more scribbles. He crossed over to the board, inspecting it. The faint stink of recently opened dry-erase markers lingered. Calendar dates of thunderstorms were scattered around the inside perimeter. There was hardly enough space above and below each date to add additional information. The center of the board was kept blank. The algorithm that Annette formed had not yet found its function.

He looked at her once more, shaking his head. In the short time that he inspected the board, Annette shifted face-forward. Her left arm hung down as her right arm folded beneath her. Nathaniel let out a quick muted sigh, stretching the hoodie around the back of Annette's swivel chair. He extracted the third violet envelope from his pants pocket, adjusted it vertically just-so against her Lite-Brite and proceeded to leave.

He heard Annette ask: "Mr. Cauliflower?"

He stopped and turned to her. "Miss Redmond, you're awake."

She sat up on the couch giving a stretch. Annette then noticed the delivered violet envelope. She asked, "Are you not coming with me?"

"I figured you're ready to tackle the violet envelopes on your own."

"Oh come on," she told him, turning her head slightly to the side. A single strand of red hair tumbled down to her waist. "What's one more consort-appointed inspiration between friends?"

"Friends?" he quizzed her.

Annette stood from the couch. Her house dress smoothed as it had before. She crossed to the desk casually picking up the violet envelope. "We never had the opportunity to finish our conversation before dinner."

"Oh?"

"You were telling me about your first life and the Dandelion Sisters."

Nathaniel puffed in defense. "I suppose you want to know more?"

"No," Annette told him. "Well, I mean yes. I do want to hear more, but . . ."

Nathaniel interjected impatiently by saying, "Yes?"

"You told me a secret about you but I never told you a secret about me."

"Oh," Nathaniel told her, suddenly feeling foolish. "I suppose you're right."

"You've been avoiding me since the last conversation."

"I have not," he countered.

"You have."

"I haven't!"

"At the end of the meal you gathered the empty plates so fast it was an urgent whirl-wind of crystal."

"Well," Nathaniel started but then stopped himself. "Now see here, Miss Redmond, I don't need to explain my actions to you." He went on defending himself anyway, "The meal came to a close and your fellow peers, including yourself, had that half-mast look."

"Half-mast?"

"Eyelids were drooping, Miss Redmond, in the same fashion as a flag is lowered on a pole when it's half - " He rolled his eyes. "Why am I saying this when it's glaringly noticeable why I cut the meal short? Everyone was getting tired. What was I supposed to do? Delay their dozing?"

Annette raised her eyebrows and looked at the envelope by way of waving a white flag in surrender. "Anyway, I figured that after what you shared, you might have been interested in what I had to share."

Nathaniel stood unyielding to Annette's imposed self-importance.

"Or would you prefer that I confess nothing? Open this envelope and be done with it?"

"Do whatever you desire, Miss Redmond," he told her, massaging the bridge of his nose with his right middle finger and thumb.

"Perhaps I can tell you a secret during the downtime in the third inspiration?"

Nathaniel pursed his lips. "How presumptuous of you to think there *will* be downtime."

Annette opened the violet envelope. She held in her hand a purple-colored peg. As she took a sip of water from her water cooler, Annette placed the peg into the face of the Lite-Brite board. She was joined by Nathaniel, who picked up the black hoodie and handed it to her.

"You'll need this," he curtly explained.

"Will I?" She made no effort to take the black hoodie.

Nathaniel rolled his eyes and helped, wrapping the bulk of it around her. He then took it upon himself to zip up the front. As he did, the office folded and unfolded as it had done the previous two times. Instead of the tumbling of Christmas ornaments or the twists and turns of an attic constructing itself, they found themselves swept in a heartless crashing of ice, snow and a bitterly freezing wind. As the pop-up book settled around them Nathaniel and Annette stood in a dismally gray winter afternoon. What limited sunlight could be seen on that day had already been blotted by clouds which rolled above them causing abundant flakes of snow. The blizzard obscured both Nathaniel and Annette's vision so that they could only see a few feet in any direction.

As she stood there in her yellow dress and black hoodie, ankle deep in the snow, Annette's eyes glazed as if she was lost in thought and perhaps instinctively returning to warmer memories. Nathaniel assumed she was envisioning the lazy summer afternoons that she and Adam would have most likely spent in the shade, sipping Mint Juleps at sunset. Perhaps she remembered how her fiancé's body warmth in the bed beside her had been all the heat that she needed through the winter nights. Or perhaps her thoughts settled comfortably before a fireplace, where she had most likely stood poking the logs and, having been in the warmth of the ever-growing flames, her soon-to-be husband would have held her from behind in the surrounding orange blaze of the fire.

Annette's mind wasn't the only one who found itself consumed. Standing there in the blizzard, Nathaniel remembered warm memories of his own.

*

One summer evening in 1808, twenty-three-year-old Nathaniel stood outside Evangeline's window. Not having been the sort of lad to watch women through glass, Nathaniel felt awkward. Still, he had made a promise with Evangeline that he intended to keep. For months leading up to this night, Nathaniel had avoided taking her back to his master's studio until Evangeline had sternly, yet playfully, stated that if he wanted to see her again, he must wisely introduce her to his additional inspired paintings. It had been an ultimatum that he could not refuse.

In those few months preceding the taunt, Nathaniel's affections toward her had developed into an infatuated craving. When he slept, he dreamed of her powdered skin, gently flexed nostrils, her short intakes of breath and heartbeat. Upon waking, Evangeline stayed with Nathaniel as he did his marketing, as he swept the floors and when he picked up a brush to clean the bristles. Had it been love that he had felt for Evangeline? They had barely spoken to one another in the conservatory. He had known nothing of her, so what was there really to love? Had it been her beautiful face? Had it been her soft, pliant skin?

"Perhaps it's more the idea of you, Evangeline," he whispered to the ever mounting number of stars as the sun had set in the frame of his loft's window. He held his own hand in his lap, pretending he was holding hers.

The only time he didn't think of Evangeline was when he felt the familiar prickling in his fingertips. As he brought the paint to his private canvases, she was there, set on a distant shelf, reserved for another time.

Evangeline found her way to Nathaniel's studio days after he had painted her. His master had been out that day, leaving his apprentice to his own devices. Nathaniel was shocked to find Evangeline at his doorstep. She was accompanied by her ever-observant chaperone.

Nathaniel insisted that he could bring the paintings down to Evangeline, but his beloved wanted to see them in the upstairs loft. She climbed the ladder as if she had climbed rickety ladders all her life and, in-so-doing, Evangeline explored her true nature: a young woman with a passion for exploratory intrigue instead of a demure world of petticoats, perfume and perfected manners.

He hesitated for a moment before offering Evangeline the first of his secret paintings. But she had come all this way, and he loved her too much to deny what she had so ardently invested her time in traveling to see.

"This one," Nathaniel turned the painting of Fiona to Evangeline on that day, "was my most recent one, and my favorite." They were standing in his attic loft. The chaperone was sitting on his chair.

Evangeline turned her head quizzically to the side. "Did you paint her from memory?" Her skin had been cleared of powder. Her hair had been tied beautifully, revealing the slight skin around the top of her neck and below her ears. She had smelled of a lavender toilette that excitedly tickled his nose.

Nathaniel shook his head. "I have no recollection of who she is."

"No recollection?" Evangeline said with a playful smile, thinking it a joke. "And I suppose it's the same with these other faces; you have no recollection of who they are either?"

Again, Nathaniel shook his head. "They come to me in the middle of the night," he confessed, "shortly after my master has gone to bed."

"How do they come to you?" Evangeline turned to the open window of his attic. She wore a violet petticoat that swished as she moved barely two steps. Evangeline was also constricted by the same corset she had worn on the first day they had met. Even though she spoke to him on that day, it was still been evident that she fought to breathe. "Do they come through the window?" she asked him. A sparrow had flitted from one sill to the next in the exterior window.

"Not the window," Nathaniel said in all seriousness.

"The ladder then," Evangeline crossed to the ladder which adjoined the loft to the rest of the flat. Nathaniel took several steps toward her, shaking his head. "Well you must see them with your eyes," Evangeline offered. "The details of each face are too defined to make up from nothing. Tell me. If they don't climb in through the window, up a ladder and if you don't see them then how-"

"Through my fingertips." A silence then passed. The mysterious "Fiona" hovered in his fingers between him and Evangeline. "No other words can describe it I'm afraid."

"Show me?" Evangeline asked of him.

Despite her request, Nathaniel didn't show her how he painted the canvases, at least not for the next few months that had followed. The more he painted in secret, the more Nathaniel convinced himself he had made the right choice in having kept the practice from her. It hadn't been normal what he painted. Nothing about the images on his canvas, or how they had appeared to him, was conservative. He also feared that, by showing her the method, it might trigger the chain reaction the Dandelion Sisters had forewarned. As a preventative measure, Nathaniel had tucked the newly painted canvas into the shadows of his rafters before going to bed.

Nathaniel had underestimated Evangeline's desire to witness the late night procedure. She kept in close contact with Nathaniel by letters, asking him to show her how he had created such masterpieces. With each correspondence, Nathaniel devised excuses as to why it wasn't timely possible. It was Evangeline's final letter, when she posed the ultimatum, which brought Nathaniel bowing to her will.

In the summer of 1808, after Evangeline's provocation, Nathaniel cut a path to her window. Though he and Evangeline were two dissimilar canvases, hanging awkwardly on the same wall side by side, Nathaniel yearned too much to be with her, which led him to linger by her window. He didn't see Evangeline in her room, but took comfort in the shine expanding from her candlelit window.

"Monsieur Cauliflower?" she said from behind him. He spun to find Evangeline out on the grounds, surprisingly without her chaperone! She scolded: "It's not like a gentleman to peer through windows at night!" Evangeline then gave a lilting laugh, taking a few steps closer. Nathaniel was at a loss for words, entranced by her noteworthy loveliness in the moonlight.

"Mademoiselle Evangeline," he asked "what are you doing out on the grounds all by yourself?"

Her eyes looked at the moon. "There are some nights that I sneak out and take a walk in the moonlight. I find the moon oddly reassuring."

"Do you?"

"There are some nights," Evangeline earnestly whispered to him, looking serious, "where, I swear, I can almost hear it sing!"

Nathaniel turned his eyes to the moon, half-expecting to hear it sing. He felt a cold chill stretch up his spine.

Evangeline erupted in laughter. "Oh come now, Monsieur Cauliflower, the moon can't sing! How delightfully gullible you are to think that the ridiculous things I say have truth!"

Nathaniel felt foolish. "Then I suppose your challenge in the last letter was simply a rouse as well?"

"Have you been visited by another painting?" Evangeline hungrily held Nathaniel's fingers. Though they had been in the same room together before on two occasions, this was the first time that they legitimately touched. He felt his heart race!

They strolled silently along the road hand in hand: the painter and his mistress. They needed no words to describe their shared affections. Nathaniel loved her, and she, he assumed, loved him. A twinkle in her eyes reminded him of the stars overhead. As the night continued on, Evangeline once again climbed the ladder of his attic loft requiring little help from Nathaniel below. Evangeline looked at him from the upper landing.

"Coming, Monsieur Cauliflower?" she whispered.

Nathaniel was uncertain whether he should or not. It was Evangeline's smile that gave him a second wind of courage. His prickling fingers grasped the rungs of his ladder, pulled him, inch by inch, closer to her. On the landing, he and Evangeline met, their noses centimeters apart. Nathaniel thought of stealing a kiss but thought better of it.

Evangeline removed his mysterious paintings from the rafters propping them on display as a collective audience to Nathaniel's future work.

A portrait was ready to be painted, his master snored through his dreams, and Evangeline was there waiting for Monsieur

Cauliflower to amaze her. With these circumstances aligned, Nathaniel lit a candle, removed a box of brushes and paints, and faced a blank canvas lying in wait. Lips pursed, eyes focused, fingers confident, Nathaniel began to paint.

First were the shoulders, then the left ear, then the right. Detail after detail, the figure on the canvas emerged. To his and Evangeline's surprise, the face proved eerily familiar.

"Why," Evangeline brought a hand up to her lips. "That's me."

But it wasn't Evangeline. Not completely. The face on the portrait wasn't young. The wrinkles around the lips and eyes were more pronounced. Cheeks that were once flushed looked pale. There was a despairing wisdom in the old Evangeline's eyes indicating a sense of loss. Evangeline slinked from the misshapen version of herself as Nathaniel's brush unremittingly sited the finishing touches. Evangeline drew closer with curiosity.

The age of the woman in this painting was imperceptible but Nathaniel guessed the age to be well over eighty, possibly past ninety! Though in the painting Evangeline's hair had grown grey and her skin frail, the general beauty of her upcoming self remained intact. She was painted old but would age relatively gracefully.

Nathaniel's brush stopped. He sat back on his stool taking a few moments to investigate the art with her.

"What does it mean?" she asked him. Evangeline looked at her painting and studied the other faces around them. She asked in wonderment, "Who are these people that you've painted and how am I associated with them?"

Nathaniel didn't know the answers to these questions. There were secrets behind the portraits: secrets that eluded them both. Secrets that could only be understood by the Dandelion Sisters who had granted him the express gift in the first place. Secrets or no, Nathaniel didn't care. Evangeline was here with him on this night and that was all that mattered.

Their eyes met. They closed the physical distance between. His kisses were gentle and she fell into them with the same ease that the moon stretched an arc against the sky. Nathaniel's fingers ventured around her waist where he found the strings of her corset which he unfurled with great passion. Evangeline breathed and did so several thousand times throughout the night while in the arms of her artist. As they made love in the moonlight, the displayed paintings looked upon them like mischievous cherubs. Afterwards, the lovers dipped into a dreamless sleep. For the first and only time in Nathaniel's timeless existence, the thought of Evangeline did not haunt him.

*

Annette had already been pulled out of her warm memories before Nathaniel had. Her eyes were focused on the environment's possibilities. At present, Nathaniel's attention was on Annette's third violet envelope in which the falling snow thinned making the visibility more pronounced. There came a rumbling sound beneath them: the typical sound of thunder that signaled the approaching end of the violet envelope. Her client had not yet arrived on the scene making him and Annette the only two souls out in this freezing site. All that passed between them was a strong wind that stirred the snow, kicking it up in clouds of frozen flakes. Nathaniel thought about saying something to lift the silence between them but thought better of it.

It was then that Annette saw someone approaching from the distance. She nudged her mentor, motioning toward the figures standing opposite.

In the time that Nathaniel had been remembering Evangeline, his glasses had slinked down his nose. He swept his eye-glasses up to investigate further. There were two "someones" looking back at them.

The two dark, human-shaped shadows in the distance were too far away to determine any exact details.

Annette raised an arm and waved saying "Hello!" but the figures didn't move. They stood there like stone sentinels, staring back.

"Miss Redmond, refrain from disturbing them!" Nathaniel scolded. "Unless your heartstrings tell you that they're your clients."

"That's them, right? The clients I'm supposed to be inspiring?" Annette asked him but the look of insecurity on Nathaniel's face made her pause. "Well who else am I supposed to inspire out here? There's no one!" Annette waved at the strangers again, calling out "Hello out there in the snow!"

Nathaniel consulted his wrist-watch then looked at the strangers. "If they are, they're too early. Your client should be on the approach but not from that direction."

Annette dropped her hand, signaling the end of the distant contact. "Well if they aren't who I'm supposed to inspire, who are they?"

After a brief second, Nathaniel said "I don't know." One of the figures stepped forward but stopped. Nathaniel squinted his eyes, hoping for a better look. He noticed that the other stranger put a hand on the first, stopping him.

There came a crunching sound in the hushed winter day snow. As the sound grew closer, Nathaniel turned his attention from the two strangers and said to Annette "Aha! Here we go!"

Annette's attention was also diverted from the two figures as a semi-truck appeared through the wall of falling snow. It was moving at a moderate pace from Annette's left headed straight for them. Another vehicle appeared to Annette's right coming straight for them from the opposite direction. The second vehicle was perhaps a smaller private passenger car. From Nathaniel's perspective, Annette turned her eyes to the strangers. As mysteriously as they had arrived, the expanse was vacant, with only the swirling of flakes.

Nathaniel retreated a step to allow Annette the opportunity to inspire by her own inner instructions. Nathaniel knew that both the truck and the passenger car were bobbing along too fast for this weather. And as the semi-truck approached, he watched as Annette studied each vehicle, no doubt astute to the fact that each set of wipers were fighting hard to sweep the accumulating frost. As the distance between the two cars decreased, he could tell that Annette knew that she and Nathaniel were standing in the middle of the road of equal distance between them.

"Mr. Cauliflower," she said to her fellow muse.

"Just a moment longer," he told her with confidence.

"But if we stay here we might get run over," Annette pondered out loud.

"Precisely the point, Miss Redmond," Nathaniel said evenly. He watched as she retreated a few steps and pushed Annette back to where she had been standing. "Stay here seven more seconds," Nathaniel told her while consulting his wrist-watch. "Seven . . ."

"But in seven seconds we'll be road-kill."

"Six," Nathaniel chimed.

"Is this punishment for the arguing we've done?"

"Five," Nathaniel said over her words.

"Mr. Cauliflower . . ."

"Four." The vehicles were both headed straight for them. He didn't have to look at Annette to realize that she found herself in an uncomfortably threatening situation, desperate to leave. But the colored peg had put them in this exact spot for a reason, and he was determined to make sure that she must stay there. "Three."

"What kind of operation is Management running here?" she yelled at him.

"Two!"

"We're supposed to be inspiring people, not causing accidents!"

"One!" The semi-truck, finally noticing him and Annette in the road, slammed on its breaks. Nathaniel grabbed Annette and reeled her off to a snow-covered curb.

Unfortunately for the semi-truck, the ice was too slick on the road for the vehicle to stop normally. It skidded along the slippery road spinning along the ice. The driver of the other vehicle, noticing the truck, also put on its brakes to avoid being part of the collision. However, it too began to slide on the road until, eventually, it spun and stopped in the opposite direction. The semi-truck driver, trying to over-correct, caused the rear bumper to slide across the road until there came a sickening crunch of metal upon metal as it struck the Mercedes, propelling it further into the falling snow, down a camouflaged ravine.

Once both vehicles came to a stop, Annette raced toward them calling out that she was on her way. The inspiration was coming to an end but she rushed regardless.

All Nathaniel could do was stand in the snow and watch as Annette tried to interfere with circumstances in which she had no control. It was clear that, with each step, Annette could feel the rumbles of thunder. Nathaniel took a breath and closed his eyes doing the only thing he could have done: whispering a word of prayer to Management. He followed Annette's path through the snow finding her at the edge of the snow-capped ravine. He watched as Annette passed the semi-truck driver who was climbing out of his truck. Nathaniel then watched as Annette found her footing, shuffling down the ravine through an exposed path to a Mercedes. The sound coming from the wreckage was a crying baby, its tiny screams piercing the surrounding storm.

Nathaniel watched as Annette reached the Mercedes. There she found a man in the driver's seat, conscious and fighting his way past the deployed airbag. Annette found the baby in the back seat, strapped safely into a car seat, wailing for its mother. Though Nathaniel was some distance away, he knew what Annette must have seen for herself: the front passenger seat where a woman, supposedly the mother, lay unconscious with a bleeding head wound.

Even where Nathaniel stood he could hear the father calling the baby's name.

"It's alright Jonas," said the father. "Everything's going to be alright. Mommy's just sleeping." A roll of thunder, this one louder than before, splintered the snow-covered ground. The baby named Jonas continued to cry so high-pitched Nathaniel thought perhaps the shrill might cause the glass to break. "Jonas, it's okay. She's just . . ." It was then that the father wailed with as much anguish as his newborn son until both screams were carried through the storm, rising up into the clouds, muted by the torrents of falling snow that cascaded upon them.

There were three horrendous rumbles of thunder that signaled the end to this segment. In those three roars Annette, realizing she was alone at the car, turned her attention at the ravine, where she spotted the driver of the semi, a portly man with a ball cap, descending the slope. But it was Nathaniel that her eyes were locked on; Nathaniel who looked toward his handiwork like an artist consulting the brush strokes of a masterpiece.

As the inspiration came to an end and Annette was deposited back into her office there was one word that echoed far beyond its rumblings: "Jonas." Annette turned to Nathaniel, who casually shed the accumulated flakes of snow from his clothes.

"We caused that accident," she said to him.

"Yes, Miss Redmond. I was there."

"We *caused* that accident by *standing* in the *middle of the road*!"

"Yes, Miss Redmond, we did. A job well done."

"A job well done?" Annette raised her voice, riding on the last shred of adrenaline.

"A successfully administered catalyst, if I do say so myself."

"How does bringing about death inspire someone, Mr. Cauliflower?" Annette asked of him.

Nathaniel looked into Annette Redmond's blue eyes and studied the stray lock of brown hair amidst the red. He wasn't sure how to respond. He had asked himself the same question at the end of each of his seven lifetimes, only to have the question go unanswered.

*

Morning arrived stealthily in 1808. Evangeline's skin was warm beneath Nathaniel's fingers. Her breathing was calm and unrestricted. Sunlight struck her hair just as it had the morning that he had first painted her in the chateau's conservatory. Nathaniel collected these details with his barely opened eyes. He learned then that the most precious moments had to come to an end, and they did in this approach: a scuffling sound was heard from behind Nathaniel causing his eyes to widen. In the excitement from the night before, Nathaniel had forgotten to store his paintings into the rafters. Much to Nathaniel's horror, he spun to find his painter standing in the loft amidst the ghostly faces in the daylight. In his painter's hands was the Fiona portrait.

"Explain this to me," the painter inquired. Nathaniel stood. His bare, toned torso and lower half were draped by unbuttoned trousers.

Nathaniel wondered how he could have been so careless by leaving the paintings on display through the night? And worse yet, how could he have been so bold by having taken advantage of Evangeline, who presently stirred from the floor boards? Both the painter's and Nathaniel's eyes turned to Evangeline who had sat up and protectively gathered the corset at her chest. The painter said nothing.

Nathaniel on the other hand assisted Evangeline from the floor bidding her to go. She scrambled down the ladder. When she reached the lower level, Nathaniel started to go down the ladder himself.

"Boy, let her go," the master ordered. Nathaniel turned his face to him knowing that Evangeline had exited into the daylight, fleeing the two artists. As the painter approached the ladder, staring intently into Nathaniel's eyes, Nathaniel clutched the rungs with his heart thudding heavily in his chest.

The Dandelion Sisters had warned Nathaniel about this moment, and Nathaniel had desperately attempted to have kept it from happening. Yet it happened anyway.

The painter, for reasons of his own, grabbed the rungs of the ladder tipping it, and the boy, from the ledge. Nathaniel grasped at the growing distance between the ladder and the loft in an attempt to connect the two again, but to no avail. Within not even a moment, Nathaniel lay on the lower landing, dead.

*

Definitely, Nathaniel had asked himself the same question that Annette Redmond had asked of him. It had appeared that the only woman who had truly known the answer had been Ninth Generation muse Annette Slocum. He hoped Annette would remember, but it was evident that the promised memories were unwavering.

Annette went on in saying, "I was a missing person's detective before I came here, Mr. Cauliflower. And that job consumed me for many years, and still does. I've spent my life avoiding the kind of messes that we've caused, obsessed with finding individuals who disappeared at the hand of an elusive person who I've nick-named the Thunderstorm Man. I almost lost my fiancé, Adam, because of my work hours. I made a promise to him three months ago that it would change. Our wedding was supposed to take place moments before I was handed an invitation by a woman in a baby-blue pants suit, your Head Muse, Fiona."

Annette turned from Nathaniel facing toward the sunlight. "That invitation carried with it a strong lead that could break the case of the Thunderstorm Man wide open, so who was I to deny it? Fiona told me that, if I went with her, I would be returned to that exact place and time as if I'd never left. So I left my fiancé, Adam Eustace McCloud, standing at the altar, waiting for me!" Annette sighed. Her back was turned to Nathaniel. "Here I am causing more destruction than before I left. Sometimes I wonder what life would be like had I taken a different road? What would have become of me if I followed my dream to become a pie maker, like you mentioned? What would become of Adam? What would become of everyone?"

"Miss Redmond," Nathaniel told her "sometimes . . . sometimes we have to trust that Management knows what's best for us. I, myself, have a hard time believing in it, but it's the only thing that keeps me . . ." he hesitated for a moment, then surprised himself by earnestly saying ". . . that keeps me cooking in my kitchen, re-assigning those colored pegs and delivering the envelopes. It gives me enough strength to make it through each day. Sometimes circumstances change, causing us to take one path over another. But we eventually find our paths. I have to believe that."

There was a silence. Annette then asked "What did you say?"

"I said that we eventually find our paths."

"No, before that."

"Circumstances change."

Annette gave a breath. "Yes, I'd heard that from Fiona when I first came here." She gasped, turning to Nathaniel. Her hair was no longer red. Instead it was brown all over. Her skin, which had been tan with freckles, was a steady pale. The facial features, which had been recognizably Annette Redmond, showed a face that Nathaniel had known for years; it was the undeniable face of Annette Slocum. "I remember," she said with tears.

"Do you?"

"I remember being a little girl with a mom and a dad, and two older brothers named Franklin and Michael. I remember being incredibly shy and living inside the pages of library books. And I remember there was a boy who rescued them for me, a young boy named Nathaniel J. Cauliflower!"

Nathaniel didn't say anything. He allowed Annette to remember all that she needed to.

"I remember when I graduated high school my father bought me a car: a champagne-colored 1979 VW Beetle that he asked me to use while traveling and exploring the world. But I didn't. Instead, I married the car salesman who sold it to my dad. I was a housewife to Lyle Slocum for ten years and, for many years I waited for you, Mr. Cauliflower. I waited for you all my life to come and fix me the way that you fixed my library books but, as I grew older, I gave up on that idea. I immersed myself into my solitude, living each moment of each day cooking Lyle's breakfast, watching Lyle's dress shirts flutter dry on the backyard line, and kept myself safely inside the confines of the books I borrowed from the library.

"I remember the day that Fiona arrived, standing at my mailbox, waving to me as if she had known me for years. And I remember the chase that happened at the library. All she wanted to do was talk to me but I was too antisocial to let her! I remember making a quick getaway for the library parking lot and how there were so many cars driving by. And how one, a blue Cadillac, struck me!"

Annette then took off the black hoodie. She held it in front of her.

"I remember after my death waking up in the waiting room and becoming a Ninth Generation muse. My first inspiration sent me to a man named Jonathan whom I handed a violin while he lodged in a hotel room. Later I found out who Jonathan really was: the very same driver of the vehicle that caused me to be here as a muse at the outset!"

Annette stepped forward. The black hoodie was clutched between her fingers. "Oh Management . . ." she said with a laugh. "I remember!" She handed Nathaniel the hoodie and said to him intently, "Thank you."

Nathaniel took the hoodie. There were many things he wanted to discuss with her, but all he could say was "Welcome home, Mrs. Slocum."

*

The thick churning bands of the approaching thunderstorm casually streaked across the sky and moon devouring the Heavens in its cold, bitter wake. The storm stretched across a highway dotted with pale orange street lamps. It clawed itself across the great field, the gale of its darkness wreaking havoc on the acres of corn and rapeseed. It settled upon a particular spot of land where it seemed to linger in anticipation of an unprecedented event. Lightning flickered in the twisting plumes as if an indiscernible mob occupied its fury carrying torches set in a concentrated inferno. The storm dared not rain, at least not yet, for fear of ruining this fine moment.

The structure which the clouds hovered over was a seedy motel with an indecisive neon vacancy sign. The night manager of the motel stepped out of the front door and, looking up in awe of the towering storm, lit a cigarette. But the storm was not looking down on the night manager. The storm's attention was upon another individual: a man named Jonathan who occupied one of the hole-in-the-wall rooms.

Jonathan was in his forties and looked as if the world had truly done a number on him. Jonathan was fast asleep on the mattress of his grimy bed. The covers had been kicked off the foot of the bed hours ago. He lay exposed in a pair of boxers and a wife-beater, sleeping soundly despite the chaos on the other side of his dust-caked window. Jonathan supported a violin and bow in his arms in the way some children covet teddy bears to ward off creatures from under the bed. Unfortunately for Jonathan, the act of cleaving to such an item of safety did not stop a monster from stepping out of the room's shadows.

While Jonathan slept, a man with gray hair and a black suit and tie appeared, watching him sleep. The man was in his mid-thirties but looked older than his age. Crow's feet expanded around his eyes. The man's glacial stare focused upon the violin in Jonathan's arms. A scowl formed across the man's face.

Jonathan was too lost in his pleasant dreams to notice he was no longer alone. He absentmindedly abandoned the violin to turn to his pillow, fluffing it a bit, and returned to his slumbers.

With the violin unprotected, the uninvited man took his opportunity. A rumble of thunder helped to accentuate the stranger's hands as they reached out and seized the instrument. A tendril of lightning shot across the sky as the man held the violin up to his icy, hawk-like stare.

The man studied the violin, taking disgust in the item, offended by its very presence in the room. He strode across the room and cracked open the window. Dangling the instrument over the several stories between them and the parking lot below, the man smirked and purposefully let the violin and bow drop through the air delighting in the sound as the wood splintered upon collision. He brought his eyes to the storm nodding at the clouds as if they had been friends for years.

Jonathan stirred from his sleep to find the violin gone. He frantically searched the covers, overturned the pillows and looked over both sides of the bed. Jonathan's bloodshot eyes settled upon the man in the suit and tie, who was still looking out the window in reverence of nature's ominous display. Rain started to sprinkle, the moist darting drops glistening the man's fierce expression.

"Isn't it beautiful?" the man asked, placing both hands on the exposed window sill. "I love watching thunderstorms. They seem to know when to arrive, heralding a sense of peace, a feeling of comfort. They never stay for very long, do they? As soon as they arrive, they're gone again. It's important, no matter where we are in life, to relish these rare moments and to take advantage of each fleeting second of its countenance."

"Do I know you?" Jonathan asked.

The man shook his head.

"How did you get in here?"

"My name is Jonas," the man answered, his attention still on the storm. "And I, like this storm, have come to give you a personal sanctuary from the grim reality of this decaying, desolate world."

"My violin," Jonathan shook his head, running his fingers through his greasy hair. "What have you done with it?"

"Violin?" Jonas' eyebrows raised in concern. He shook his head, giving his attention to Jonathan. Jonas then looked Jonathan squarely in the eyes and said with a well-rehearsed, almost convincing lie: "There is no violin."

Jonathan nearly took Jonas at his word but then tried to piece his memories together to prove the interloper wrong.

"No. I remember. I woke up and she was standing there, right where you're standing! She was wearing a housedress and slippers. She was holding the violin and bow in her hands. I thought it surreal seeing her – the woman that I had hit and killed with my Cadillac all those years ago in front of the library, holding a violin!"

As Jonathan tried to make sense of how he received the instrument, Jonas sported an unyielding poker-face. Jonathan shook his head, dismissing the idea that the woman he'd killed had, indeed, been standing before him. At last he asked Jonas: "It seems improbable, doesn't it?"

"Of course it's improbable," Jonas consoled. "You ran over the woman with your car. Your mind fabricated an elaborate dream in which she returned to you to issue a peace offering." Rain fell hard outside the open window flooding the sill and moistening the carpet. "The mind is a creative organ, Jonathan. It's most deceitful when you dream, telling you comforting lies to help cope you with awful situations. No doubt you've tried to trace the events. If you hadn't heard the mysterious violin music that haunted you since childhood, you wouldn't have been so obsessed with procuring the violin which led you to accidentally hitting her!" Jonathan, who had turned his eyes to the covers in contemplation, shifted his eyes back to Jonas. "Oh yes, Jonathan. I know about the violin music. I know that you heard it when you were a boy working your arithmetic. I know how you climbed up to the attic and found your father's trumpet . . . and how shortly after you found the violin in a music store . . . and how after promising your parents you'd do better in school, your parents gave you lessons for the trumpet instead. And how, ever since, you've harbored a deep loathing. Then, many years later, you were given advice to buy the violin, which you did, only to have had it snatched from you when some twit of a housewife decided to dodge cars in front of the local library!"

Jonathan's eyes were wide as Jonas recanted the trials of the violin music's involvement in his affairs. "Who are you?" Jonathan asked him.

"Someone who's been waiting far too long in the background, Jonathan. Someone who's seen what tragedies were thrust on you. The original haunting music was never supposed to have entered your life from the beginning. Imagine, if you will, a life without the ghostly music tormenting you, causing such grief; a life unhindered by the obsession for the violin. A normal existence where you could chart your own path instead of having it dictated to you by echoes of an unnamed source."

"That music was supposed to come to me," Jonathan told Jonas. But even with these words Jonathan's voice faltered.

"Or so you've raised yourself to believe." Jonas put a comforting hand on Jonathan's shoulder. As he did, Jonathan's eyes went to Jonas' hand, staring at it without reflex to pull away. "It was a terrible mistake that I've come to rectify. Remember the days when your children loved you, when you made your wife laugh, when you were in control of your own future. A future regretfully taken from you by the violin music. But I can give it back. I can make it happen where the violin music never came to you."

Jonathan's eyes suddenly swelled with tears.

Jonas, knowing full well of his magnetic effect, went on: "In place of sitting here in a motel room wishing for the things that could have been, I can make it so that you can actually live the future you've dreamed of. You'd like that, wouldn't you?"

Jonathan nodded slightly, a small movement heightened by a dramatic roll of thunder and a flash of lightning.

Jonas smiled. "Come with me, Jonathan. We can make everything right."

It was during this conversation that the night manager, finishing his third cigarette under the aid of an umbrella, spotted the dismantled violin and bow from below Jonathan's window. The night manager scratched his head in confusion, picked up the instrument and carried it inside, setting its pieces behind the check-in counter.

Jonathan, now dressed, crossed through the lobby with Jonas. The night manager hadn't seen Jonas come in or out that day and certainly didn't remember him checking in. He watched Jonas closely with suspicion.

The manager's troubles were truly exacerbated when Jonas told Jonathan: "Wait here." Jonas then crossed to the night manager at the front desk.

As Jonas approached, the manager felt a sickening feeling creep upon him, which only worsened as Jonas handed him a violet envelope with the number "6" scrawled on the back.

"Do you see this envelope?" Jonas asked.

The night manager nodded.

"In three days time," Jonas turned his eyes to a wall calendar which read March 22nd, "a woman named Annette Redmond will be here looking for me. She'll have many questions, I'm sure. You won't answer her questions. You'll hand her this envelope. Understand?"

The night manager nodded even though something inside of him urged against it.

"If you open the envelope before she gets here," Jonas' gray eyes bore holes into the eyes of the night manager like a crazed wolf staring at its prey, "I'll know. And trust me, you don't want that to happen. Do as you're told. Give her the envelope and we shouldn't have any problems, yes?"

Again, the night manager nodded.

Jonas reached into the jacket pocket of his suit. As he did, the night manager could detect a key dangling from a silver chain on the outside of his dress shirt. Jonas handed the night manager a hefty roll of tightened dollars bound by a rubber band.

"For your troubles," Jonas told him and was out the door with Jonathan.

The night manager stepped to the glass of the front door. He watched as the two men disappeared into the night, into the squall, which seemed to accept them both graciously under its silk waterfall-threaded cloak. The storm, seemingly satisfied with its entertainment, continued on its path looking for other random moments in history to feast its yearning eyes and steadfast appetite.

CHAPTER 8: PATERNAL RATIONALITY

    There was a sense of comfort that Nathaniel felt in the Nine Greatest Muses under one roof. It was something akin to a parent having all of his grown up children back in his supervision, if merely for a short holiday, and those children having two distinct identities: who they had been, and who they would eventually grow to be. Nathaniel had never been a father but he entertained the idea on occasion.

    He predicted the kind of dad he would have been. Nathaniel would have been the parent who would sit on metal bleachers during his son's Little League games or would dote on his daughter by attempting high-quality sales during Girl Scout Cookie season. He would have participated in impromptu tea parties, Pine Wood Derby contests, parent-teacher conferences, attended ballet recitals, stared through amateur-crafted telescopes beneath starry skies, created misshapen snowmen and extra events that real parents had experienced with their children. He would have been proud of any endeavor his children would have tried, at any age or phase in their life, so long as they were following their dreams, however fleeting or long-lasting.

    In all probability, Nathaniel would not have been physically affectionate toward them, save for a kiss on the forehead after bedtime stories or an occasional congratulatory embrace. Not because he would have loved them any less than they had deserved, but largely due to his not being a demonstrative type in any of the seven lives led. Nathaniel would have been more like a grandfather clock, wisely witnessing the events that occurred in the time that he catalogued.

In the department he was able to explore the notion of parenthood in some capacity. He felt protective of his people, proudly gauging an employee's spiritual growth, ending in a swelling pride as the muses retired to their chosen destinations. He did not mourn when each muse passed on. Nathaniel felt satisfied with each retirement knowing that he accomplished the missions per capita. Nathaniel moreover practiced his paternal prudence when he rotated colored pegs clockwise and counter-clockwise, reviewing relationships of other fathers who blossom in the sordid lives of their transitory clients.

It was a circulated belief among Nathaniel's progenies that, when a colored peg was rotated counter-clockwise, a muse could appraise a client's life from the moment of birth leading to the moment of inspiration. If the corresponding peg was rotated clockwise, the muse was given the option to watch a client's life subsequent to the motivation.

In the past, Seventh Generation muse Lucas Richardson had known this feature better than anyone. In his former role as a regular muse, Lucas had taken on the added responsibility of the department's "welcome wagon" for new hires. While he had taken strides to make his coworkers feel at home, Lucas gave special interest to an anti-social Ninth Generation muse, Annette Slocum, who had recently begun her tenure.

By that time, Annette had not even begun to scratch the surface of her initial employment, timidly branching out from her anti-social behaviors. Though Annette had been placed into an employment forcing her to interact with strangers, it was Lucas whom she attached to fairly quickly. They had formed a unique bond. What made their friendship exceptional had been a simple aspect: Lucas had liked to talk and Annette had not; but, if Annette did have something to say, Lucas would have listened intently, earnestly engaging himself on her every word.

Though Nathaniel's interactions in the department had been brief in that time period, he overheard a conversation between Lucas and Annette regarding the eventuality of peg-rotations. The conversation had taken place well before they had developed into two of the Nine Greatest Muses in history.

Nathaniel had heard Annette speak. "Someday I hope to actually meet this Cauliflower guy to get his recipes."

Nathaniel, who had entered the department to deliver more envelopes to postboxes, and to clear the dishes from a meal, lingered by the door, eavesdropping. At this point in history, Annette had not yet inspired Nathaniel in the root cellar. But to Nathaniel, the memory had been fresh in his mind, as it already happened to him.

"I know, right?" Lucas had answered her. "Fiona said that when she visited his office, she found an entire gourmet kitchen which spanned for half a mile! Imagine the amount of counter space and storage! She said he had at least a hundred rolling pins, and five times as many pots and pans. She didn't see any cookbooks, though. He must have them all memorized."

"Every recipe?" Annette had scoffed. "Memorized?"

There had been silence between them. Nathaniel had assumed that either one, or both of them, had been distracted by a memory. He had turned to go but heard Lucas say, "*Anyway*. I only have one peg left."

"One peg?" Annette had asked.

"Only *one*, and you know what *that* means. I'll be out of here: long gone. Vamoose. Finito. No more."

"Lucas?" she had asked him. "What memories come back to you?"

"All sorts of memories, really," he had told her thoughtfully.

"I didn't mean to pry." There had come a sound which had spurred Nathaniel. He had assumed, from the noise, that Annette had been guided from her swivel chair. Nathaniel's assumptions had been confirmed as she had asked Lucas, "Where are we going?"

Nathaniel had rushed down the hallway to the conference room where he stood with his back against the wall. As Nathaniel had ducked into the conference room, Annette and her companion had crossed from her office into his. Their voices had been slightly muffled but Nathaniel had been able to make them out.

"The first day I got here, Annette," Lucas had explained, "the *very* first day, Fiona showed me the instructional video in the conference room and then led me to my office, where I found the Lite-Brite board. You'll see, Annette. At the end of every employment, Fiona empties the Lite-Brite board, sweeps the office of any personal belongings, and prepares for the next muse. But mine *wasn't* empty, Annette! There, in the face of my Lite-Brite board, was a colored peg: one harmless little green peg. At first I didn't think anything of it and figured it was left over from the previous muse, right? But no, this peg was different."

Nathaniel had remembered how Lucas' peg had found itself there in the Lite-Brite. But Nathaniel had thought to himself, *"Another memory for another time, Nathaniel."*

Annette had asked Lucas "This is your peg?"

"Spectacular, isn't it? What it was doing in my Lite-Brite, I'll never know, but the point is this: after Fiona helped with my first inspiration, I twisted it counter-clockwise."

"What did it show you?"

Lucas had rushed out from his office, jogging down the end of the hall to Annette's workplace.

Nathaniel had peeked around the corner watching as Annette had trailed behind her friend. After they had disappeared into Annette's office, Nathaniel had taken a few steps down the hall to listen more closely. He had watched from the office door as Lucas had inserted the peg into a random spot on Annette's Lite-Brite grid. Lucas had tightened his grip on Annette's hand and, with the fingers of his spare hand, rotated the peg counter-clockwise. Annette's office had folded and unfolded taking the two muses backwards into Lucas' timeline and leaving Nathaniel to stare at her empty office.

The first half of Lucas' life had started before Lucas was born. Even when Lucas had been inside his mother's belly, and all through his childhood years, his father had played the guitar to sooth Lucas' anxiety. Lucas had only been in the sixth grade when his father had died of cancer, and the only respite Lucas found was the sound of someone else's guitar playing in the distance.

Lucas had soon ascertained that the owner of the guitar had been a young man named Gabriel: a boy in his English class. Their heartfelt friendship had been fueled by Lucas' desire to learn the instrument that Gabriel had easily strummed. There had been an intimate moment that Nathaniel had never forgotten upon preliminary examination of Lucas' peg after inspiring him: Gabriel had placed his hands on Lucas' while having tried to form chords. It had been obvious that they had shared an unspoken, requited love for one another that was severed when, one day, Gabriel and his family had moved without providing a forwarding address.

Many years later, after Lucas had become an adult and an established music teacher in Portland, Oregon, he found Gabriel on the internet. Gabriel had been living in New York at the time working in the World Trade Center. Lucas had been determined to keep his friend close. Gabriel had written saying that he felt the same. They had plans to reconnect in person and it seemed that, in their adult world, nothing could break their attachment.

Lucas had awoken one September morning in 2001 to news of the terrorist attacks. Nathaniel had remembered seeing Lucas' heartbreak, feeling empathy for his client, understanding that kind of anguish himself due to his own loss with Evangeline. How he had wanted to be there for Lucas, to tell him that he was not alone! Perhaps, Nathaniel had considered, they may have been able to grieve together!

Lucas' peg had one final scene in the first act in which Lucas had been sorting music in his classroom. Second Generation muse Nathaniel J. Cauliflower had appeared in his classroom doorway. Nathaniel had remembered this remote moment fondly. Lucas had asked if he could help the stranger, to which Nathaniel had said to him, "I sure hope so." Nathaniel had handed Lucas a violet envelope. Inside had been a guitar pick. With that, it had been the end of Lucas' first half of his green-colored peg.

"Wait, that's it?" Annette had asked as they had been brought back to her office. Nathaniel had been outside of her office door listening to the exchange.

"No, there's more. There are just too many memories, you know?" Lucas had told her.

"Nathaniel J. Cauliflower was your muse," Annette had pondered out loud.

Nathaniel had stopped listening, getting to the business of the dishes and delivering envelopes. Nathaniel had hated himself for not coming forward. There had been a reason for his avoidance. It had been an excuse that he had intended to resolve someday. But that "someday" had not been that day, nor would it be anywhere in Lucas earliest employment. Nathaniel had even shied from telling Lucas during his former client's retirement party.

*

Nowadays, as Nathaniel delivered the envelopes to the post boxes of his Nine Greatest Muses, he stopped by Lucas' office. What had once been made up to be a starlit cedar balcony perpetually caught in a mid-spring evening was replaced by the Hall of Thunderstorms, with its nine black-stained wooden archways. Lucas stood contemplating an approaching thunderstorm. There was a short-lived look in Lucas eyes that reminded Nathaniel of Jonas. The stare was broken as Lucas looked toward Nathaniel. Lucas smiled.

"Mr. Cauliflower," he said. "Welcome to my new office. I have to admit that, even though it's not the balcony that I had before, I kind of like it. Thunderstorms are soothing, you know?" Lucas brought his eyes to the archway.

"Yes," Nathaniel looked upon the thunderstorm, "I suppose they are."

"I hear that Annette's back," Lucas went on. "Well, I mean she's been here since we all got here, but in a different form . . . as Miss Redmond, you know? I hear she remembers being her old self again, before she was reincarnated. Rumor has it she remembers everything from being Annette Slocum: of the people she knew while she was alive, of her clients, even the muses that she worked with. I drop by her office on occasion but she's away on envelopes. She hasn't said hello, but I'm sure she'll be in eventually." Lucas was saddened about this but brushed it aside with a single word: "Anyway!"

"It's my fault, Mr. Richardson," Nathaniel told him. "There was a slight hiatus in her work. She has to catch up with the rest of you."

Lucas shrugged his shoulders, turning from the archway to his desk and swivel chairs. "So what brings you into my office today? Normally you leave the envelopes in my postbox before I even see you!" Lucas sat in the swivel chair behind the desk.

"Well," Nathaniel started.

"Please, Mr. Cauliflower, have a seat."

Nathaniel sat in one of the swivel chairs. "I know it's a bit late for this, really, but I wanted to tell you something."

"Oh?"

"About . . ." Nathaniel took a pause, ". . . about why I had never introduced myself after having been your muse."

Lucas scooted to the edge of his swivel chair.

"As you know . . . I, too, was a muse in this department, like you, a very long time ago. It was after my second life when Management gave me an office and a Lite-Brite board. Nearing the end of my own board, I was given a green-colored peg. That peg was yours. When I inserted it into the Lite-Brite, it delivered me to the morning of 9/11, to a specific cubicle, and individual. There was a framed picture of two young boys holding a guitar and, having sat below the picture, was a lone guitar pick. Management assigned me to take that guitar pick so that it may be forwarded to the proper location in the second half of the inspiration. So, I did what any normal muse would do. I pinched the guitar pick and held it in my hand. There was a young man at that cubicle who, from my assumption, was an adult version of one of those boys in the picture."

There was a glistening in Lucas' eyes.

"Gabriel never knew I was there, Mr. Richardson. But I *was* there . . . in the building, in his cubicle with him, when the first plane hit. He sent a quick e-mail telling you that he loved you. And I was there as he was thrown from his cubicle into the pandemonium."

Tears streamed down Lucas' cheeks.

"I'm not saying this to bring you more grief, Mr. Richardson. I'm saying this because you deserve to hear it. We deserve to have a token of something positive in our life, and sometimes in our afterlife, to keep us going." Nathaniel reached into his pocket and took out the same guitar pick, placing it on Lucas' desk.

Lucas reached for the object. "This was the item in my ivory box. It's what gave me my memories." He looked at Nathaniel. "I can keep it?"

Nathaniel nodded. "This guitar pick won't return Gabriel to you. It merely serves as a reminder that, whenever you are feeling alone, you were . . . are . . . loved. By Gabriel, your muses here, and Management."

"Why did it take you this long to say this?"

Nathaniel stared at the surface of Lucas' desk, gathering the strength to tell him what he had wanted to share for Generations. He said, with mounting courage "There are two reasons. Until recently, I've found myself shutting out those memories from before, and have been quite successful." Nathaniel felt inside his other pocket and took out a glow-in-the-dark star, fiddling with its distinct edges. "Ever since Miss Redmond came along, I find myself less able to keep those memories hidden. She has that inquisitive nature about her."

"Yes," Lucas smiled. "She does."

"The other reason . . ." Nathaniel frowned. ". . . Why I never came forward . . ." He felt along the contours of the glow-in-the-dark star as if massaging a worry stone. "Right after I handed you the guitar pick, I returned to my office in the department. I expected to find more envelopes in my postbox, but instead I found Fiona who stood by my door. She had told me that Evangeline had opened her final envelope, and that Evangeline was standing in front of a mailbox with a misdirected letter. Whenever I think about inspiring you, the memory is paired with Evangeline and her downfall."

Nathaniel, upon confession, recalled that rainy afternoon.

*

Nathaniel entered Evangeline's final inspiration and watched from afar, so as not to disturb her work. The churning, turquoise bands of the approaching thundercloud attacked the morning's pristine spring sky in the same fashion that certain dread gradually constricted upon Evangeline. The passing years had taken such a toll on

Evangeline that her exact age was indiscernible. Crows-feet were petrified around her glassy blue eyes. Her hair was a stringy mass of spider-webbed strands which whipped this way and that in the ever-growing ominous breeze. She wore a white cotton lace dress circa the nineteen twenties. It had a floral pattern which, upon the wind striking it, came to life in a maddened rabidity of disturbed petals. She held an envelope in her gnarled, arthritic right hand which she had been assigned to place in the mailbox in front of her. By now the sky had turned black. The fear inside Evangeline had darkened as bleak as the tumbling clouds overhead.

Nathaniel approached her from behind cupping his hand over her own. Evangeline's eyes fluttered closed and a single tear traced along her wrinkled cheek.

"Evangeline," Nathaniel whispered to her. Nathaniel was in his early thirties and sported a bald head and a shaved face. His brown eyes were encased behind brown frames. He adorned his usual dress shirt, matching brown tie, suspenders and dress pants. He stood behind her affectionately. His voice was calm and reassuring. "Breathe, darling, and it will all be over in a moment."

"You shouldn't have come here," Evangeline told him.

"I had to . . ." he told her on that day. "I had to . . ."

*

Nathaniel stood from the swivel chair and excused himself from his muse's company.

"Before you go, Mr. Cauliflower," Lucas asked. "I have to ask you something. You've lived seven lives. When you inspired me, you looked as you do at the present. Have you always looked the way you do? In every single one of your lives, have you always had a bald head, glasses and suspenders?"

Nathaniel shook his head. "No, in fact I looked vastly different in all of my lives. I had different hairstyles, features, and went by different names. In the afterlife, however, I inevitably, between every life, looked the way I do currently. I suppose you could say that with my lives led, and of the incongruities, Management needed an element of consistency."

"That has to be disorienting, you know?" Lucas asked.

"I suppose I've gotten used to it."

"Thank you, Mr. Cauliflower, for the guitar pick," Lucas told him, "thank you for being my muse and for being there for Gabriel."

"It's my pleasure, Mr. Richardson."

"And hey, if you see Annette around, tell her to stop by."

"I'll certainly do my best."

As Nathaniel left Lucas' office, Lucas turned to the thunderstorm he had been watching earlier. Nathaniel realized that he had not given him his assigned envelopes. He placed them into the postbox as he had habitually done for Generations. Postbox after postbox, Nathaniel had delivered the envelopes to the rest of the Nine Greatest Muses, settling on Annette's office.

He stepped inside her empty cathedral walking close to the dry erase board.

She had made considerable progress in her detective work with the Thunderstorm Man. The last time he had seen the board, only dates of thunderstorms had been listed around the perimeter, and the center was left blank. Since he had seen it last, Annette had matched pictures of three nameless individuals to three thunderstorms. Beside each name had been a numbered violet envelope starting with "9" ending with "7." What perturbed Nathaniel the most was a recent photograph of *him* that had been placed in the middle, with lines connecting him to the three victims! Fastened beside his photograph was the invitation that he had given to Fiona shortly after the colored pegs had fallen. Its wax seal was broken.

Oh how Nathaniel wished he could get inside Annette's mind! Even though she had Mrs. Slocum's memories, Miss Redmond was inside somewhere, tinkering at this project. It concerned him that, even though his picture was smack-dab in the middle of it, she was not consulting him with its vague details.

Annette's office folded and unfolded depositing her into her swivel chair.

"Mr. Cauliflower," she said after seeing him. "I suppose you and I need to have a chat."

"Yes, Mrs. Slocum," Nathaniel said, looking at his own photograph. In the years that he had imagined himself to be a father, he had never pictured himself one that could not have been trusted. But he had supposed that not all fathers could be the heroes that their children idolized. Some parents, no matter how hard they try to win their children, are looked at with suspicion.

He scowled at Mrs. Slocum adding, "I suppose we do."

CHAPTER 9: A NARRATIVE EXPRESSED BY AN ACCUMULATION OF CHRISTMAS ORNAMENTS

"I see that you're back to your old reading habits," Nathaniel observed from his exposed memoirs manuscript on Annette's desk. He coolly flipped through to the details of his second life. He grimaced while spying the words "kerosene lamps" and "uncontrolled vengeance." He quickly closed the pages.

Annette explained, "There was a time as Lyle's housewife, when I could read at least fifteen books in a single month. After Lyle left for work, and the housework was finished, I walked to the nearest library, immersed myself in fictional worlds, avoiding my own life."

"I know," Nathaniel told her.

"I stayed up late through the night reading at the kitchen table. Oh, how I enjoyed those quiet evening hours. When the rest of humanity was sleeping, I partook as a nocturnal bibliophile exploring the convoluted pathways of an author's chapters!" Annette, suddenly catching herself taking almost too much delight in the prospect of a good read, changed the direction of their conversation by asking "What about you, Mr. Cauliflower. Any good books on your bookshelf?"

"I've read a few."

"What are some of your favorites?"

There was a small number of titles that came to mind; titles that had been the ones that he had rescued for Annette in his most recent life. He had the works which he rescued. Though he had never seized the opportunity to be friends with Annette, or to know her personally, Nathaniel read her library books in hopes of capturing who she was through the words that she had so comfortingly relied on.

"I suppose you could say that I like any tale and how it develops," Nathaniel offered. "The memorable stories are more than words on paper. The most intriguing stories are a client's life when their peg is rotated. You can understand where I'm coming from, can't you? When you were here before, as a Ninth Generation muse, you rotated your share of colored pegs in hopes of gaining better insight into the human condition."

"I remember rotating several pegs." Annette nodded. "I remember Jonathan's green peg, where I understood why he was destined to receive the violin. I recall the cream-colored polka-dotted peg of a waitress named Doris who was inspired by dropping a donut to the floor of her diner. Doris was ringing the doorbell of my ex-husband Lyle with the intention of wooing him with hand-crafted funnel cakes. I even turned Lyle's purple peg inspiring him to answer the doorbell that Doris, with funnel cake in hand, was ringing. I remember a man named Patrick, whom I inspired by admonishing that he watch sunrises instead of sunsets. He was Lucas' replacement. Then there was a blue-colored peg, which belonged to a bookseller named Adam Mansfield who worked in a privately owned bookshop called *The Muse's Corner*. Of course, that was before Adam Mansfield and I were both reincarnated. Adam Mansfield reincarnated into the man who later became my fiancé: a handsome ice-sculptor named Adam McCloud. In the same fashion as I reincarnated into Annette Redmond. Did you know that he and I, in our new lives, found one another again underneath the light of a streetlamp one snowy Christmas Eve night? That was right after I saw you and Fiona in the graveyard. After I instinctively waved to you and you returned the wave." Annette was lost in thought, thinking of the colored pegs that she had turned in her past employment.

Nathaniel did not answer.

Eventually she added "Which is why I have to turn them again."

"Do you?"

"Yes, Mr. Cauliflower," Annette told him. "I have the first three colored pegs from my violet envelopes, which you gave me, but I need access to the other pegs."

Nathaniel asked bluntly "This wouldn't have anything to do with the dry erase board would it?"

Both he and Annette looked at the dry erase board where the faces of the three victims, along with Nathaniel's picture, were tacked.

"You don't recognize any of these faces?" she asked him.

They studied the display like art students contemplating an oddly tinted relief painting.

"No, I don't recognize any of these faces," Nathaniel sighed. "Should I?"

"This right here," Annette pointed to the picture of a middle-aged woman wearing thick black glasses whose eyes had been magnified several times over by the lenses. "This is the waitress named Doris whom I inspired in the diner with the donut." She jabbed an index finger to the picture of a man with a comb-over and a handlebar moustache. "And this is my ex-husband Lyle from my former life."

Nathaniel looked closer but said nothing.

"Lyle!" she clarified. She waved her right hand in a circular motion to help get Nathaniel's gears to move as clearly he wasn't seeing it.

Nathaniel still said nothing.

"Come on, Mr. Cauliflower. Lyle, who I inspired to answer the door while Doris was ringing the bell with the funnel cake in hand?"

"Okay?"

"And this individual. She was the first to disappear. Surely you remember her!" Annette tapped the picture of a young woman with a name and face that Nathaniel didn't recognize. "You assigned me these colored pegs, Mr. Cauliflower. Doris and Lyle were my clients that you delivered to my postbox when I was a Ninth Generation muse. This third woman may have been the client that Jonas was supposed to inspire on his twenty-second envelope but took with him instead! Don't you see?"

"That handlebar moustache is hideous. Who couldn't forget facial hair like that?"

"You don't remember reassigning the others?"

"No," Nathaniel shook his head. "These faces don't mean anything to me."

"Even this third woman?"

Nathaniel sighed, getting frustrated. "No, Mrs. Slocum. I don't recognize the face of . . ." he read the victim's name out loud, "'Sarah Milbourne.'"

"You assigned Jonas' last envelope. You must have seen something about who it was or where they were from. Sarah Milbourne: disappeared on July 17th, 2005."

Nathaniel shook his head.

"Who was it, then, that you assigned to Jonas? Who did he neglect?"

"I don't remember."

"Three of these people, Mr. Cauliflower," Annette explained "all three of them disappeared on a day of a thunderstorm. There were eye-witnesses on those days who gave statements about a man in a black suit and tie, with grey hair, that had been seen with them! At some point during the thunderstorms, they went missing with no indication as to where or when. Empty violet envelopes were left with numbers listed on them." She pointed to each name and corresponding envelope. "Sarah, '9.' Doris, '8.' Lyle, '7.'"

"What are you saying, Mrs. Slocum?" Nathaniel wanted to know, looking unconvinced. "That Mr. Rothchild is out there plucking people from history?"

"Really?" Annette scowled at his blatant skepticism.

From Nathaniel's perspective, even though she looked like Mrs. Slocum, there was an undeniable side of Miss Redmond that resided within her.

"I need to turn the other pegs again, Mr. Cauliflower, to see if there truly is any connection. I'm a detective; it's what I do! I've been working this case for years and the only real piece of solid evidence is you. Looking at it through my 'Redmond' eyes, it didn't make sense, just a bunch of pieces that didn't add up. But I have the advantage of knowing *two* of these individuals as Annette Slocum. You are my key to this padlock, Mr. Cauliflower, and if you won't help me turn these colored pegs, I'll find a way to do this on my own."

"Mrs. Slocum," Nathaniel tried to reassure her "if Mr. Rothchild *were* extracting people from history, more colored pegs would have fallen." He turned his eyes to her cathedral ceiling and to the doorway leading to the rest of the department. "Everything seems fairly quiet here to me."

"I would like to investigate all the same," Annette countered. She reached in to her desk drawer taking out the three pegs, holding out the first one. "Please turn them with me, Mr. Cauliflower, so that I can prove to you the method to my madness!"

"We don't have time, Mrs. Slocum. We still have many more envelopes to work before we can get you to your wedding."

Annette considered his words. "If we turn these pegs, and the others, and there's nothing to suggest Jonas' involvement, I'll work as many envelopes as you want. I'll go to my wedding day with my fiancé. But if it turns out that there *is* something happening, proving more pegs are about to fall, I want to stop it before it spreads." She re-inserted the blue peg into an empty slot on her Lite-Brite saying "It's a means to an end, Mr. Cauliflower."

"I suppose it is." Nathaniel felt unsettled by this exchange. He hoped that Annette was wrong, however her frame of thinking was irrefutable. He didn't recognize the face of Sarah Milbourne, but he couldn't negate that the face of Sarah Milbourne didn't mean something to Jonas.

Annette rotated the peg counter-clockwise saying to Nathaniel, "Here we go."

The life of the bowling alley attendant, Luanne, arranged itself like Christmas ornaments set on parade in a delicately-strung garland of memories. Rustling red tissue paper ignited the prologue as a gift box was opened, revealing its prize.

"Look, honey," said a mother as she cradled her newborn in a heavy navy-blue blanket. She held a polished brass ornament in front of her and the baby. It was in the shape of a sleeping cherub on a cloud. Dangling beneath the cloud were three brass discs embossed with brief messages, which the mother read aloud to the child. "'First Christmas,' and then 'Born July 16th, 2029,' and then 'Louis.'"

The baby looked at the ornament with gleaming eyes. The lights on the Christmas tree beside them reflected off the brass ornament and the light bounced from the ornament to the baby's cheeks.

Annette voiced concern. "Louis? Did I miss something? Did we turn the wrong peg?" She looked around the client's room for any further signs that they were reviewing the wrong client. "It should be Luanne that we're watching, not Louis."

"This *is* Luanne," Nathaniel told Annette.

Annette gave her attention to the baby. "But how can that be? Surely her mother knows what gender her own daughter is."

"Oh, I'm sure the mother knows the gender. Perhaps it may not be the gender that the baby is *presently*."

"Interesting," Annette gave a subtle nod.

Nathaniel glanced at Annette then to the mother and child.

Time moved through many Christmases in their client's life. Several varied ornaments were given to Louis: a clay tablet with an indentation of a foot to commemorate the year of his first steps, a miniature yellow school bus in honor of his first day of school, a soccer ball to immortalize the moments of his afternoon extra-curricular activities, a small diploma with a thin red ribbon in celebration of his graduation from elementary school, and a wooden, hand-whittled angel made of polished rosewood to signify the transition from youth to manhood in the junior high years. These years flipped in front of Annette and Nathaniel in quick succession with the fluidity of notes and chords being sung by carolers during the holidays.

In Louis' earliest decade, gender between boys and girls was almost imperceptible if it were not for the differences in clothing and hairstyles. Louis seemed blissfully unaware that he was different from the opposite sex. But when puberty caused a drastic divergence in their physical paths, Louis looked in the mirror half expecting his own body to confirm with the females. While females began to grow well-defined breasts and developed women problems of their own, Louis' chest remained as it always had been. And then there was the pitch change of his voice! Time stopped in front of fourteen year-old Louis as he stood in front of his bathroom mirror studying his toned physique. He was shirtless, wearing only a blue towel around his waist. His long brown hair had been tied up in a ponytail, which framed his increasingly chiseled jaw-line. To add insult to injury, his face was spotted with a thin layer of hair. He angrily studied the facial hair, tightening his grip on a hand-held razor.

"Who are you?" Louis, with a deep voice, asked himself in the mirror.

"Louis?" his mother called from beyond the bathroom door. Louis shifted his eyes to the closed door. His mother went on: "We're leaving the house in fifteen minutes. Put a move on, buster!"

Louis brought his eyes to the mirror, frowning. He sprayed a bit of shaving cream on his left hand, smearing it across his face. Taking the razor, Louis rid himself of the hair on his cheeks, chin and Adam's apple.

More years raced by in front of the muses settling upon a moment in time when Louis, in his early twenties and living in his own college dorm room, unpacked his holiday decorations. He was in the living room of his apartment with a fake eight-foot tree. Snow blotted out the rest of the world as he applied the ornaments and strung white lights. Louis' diverse collection of mismatched ornaments was a shrine of assorted accomplishments: a miniature silk top hat to signify his high school prom, a rusted stopwatch with roman numerals in regards to his transition spent in the first year of college and, his most recent ornament, a blue glass ball with the names 'Louis' and 'Halia' connected by a heart. He held the blue ornament to the light, examining it closely.

"And you say that every year your parents give you a unique ornament?" Halia asked as she fastened hooks to his ornaments. Halia was in her late teens. Her long black hair waved freely between her shoulder blades. Being from Hawaiian descent, her skin was naturally tan. On this day, she wore a gray wool turtle-neck and a long, flowing blue skirt.

"Yes," Louis told her, still looking at the glass ornament dangling from his index finger, "every year for as long as I can remember." He put the ornament in an empty space on the branches.

"Oh look!" Halia exclaimed. "I think I may have found the first one."

From both Annette and Nathaniel's perspective, Halia held the brass ornament that had first been introduced at the beginning of Louis' life. Louis held Halia from behind, placing his chin on her shoulder. They silently admired the ornament together.

The following scene was of Louis and Halia again, only this time the lights from the city caught the crystallized frost on the windowsill. The tree was aglow. A space-heater hummed happily. The two lovers explored one another's bodies. Louis' touch was warm as he reached under Halia's turtle-neck. He lifted the shirt from her figure exposing her skin and the straps of her brassiere. His fingers were gentle as he unhooked the support.

He continued to undress Halia. She trembled at the upcoming prospect, undressing Louis, unbuttoning his shirt and dropping it to the ground. She then removed his pants and boxers until they both stood staring at one another taking in the full effect of their anatomy.

"This is me," Halia said with a slight shrug of her shoulders.

"You're beautiful," he told her, looking reverently at her breasts. It was a look that reaffirmed that this was the body that he had wanted, not just sexually, but on his own figure.

"So are you," Halia said earnestly, wiping away his tear. Halia wasn't sure why Louis was crying but she found it endearing.

The relationship progressed exponentially in a matter of seconds. Louis and Halia explored the sexual intimacy of their partnership as well as the domestic. It was evident that, with each passing day, Louis' desire to have the same female figure of his fiancé, and later wife, grew to an uncontrollable, yet unspoken, yearning. The greatest blow to his ego came at the birth of his two children: identical twin girls. It was a balmy afternoon as he sat next to Halia on a park bench, looking into the squinting eyes of his daughters.

"Aren't they breathtaking?" Halia asked Louis.

Louis swallowed his bitterness and smiled. "They take after you, no doubt about it."

Time passed and the relationship grew colder. The physical aspect of their relationship disintegrated. Louis felt a sense of disgust when Halia touched him. When Louis was asked what was bothering him, he shrugged it off. He told her he was growing older and tired, that he didn't have the spunk that he used to. It was a barefaced lie. He fantasized, late at night, about being a different gender. He would lay awake in bed and daydream about being a woman. Dreams manifested themselves as visible thought bubbles to both Nathaniel and Annette, who watched the hovering ideas as they swam inches above him like swirling cotton-candy-like clouds of joy. As Louis slept, the thought bubbles dissipated. It didn't change the fact that, no matter how much he dreamed of being someone different, he was who he was when he woke.

"It's not that I want to be someone different," Louis told the marriage counselor one afternoon during a private session. "It's that I want to be the *real* person beneath this uncomfortable, ill-fitting skin." It was the first time that he gave a voice to the feeling. "Normal people aren't supposed to feel this trapped within their bodies. I can't keep living with this much resentment, and this much hatred. I feel," he stopped, thinking of the right words.

The therapist, a middle-aged woman with make-up and hairstyle perpetually stuck in an eighties frizz, allowed Louis as much time he needed.

"I feel . . ." Louis looked to the carpet beneath him, giving a laugh. " . . . Like I'm a woman, stuck inside a man's body."

"Do you think you'd be happier if you were a woman?" the therapist asked.

"I think I would be happier," Louis answered. He turned his eyes to the therapist. "Yes," he said earnestly. "Yes, I believe I would be."

The therapist then inquired, "Have you given any thought to gender reassignment?"

"No!" Louis was quick to respond, but his second "no" was not filled with nearly as much zest.

"What you appear to be suffering from is what medical journals call 'gender dysphoria.'"

"Gender dysphoria?"

"The feeling of being uncomfortable as a certain gender, perhaps believing that you should have been born the opposite sex . . . this is not an uncommon feeling. I have several individuals who feel the same as you do. The question is, if you feel that you are a woman trapped inside a man's body, how far are you willing to go to change it?"

Upon researching his situation he found that the therapist had been correct in saying that Louis was not alone in his thoughts. People in his situation were growing in numbers, a statistic that revitalized him. Based on his research, some individuals went so far as taking hormones, changing their wardrobe and way of life without actually shifting genders. He found those who went the full route, having the surgery that would permanently alter their physical attributes. He read success stories of individuals having already gone through the transition. To any commonplace onlooker, the materials perused would have felt obtrusive, abnormal and 'in-your-face' about such anomalous taboos. When it came to Louis, he found himself more and more curious, intrigued at the idea that he could finally reach the life that he had always wanted to live. It gave him an unfamiliar sense of optimism that he had been deprived.

"I'm not understanding what you're telling me, Louis," Halia said with concern.

"I've been doing a lot of research into this subject, Halia," Louis tried to explain again "and I firmly believe that this is something that I have to consider."

"Becoming a woman . . . ?"

"Yes, Halia. Becoming a woman."

"Do you know how insane that sounds?"

"I'll tell you what's insane, Halia," Louis countered "having lived this long feeling this way, and thinking that I'm cornered in the wrong body. What's insane is how I feel when I look at you, when I look at any woman and think how bitter I am! What's insane, Halia, is how much I hate who I am when I look in a mirror, how disgusted I am with my own body!"

Halia tossed her hands in surrender to straighten the children's toys in the living room.

Louis went after her. "I have to do this, Halia. I have to at least try. And I want you to go on this journey with me."

"Now that notion *is* insane, Louis, thinking I might go on this 'journey' with you." She did not look at him as she spoke, but instead turned her attention to the toys, tossing them forcefully into the toy chest beside the entertainment stand. "What about the girls? Have you thought about them? Have you thought about how they will feel if they have to watch their father pop hormone pills, wear women's clothes, and transition from one sex to another? What do you think they'll say when the doctor chops off your manhood?"

"That's not how the surgery works, Halia. Yes, the testicles are removed," but before he could explain, Halia swooped beside the sofa to swipe a rogue toy.

"I don't want to hear it!" Halia shouted. "I don't want to *hear* it, Louis!" She cried, facing her husband. "You can't do this to me. To our daughters. To . . . us! You and me!"

"Halia," Louis approached, reaching for her. "Halia, listen to me. If I don't do this, if I don't at least make an attempt, I'll die. And I don't want to die, Halia. I want to live."

Halia scoffed. "And you can't live the way that you are? With me? With the kids?" She clutched the toy in her hands as if fixing to strangle it. "Then I suppose I have no choice, Louis. If you want to live in this new lifestyle, do what you have to do."

"Do you honestly mean that?" Louis asked.

"Yes, Louis. I mean that. But you have to know: if you do live as a woman, as far as the children are considered, you'll be dead to them. I refuse for you to subject them to this monstrosity you're about to create for yourself."

Louis was visibly taken aback by this.

Time sped forward through the ending of their marriage to the gut-wrenching custody hearings where Louis fought to keep his children. Halia gained sole guardianship. Though filled with anguish, he went to the west coast, keeping with him photographs of his daughters. Nathaniel and Annette watched the long process of Louis' transgender passage. They were with him as he visited therapists and as he began taking hormones. They were with Louis as, after two years, the physical reactions to the hormones took effect. His voice was higher-pitched. His skin was softer. His upper body strength decreased and his body fat grew leaner into a womanly figure. The muses were there as Louis dressed as a woman, functioning in society as the gender he had often dreamed. Louis maintained a steady job at his local bowling alley, went to school part-time, and volunteered in his new community. Louis immersed himself in support groups of like-minded individuals, connecting with others on the same path. When he visited the therapists and doctors' appointments, he did so alone. Often, he would pull out the pictures of his children and wish he were a part of their lives as the person he wanted his children to see him as: a happy, thriving individual who chased dreams to the bitter end.

After receiving three letters of approval from the appropriate therapists, Louis achieved his dream. After nearly four years, and after working so closely in discussing everything with the mental health doctors and also his surgeon, Louis closed his eyes and opened them as Luanne.

As the years went by, Luanne seemed to adjust well to her new lifestyle. However, with each passing day, she felt numb. In all those years, Luanne had been so concerned in finding herself that she abandoned her collection of Christmas ornaments. Each Christmas that passed, she would forgo the fake tree and ignore the holidays. Luanne found herself drifting farther and farther away from the original hope of reconnecting with her children. She had achieved being a woman, definitely. But what did it mean now that she didn't have the most important women in her life to share it with?

These thoughts, and more, flooded her mind until one afternoon when Luanne found a Christmas ornament sitting on the counter of her bowling alley work station. The ornament was a crushed soda can with the face of Santa Clause crudely painted on it. A red ribbon was attached to the top, enabling the ornament to dangle perfectly on any tree branch. When she held it, Luanne smiled. It appeared that, from that moment on, everything was going to be okay.

Luanne's life reached its midway point and the muses were deposited back into Annette's cathedral office. They sat in silence for several moments before Annette said anything.

"I had forgotten how raw these colored pegs can be once turned."

"Now you see why I like to review the lives of our clients over reading a good novel," Nathaniel answered. "The truth, however odd or inconsistent it may be with how we normally view things, is far more intriguing than any work of fabricated fiction." He sighed and asked "so are you satisfied, Mrs. Slocum?"

"Satisfied?"

"There was not a hint of Mr. Rothchild inside Luanne's life."

"Oh," Annette said, lost in her own thoughts. "I suppose I am. For now. But I would like to review the others."

"Of course you would," Nathaniel said dryly. He stood from the swivel chair and started to leave. "We have envelopes that need attending, and more clients to inspire. Luanne's life is one story in a cluster of millions of others that need our care."

"What would I see if I were to turn your peg, Mr. Cauliflower?" Annette asked.

Nathaniel turned his eyes to the manuscript on Annette's desk. "It's in there on those pages," he told her, "If you're really that interested in knowing."

"Even your seventh life when you rescued my library books?"

Nathaniel didn't answer Annette's question. He was already out of her office door headed back to his own. Once safely in his own office of seven obsessions, he closed and locked the door. He pressed his back against the door, closing his eyes, and thinking on what he had seen in Luanne's peg. He took several deep breaths, righting himself. Within moments he was in front of the cabinet of rescued library books. He pushed several aside and, from beside a copy of Geoffrey Chaucer's *Canterbury Tales*, he removed a bundle of pages. On the pages was scribed the details from his seventh life; pages that he had taken from his manuscript when he cleaned the department before the Nine Greatest Muses had arrived.

"Someday you'll be ready for our story, Annette," he said to the pages. "But not now."

*

"Excuse me," there came a voice from the other side of the desk. Luanne, who had been spraying the shoes with disinfectant, turned to find a middle-aged man with stark white hair. He was wearing a black suit and tie. "My name is Jonas, and I was wondering how much a typical game would cost? My friend and I are interested in rolling a few bowling balls, hoping to work on our strike record."

Luanne turned to the aforementioned friend. Jonas' friend had their back facing the counter. He was wearing a black hoodie with the hood obscuring any details of the face.

"Well," Luanne told Jonas "it depends on how many games and how long you intend on playing?"

Jonas glanced over Luanne's right shoulder where he spotted the Christmas ornament resting on the counter. He then looked at Luanne and smiled. "I suppose however long it will take for me and my friend to perfect our method."

CHAPTER 10: LOVERS, REVERSED

Warm rain poured worryingly during the summer afternoon in 2009. It was a storm with scattered rumbles of thunder which sporadically germinated throughout the atmosphere's hovering clouds. Jonas and his partner in the black hoodie occupied the same dry space underneath a black umbrella. They looked out onto a graveyard: the hallowed ground precarious with thick, wet mud. There was a man in the distance who was on his knees in front of a grave mourning the loss of a loved one.

"Why are we standing out here in the rain?" Jonas' accomplice asked. "Are we here for the man kneeling at the grave?"

"No," Jonas responded. "We're here for the woman in the car."

"What woman?" came the reply "what car?"

A Honda Civic pulled up a little ways from their right. The red and white tail lights flickered as the vehicle was put into park.

"The story between Doris the waitress and Lyle the car salesman goes as follows: our bereaved bachelor here has frequented Doris' diner several times. For the past three days our waitress has been secretly admiring the newcomer, but Lyle hasn't yet acknowledged her. For the first three days Lyle's come and eaten his eggs, paid his bill and left without even batting an eye. That was, of course, until a donut was dropped to the floor of the diner, causing Lyle and Doris to have locked eyes and briefly connect. Here she is, watching Lyle from afar again, and before her bravery with the funnel cakes, hoping for more of an association. Also, at this exact moment, a previous version of Annette Slocum, working her second inspiration in her first term as a Ninth Generation muse, is appearing in Doris' car in miniature grasshopper size offering one a word of encouragement to her client. In a few seconds, Doris will be climbing out of her vehicle and fighting with her umbrella. According to what I've been told, an obsession with baking funnel cakes will ensue, which Doris will make for her stranger, ultimately bringing her to Lyle's doorstep to ring his doorbell which will lead to a beautifully Management-constructed happy ending."

"But we are here to change that?" the hoodie-clad cohort inquired.

"We are."

"How?"

"Did you know that when Doris was a young lady in elementary school, that she created Valentine's Day boxes?"

"I didn't, no."

"Oh yes," Jonas nodded. "Every year each box had gone from being made of macaroni shells to hand-carved, erected more and more elaborately. Year after heart-breaking year, the boxes remained empty. Our lovesick waitress has been waiting to find someone to capture her heart. Well, that day's arrived! Our advantage here is that Doris suffers from low self-esteem, and her extreme affections haplessly attach themselves to anyone who gives her even the slightest interest. This feature will help enable my plan to entice her with a valentine." He withdrew a piece of folded red construction paper that had been snipped into the shape of a heart. "I'll intercept, hand this belated token of love, and we'll have her."

The driver's side car door opened. An umbrella shot out from the interior, puncturing the rain like the tip of a sword. Doris fumbled with the umbrella until it spread wide.

Jonas took out a second piece of paper from his pocket: a violet envelope labeled with a handwritten number. He turned to his acquaintance in the black hoodie handing him the violet envelope. "I'll expect to see you at our home after placing this on the empty driver's seat."

The figure in the hoodie nodded.

Jonas abandoned the umbrella, bid his colleague farewell and headed toward Doris with the valentine in hand. Jonas claimed this victim amidst an ostensibly neutral storm, creating his own love story in a malevolent line of attack.

*

Nathaniel had once overheard Harriet when she had said to Fiona: "The energy efficient light bulbs, the instructional video, the water coolers, you treat them as if they're just as important as our clients."

"Ah, but they *are* just as important as our clients," Fiona had told Harriet.

"But they don't have skin, brains, a beating heart, souls . . ." as Harriet had gone on, Fiona had carried a ladder out of the conference room down the hallway past the doorless offices. Nathaniel, who had been delivering envelopes to a muse's postbox, hurriedly ducked into an office door to avoid contact. Harriet, having been unaware of Nathaniel's nearness, said "They don't have a projected purpose Fiona, but you're acting as if they did."

"Just like one of our clients, Harriet," he had heard Fiona explain "If one little cog is missing, broken or obsolete, then circumstances would change. Management has things the way they like it for a reason, from a client that we inspire down to the energy efficient light bulbs in the hallway. Everything that we encounter deserves recognition."

"I'm not trying to be difficult, Fiona."

"Not being difficult at all, Harriet."

Nathaniel peered around the corner. With their backs turned to him as they crossed down the hall, Nathaniel delivered the envelopes to the last postbox without being noticed.

"Only one more peg to go before I retire, and if I'm going to take over your position, I need to know these things."

"When I started as a First Generation muse, Harriet, and was employed as Head Muse after the initial employment, do you think anyone passed down a guide book? Sure there was the demonstration about the Lite-Brite board but I personally formulated my own procedures as the need surfaced."

"Management must have taught you *something*, Fiona."

"There are many things that Management taught me, Harriet," Fiona had sighed, "and many things I wish they had, but didn't. Alas, like the lives our clients, we are only given enough to continue on our own path. It's up to us, as it is for them, to figure out our own answers."

This conversation had taken place right before Jonas appeared at the conference room door with news that he had neglected his twenty-second envelope.

In the present day, Fiona sat in her respective office. Fiona, who had once shown advertised managerial authority with dignified poise, showed physical signs of her exhaustion. After over ten generations as acting Head Muse, she was ready to retire. A smile formed on Fiona's face as Nathaniel brought the last bin of reassigned white pegs. Seeing them meant Fiona's freedom would be granted and Harriet's tenure of being Head Muse would rapidly initiate.

"So this is the last of them?" she asked.

"These are," Nathaniel told her.

He delivered the latest bin of purple pegs to Harriet who had been ready to take the role off her mentor's hands, eagerly awaiting the coronation. With bobby pins puncturing her immovable hair bun, she bore a complacent look on her middle-aged face resembling a determined, sanctimonious rule-abiding sentry. Harriet was stringently unbending in her initiative to tolerate Management's orders. It wasn't that Harriet was set on running the diplomacy with a stricter hand; the truth of her motivation was much simpler. Due largely to the physical abuse endured in her previous marriage, Harriet was terrified of the living world and longed to stay in the safety of the afterlife.

Anna Pavlova practiced in her studio as Nathaniel brought the reassigned pink-colored pegs. The ballerina's back was to him with one hand on the barre as she dipped into a graceful plié. He reverently watched her dance for several minutes, propping himself against the office's doorframe. When she bent to the doorway, Nathaniel was gone. Paul Lawrence Dunbar raised his eyes from a newly-written poem when Nathaniel entered with the final bin of the reassigned cream-colored pink polka-dotted pegs. Mr. Andrews, while pacing the deck of the reconstructed Titanic as the ship, nodded to Nathaniel who delivered the red-colored pegs.

Lucas' office was colder then Nathaniel remembered when he entered with the reassigned green pegs.

"Annette has yet to come by," Lucas told him.

"Our retirement party will be upon us soon, and hopefully she will reconnect then."

Lucas looked to the window. "I hope so." He sighed heavily. "I feel so lonely, Mr. Cauliflower. I thought that, when I went to Heaven after retiring the first time, I wouldn't feel this way anymore. But it's still there: the loneliness. I wish I had someone to talk to, you know?"

"I know exactly what you mean, Mr. Richardson. More than you can understand."

He started for Lucas' door but turned back to see his client before exiting. In Lucas' right hand, the guitar pick was being massaged. Watching Lucas with the guitar pick, Nathaniel wondered if it had been a mistake giving it to him.

Nathaniel visited the next to last office of his tour: the living Grecian beach, basking in afternoon sunlight, of which Icarus was engaged, staring off into the cloudless sky.

Icarus said Nathaniel, "Thank you for a familiar landscape, Mr. Cauliflower."

Nathaniel brought the remaining bin of reassigned yellow pegs closer. "I hope the office is to your liking, Icarus."

"Oh," Icarus pondered, "it's as if no time has passed since I last stood at this shore with my father. It's not the real rocks and sand that I stood at before my initial flight, but it's enough to bring back memories of more idyllic days."

Nathaniel proceeded to go but Icarus had more to say causing a misstep in the postmaster's walk.

"I take comfort in knowing that I'm not the only one who was meant to soar to such heights, only to have gravity pull you down."

As these words were spoken, a memory swept over Nathaniel concerning his life's conclusion in 1808.

*

Twenty-three year-old Nathaniel watched as the painter, and the loft, became smaller in perspective as he scrambled to right the falling ladder. Nathaniel felt a sense of panic in the moment between him falling through the air and colliding with the floor. It was a short-lived panic as the Parisian sunlight was ripped from his vision. When he opened his eyes again, he perceived a rotunda void of personal items. The only thing it contained was an oculus with a lone ray of sunlight shining around him. His gaze then caught sight of a woman in a cream-colored paints suit.

"Hello Mr. Cauliflower," the woman said to him. "My name is Fiona, and you've been hired by Management to be a muse." She offered a hand to help him.

"A muse?" he asked her, righting himself with her assistance.

"Precisely," Fiona confirmed. "Would you follow me please?"

*

Nathaniel knew what it was like to fall to his death, Icarus had been correct. Icarus had fallen to his death twice. The primary time had been when Icarus and his father Daedalus planned to escape from Greece. Daedalus had been a great inventor during the Bronze Age, favored in the court of the Great King Minos of Crete.

Minos had a labyrinth in his palace that had housed a horrific Minotaur which had been half man, half bull. For sport, Minos had brought many epic heroes into the labyrinth to battle the beast and find their way out of the labyrinth. No heroes had made it out alive. When the champion named Theseus had appeared, Minos had been shocked when the conqueror made it successfully through the labyrinth. To have made matters all the more spectacular, Theseus had brought Minos the head of the Minotaur, throwing it at the king's feet. Minos had been so flustered by the success that he sent his men to investigate the labyrinth to see how Theseus could have found his way in, and out, so effortlessly. His men had discovered a string that had been tied to the labyrinth's entrance.

"When you created my labyrinth to house the Minotaur," Minos had consulted Daedalus that afternoon, "you told me that you made it so perfect, so confusing, that even the most intelligent warrior couldn't flee from it alive. Yet, here we are with a dead beast and a proud vanquisher. Explain how this happened?"

"Perhaps Theseus had more wits about him than the others," Daedalus had told the king.

"Or perhaps he had been informed by someone how to effectively navigate the routes." Minos had held up the string. "Theseus was given a string to tie to the entrance. As it unspooled, he was able to create a clear path from the entrance to the center where he discovered, and slaughtered, the Minotaur. It was this string, given to him by you, the inventor of the labyrinth, which gave him the advantage to find his way out!"

Daedalus had looked at the string, feeling a sense of alarm rush through his blood.

"You've made a fool of me, Daedalus," Minos had spat. "And for what purpose? Did you think that Theseus would carry you and your son on the boat back to his homeland?" Minos had tossed the string to the dirt ground, stomping on it several times to prove his control.

The shouting had brought Icarus into the room who had been no older than eighteen.

"As punishment, Daedalus, I'll take the life of your son in exchange for the life of the Minotaur."

Daedalus had begged forgiveness through tears, shaking his head maniacally. "Please, King Minos! Please! Not Icarus!"

Athenian guards had entered Daedalus' home and pried the inventor from Minos. Icarus had started to flee but they took him as well. Minos had been alone in the room. He had looked at the string on the ground, examined Daedalus' dingy home, and departed with his cape fluttering luxuriously behind him.

"The wind on this beach reminds me of the wind on the day of our escape from King Minos' court," Icarus said to Nathaniel. They were both staring into the clear skies and crystal-blue waters of the roaring sea. "On the night of our imprisonment, father constructed two pairs of wings; one for me, the other for himself. As the sun rose on that day, father told me not to fly too high or the sun would melt the wax on the wings. If I flew too low, the water would weigh me down.

As he tightened the leather straps around my shoulders, he asked if I was listening. I told him I was but, truthfully, I was too excited to feel the wind rush against my face to care, to feel like a bird in mid-flight." Icarus shifted his eyes heavenward. "I kicked myself into the wind. I shouted with hilarity as the beach disappeared beneath me. There were sea birds in the sky but I flew far above them to prove that I was more powerful. I wanted to kiss the clouds. I wanted to say hello to the Gods in the stars! I flew higher and higher! The wind rushed across my face and through my hair! It was almost deafening! I felt free, uninhibited! I heard my father screaming for me. He too was in the sky shouting for me to not fly too high. I turned to look at him feeling smug. I was defying the laws of gravity! What did I care?"

"And then the wax melted," Nathaniel confirmed.

"I plummeted," Icarus nodded. "The clouds were swept into a vortex. The sea birds cawed condescendingly as I descended. I fell headfirst into the rampant ocean and promptly drowned. I found myself in the Underworld faced with many abominations while in the company of . . ."

Icarus paused and did not refer to the Underworld or who he had encountered. He asked "If you were given the opportunity to rework a specific moment in your life, Mr. Cauliflower, would you?"

Nathaniel frequently wondered how things would have turned out had he not kept the paintings on display, but he didn't share this with Icarus.

"When I was a Third Generation muse," Icarus went on "I was assigned to work the resulting colored pegs of Evangeline's neglectfulness. The circulating rumors of your affair were fresh, and I tried to be empathetic. If I may be so bold," Icarus looked at Nathaniel "did you ever find her again?"

"Evangeline?" Nathaniel sighed. "No. I never found her. Eventually I gave up searching, hoping that, someday, Management would return her to me."

"So then you would?" Icarus asked again, "you would change a moment in your life to have her in your arms?"

Nathaniel didn't answer. He simply stared out at the sea while thinking of his beloved.

"Oh to have that kind of love for someone," Icarus thought out loud. "When I was alive, I loved both men and women, I didn't discriminate. I suppose you could say that I loved Persephone in the Underworld. She was filled with such beauty and hatred. Prior to meeting Persephone, before my fall, I was in love with a young Greek man named Castor. Mr. Richardson reminds me of him. I wonder what would happen if I were to befriend Mr. Richardson. I've seen the way he looks at me."

"You should explore that," Nathaniel then started for Icarus' office door.

"I hope that you find Evangeline again," Icarus told him.

Nathaniel sighed and said, after a brief hesitation, "Me too."

The last bin of reassigned orange pegs was delivered to Annette. No doubt Annette was currently on an inspiration as her office was not in use. Though Nathaniel had seen little of her since they rotated Luanne's blue peg, he tracked Annette's progress. He was content that she had maintained an unprecedented momentum.

Nathaniel wheeled the bin alongside her desk and studied the dry erase board. Not much had been added save for a bit of commentary that she had scribbled with a blue marker that read: "What are the envelopes counting to? How many are there meant to be and why?"

Her cathedral office had begun to grow a garden of yellow tulips. Trails of yellow roses climbed the walls and columns. Nathaniel stepped to a rose and placed his nose to one of the yawning petals. Closing his eyes as he sniffed, he couldn't help but to remember the fresh roses that were in Evangeline's room when he had seen her in his second life in the year 1923.

Evangeline's voice rang clear in his mind as he smelled the rose: "Promise me you won't go after your painter, Nathaniel. Promise me that you'll stay safe inside my home. Together we can live the rest of our days." Her frail voice was that of a woman well over one hundred years. "Promise me that, whatever happens, you won't let the darkness in your heart overtake you."

Nathaniel, who was eighteen in his second life, and an immigrant from Russia, responded in a thick accent "I promise." He knew his appeasing words were a lie. They were also the last words that he would speak to her before being murdered a second time.

*

Nathaniel felt a hand touch his right shoulder. He spun to find Annette.

Annette said, "Hello."

Nathaniel said quickly "Hello, Mrs. Slocum."

"The flowers sprouted thirty envelopes ago," Annette told him. "Thank you for adding them."

"I didn't add them," Nathaniel retorted. "They must have grown on their own accord."

"Have you come to help me turn a few more pegs?"

Nathaniel studied her. "Mrs. Slocum . . ."

"I need to see for myself if Jonas is responsible for stealing these people during thunderstorms," she told him. "Plus, if I return home, there may not be a wedding to return to."

"What do you mean?"

"The night before my wedding day in 2016, the night of the bachelor party, there was a thunderstorm. Adam was out with his guy friends at a local billiard hall. Whenever there's the slightest roll of thunder, or hint of lightning, I've asked him to call me and check in. And to continue checking in until the thunderstorm has finished. It's sort of our thing. And it brings me comfort from my paranoia. It's one thing to be apart from your lover for a single night knowing that you'll see him standing at the altar. It's quite another to believe that, if the Thunderstorm Man truly chooses inclement weather to snag his victims, he might abduct someone close to the detective working the case."

"You're concerned that, if he's responsible, Mr. Rothchild may have taken Adam?"

"Or may take him at some point," Annette confirmed. "I can't return to my wedding day until I know for a fact that I've completed this open file."

"You've loosely based the evidence on Mr. Rothchild."

"For now," Annette told him. "But, if you'd allow me to gather more information by turning pegs perhaps I can prove to you that I'm justified." She took a step closer to him, saying solemnly, "Wouldn't you want to do everything in your power to protect your loved ones from someone who may want to do them harm?"

"I suppose I can see your logic. I've already ordered the pegs to be delivered from Management's personal library. Until then, we'll rotate the remaining two we have."

Annette reached into her desk drawer and pulled out Phillip's red peg and the blue peg corresponding to the blizzard. She put the red peg into the Lite-Brite. Nathaniel touched his hand gently to her wrist.

"If we rotate these pegs, and we don't find anything, promise me you'll return to your wedding day, close the case and revisit your pie-making aspirations."

Annette nodded in agreement. The red-colored peg was rotated counter-clockwise. They disappeared from the office into the life of Phillip: the boy destined to witness the glow-in-the-dark stars.

As soon as they left, Icarus appeared at Annette's doorway making sure that the coast was clear. He wore a black hoodie which he carefully zipped. Icarus' eyes caught sight of Lyle Slocum's photograph on the dry erase board. With both hands, he reached and pulled the hood over his head. Wearing a sly grin, he walked down the hall to his own office.

*

The rain pounded onto the Slocum house in 2009 as two figures, Jonas and his friend in the hoodie, were on the front porch.

"When I stood here previously," Jonas told his escort, "I had a copy of Oscar Wilde's *Dorian Gray* that I intended to give Annette as a gift. I discovered the identity of the individual who repaired her library books when she was a little girl, and I intended to take her from this place and show her who repaired them. But her husband intervened. He guided me into my car and I drove off, defeated."

Jonas moved his gaze to the lawn, and to the tumbleweed-type bush that haunted the mailbox, where the mailman pulled up in his carrier truck. Jonas and the mailman exchanged glances. The mailman gave a slight smile, stuffed the mail into the mailbox and drove to the neighboring address.

"Today, I have no intention of being defeated," he told the hoodie-clad individual. Jonas held in his hand an electric screw driver which he plugged into an outside socket. He held the electric screw driver aloft pressing the trigger button bringing the mechanism to whirl. He wore black leather gloves to avoid leaving fingerprints.

"Why don't we ring the doorbell?" asked the hooded individual.

"No amount of ringing the doorbell is going to pull Lyle from his depression. At this moment, he's sitting in his recliner dozing in misery while watching old re-runs of television shows. He's heard the doorbell ring several times and has yet to budge. If we're going to get his attention, it's time to take our own direct measures."

With a simple flat head screwdriver, no bigger than his ring finger, Jonas spied a little latch near the knob and pushed in. He removed the knob setting it on the porch floorboards. He removed the exterior rose plate. There was a mounting plate underneath attached by two screws. Jonas took the electric screwdriver, gave it a few spins, and touched the tip on the end of each screw. Both screws fell to the porch. Jonas then pushed the other side of the doorknob out from the other side and removed the lock. Soon there was a gaping hole where the doorknob had been.

Jonas smiled. He pressed his left hand against the door causing it to swing open.

"Admittance arranged," Jonas told his friend in the hoodie who had crouched down with him during the process. Jonas wrapped his tools. They both stood at the same time. Jonas opened the door wide, allowing a view into the foyer. "Now it's time to collect who we've come for. After you, friend. Don't worry; there are no guard dogs to drug, no trip wires to avoid. It's only a house filled to the brim with past memories.

His friend went in first.

Jonas then crossed the threshold. He spotted a framed wedding picture of Annette and Lyle. He removed the picture from the frame holding the flimsy photograph to his eyes. With his hands still gloved, he tore the picture in half separating husband and wife. He held up Annette Slocum's half studying it in the waning light of day.

As the rain cascaded the windows of the house, Lyle slept in the living room recliner as the single withering occupant in the abode's peeling, faded wallpaper of bad dreams.

Jonas who was still in the foyer, looked at his feet where he found a funnel cake had splattered on the floor. He kicked it aside. "Funnel cakes," Jonas sneered. As the rain sounded, Jonas indefinitely interrupted the love story that Management had strategically set into motion.

*

Several days later in 2009, an eye witness confirmed to a detective named Annette Redmond that he had been the one delivering the mail when he noticed two men on the porch. Upon further investigation, detective Redmond found the empty frame with Lyle's half of the picture sitting on the carpeted floor. She then spotted a discarded violet envelope on the recliner in the living room that read "7."

"Detective Redmond?" asked one of the officers who dusted fingerprints. "What do you make of it?"

"I'm not sure, to be honest," was her response. "Someone's out for a laugh and I'm not finding the humor in it."

She pocketed the photograph of Lyle Slocum into an evidence bag and added it to her case files. It was the same ripped photograph that, many years later, in 2016, ended up on her dry erase board in her cathedral office after she had been brought back as one of the Nine Greatest muses in history.

CHAPTER 11: A BOY AND HIS STARS

The retelling of Phillip's life began with stars. Not the common stars as one might find in a nighttime sky while casually adjusting eyes upward or by utilizing a telescope to map out the specifics of a glowing dot. The stars introduced at the beginning were far smaller and didn't give off any light. They existed on the left forearm of Phillip's father who held his two year-old son late in the night. Young Phillip had developed an awful cold, and was filled with such congestion, that nothing short of his father's loving embrace could cure it. Having already applied vapor rub to the toddler's chest, his father cradled his son in his arms and now soothingly rubbed his back. Phillip's chubby face leaned against his father's left shoulder peering at the stars on his father's arm. His young eyes blithely studied the stars while his tiny fingers traced the inked, pointed angles. This instant would be Phillip's most treasured childhood memory.

As Nathaniel watched this, he felt a fluttering in his heart; a yearning to have a moment like this one day. He gasped, hoping that the intake of air might stifle the urge to feel any kind of emotion. He was pleased that it worked.

"Are you okay?" Annette asked, witnessing his reaction.

"Acid reflux," Nathaniel lied.

"There may be some antacids in the department's common bathroom," Annette offered.

"I'm good, thanks."

Time skipped forward with the propulsion of a rocket ship exiting the atmosphere. The second scene was of several months later when Phillip lay in his crib trying to fall asleep on his own. He was healthier in this moment than he had been previously. Phillip's eyes gazed at the revolving mobile above his crib where miniature planets in the solar system spun with the power of AA batteries. As the view of the room expanded, the crib and the solar system were only a minute fraction of the outer space surrounding him. The entire room was dotted with glow-in-the-dark stars which shined dimly in the encroaching darkness. There was also a slowly twirling nightlight that showed a circling panorama of nearby constellations and remote galaxies varying in shape, size and luminosity. Phillip's private universe expressed the impression of a forever expanding space centered on the little tyke as he finally closed his eyes, ending each day in the hypnotizing cosmos.

Phillip grew older, as all children do. He developed into a young lad with apricot-colored hair, brown eyes, and slightly chubby physique. When he was in the fourth grade he, and his class, visited the local planetarium where Phillip's father worked. It was here that he officially learned the terminologies regarding the spinning, twinkling objects on his bedroom walls.

He educated himself about the volatile temperament of the immense powerhouse bonfire known as the Sun. He was enthralled by Mercury's scarred, cosmetic appeal as it orbited the fastest of all the planets, yet rotated equally as slow on its axis. Phillip gaped while discovering that Venus, although being the shiniest, most recognizable planet to the naked eye, possessed a dense atmosphere of poisonous greenhouse gas. He marveled at how Earth was protected by an invisible magnetic bubble known as the "magnetosphere" which sheltered his home from space debris and emission particles ejected from the neighboring star, and how, because of that field, colorful auroras could occasionally be witnessed near the poles. He bit the skin around his right-hand thumb as the expansive scarlet terrain of Mars was explored by a mechanical robot. He widened his eyes further at watching tumbling varied asteroids as they spun around in a gravitational belt between the red planet and the gas giant Jupiter. He was amazed as the show took him inside the Great Red Spot, delving the audience further into Jupiter's gaseous, churning atmosphere of liquids and metals. The screen danced from moon to moon, briefly touching on each of the sixty-three smaller satellites that orbited the planet. Phillip gazed wondrously at Saturn's rings, marveling at how, from afar, they seemed solid, but flying closer discovered there were hundreds of discs, each consisting of their own collections of billions upon billions of spinning icy rock particles. Uranus was next: a brilliant blue sphere with an atmosphere of methane gas storms, and how its axis was tipped on its side, causing its rings to run vertically. Neptune winded him as it described how the planet's gales were the fastest recorded gusts in the solar system. At last there was Pluto, re-classified as a dwarf planet, along with its only orbiting moon, Charon, in the Kuiper Belt of other smaller ice chips, each rotating on their own, obscure axial tilt.

  This virtual tour ignited Phillip's curiosity. He visited the local library in hopes of procuring more books on the subject. Over the years, Phillip's fascination with the universe expanded with his new-found knowledge on rotating, fantastically plumed, glittering galaxies; some were small clusters of moving stars in a tight, dwarfed system. There were irregularly shaped galaxies that had no true form while glowing brightly in a concentrated white center. Other galaxies were scintillating metropolises shaped like suspended discs. Some as whirling spirals, some were shaped as elliptical spheres. A few had energetic centers shooting matter into space!

Phillip soaked in the vibrant colors of surrounding nebulas. He imagined himself rocking inside the warm, inviting reds. Phillip flew through the blues as rich as a mid-afternoon sky. He gowned himself in the rich silken purples and gold, resting upon fields of soft greens and picking apart the present yellows, holding them in his hand like plucking tulip petals. It was in these nebulas that he, himself, felt responsible for the birth of every star, playing a proud parent in the colorfully illuminated nurseries.

As the years soared by, and his astronomical education expanded, Phillip was overjoyed at learning the nature of stars, and how there had been many classifications and sizes starting from the small brown dwarfs to stars similar to Earth's yellow star all the way to massive blue giant stars. He was enthralled at the varying life-spans of each star, awestruck by the idea of novas and supernovas.

In his education through his teens, Phillip grasped the concepts of elements listed on the Periodic table and their relationships with the universe. He learned of Einstein's Theory of Relativity, of Stephen Hawking's genius, theories surrounding the ideas of multiple planes of reality, wormholes and multiple universes. He researched different theories about how the universe may have originated and pondered where the universe was headed. Some believed the universe would eventually stop expanding and retract upon itself, while others counter that perhaps the universe would rip apart.

All of these ideas and more flooded around Nathaniel and Annette by way of colors, sounds, phantom voices reciting textbook theologies, visions of exploding stars, glowing galaxies teetering too close to one another, raging storms of hydrogen and methane, living constellations at war, whizzing comets, dipping asteroids, startling eclipses, raging plumes of coronal mass ejections, solar flares, spinning satellites, images of Phillip's astronomy teacher giving lectures on the quantifiable speed of light, multitudes of mathematical equations measuring distances from one object in space to another, and the plethora of knowledge sweeping from the first astrologers in history to the most recent.

Standing in the center of this multihued bedlam was the evolution of Phillip who grew to be eighteen. In his late teens, he was confident and more aware of himself than ever before. It showed the meaningful relationship between him and his father and the growing collection of books, star charts and telescope equipment. Phillip's early adulthood revealed a storyline in regards to the relationship between Phillip's arguing parents, who were on the cusp of their own supernova, set to negatively ignite at even the slightest provocation.

The tale was muted by pitch-blackness and a stillness void of everything previously viewed. There came a rustling sound in the darkness which Nathaniel determined was Annette spinning in place.

"What happened?" Annette asked into the void. "Did someone snag a power cord or something? Did we sink into a black hole?"

Annette's question was answered by the sound of scratching leaves on the side of a road as they were upturned by a pair of shoes. A faint gray light appeared, expanding to an autumn afternoon when Phillip walked home from school.

In his nineteenth year Phillip's five o'clock shadow matched the spiked cherry tinge of his textured hair. It was hard to deduce his exact body shape considering that he wore a bulky maroon hoodie with a sagging hood around his nape. He also donned frayed, loose-fitting blue jeans and absentmindedly kicked the leaves with his scuffed Doc Martens while listening to music through a pair of headphones attached to a cell phone.

Phillip found himself in his own driveway. He flipped the opening of the mailbox removing a wad of envelopes. Carrying the mail with him to the single story, gray-siding coated house, he passed by the closed single car garage and took out keys from his right jeans pocket. An aroma of fresh-burning leaves traveled on the wind and he briefly look up to determine the source of it.

The scene switched to the inside of the house focusing on Phillip as he entered the foyer and set down his school bag and mail. In his bedroom, he sat on the edge of his plaid brown and blue bedspread. He was too busy untying his laces to notice that his room was not the same as it had been that morning.

Annette was aware of a change and she examined it scrupulously. She touched the bare walls. She crossed to Phillip's desk where there were no signs of the school books and pictures regarding the universe.

"Where is everything?" she asked.

As if Phillip heard her, he stopped untying his shoes and observed the room.

"What the . . .?" Phillip asked. He crossed to his walls looking for his research. He checked his desk drawers, the closet, under the bed, underneath the mattress and box springs, but to no avail – everything associated with the universe, and its splendor, had gone missing. He heard a faint tapping against his window as if a few rogue pebbles were being tossed at the glass. He parted the curtains to find the source of the burning he had smelled in the street. With the words "It can't be," Phillip retreated from the glass.

"What is it?" Annette approached the window.

Phillip sprinted from the room with his shoelaces whipping back and forth.

The sound wasn't from pebbles hitting Phillip's window. It was the sound of a crackling fire in the backyard. Burning in effigy was a mountain of personal astronomy items! The green trunk from Phillip's bedroom was dragged by his mother to the inferno. It contained his modest collection of literature, star-charts, glow-in-the-dark stars and the mobile, all sentenced to execution.

"Oh, Mr. Cauliflower, you have to come see this." Annette brought a hand to her mouth.

Nathaniel said to Annette: "There's no need, Mrs. Slocum. I've seen it."

Nathaniel and Annette stood in the backyard as Phillip stumbled through the overgrown grass to reach his mother. Inch by inch, she dragged the trunk closer to the fire.

"Stop!" cried Phillip. "Mom, why are you doing this?"

It appeared that his mother didn't hear him or, if she did, his words went ignored.

Phillip tripped over his shoe laces and fell to the ground, grasping the strap on the opposite end of the trunk. Feeling resistance from the other end, his mother whirled, glaring at her son.

She was a portly woman in her mid-forties who had forgone her thin figure years ago masking it with frumpy jeans and a sweatshirt with a local college football team logo. Her shoulder length black hair was mixed with rascally gray strands. Her bloodshot eyes were filled with rage bringing Phillip to shrink back slightly with his hand still on the trunk's side handle.

"Dad's going to be furious when he gets back," he explained.

"Your dad's not coming back, Phillip," she answered coldly.

Phillip cocked his head slightly to the left. "What are you saying?"

"He's gone, Phillip."

"Where did he go?"

"To the stars and galaxies that he loved so much," she sneered, tugging on the trunk. "Let go."

"Wait," Phillip begged.

For a moment, his mother hesitated.

"What happened to him? Is he dead? Is that what you meant by him going up into the stars and galaxies? Because, surely, he didn't join any astronauts on any space shuttle visits!"

His mother tugged at the trunk again. Seeing that Phillip wasn't going to let go without a straight answer, she dropped her end and charged at him. As she fought to pry his fingers off the handle, Phillip shouted.

"What is wrong with you? Why are you acting this way?"

"For the past thirty years it's all he's cared about: those damned stars! Do you think out of those thirty years that he's loved me as much as he's loved those stars? *Do you*?"

"Dad's been here for us, mom. He's been a wonderful father!"

"To *you*, Phillip! A wonderful father to you! Ever since you were born, he's taken such a liking to you. When you visited the planetarium and started taking an interest in his obsession, he pampered you, showering you with love and attention as if you were as important as the stars above him! But where does that leave me, Phillip? Where does that leave me? Who sleeps in an empty bed every night while he's off staring up at the stars? I, who have asked him time and *time* again to be a normal father, being home for dinners and reading you bedtime stories, and to love . . . to love me more than his own beloved galaxies?"

His mother collapsed on the ground, sobbing.

Phillip, sensing that his trunk was safe, let go of the handle and held his mother, rubbing her back soothingly as his father had done for him in his toddler years.

"I had to do it, Phillip," his mother was choked with tears. "I had to. I couldn't let it go on any longer. I couldn't . . ."

"Where is he?" Phillip asked. He brought his eyes to the blaze. "Please tell me he isn't in there with all of the rest of his belongings, mom. Please!"

"No, Phillip!" He mother gasped at the audacity. "Are you kidding? I would never do that to your father, no matter how little he loved me."

"Then where is he?"

"At the planetarium, I'd wager, where I told him to go. So that he could continue his love affair with the 'other woman' he truly adored. He packed a few bags this morning asking that I send him the rest. Being his faithful wife, I'm sending him his things! As ash and dust through the air!"

Phillip surrendered the trunk to his mother. What he treasured most wasn't the books, glow-in-the-dark stars or the mobile; it was his father who had brought it into his life.

Running through the planetarium he asked if anyone had seen his father. When he came to his father's desk, he noticed that a new owner had taken residence: a thirty-something man with horn-rimmed glasses named Melvin. Phillip felt it surreal that his father had abandoned the planetarium. Baffling him more was that no one knew where his father had gone! There were no leads, no clues or any footprints for him to trail.

Phillip grew into a middle-aged adult who gradually stopped focusing on the stars. He worked in a warehouse during the evening hours, enslaved to a schedule that ushered him through the starlit nights. As the years extended, Phillip, miserable and alone, forgot his father's significant cosmic anomalies.

He was in his late thirties when his mother, and her belongings, were moved into a retirement community. Phillip made it his responsibility to settle the affairs of his childhood estate during the day. During the afternoon hours, before he left for work at the warehouse, Phillip held showings so that the home might find a future owner.

Time slowed on a bright, sunny spring day. Phillip looked out of his boyhood bedroom window vaguely remembering the day of his mother's fire. He wore a black polo shirt, fitted jeans and freshly-shined black loafers. He appeared as he had when he was eighteen, except for a few extra wrinkles that spotted his face. His hairstyle was the same from his youth, as was his facial hair.

The doorbell rang.

Phillip met a charming married couple scouting for a home. He showed them the four bedrooms, family room, kitchen, garage, and basement that had been made up into an extra recreational area. As he accompanied the couple on the main floor discussing price he heard a scuffling in the attic. The couple heard it too. The scuffling only lasted for a second more before falling silent.

"Squirrels or perhaps the settling of the house," Phillip explained with a smile.

"But that's not right," Annette told Nathaniel. "We were in the attic at night. There were stars outside of the window. It was dark outside."

Daylight decreased considerably, blanketed by thick storm clouds. The married couple poked their heads out the front door to see the oncoming storm and excused themselves. As the couple drove off, the clouds were so darkly ominous it was as if a windy mouth of a cave was closing in. Once by himself, Phillip returned to the house closing the front door and windows. Street lamps began to flicker a pale yellow.

As before, there came a shuffling in the attic.

Phillip could hear a woman and a man talking along with the scraping of objects along the attic floor. They were voices that Nathaniel recognized as their own as they had first been brought to inspire Annette's client.

"It doesn't make sense," Annette told Nathaniel. "There were stars outside of the window. Not streetlamps."

"Perception can be a powerful thing," Nathaniel told her. "Perhaps they really were streetlamps outside the window, flecking the blackout in the midst of the neighborhood and city."

"Oh come on, Mr. Cauliflower," Annette scoffed. "Also, there was frost on the window when we were up there."

Nathaniel motioned toward the windows which had fogged due to the drastic temperature change.

"That's us in the attic," Nathaniel told Annette. "That's our client, listening to us move his trunk around, positioning the contents about on display."

While Phillip hesitantly reached for the pull string of the closed attic door, his story concluded, depositing Nathaniel and Annette back into her cathedral office. They were once again surrounded by stone walls, great arches and a garden of yellow flowers.

"So his mother saved the trunk," Annette pondered.

"It appears she did, and to our benefit." Nathaniel hurriedly left Annette's office.

"Wait!" Annette called. "We have to turn the third one!"

"The other muses are finishing the last of their envelopes," Nathaniel answered "so should you."

"But what about the other colored pegs?" She asked. "When are they set to arrive? Also, there was a thunderstorm on that peg when we left. We have to see if Phillip was taken during it!"

Nathaniel closed himself inside his quiet office. He shut his eyes taking several deep breaths. After he gathered himself, he spotted Fiona at his desk.

"Forgive the intrusion, Mr. Cauliflower, but I've completed the envelopes you've assigned. I was hoping we can discuss the arrangements for the upcoming retirement party."

"Yes, of course," Nathaniel waned a smile.

"Before we get started, this arrived for you through your oculus ceiling." Fiona handed him a blue envelope from Management.

Nathaniel opened the envelope. It was regarding to the colored pegs he had requested from Heaven's library, those belonging to Annette's victims. Inside were index cards. On each had been printed a single message from Management that read: "Inquiry not found."

"All of them?" Nathaniel asked out loud.

"I'm sorry?" Fiona asked.

"Nothing," Nathaniel pocketed the pegs and cards. "It's nothing." He approached his desk.

"You've been rotating pegs with Mrs. Slocum, haven't you?" Fiona put a comforting hand on his shoulder. "I could see it when you walked in here a moment ago, a look in your eyes of such tragedy."

"It's nothing."

"Does she know yet?" Fiona asked. Nathaniel looked at her with a furrowed brow. "Does she know how Luanne and Phillip are connected?"

"No," Nathaniel said sullenly. "And she's not going to."

"Why are you so determined to get her home, Mr. Cauliflower?" Fiona asked.

Nathaniel sat in his swivel chair opposite his Head Muse. He adjusted the three Lite-Brite boards just-so. "Obviously we can't settle on a meteor shower and cherry blossoms for this retirement party, Fiona. We have to be more creative and foreswear any decorative reservations."

Fiona sat in the swivel chair opposite him awaiting him to say more.

Nathaniel took in a deep breath. "She was my muse when I was a little boy in my seventh life. I want to keep her safe. The longer she stays here, she's in danger. It's better for everyone if, after she inspires her envelopes, I take away her memories and send her back to her esteemed fiancé."

"Before I set out to retrieve her," Fiona reiterated, "I had asked if you had known what it would have meant having brought her back here."

He shifted the conversation by saying, "So . . . about the retirement party . . . where shall we start?"

*

Phillip reached for the pull string on the attic door. As his fingers clasped around it he heard a knock on the front door accented by band of lightning. He abandoned the attic and opened the front door. Standing on the porch, shaking the rain off of his umbrella, was Jonas and his partner in the black hoodie.

"Are we late for the open house?" Jonas asked. "This is as good a time as any to stop in where it's dry, take a look around."

"Why not?" Phillip invited Jonas and the hooded individual through the door.

"Oh, this is nice!" Jonas chimed to his friend as they surveyed the foyer. The front door was ajar framing the ferocious storm. "Perfect little haven for our humble home, isn't it, my friend?" He turned to Phillip. "We'll take it."

"Take it?" Phillip raised an eyebrow. "You've only seen the foyer."

"Believe it or not, I used to live in this house, a very long time ago."

"Did you?"

"Oh yes," Jonas told him "with my wife and son before she kicked me out. I suppose you could say I've returned to reconnect with old memories. To see if I can shake these walls for some answers."

Phillip measured Jonas who looked well beyond his years in the storm's light.

"Like I said," Jonas smiled, teasing off his suit jacket. His sleeves were unbuttoned showing a convincing, albeit bogus, tattoo of stars, which had been drawn on his forearm by a water-proof ink-pen. He offered a Faustian handshake to Phillip. "We'll take it. Today. At any asking price."

CHAPTER 12: YURI ABRAMOVICH'S FORETOLD FUTURE

After Nathaniel had fallen from his attic loft in 1808, he was greeted by Fiona, and given orientation for the department procedures.

"You're no doubt wondering what this place is, Mr. Cauliflower," Fiona, wearing a cream-colored pants suit, told him as they walked the hallway past the other offices to the conference room. At this point in the department's history, the offices were nothing more than barren rooms with egg-shell white walls, a simple desk, swivel chairs and strange, horn-shaped devices with turntables. The department had an aroma of freshly applied paint: a pleasant bouquet of fresh-picked roses which cloaked the smell of the lacquer. Above their heads were impressive hanging crystal chandeliers with flickering candles. As Nathaniel inspected these details, Fiona went on in saying: "It's a very special office, for a very special function. You, Mr. Cauliflower. I've been instructed, due to the unexpected circumstances, to train you."

"Train me to do what?" Nathaniel had asked.

Fiona had showed him the vestibule which led to the conference room and its table.

Nathaniel stepped inside and found that the conference room walls, like the walls of the offices they had passed, were bare. There was a single chandelier which hung from the ceiling. The only other decoration was a single, horn-shaped device with a spinning turntable. There was also a large, square-shaped unmarked sleeve. He looked at Fiona questioningly.

Fiona explained about the original muses and how Management had, not long after the initial muses had departed, orchestrated an alternative plan.

"A muse in training," Fiona described, "is given a Victrola Gramophone record player. A muse is also given specific sleeves. Inside each sleeve," Fiona picked up the sleeve from the table extracting a shiny, thin black disc with a hole in the middle, "is a record. Upon its center is a label which has a name of a corresponding original muse. The record goes onto the turntable like so. The record player is activated by the crank on the side here. Wind it to the right until you feel a slight resistance then release this brake lever to begin the turntable spinning. Once the record starts to spin, there's a steel needle at the end of the reproducer." Fiona showed him the arm with the needle motioning that it be placed on the almost invisible ridges of the record. "A needle which, when touched to the record in this groove here, provides a certain song, which is the exclusive melody of a person's life. The sound comes from the funnel-shaped horn, which stretches upward, spreading the sound outward for all to hear. When the initial song plays, the muse is taken to a specific person, place and time. Once there, a muse is given an imperative task: to provide a catalyst of inspiration to the living."

"To the living," Nathaniel repeated.

"Would you like to try?"

"Will it take me to Evangeline?"

"Truthfully, this may or may not," Fiona told him sympathetically. "You see, Mr. Cauliflower, time is circular. This record could take you backwards or forwards through time which means that there are no guarantees as to where its music will transport."

"Then what's the point? If it won't take me to her, why show me this?"

"Even if this record, or any record, were to take you back to Evangeline," Fiona calmly explained, "you would have a handful of seconds with her. Even then, she may not see or recognize you. Management has informed me, and what I've seen for myself, catalysts come in different forms. They may, or may not, constitute face-to-face contact."

"A few seconds isn't enough time," he shook his head.

"There's a way to spend more time with her if her record is found and played." Fiona reassured, trying to sell him on the idea. "After a catalyst has been executed, a record can be rotated backwards and forwards. When the melody plays backwards, you can review a client's life from the moment of birth to the moment of the inspiration. When the melody is played the right way, you can review a client's life from the inspiration to their death. Be aware, you will be viewing the life as a spectator. You cannot touch, or speak to, a client when reviewing a life. They cannot touch, see, or speak to you."

Nathaniel slowly reached for the crank and steel needle. His eyes were moist with a thin layer of tears. He stopped.

"No," Nathaniel whispered. "No, it's not enough."

"Management has placed you here for a specific purpose, Mr. Cauliflower. You have to believe that everything happens for a reason. Your death is only the beginning, my friend."

"I'm not your friend," Nathaniel recoiled from her and the record player. "I want to see Evangeline again."

"It's too late for that," Fiona told him, smothered in empathy. "I'm sorry."

"You said time was circular." Nathaniel reiterated. "Management brought me here to the afterlife. If Management can do that they can permanently bring me to her."

"Mr. Cauliflower, please," Fiona consoled.

"Stop *calling* me that," Nathaniel ordered. "I feel as if ever since the Sisters in that circus tent have called me that, I've been cheated!"

"The Sisters?"

"You say you've done this once before? How many other people have come into this office? How many other muses have listened to this ridiculousness?"

"Aside from me, Mr. Cauliflower?" Fiona took a breath and said, "No one else."

"It's not fair, Fiona." Nathaniel shook his head incredulously. "I feel as if I'm being chastised for something that isn't my fault; it's as if I've stepped into a corner of Hell."

"This isn't Hell," Fiona told him. "Nor is it Heaven. No, I'd rather be here than Heaven any day."

"Send me to her," Nathaniel begged. "Please, Fiona. Send me to my Evangeline."

"I can't do that, Mr. Cauliflower."

Nathaniel took the record in his hands, hoisted it, demanding like a snappish adolescent: "Do it I say." He brought the record down to the ground, shattering it. "*Now!*"

Fiona was unaffected by his actions. "You don't know what you are asking, Mr. Cauliflower. There are consequences that could arise from prematurely sending you through reincarnation. You may never find her. You may wander aimlessly through your next life without any contact with her. You won't remember anything from your previous life wherever, and whenever, Management might send you."

"I don't care," Nathaniel looked at Fiona with burning bravery. "No matter where and when I go, I'll find her."

A blinding white light erupted from the hallway.

"Very well," Fiona sighed.

There came a sound of fluttering envelopes above them as Nathaniel headed toward the conference room door. In response to the noise above, Fiona stopped him. "Before you go, Mr. Cauliflower, I must warn you. You've shattered a record that corresponds to a person's life. Records are delicate things and cannot be perfectly restored. Following your death in your second life, you'll be brought back here to finish your term as a muse. Management will then present you with a new task as penance for your breaking of a record and, thusly, the severing of a bond between a muse and a client. Do you truly want to be in that kind of position?"

Nathaniel turned away from the white light, considering his punishment.

Fiona added, "Management has told me that if you stay here and do your regular term as a muse, they can ignore the upset you've caused. If you choose to reincarnate, Management will have no choice but to serve your sentence. The choice is yours."

"Is it? The upset *I've* caused? It's because of those Dandelion Sisters I've been put into this situation. For all I know, you might even be working this operation alongside them!"

"The question you have to ask yourself, Mr. Cauliflower, is how much heartache your love for Evangeline is worth?"

"My love for Evangeline runs deeper than any love I've felt," Nathaniel told Fiona. "I'm willing to suffer whatever punishment the 'Sisters' or 'Management' gives me to be with her." Nathaniel then said "When I return, if you and Management know what's good for you . . ." He stared into Fiona's eyes, "Don't call me 'Cauliflower' again."

Nathaniel crossed through the swirling illumination, disappearing from the hereafter. Only the dim light of the chandeliers remained.

Fiona carefully picked up the broken record and piled the pieces.

"That didn't go as well as you'd expected, I can imagine," Fiona told Management. "Perhaps instead of records, we need an instrument of transport that is a bit more durable?"

*

Retirements in the department were fantastical affairs that occurred at the end of a muse's employment. Parties consisted of the basics: cherry blossom in mid-morning sunlight, closely passing meteor showers, orbiting planets, undulating oceans with tidal waves, expansive fields of wildflowers, mismatched tables and chairs for a dinner party of a thousand dishes, a colossal Ferris wheel and catalogued moments that gave vision to a muses' unrealized hopes and dreams. Public speakers gave words of wisdom in a made-up auditorium. Cakes were wheeled out at the celebrations. The retiring muse had to make a choice as to where they would visit: to reincarnate or to reside in Heaven. With the decision having been made by whomever the wish was granted, a swirling white light would erupt in the waiting room at the end of the hall. Stepping through the swirling light the retiring muse was taken wherever they had decided to depart.

The retirement party for the department's Greatest Muses required equal deliberation and care. Fiona and Nathaniel tirelessly negotiated formulated designs for the festivity.

". . . and we've reached the dessert portion of our planning," Fiona pleasantly told Nathaniel as they sat in his office under a beam of sunlight entering the oculus.

"Perchance we might switch the cakes for pies?" Nathaniel offered.

"Pies?" Fiona asked.

"We have an aspiring pie-maker in our company. In my opinion, it would be advantageous to offer her a temporary position of appropriately dabbling in an art she's fantasized."

"You are speaking of Miss Redmond?"

Nathaniel nodded. "We can take surveys of which pie the muses would like to wish from?"

"You're hoping that this will trigger something, aren't you, Mr. Cauliflower?" Fiona spoke earnestly. "That if she speckles herself with flour and sniffs the aromas of the baked pies she'll want to explore that side of herself after she leaves?"

"Isn't that what this place is known for, Fiona?" Nathaniel asked. "Having them arrive one way and depart enlightened?"

Fiona smiled proudly.

Nathaniel cleared the strewn paperwork.

"You and I have been here the longest," Fiona told him. "It makes me sad that we'll soon be taking divergent paths. For many generations, I've found myself watching muses retire through the waiting room door, venturing off on escapades. I wonder what will become of me once I blow out my candle at the end of this retirement party."

Nathaniel sat on the edge of the desk listening respectively.

Fiona sifted through the paperwork, airing a concise list for her own personal adjournment. Her retirement party was believed to be the biggest celebration that the department had ever seen.

She asked him, "Where will I go? What will I do?"

"Rest, most likely," Nathaniel accepted the list.

"Well, yes. But after that?" She sighed. "I've spent almost my entire existence catering to inspirational needs. When it comes to focusing attention to myself, I'm at a loss. Who will I become?"

"You'll find your direction," Nathaniel reassured. "You need to have faith that Management will be with you."

"What is it like walking through the waiting room door into the unknown?"

Nathaniel sighed deeply, searching for the words. He flipped through her requests. One word came to his mind, and that was: "Exhilarating."

Thinking back on all the times that he had passed through the light in search of Evangeline, Nathaniel supposed the word "exhilarating" was the closest. His memories settled upon his journey into the nameless mist, into the outer crest of his second life, having worn a foreign skin surrounded by an absorbingly surreal storyline. It had unfolded on a gray, murky summer afternoon in 1921, as a lone immigrant ship had drifted by the gargantuan Statue of Liberty, completing its destination to the promising shores of a culturally flourishing America.

*

Yuri Abramovich was eighteen years old when he set eyes on the Statue of Liberty. He sported short-cropped, messy brown hair, intense deep-set brown eyes, distinctly toned nostrils, narrow lips and angular jaw. His exposed ears were perceivably a size too large for his boyish face, which glistened with moisture as he stared into the thin sheet of falling rain. Having lost his family in the disastrously altering communist government at the end of the recent Russian Revolution, Yuri had found that his hatred of the new Bolshevik regime ran so deep that he abandoned his demarcated heritages in search of a new option. He took roots on an aspiring continent guarded by an oversized symbol of a woman clad in robes holding a torch heavenward who embodied a better, and more conducive, administration.

America was not without its own setbacks. It had been a few short years since the end of World War I. The country had undergone a severe recession. Thankfully, several austere titans were there to restore the vast country: President Warren G. Harding, automobile expert Henry Ford, oil enthusiast John D. Rockefeller, financial philanthropist J.P. Morgan, newspaper publisher William Randolph Hearst, electric intellect Thomas Edison, government secretary Herbert Hoover, Hollywood's originator D.W. Griffin, America's most profound ballplayer Babe Ruth and many others who assisted in the nation's rebirth. Even if it meant living in a cramped, poorly lit brick tenement building with other immigrants, America was on the rise once again, and Yuri had come to reside within its pervasive opulence.

In his first month, a full moon hovered symmetrically above an alley between his tenement building and the one beside it. There were several laundry lines connecting the two buildings; taut string bridges enswathed in shirts, pants, dresses and under-things. Yuri exited his building for a nightly stroll in the city, hoping for a bit of fresh air before bed. He didn't give the alley a second thought until a sound forced his skin to shiver.

"*Yuri...*" called a voice from the shadowed corridor.

He took a few steps back, inspecting the alley. The moon acted as a light bulb igniting the stacked, wooden pallets on the ground. The crates were made of thick planks spaced far enough apart so he could see straight through. There was no one in the alley that could have called his name. He started to leave, thinking it a trick in the wind.

"*Yuri...*" the voice spoke.

Yuri spun and stepped in front of the alley. His eyes scaled the walls, wondering if someone were calling to him from an open window. He spied the laundry several floors above. The fabric fluttered slightly, teased by the balmy summer breeze. Yuri witnessed as a stray, loosely draped white cotton shirt tumbled to the ground. He stepped into the alley catching the shirt with his hands. Though it was still damp, it smelled clean with a hint of soap.

As Yuri stood in the alley, taking in the smell of the newly laundered shirt, other fabric descended. He tried to recoup as many as he could from the dirt and grime of the alley floor but the clothes fell in such abundance, and so fast, that Yuri possessed little luck. As the clothing piled around him, they churned into a shape that towered quickly. Afraid he found himself in the heart of a growing dust devil, Yuri scrambled toward the alley's entrance.

Rushing to the street, he turned to find that the shape had built upon itself but not in the form of a funnel. The clothing, which was made of individual pieces before, was hurriedly stitched by dark, phantom-like thread. The shape was distinctly a staked circus tent. As the last of the clothing fit into place on the improvised tent's rooftop, a front flap opened revealing a pitch-black core. Coming from inside was the voice that had whispered his name: *"Yuri..."*

There was an erected plank of wood by the opening which read:

Dandelion Sisters
Admission: Three Dandelions

Yuri checked beneath his feet finding a patch of dandelion weeds which tried to reclaim the paved street. He picked three dandelions by hand.

Yuri then spotted two men, and a leashed greyhound, exiting the tent. One man was dressed in a green three-piece suit, cufflinks, and brandished a walking stick with a silver tip in the shape of a brain. The second gentleman was much taller than his predecessor, bulkier in muscle mass. From Yuri's perspective, the more brutish looking fellow was perhaps the other gentleman's bodyguard or strongman. The greyhound was attached to the taller man by a black leather leash. The greyhound spotted Yuri and whimpered at the sight of him. The leash was yanked hard and the dog snapped to attention.

The man in the three piece suit studied Yuri. Yuri was taken aback by the man's eyes. They startlingly resembled the shining blue eyes of a wolf. The stranger nodded to Yuri for him to enter the tent. Seconds after this brief interaction, the two men, and the greyhound, circled around to the back of the tent, disappearing into the opposite end of the alley. Yuri and the Dandelion Sisters were alone in the constrained lane.

He stepped inside the tent. There was a kerosene lamp lit before his arrival which brought the room to a warm, orange glow. Yuri found a lectern with carved dandelions on its wooden base. On the desktop was a quill, bottle of ink and an open ledger. Also on the lectern's surface was a ring of hardened wax which Yuri assumed had been left from the previous visitor.

He lifted the quill, dipped the tip into the ink and signed his Russian name below the present name of "Nathaniel J. Cauliflower." Following suit from the previous entry, he filled in the year and his age. When Yuri set the quill onto the desk, a voice spoke.

"You've come," said a young female voice from beyond the shadows of the kerosene lamp's illuminated range. "At last, you've come."

"Have you been expecting me?" Yuri asked, his voice rich with his homeland accent.

"Oh, we have, Nathaniel J. Cauliflower."

Yuri looked behind him expecting to see the "Cauliflower" to whom they referred.

"It is you, Nathaniel J. Cauliflower, though you may not realize it. But you will. Oh, you will remember who you were, I can assure you."

"I can't see you in this darkness," Yuri asked the voice. "Won't you come into the light?"

There was a stirring in the shadows. The vision of a young blond girl who had been no more than ten appeared. She was barefoot and in a donned white cotton dress. Having crossed into the light to be seen, she didn't approach further.

"You have the dandelions?" the girl asked. Her voice was young and pure.

Yuri held out the dandelions but she didn't approach to claim them. He instinctively placed them on the floor. He stepped back to allow her access.

The young girl timidly stepped forward, scooping the dandelions, returning to the dark.

"Wait!" Yuri pleaded. "Tell me more about being this Nathaniel J. Cauliflower of whom you speak. Who is he and why do you think I am him?"

The young girl stepped into the light holding one of the yellow dandelions. "You are the reincarnation of yourself, Nathaniel J. Cauliflower. You've been given a different name, identity, and alternate set of memories which cloud you from the truth of your true purpose."

"What purpose?"

"To find her again."

"To find who?"

"To find the woman whom you've dreamed of every single night since living as Yuri Abramovich," the girl had explained. "The woman in the petticoats and the corsets? The woman who haunts your dreams? Your own succubus: the woman named Evangeline."

The name stirred something within Yuri.

The young girl receded and was replaced by a middle-aged woman in the same cotton dress as her forerunner. The middle-aged woman, too, was blonde; an older version of her younger self. She carried in her hands a yellow dandelion with exposed, gangly roots.

The middle-aged woman told him, "After much searching, you will find Evangeline again. The number to remember is two thousand, three hundred and seven."

"Two thousand, three hundred and seven?"

"Yes, Nathaniel J. Cauliflower. On that day, you'll see Evangeline. You'll recognize her. She'll recognize you. But there is a caution to these words." The woman ducked out of the light.

"Caution?" Yuri asked. "What caution? Where are you going?"

An old, haggard crone stepped into the light. Her frail, bruised skin had grown thick with veins. She had lost her eyes many years prior, leaving empty sockets. A few of her yellowed, crooked teeth had remained. She resembled nothing more flattering than a walking, talking corpse. She held in her claws a dying dandelion thick with white, wispy seeds on the verge of floating away. Her voice was coated in rotting mucus.

"Evangeline will not be the only one who will recognize you, Nathaniel J. Cauliflower. For with rediscovering your old love comes rediscovering your murderer! You'll see and recognize him! He'll see and recognize you!"

"Leave me alone!" Yuri shouted. "I don't want to hear any more of this! I'm not Nathaniel J. Cauliflower! I'm Yuri Abramovich!" He grabbed the ledger to show the old woman proof. He gaped at the page in front of him. Where he had previously written his Russian name the name "Nathaniel J. Cauliflower" appeared in its place. "What witchcraft is this? How did you change what I'd written?"

The hag started to approach him.

Yuri stumbled to escape her grasp, scrambling backwards to the tent's entrance.

"I wish to take back my dandelions!" he ordered.

"That's not possible, Nathaniel J. Cauliflower. Once the payment has been made, and once the name, date and year have been scribed in the ledger, there's no turning back to what you were before."

Yuri ran through the open flap back to the city street in front of his tenement building. Once he made it safely outside, he looked over his shoulder to the alley, finding the exposed pallets on the ground. The tent had vanished. The separate articles of clothing had returned to their line. There were no dandelions beneath him.

Yuri stared at the moon which looked at him. It was then that Yuri noticed a trace of the Sisters' existence, which came in the form of the number "2,307" burned into his retinas, in the same lasting impression of blinding sunlit metal might linger for a moment or two. But the number didn't fade. The digits were still there like a sucking leech. Little did Yuri know that the numbers had a far more baleful arrangement for him than he could ever expect.

CHAPTER 13: HOW THE KEROSENE LAMPS CAME INTO PLAY

"And then what happened?" The question was asked by Lucas as he lay on the department's fabricated Grecian beach. He was being held from behind in Icarus' arms. They were in this affectionate position for some time while staring into the horizon sharing the details of their own lives before they had become muses. Icarus had been telling Lucas of the Bronze Age and his fall from grace to the churning waters when the wax on his wings had melted.

"I woke up in the spirit world," Icarus explained.

"Here?" Lucas wanted to know. "In the waiting room?"

"No. In the Underworld. A place filled with rusted metal lintels, chipped paint, grinding gears and atonal melodies. There was a boatman: an animatronic gondolier whose half-rotted painted face disclosed a brittle human skull underneath. He was motionless and possessed a tiny slot which required a form of payment to start him moving. I opened my clinched right fist and found two Grecian coins which I fit into the slot. The boatman sprang to life, jiving with rickety motions. He motioned to a wide canoe on a river's edge which bobbed on currents of putrid sewage. I climbed into the boat. The mechanical captain boarded with me. As the boat rode along a bumpy track through a series of tunnels, the creature talked mainly to himself reciting the things that had been, and of all the souls that had once shared the sojourn."

"It sounds so strange."

"A name was welded into his forehead: 'Charon.' A titled subway sign named the flowing sewage beneath the boat: 'The River Styx.' I recognized these titles from the Grecian belief of the afterlife. They confirmed that my motorized chauffeur was delivering me to the gates of the Underworld. The longer that we travelled, I slowly accepted the fact that I was dead."

A warm waft of air caught the fabric of Icarus' black hoodie. Icarus' curls also shifted in the fluctuating wind. The Grecian Adonis soaked in the comfort of having Lucas in his arms.

"We passed through various corridors of other animatronics which sparked and fizzled at the slightest movement. I observed that the rooms in which we floated were, at one time, filled with some sort of colorful amusement; a history of vibrant colors, fresh paint, regularly replaced light bulbs, of joyous chanting songs of glee. Those days had ended, leaving behind a contrasting version, almost monstrously malformed. We entered the final room and approached a wide set of closed double-doors, on which was painted a cheerful yellow sun with a slashed and morbidly scarred grimace. There were two groups of statues poised on jutting platforms beside the doors. The group to the right was made of two motionless, lifeless, mannequin men and a wax dog on a leash: one man wore a green three-piece suit and held a cane. The other mannequin was taller and muscular. The man with the cane had a pair of eyes that were almost canine. They seemed to stare as the boat glided by."

"And the second group of statues?" Lucas asked.

"Were made of three identical girls carved out of rosewood. Their hands were cupped around oversized wooden dandelions."

"Who were they?" Lucas asked.

Icarus paused for a moment remembering the features. He went on without answering Lucas' questions. "The doors, which were initially closed, screeched open on their hinges showing total blackness ahead. The boat glided on, leading me into the cold, stale kingdom of the Underworld."

"So much more fascinating than how I found out I was dead," Lucas sighed.

"What did you see?"

"I hoped that Gabriel would be waiting for me, prepared to lead me through Pearly Gates or something, you know? Alternatively, I found a waiting room," Lucas stated plainly "with nine identical chairs, and a woman in a cream-colored pants suit who introduced herself as Fiona. Even after I retired the first time, after my Seventh Generation term, I expected to see Gabriel. But no. Management had alternate plans for me."

Astray in his own misery, Lucas grew quiet.

Icarus shifted so that he could see into Lucas' eyes. "Do you wonder what would have happened if the attacks never occurred?"

"Every waking moment."

"Would you . . ." Icarus fixed to say but stopped. Promptly swallowing his apprehension, he finished the question. "If you were given the opportunity to go back in time and stop the moment from taking place, would you?"

He studied Icarus. "No. Because then I wouldn't be who I am today. And I wouldn't be sitting here on the beach with you."

Icarus solemnly studied him for a moment then smiled. He kissed Lucas gently on his forehead. The subtle moment was felt by both and needed no additional accompanying words.

Lucas thoughtfully moved his eyes back to the water of the sun-speckled sea. Though he had answered Icarus' question there was an unnoticed look in Lucas' eyes that had showed otherwise.

Annette stood at the doorway of Icarus' office looking in on the two men as they snuggled on the shore. She had overheard pieces of the conversation while crumpling two sheets of white paper with an increasingly balled fist.

Nathaniel was staring into the office with her. "Homophobic?" he asked. "Or jealous?"

"Neither," Annette lied.

"Would you mind then not crumpling the two remaining pie surveys?"

"I've been too busy to reconnect with Lucas," Annette told him contemptuously. "I've got the time but I found he has a new friend."

"So he has," Nathaniel observed.

"It doesn't bother me that it's a guy, you know," Annette scoffed. "I know Lucas is gay and I'm proud of him. What bothers me is . . . the person he's with isn't me. Though I haven't seen him since our last group dinner, I've been thinking about my best friend. Thinking about him, and his life, and how he's coping. He seems to have changed in some way. I can't put my finger on it." She shook her head slightly and looked at Nathaniel. "It's the office he's in. The Hall of Thunderstorms?" Her attention moved back to Lucas. "Do you think that by staying in Jonas' old office that it's somehow negatively affecting him? That maybe some part of Jonas is still in that office?"

"There are studies that show humans thrive more positively in direct sunlight than they do in prolonged overcast weather. As I recall, Mr. Richardson has always housed a deeply buried dark streak. I think we all house that kind of streak, to some extent."

"Maybe you're right."

"Come," Nathaniel held out an arm. "I have something that'll take you out of your routinely anesthetizing paranoia."

Annette considered Nathaniel's arm. She frowned and left Icarus' office without its support.

*

Two years had passed since Yuri Abramovich had visited with the Dandelion Sisters. America had been mesmerized in a whirlwind of scantily attired flappers, blossoming jazz and flickering motion pictures. The Roaring Twenties had seen an unparalleled growth in automobile manufacturing, the expanding use of telephones, electricity and inspiring radio broadcasts. There had been an intensification of liquored speakeasies, dizzying dance clubs and intrigue surrounding many fashionable celebrities. Even the skyline of the cosmopolitan capitals had been dazzling in a widespread architectural style respectfully referred to as Art Deco.

Though Yuri had originally come to America to be a part of its economic development, he found himself taking an unconventional route: being obsessively immersed in the painstaking application of repairing over two thousand some-odd damaged kerosene lamps.

The numbers "2,307" were etched into his vision and miraculously counted down with each repaired lamp. Closer to the final count, when the numbers reached to lowly ten digits, Yuri began to wonder what sort of compensation awaited him. The Dandelion Sisters had been accurate in describing his dreams of the Evangeline woman. Though he had no solid memory of her, the specter image of Evangeline was burned in his mind. The notion that Yuri had been another person in previous life spurred his curiosity. For many nights he puzzled at the mere thought of Evangeline. If she had been his true love, how had he so easily forgotten her? It was a question that he pondered well into the night as he strolled through the neighborhood and, especially, as he looked into the empty alleyway where the Sisters had been presented.

The answer came one autumn afternoon in 1924 as Yuri put the finishing touches on kerosene lamp number 2,307. The numbered countdown was complete which left the impression of a single, stable zero digit in his vision. The shop in which he worked was a small, but adequate, space with a glass store front window. It housed wooden shelves topped with kerosene lamps in varying states of needed repair. Yuri's heart raced at the prospect of the fate that was sure to unfold from the lamp's refurbishment. When Yuri finished it, he leaned back in his chair inspecting his work properly. He wasn't sure what to expect from its completion. Months before, Yuri had found the particular broken kerosene lamp in a back room, half hidden behind tool crates. He had assumed that the kerosene lamp had been there prior to his employment start date. He had no information as to whom it belonged except for an outdated numbered stock tag. He had searched, and failed, to find its matching receipt in his records. Therefore, he had no way to meet the owner unless they came in to reclaim it. Yuri frowned disappointedly and sat the finished kerosene lamp on a shelf with several others.

He heard the door to the shop open. A well-groomed chauffeur entered. He was dressed in a grey suit, matching slacks, polished shoes, black suede gloves and a hat. The driver respectfully removed his hat as he closed the distance. As he did so, Yuri noticed that the chauffeur had a full head of black, slick-backed hair and was slightly older than Yuri, by a few years. It was an interesting contrast between the two men in regards to decorum but the conversation remained pleasant.

"Good afternoon," said the chauffeur. "I've come to pick up an order that, I believe, was supposed to be finished today." He handed Yuri a folded receipt.

Yuri unfolded the paper. Studying it severely, he nodded and said in his Russian accent: "I'll get it for you. One moment."

The chauffeur nodded.

Yuri returned to the shelf in which he had, several seconds prior, shelved the order. Yuri consulted the slip to the lamp's numbered tag. His pulse quickened. Based on the slip's information, the chauffeur had come to retrieve the same kerosene lamp that belonged to a woman named Evangeline!

Yuri lifted the kerosene lamp from the shelf with shaking hands, wrapped it in discarded newsprint and placed it inside a hay-cushioned wooden box for safe-keeping during the chauffeur's travels. Yuri suddenly recalled the Dandelion Sisters' warnings. He didn't look at the chauffeur as his customer paid for the lamp and thanked Yuri for his time. Yuri dared not pay attention as he heard the sound of the chauffeur's footsteps as they approached the shop's door.

"Mr. Abramovich?" the chauffeur asked.

The lingering orange afternoon light poured through the window casting the driver into silhouette.

"Mademoiselle Evangeline requested that you accompany me back to her chateau in the countryside."

"I'm sorry?"

"She mentioned that you would be expecting this request. I see that, perhaps, you weren't aware of the standing invitation. The fault is mine. I assumed you had already received notice, otherwise I would have reminded you before starting to leave."

"No, sir. I haven't received an invitation." Yuri nervously looked around the shop indicating the work that needed to be done, showing distinct reservations about venturing further into this mystery.

"I can assure you, Mademoiselle Evangeline is extremely kind and, if I may be so bold, anxious to meet you."

"I'm not dressed for any kind of company," Yuri blushed. Indeed, he wasn't. Yuri wore a tattered dress shirt and slacks that had not seen a good wash in days. His face glistened with perspiration and dust. His face was badly in need of a shave.

"Don't worry, Mr. Abramovich. She wants to see you as you are."

Even though the chauffeur's words were meant to reassure him, Yuri was apprehensive. "Why is she so interested in meeting me?" Yuri asked, knowing full well the answer.

To which the chauffeur shrugged. "She didn't say."

A sleek black Model T Ford was waiting for Yuri. He had seen vehicles of this caliber in the past two years but he was never invited to sit in one. As Yuri inspected the vehicle, the chauffeur turned the crank, starting the engine. It roared to life before Yuri's eyes like a beast stirred from its catnap.

"Mr. Abramovich?" The chauffeur asked from the driver's seat.

Yuri hesitantly reached for the helpful extended gloved hand.

As the sun set on the horizon, Yuri spied over his shoulder at the abating buildings. He closed his eyes, enjoying the rush of cold wind as they drove from the city to the countryside. The fetid urban smells were replaced with the sweet scent of fresh cornfields. As the vehicle traveled, Yuri imagined Evangeline. He imagined her to be stunning with sparkling eyes and a warm smile. This image of her aged rapidly in his mind as if witnessing the rotting of fruit. The face of his dream woman grew grotesquely old and it frightened him.

He looked at the chauffeur who watched the empty road in advance. Yuri saw the stars and took comfort in them. The moon hovered in the sky, cresting on a distant hill and a grand French chateau. Yuri sat up in his seat to inspect the approaching monolith edifice which was decorated in exterior gas lanterns. As they pulled onto the cobblestoned road which led to the house, Yuri clutched the box with the lamp. He protective more of himself than the trinket inside! An unnamed stirring ignited within him which no amount of twinkling stars or constellations could have stopped.

The mansion loomed, surpassing the stars. White headlight spears washed the Baroque exterior and extinguished upon reaching the garage and stables. When the Model T was parked, Yuri exited uncertainly with his fingers clutched to the lamp's box. He couldn't help but to gawk at the moonlight-reflected windows.

"This way, Mr. Abramovich," the chauffeur said with a smile while showing him the front steps.

Candlelight carved the estate's central rooms to a tepid, orange smolder. In the limited light, Yuri was intimidated by the fierce Baroque paintings and dramatic bat-wing-esque like curvature of the furnishings. There was no laughter, or music, nor any accompanying sound emulating joy. There was only the sound of the chauffeur's and Yuri's footsteps upon the tiled floor as if they were passing through a spacious underground tomb.

The chauffeur led Yuri up an elaborately carved staircase which, in the narrow brightness, looked like prearranged delicate, yellowed bones. He led Yuri down a claustrophobic corridor with faded, ripped wall paper and ancient alert stern-faced portraits. They stopped at a dust-encrusted closed door, which the chauffeur opened.

"Mademoiselle Evangeline waits for you and your kerosene lamp."

Yuri timidly looked at the chauffeur who had been convivial. It gave Yuri a sense of hope that his mistress possessed the same qualities despite her choice in home decorum. Yuri thanked the chauffeur and stepped into a bleak room where the moon glowed through moth-bitten curtains. He swallowed, squinting into the ascetic crypt.

"Come closer, Mr. Abramovich," called a woman's voice from the window. His eyes adjusted slightly, noticing a hand having waved him forward. Yuri did as instructed.

A wingback chair jutted from the murk. He made out an arm which was attached to the visible hand. There was a table beside the speaker. On it was a set of matches, a flat wick and a bottle of kerosene. There was also a turquoise glass vase stabbed with wilting yellow roses.

"Have you brought the repaired lamp?" She asked.

He sat the box on the floor and unpacked the kerosene lamp. With a trembling hand, Yuri reached for the wick, which he fit into the lamp, and gently poured in the kerosene. Yuri then ignited a match and touched the tip to the wick. The glass neck was placed on top. He pinched the crank.

The purple room, and the occupant, were exposed. She appeared to be a gracefully ripened woman well above one hundred years old. Her tired eyes looked at Yuri while gripping a leather-bound volume of Geoffrey Chaucer's *Canterbury Tales* in her quilt-laden lap.

At first she looked at him without recognition. Yuri, in turn, didn't recognized her. But that moment was replaced by another as they both gasped. Yuri had seen her before but not in person; it had been in the form of a painted portrait in 1808 when he had been a painter in Paris named . . .

"Monsieur Cauliflower!" Evangeline smiled, increasing the depth of the facial wrinkles.

"Mademoiselle Evangeline," Nathaniel said in his Yuri Russian accent. He suddenly felt uncomfortable in his eighteen year old body. Nathaniel now saw the world through the eyes of a man he had once been. It both delighted and filled him with fear. "It's me: your painter, your Nathaniel J. Cauliflower."

*

"The last time I saw this kitchen was before orientation," Annette said to Nathaniel as the kitchen's lights flipped on one by one showing the sterile cabinets, drawers and countertops. "I remember that you banished me from this place after ruining your floor with the dropped chocolate Ganache *and* disrupting the silence with the tumbling of broom handles from the storage closet." She turned to Nathaniel and asked "Why the change of heart?"

"You have a purpose for being in here now," he answered. "A retirement party is nipping at our heels and you have some pies to construct."

"And let me guess," Annette smiled and chided playfully. "You'll be breathing down my neck hoping I don't make too much of a mess."

"No, Mrs. Slocum," Nathaniel replied, not soaking in the humor. "I have my own cooking. I figured as we are baking and cooking for the same party, we might as well share the kitchen."

"Share?"

"Share."

"This kitchen?"

"This kitchen." Nathaniel repositioned his drooping glasses to the bridge of his nose. "Is there a problem?"

"Well," Annette shrugged. "It's just the last time I was in here you bit my head off with the slightest disturbance. Making a pie, let alone seven of them, is going to be messy, what with the flour, the dough . . . the fillings!" She propped herself against a counter folding her arms. "Sharing a kitchen could make you volatile. I don't want to be a part of it."

"It won't make me volatile, Mrs. Slocum," Nathaniel barked.

Annette pursed her lips accusingly, pointing her right index finger. "See? We haven't even gotten started yet and already you're on edge."

Nathaniel blushed.

Annette sighed solemnly. "I like it when you're not so frustrated. I wouldn't be lying if I said that sometimes I enjoy being with you when you're not temperamental."

Nathaniel was flattered by her backhanded comment. "An unavoidable aspect of cooking is untidiness. Sometimes a kitchen can become a messy place when I cook too, Mrs. Slocum. Half the joy of creating slight disarray is in knowing it can be cleaned."

Annette took in Nathaniel's words. "Okay, Mr. Cauliflower, let's share a kitchen. But any grouching, any at all, and I'm out."

"Agreed." They shook on it and went to work.

As Nathaniel worked the simmering pots on stove tops, Annette handled the assorted pie fixings, including fresh fruit and various spices. Annette was pleased to discover that Nathaniel supplied a few colorfully illustrated, easy-to-understand cookbooks. They each created their own meals for the upcoming retirement celebration peacefully sharing the kitchen.

From over his right shoulder, Nathaniel watched her roll the dough with a flour-covered rolling pin. A strand of her brown hair fell out of place. She wore a frilly white apron over the yellow housedress and looked seriously deep in concentration. Surrounding herself with her untouched passion, Annette let loose a smile as she formed the crust and fit it into a circular pan. She was elated filling it with a mixture consisting of freshly cut Granny Smith and Gala apples coated in flour, cinnamon, nutmeg and cloves. She seemed to take even more joy in attempting her first lattice covering. He turned to his soup dipping a ladle to stir the surface.

Annette looked up from her attempt at a lattice crust and to Nathaniel. He added a pinch of pepper and seemed to stir in his own melancholic memories while circulating the soup's consistency.

*

The memory Nathaniel remembered while stirring the soup was this: Evangeline and Nathaniel sat in the light of the kerosene lamp. She was considerably older than he and he, despite having his old memories, was still inside the young body of a boy named Yuri Abramovich.

"The estate was moved from Paris at the turn of the century," Evangeline told him on that night. Her eyes studied the roses on the table as she recounted the past events. "Brick by brick: all of the portraits, all of the furniture, all of the memories. In the beginning, the estate looked as beautiful as you remembered it. Throughout the years, it's fallen apart. It's been one hundred and thirteen years since I saw your face in 1808. But I see it in my dreams, watching over me as I sleep." She showed him the copy of *Canterbury Tales*. "This book is what I was reading when we were young. Every year around this time I read it on the anniversary of your death, in memory of you."

"One hundred and thirteen years . . ." Nathaniel pondered in Yuri's Russian accent. "You've been alive all these years? How old are you?"

"Oh," Evangeline looked away, bringing a frail hand up to her wrinkled lips. "I'm old, Nathaniel. So old. Each day I wish it was my last so I can escape this flesh and reside in Heaven where I envision myself eternally young. Each passing day, month, year and *decade*, I wake older and older. Every time I close my eyes, even for a second or two, I see a circus tent on a field of dandelions with its front flap open . . . darkness inside. In my dreams, my feet are made of stone. I have no idea who or what is inside, but it calls to me in every dream, whispering my name." Evangeline seemed anxious by this lingering vision. It was evident from the anguished sound of her voice choked with emotion and tears.

A cold shiver ran through Nathaniel as he heard this.

Evangeline composed herself adding: "There were rumors of your coming here to America as a Russian immigrant, of your kerosene lamps. How I hoped that I would see you again. I hoped that, upon seeing you, the vision of that persistent tent would dwindle, if even in slightest."

"And has it dwindled?"

Evangeline slowly closed her eyes. For a brief moment it seemed as if she noticed the tent, but a serene look eventually spread. Nathaniel assumed now that he was here, her thoughts and dreams would be free of the Sisters' dandelions. Evangeline remained in this position, succumbing to a sound slumber.

Nathaniel removed *Canterbury Tales* from her lap and gently covered her with the heavy quilt. He felt cheated by the turn of events and equally enraged that Evangeline had felt the same. How he hated the Sisters but how he was also grateful for them. If the Sisters had not come to him in the alley, then Evangeline would be suffering nightmares. As much of a disease that the Sisters had been, they were also the cure. In Nathaniel's mind the negative and positive cancelled out making their purpose annoyingly futile. Despite how puzzling the Sisters had been, Nathaniel's true enemy was the painter that had murdered him. The hatred toward his master filled him with such breathless seething anger! Nathaniel wondered if the painter had suffered the same fate as Evangeline. He wondered if the painter was alive and perpetually aging in his own gruesome manner.

"If anyone has to pay for what's been done to you, it's the painter," Nathaniel had whispered.

Evangeline opened her eyes which resounded with chilling terror.

"What is it, Evangeline?" Nathaniel asked, alert to her needs. "Tell me what's troubling you?"

Evangeline slowly shook her head.

"He's alive, isn't he?" he had asked.

"Please, Monsieur Cauliflower, don't dig any deeper. Stay here with me in my house. I can give you a life of luxury. I can provide anything for you with a wave of my hand. All that I have can be yours. The only thing I ask is not to go searching for answers . . . for him!"

"He's here in America, isn't he?" Nathaniel asked. His voice was quiet but menacing. "Here in the city?"

Despite her inner protests, Evangeline barely nodded. Mournful tears streamed her cheeks as she wailed. Talking about the painter brought Evangeline pain. It hurt him seeing her in such agony. Nathaniel soothingly hushed her and tenderly stroked her gray hair. He removed one of the roses from the vase and held it between them. He tickled it lightheartedly against her nose. Evangeline didn't smile nor did she show signs that his gesture made her happy.

All she had said was: "Promise me you won't go after your painter, Nathaniel. Promise me that you'll stay safe inside my home. Together we can live the rest of our days. Promise me that, whatever happens, you won't let the darkness in your heart overtake you."

"I promise," Nathaniel had told her. Though he knew his words were a lie, Nathaniel said them to her anyway. These words brought about a smile on Evangeline's face and temporarily comforted him from the heavy desire for uncontrolled vengeance.

He sat with Evangeline for at least an hour longer patiently and silently watching as she fell into an idyllic slumber. Nathaniel studied her face, the shape of her jaw and the line of her exposed, wrinkled neck as it extended to her left shoulder all the way down to her arm and eventual hand that had earlier waved him to move forward. There was a subtle occasional breath that could be heard from her partially opened lips as she slept. Evangeline was a shadow of her former self, but he found her as stunningly beautiful as she had been in 1808.

Nathaniel shifted his focus onto the roses in the vase and eventually settled on the iridescent kerosene lamp he had delivered. The numbered zero could still be seen on his retina. It bothered him in knowing that, even though the prophecy came to fruition, and even though Evangeline's dreams were healed, Nathaniel remained inflicted. The Sister's prophecy hadn't truly come to pass, at least not yet. It was then that, as he thought this to himself, a flash of white lightening tore beyond the window's glass. He crossed to the window where he noticed the sky was blotted with approaching storm clouds. The yard's grass could be seen as the lightning flashed. Sitting in the middle of the yard was a second glowing kerosene lamp which had not been there prior. Farther away was a third lamp which was followed by a fourth. A fifth lamp was placed even farther.

With the storm fast approaching, Nathaniel wrote Evangeline a brief note stating that there was unfinished business to attend to in his life as Yuri Abramovich. He fled down the hall, descended the grand staircase and found himself at the estate's foyer door. As he stood on the veranda, Nathaniel gained better perspective. The kerosene lamps were placed in such an inexplicable way as to suggest a path to the city. As he contemplated how this could be possible, he heard a voice behind him.

"Can I drive you, Mr. Abramovich?"

Nathaniel spun to the chauffeur at the door. "Please," Nathaniel said in his Russian accent "I have to follow the kerosene lamps."

"The kerosene lamps, sir? What kerosene lamps?"

Nathaniel turned his eyes to the road where the kerosene lamps showed the appropriate direction. Oddly enough, the kerosene lamps were meant for Nathaniel's eyes only.

The chauffeur obliged regardless, taking Nathaniel past the kerosene lamps that only his passenger had been able to see. He retraced the path of the supposed "evenly situated lamps" to the city.

Rain punched hard on the surrounding vehicles, streets and buildings but the fire in the kerosene lamps seemed unaffected. As they passed each lamp, Nathaniel counted in his head. They passed Nathaniel's tenement building and drove by his shop where the chauffeur had earlier retrieved him. A final kerosene lamp was seen sitting on the stone steps of a nondescript three story townhouse. The windows were dark and proved no signs of waking life.

Nathaniel thanked the chauffeur for his time and started to exit the vehicle.

The chauffeur stopped him by saying, "Mr. Abramovich, I don't know what's happening here tonight and I'm not sure what you've seen that brought us to this location, but I urge you to think of Mademoiselle Evangeline and her love for you."

Nathaniel considered the chauffeur's words carefully. "I won't be gone but a minute," he reassured his driver.

The storm hovered above them in wait for the showdown between the painter and his apprentice. As Nathaniel approached the door to the townhouse, he was not expecting it to be already cracked slightly ajar for him. He lifted the glowing kerosene lamp from the front steps and carried it with him.

The noise of thunder and rain was muted as Nathaniel crossed through the darkened foyer. It was most definitely the home of the painter. Every wall was plastered by framed landscapes and faces that his master had painted. It even reeked of the painter's sweat that had secreted out of him while having slept in his nightly drunken stupors. Nathaniel spotted a flight of stairs with a back window which overlooked the stormy sky. Sitting on the top landing was the unleashed greyhound that he had seen two years earlier. It whimpered upon seeing Nathaniel. Its eyes reflected the dim lamp light. As Nathaniel approached the stairs, the greyhound nudged its head up further into the house. Nathaniel followed close in the wake of the dog's footsteps. His ascent was accented by flashes of lightning.

He found a room filled with familiar faces: the portraits that Nathaniel had painted, and hidden, in the Parisian attic rafters. They lined the four walls of the tiny gallery, staring inward. In the center of the room, growing from the floor, was a patch of dandelions. Above the dandelions was a figure who stared out the window to the storm.

"Here we are again," the figure said to Nathaniel. "In the same room with the same faces looking over us." Somehow the painter had known his long-awaited apprentice was coming. The murderer was older than Evangeline and resembled a rotted skeleton canvas with flesh barely hanging on to the bodily frame underneath. "You look different than I remember," his painter told him. "I suppose I look different as well."

Nathaniel held the kerosene lamp aloft. "I've come to ask you a question."

"Have you?"

"Why did you murder me?"

"Oh," the painter smiled menacingly, "for the paintings. They were unlike any other paintings I'd seen. The technique was almost too perfect, flawless! I knew that if I murdered you and sold them as my own, I would be well off. After you died, I sold them to the highest bidders, sending them each on their own separate ways. The buyers offered handsome sums for the paintings which led me to an early retirement. But with the sales, my nightly dreams worsened. When I closed my eyes, I saw a circus tent resting upon a field of dandelions. And every year since your murder, the paintings mysteriously, on their own volition, were in my possession. I came to learn that each patron had suffered their own demises due to their purchases. They bequeathed the cursed paintings to me in their wills. Year after year the paintings accumulated until tonight when the final painting appeared." He crossed to one of the walls where he introduced to Nathaniel the painting of the aged Evangeline from 1808. "I knew that, upon accumulating this canvas, you wouldn't be far behind."

Nathaniel studied Evangeline's portrait, feeling a sense of sorrow.

"It's unnatural to have lived as long as myself and Evangeline," the painter told him.

"We've been punished enough," Nathaniel said to Evangeline's painting.

"That we have."

"I often wondered what we would say to one another when our paths would cross," the painter told him. "What questions would be asked, what venomous insults would be spat, or who would end up killing who first?"

"What you're describing?" Nathaniel chided, "It's unhealthy to live with that kind of pessimism."

"And what are you filled with, boy?" The painter sneered. "What does Evangeline's beloved 'Monsieur Cauliflower' feel within him?" Before Nathaniel had time to react, the painter snatched the kerosene lamp from Nathaniel's hands and tossed it across the room. The glass shattered. Flames stretched from the wick to the floor and then to the walls. A hellacious blaze engulfed the room.

Nathaniel scrambled to flee.

The painter had other plans for him. Surprisingly agile, he shoved Nathaniel to the ground, pinning him face up from the floorboards. Nathaniel tried to free himself but the painter's body was encompassing. His enemy's hands were brought to Nathaniel's neck and he squeezed hard. Nathaniel fought to regain a sense of power but was not able to breathe. Thusly he was not able to fight. He looked into the hollow eyes of his painter. The portrait of Evangeline stared judgingly at him in the surrounding flames.

"It will be done in a moment," the painter told his apprentice. "You'll die. I'll die. The paintings will burn and this nightmare of our long, overly drawn out hatred and misery will cease!"

The passion play of Yuri Abramovich and Nathaniel J. Cauliflower did cease. As Nathaniel stared at his painter's face, the zero digit that had been engrained into his retina faded. All that was left of his life were seven brief seconds as the flames consumed the room, and the two men, who took the blight of the Dandelion Sisters with them.

*

Annette and Nathaniel survived their sharing of the kitchen. With the kitchen cleaned from their mess, Nathaniel showed Annette through the velvet curtain to the rotunda office past the 2,307 kerosene lamps and portraits.

Before she exited through his office door, she asked "Have you had the chance to order those colored pegs from Management yet? The ones for Jonathan, Doris, Lyle?"

"I have."

"And?"

Nathaniel didn't have the heart to tell her the truth. "I've reviewed them. No signs of Mr. Rothchild."

"I trust you, Mr. Cauliflower. If anything does present itself, promise me that you'll tell me."

"I promise."

"Like you promised Evangeline you wouldn't visit the painter?"

"That was different," he explained.

With that, he shooed her out of his office and closed himself into his constricting obsessions. He studied the portraits and remembered his second life. Nathaniel looked at Evangeline's portrait and said, "I lost you, Mademoiselle Evangeline. Someday I'll find you again, in a timeline that's agreeable to us both, and you'll remember me. Even if I have to search for seven more lifetimes; I'll find you."

*

After Annette left Nathaniel's office, she stopped to check on Lucas. He was standing in his office of nine thunderstorms with Icarus. Their backs were turned to Annette but their words were audible.

"I had a good time on the beach today," Lucas told Icarus. "Thank you for keeping me company."

"Here," Icarus removed the black hoodie and wrapped it around Lucas. "This'll keep you warm in this cold office."

Lucas told him. "I know this hoodie well."

Icarus kissed Lucas affectionately on his forehead and left the office passing by Annette. They shared an untrusting look. She watched Lucas in his office as he straightened the black hoodie. He crossed to one of the porches and looked out onto an approaching storm. There was a licorice-like shade in his eyes. It worried her.

By the time Lucas turned to the doorway, Annette was gone. He didn't know she had been standing there. He wondered, as he often did, why Annette hadn't been to see him yet. There came an unfamiliar rumble that he had not previously heard, and a flash of lightning that he had not previously seen. There came a sound of plastic colliding with wood somewhere beside the desk. Lucas looked to his feet where he spotted a single purple colored peg resting by its lonesome.

"Where did you come from?" Lucas asked, thinking perhaps it had come from his Lite-Brite. He bent down and picked it up turning it this way and that. He considered a startling alternative to where the peg had fallen from and shifted his stare to the lately developing storm. An arctic breeze, which had not previously been felt, ripped through one of the porches. In an effort to keep warm, he zipped the hoodie and positioned the hood over his head obscuring his face. A new storm approached in all nine of the horizons. Thunder roared as if nine different run-away trains were derailing. Electric fingernails scratched with the ferocity of nine different power grids gone haywire. Lucas couldn't help but to smile at the understated amendment in the atmosphere, welcoming it almost a little too devotedly.

CHAPTER 14: THE FALL OF THE HOUSE OF MUSES

Though Nathaniel had never been a father, he sometimes imagined his pretend children opening their fictional eyes on Christmas morning. He imagined being forced from his slumbers at his children's attempt to wake him before sunrise. He envisioned himself sipping a cup of coffee as his children would excitedly tear apart the multi-colored wrapping paper, nodding as they would have fun with the received toys. Nathaniel pictured himself shoving the discarded balls of used paper into trash bags while recalling the memories. Having never been a dad, and never having the opportunity to share such happy moments with any family in such a capacity, Nathaniel made up for it by reveling in the taxing, yet equally worthwhile, task of executing retirement parties for his muses.

The retirement party for the Nine Greatest Muses began with the Westminster chime from a limited edition Steinway grandfather clock which had blocked the closed waiting room door. Each muse's eyes opened with the striking of the clock's twelfth hour. The women muses were gifted garment boxes with evening gowns. The men were proud owners of freshly pressed black tuxes, bow ties and cummerbunds. Though they were in their respective offices, the spaces in which they occupied had been sectioned by opaque theatre scrims. Wearing the established dress attire, the muses pulled open their drapes. There was a distinct separation from the muses' workspace to the extravagant retirement party that awaited them.

The department's offices had been reformed into nine different attractions: a manifested Mardi Gras, the Feast of Fools from Medieval France, Rome's nineteenth century Carnival, a modern day German Oktoberfest, an Australian flowers and fireworks festival, elongated dragon-shaped racing boats during the Duanwu Chinese New Year festival, an energetic Day of the Dead in Mexico, and an Irish Festival for Saint Patrick's Day filled with emerald cliffs, frothy beer and energetic storytellers reciting local fairy tales. A food emporium held Spanish Gazpacho soup, Greek lamb, eggplant moussaka and stuffed zucchini. There were extravagant delicacies including Icelandic cooked puffin in a buttery milk sauce and Asian sea urchin with sturgeon caviar and white rice. For dessert was an Istanbul gold leaf cake.

These attractions were brimming with crowds of dreaming clients who had been inspired by the retiring muses. Though the foot traffic was breathtakingly claustrophobic, the overall feeling of the shindig was a collected array of harmonious synchronization.

Nathaniel, who continued to wear his typical corduroy pants, buttoned dress shirt and suspenders, watched his muses with a parental eye. Noticing that one muse wasn't in attendance, he went to investigate. The curtain of the fireworks festival closed behind him silencing the small tulip-dotted office from the party's boisterous noises. He found Annette sitting in her swivel chair with her feet propped up on her desk. Annette was wearing her wedding dress. Her attention was so focused on the dry erase board that she didn't realize Nathaniel was with her until he crossed in front of line of sight. Seeing Nathaniel, Annette shifted as if waking from a daydream.

"Mr. Cauliflower," Annette smiled.

"You're missing your retirement party," he said dryly.

"Yes," Annette told him. "I woke from a nice dream and found my dry-cleaned wedding dress. I prepared to attend the event, honestly I did."

"And yet here you are as the event goes on without you."

"I was going to attend," Annette sighed "but three things stopped me: the first being that, even though I'm social as Miss Redmond, there's a Slocum side that's anti-social. I've been in a personal battle trying to decide whether or not to make small talk." She motioned to the dry erase board. "The second: I have unfinished business. I can't leave without turning a specific peg."

"Oh?" Nathaniel asked. "What peg would that be?"

Annette held up a purple peg. "The peg of Jonas Rothchild's dad, from the blizzard accident."

"That peg," Nathaniel looked grave.

"Yeah, I was thinking that, before I retire and go back to my wedding day, I might want to give it a good tug as I probably won't have another opportunity."

"You want to turn the peg *now*?" Nathaniel said in amazement. "You'll miss the entire get-together."

"If it means possibly cracking a long-standing missing person's case," she shrugged.

"Well," Nathaniel surrendered "if we turn the peg right this second, we might have enough time to catch the masquerade ball near the end."

Annette perkily jumped from her swivel chair and extracted the pistol from her holster.

As the colored peg was rotated counter-clockwise, Nathaniel sized Annette up as she, enthusiastically, raised her eyebrows and held the pistol aloft. He rolled his eyes, sighing pensively as the office refolded.

*

A field of yellow dandelions, shining brilliantly in the summer sun, swayed on a warm spring morning. Clouds drifted lazily overhead. To any commonplace witness, the dandelion-drenched day was what life was worth living for, yet Annette clutched her pistol anxious to fire it.

Three young girls, spinning carefree, giggled as the hems of their dresses brushed through the patch of dandelions. Annette scowled, suspecting the worst behind this display of innocence. While two of the girls whirled on, one paused, bent and consulted a single dandelion attached to the ground.

"Come on, Kathleen!" called one of her friends.

"You two go. I'll catch up in a minute," Kathleen told them. Her friends giggled and frolicked through the field without her. Kathleen, nearing her late teens, was a radiant girl with apricot colored hair. The fabric of her dress was light blue and flapped in the breeze as she picked the single dandelion holding it to her nose.

Thomas, no older than twelve, watched her from afar, resting his elbows on the partially barbed, wooden fence at the field's edge. He stared longingly at her as Kathleen brought the dandelion up to her left ear fitting it carefully between the strands of her hair.

Unmindful that she was being watched, Kathleen then dove off into the sea of dandelions, joining her friends.

Young Thomas followed her recent path through the field, approaching the spot Kathleen had been standing. Thomas' gray eyes scoured the weeds for the perfect dandelion. He found several prospects but only seemed interested in one where a stubborn bee perched on the petals. Thomas sat and patiently watched as the bee picked pollen. As the bee buzzed away, he picked the single dandelion and held it to his nose, taking in the subtle scent of spring. Casting his eyes out to the field, Thomas watched as, in the distance, Kathleen caught up with her friends. Eventually the three girls disappeared into the horizon. As Kathleen had done, Thomas fit the dandelion adoringly above his left ear. He was pleased in knowing that he had seen her that day even if it had been for a handful of seconds. Although it was evident that Thomas loved Kathleen, he primarily resided in Kathleen's peripherals as an observant bystander.

Time traipsed forward to another moment. Kathleen was in the company of dandelions and Thomas, an outsider in her life, observed from a distance. From Thomas' perspective, Kathleen was contentedly covered by the dandelions while lying on the ground with a navy blanket beneath her and an open book was poised in the air by her fingers. Kathleen had a private picnic on the blanket which included a cold turkey sandwich, a glass bottle of fizzy soda, a strand of green grapes and a slice of gooseberry pie. Her eyes, which were almost the same jade of the grapes, keenly explored each paragraph the book had to offer.

This is how the afternoon went until the sun started to set. Kathleen closed the book, picked a second dandelion and put it into the page she'd last read as a bookmark. She folded the blanket and the remains of her meal. She abandoned the field leaving Thomas the chance to climb the wooden fence in pursuit of the lasting traces of her memory. There were tell-tale signs of her picnic: a single discarded napkin, two grapes that had wandered from the blanket and a small patch of crunched dandelions that had snapped under Kathleen's weight. Thomas collected a recently squished dandelion and, like the first, held the petal up to his nose taking in its scent. He tucked the dandelion safely behind his left ear thinking of Kathleen and his undying, unspoken feelings for her.

As time moved forward, the field remained but, atop the dandelion weeds, a carnival was hammering their posts. The beauty that once had been was soon ruined by tire tracks, muddy footprints and a wave of announcement flyers that were kicked by the wind. For several consecutive days, piece by piece, sign by sign, attraction by attraction, the carnival rose like a fiendish creature clawing from the earth. Kathleen stood disconsolately at the wooden fence as the carnival invaded her paradise. As a mid-afternoon sun dipped to the skyline, its yellow face malevolently burned orange. Eventually there was nothing left of the daylight but the pale bastard light bulb cousins which shamelessly coaxed the townsfolk from their houses.

Kathleen pressed against the wooden fence this time wearing a pale green dress that changed colors due to the carnival's oscillating lights.

As her two girlfriends chimed with excitement, rushing over the fence into the field toward the amusement, Kathleen anxiously bit her lip and went with them. Stopping briefly at the main entrance of the carnival, she looked to hesitantly see that her beloved yellow garden had been heartlessly trampled. Despite this setback, she spied a small patch of dandelions that had been spared. She picked one and brought to her nose. Kathleen carried the dandelion with her, walking into the land of blinding lights, inharmonious bells and crying carnival barkers.

Thomas, who had been following Kathleen close that night, spied the same patch of weeds and plucked one. He dug through his pockets where, days ago, he had pocketed the others, having begun his collection of dandelions. It was clear from the look in Thomas' eyes that he hoped he and Kathleen would someday collect more together.

"Let's not hog them for yourself, kiddo," came a man's voice. Thomas looked from his three dandelions to see a man dressed in a pea-green, three-piece suit. The stranger's eyes were almost golden in the carnival's light. His black hair was carefully combed and sculpted with mousse. Extending from his right arm, the man held a black ivory cane. On the top rested a miniature silver-cast likeness of the human brain. Thomas wasn't sure what to say as the man appeared from nowhere!

Both Nathaniel and Annette recognized this figure. Nathaniel had once seen this man in his second life as Yuri Abramovich. Annette knew of him from having read Nathaniel's memoirs. Nathaniel's nostrils flared as he attempted to sway rushing emotions arising from this correlation between Thomas' story and Nathaniel's.

The stranger crouched down, keeping himself balanced with the cane. As he did, the hem of his pants raised an inch or two, exposing pea-green socks. Snatching three dandelions of his own, the man was erect again. Without another word to Thomas he strode confidently, and purposefully, through the field.

Thomas' attention was drawn to a solitary circus tent.

The man in the three-piece suit stopped at the tent's entrance and spoke to a larger man.

"See that we're not disturbed, Mr. Moaning," said the first man to his friend, who held a single leash attached to a whimpering greyhound. The man with the cane told the dog: "Be a good puppy for Mr. Moaning, Cerby."

Cerby flinched at the approaching hand. After a quick pat on the dog's head, the man in the suit disappeared through the flaps of the tent.

Mr. Moaning and his greyhound stood so rigid, Thomas wondered if perhaps they had quickly become made of immobile wax. There was something oddly ancient in both Mr. Moaning and Cerby's eyes that pulled Thomas to them, both Nathaniel and Annette could see, as the pop-up book of her client's life spared no details. A wooden sign was staked into the ground by the tent which read:

Dandelion Sisters
Admission: Three Dandelions

The letters on the wooden sign were bright red as if written in blood. Thomas shivered at the thought. He consulted the number of dandelions he'd collected in the palm of his hand.

Voices were heard from the tent. Abiding his curiosity, Thomas crept closer to the tent to hear better what was being said. Mr. Moaning's fierce brown eyes were strict enough to keep the young boy from eavesdropping.

"Is it true what the sign says?" Thomas asked Mr. Moaning, "three dandelions for admittance?"

Mr. Moaning nodded.

"Seems a bit cheap for any cost of service, don't you think?"

Cerby made to introduce himself to Thomas, whimpering as he placed his paw forward, but his owner snapped the leash. The canine returned to its normal, stationary stance.

The flap of the tent opened and the man in the three-piece suit appeared with his black ivory cane in hand.

"Mr. Jolly, there's one more thing," said three female voices in unison; voices that brought chills to, not only Thomas, but to both Nathaniel and Annette.

Mr. Jolly re-entered the tent.

Thomas snuck a peek before the flap was closed. In what little time he was allowed to look inside, Thomas spotted a single glass vase with a dandelion that had turned white on the verge of shedding its seeds.

"Who are they?" Thomas asked Mr. Moaning with the same wonderment as Scrooge inquiring as to the name on the gravestone.

Mr. Moaning, however, remained silent.

Mr. Jolly appeared from the flap turning his wolfish golden eyes to Thomas' level. A wide, mischievous, inhuman grin spread across Mr. Jolly's face showing his rotted teeth.

"Your turn, kiddo," said Mr. Jolly. "Come, Mr. Moaning. We shall discuss what they had mentioned on the way." The two men walked with Cerby leading the procession. Mr. Jolly looked behind him and turned his golden eyes to Thomas. The smile widened across Mr. Jolly's lips. Mr. Jolly, Mr. Moaning and Cerby disappeared into a thunderclap.

"Thomas . . ." spoke the three female voices.

Thomas reeled to the closed flap entrance; fabric that opened on its own as he stepped through.

Annette started to follow. Nathaniel reached out and touched Annette's arm.

"I must warn you, Mrs. Slocum, seeing the Sisters can be a tad startling."

"I've read about them in your manuscript."

"Reading about them is one thing. Seeing them in person is entirely different." He motioned to her pistol. "You won't need that. Remember that we're watching a story that's already taken place. Whatever you see in there, however frightening, it doesn't constitute firearms being aimed."

Annette gave a nod, placing the pistol into the holster. She and Nathaniel stepped through the tent. The two muses were not a part of this interaction. They were there as Thomas' support. The flap closed behind the boy and his muses like a scorching electric blanket on a cold winter's evening.

Thick cloudy layers of incense swirled within the tent's perimeter. Nine kerosene lamps had been placed in a circle on the floor which heightened the tent's faded colors. In front of him Thomas noticed the three Dandelion Sisters who stared with a lack of emotion. The triplets were beautiful with flowing red hair. They wore elegant golden robes matching in fabric and color. The young women chanted in equal breath, intonation, and message.

"Thomas," said the three women "welcome. We have waited so very long."

Thomas was instructed to scribe his name on the ledger. The exposed booklet on the dandelion-carved wooden lectern had been scribbled with several entries. The name "Nathaniel J. Cauliflower" was listed a total of six times, each with different dates and ages. Thomas didn't see Mr. Jolly's name on the roster. He wondered why. Regardless, out of inquisitiveness for what the Sisters might say, Thomas added his own information with the ink and quill.

"Who are you?" Thomas stood as if he were on trial.

This question bothered Nathaniel. He shifted his weight from one foot to another.

"Moirae," answered the women. "Owners of apportionment, Fates . . ." upon speaking "fates" the flames inside the kerosene lamps flickered.

Thomas replied, "Fates?"

"Did you bring the dandelions?"

Thomas held his dandelions to the three young Fates. There were three empty glass vases on the elongated desk in front of them.

"In the vases . . ." spoke the Fates "if you please."

The dandelions were placed in separate vases. What happened then forced Thomas' eyes wide. In front of the Fate on the left, the dandelion grew back its root. The middle dandelion, in front of the second Fate's vase, which had been crushed in his pocket moments ago, resorted back to full fair radiance. For the Fate on his right, the third dandelion's petals turned white and frail, its seeds threatening to flutter at the slightest breath.

"Shall we begin, Thomas?" the Fates asked.

"Before we do," Thomas interrupted. The three young women's eyes brightened as blue as a crystal ocean at his words. "I would like to know your own names, ladies. You know mine. I'd feel at ease if we were properly introduced."

"Clotho," spoke the Fate on the left.

"Lachesis," spoke the Fate in the middle.

"Atropos," spoke the Fate on his right.

In this occurrence, the three women spoke separately. The rest of the fortune went on in unison. Thomas was surprised as the three women aged five years in a manner of seconds after reciting their names.

Clotho removed the dandelion root from her vase holding it out. She extended the root at least three feet as if it were elastic.

"See here, Thomas," spoke the Fates as Clotho displayed the dandelion roots. "The thread of your life: History from joyous beginning to bitter end. How you've loved the girl Kathleen in secret. How you've been consumed by dreams and thoughts of her; you've suffered torturous restless nights of fantasies. Though you may not be with her at present, you'll be with her one day, and you'll be happy. There's hope for you, Thomas. Connected hearts, kindred spirits, a marriage . . . and a child."

"Can it be?" Thomas asked them.

After the fortune, the women aged by thirty years blossoming into palpable womanhood. Their cheeks flushed, their breasts more defined beneath the fabric, their fingernails were long and kept. Thomas wondered if they were done aging, fearing how much older they might appear.

Lachesis held her dandelion to the light where the yellow petals grew brighter. "Rewards will be plenty, Thomas, if you heed our warning. The child must only be influenced by you. And only be affected by *your* influence. There will come a time when a metaphorical storm cloud will pass into your skies. Death will overtake someone dear to you, but despair not. There'll be wealth, oh yes, plenty of that. And power. There will be plenty of love and family. Despite these maladies and treasures, Kathleen will remain with you until the end."

As the second Fate finished, the women aged fifty more years. Their breasts sagged, their cheeks shriveled hollow and their skin decomposed. Thomas stood with his mouth agape and horror writ large across his face. The women were disgustingly repulsive. But the passing of age didn't stop there. The Sisters withered into wicked-looking crones with coiled fingernails.

"They're hideous," Annette told Nathaniel while staring at their new form, "Absolutely repugnant!"

"Enough of this!" shouted Thomas who spun to the tent's flap. But the fabric was not about to let him free. No, there had been many last-minute escapes in the past, but the Dandelion Sisters were not about to release him without uttering the critical instructions. Atropos, the third Fate, lifted her own dandelion. With her disfigured fingers, she angrily plucked the tiny, white seeds from the root.

"One day Thomas," continued the Fates, "your son will graduate from his educational institution and you will hand him . . . this . . ." Atropos brought out a silver chain which held a key with the top portion shaped like a dandelion. The fingernails that held the key were black with mold and gnarled like driftwood chopped by a furious white-water rapid current.

Seeing the key, Annette gasped. "I've seen that key before!"

"Have you?" Nathaniel asked.

"I'll hand him nothing!" Thomas screamed.

The women shouted with fury. The skin on their faces hung loose. Their eyes shriveled into empty sockets. "Do as we say, Thomas, or you'll rot along with us!"

Thomas looked at his hands and shrieked. They, like the Fates, aged exponentially. Thomas reached for the dandelion key but his joints were already deteriorating causing him to wince in pain. The harder he reached the more he felt constricted by the maladies of age. Initially the effects were physical but, as seconds passed, Thomas felt his sanity begin to quiver.

From Nathaniel's perspective, Annette looked doubtful that he'd make it out alive.

Thomas seized the key. Youth swept through his lungs and swam through the blood in his veins. The twelve-year-old Thomas shielded his eyes from the festering Fates by fleeing to the flap which miraculously swung open.

Normalcy awaited him: laughter, bells, whistles and the cries of carnival employees! Without hesitation, Thomas soared through the flap, escaping his captors, rejoicing in the warm night air toward civilization. Thomas' eyes set on a familiar and reassuring face.

Kathleen stood with a prize teddy bear in one hand, cotton candy in another.

"Is everything alright?" Kathleen asked Thomas as he ran past her out of desire to be far from the tent.

Seeing her face reminded him of the transformations he had witnessed. As he looked over his shoulder, Thomas discovered that, where the tent sat previously, was only the empty ground. On that ground were crushed dandelions.

Thomas breathed deeply, looking at a concerned Kathleen. He looked at his hand where he saw the silver dandelion key. Thomas ran from the carnival with key in hand, frantic to return home. Hoping that the farther he ran, the less chance the Fates' words were to come true.

A light dusting of snow filtered through the clouds on a January Saturday afternoon twenty years later. Boots of pedestrians crunched indents in the freshly fallen flakes. Streets were slick with ice bringing the traffic to move at a congested pace. It was on a typical residential street when thirty-two year-old Thomas' Mercedes was suddenly rear-ended by a second vehicle. While inspecting the damage, his blushed chiseled cheeks puffed warm air into his gloveless hands. His head was covered by a black fedora which caught the drifting flakes of snow. The visible hair atop his head showed a bit of white. His eyes were as gray as the afternoon around him.

"I'm so sorry," said the other driver. She was flushed and flustered, tightening a red scarf around her neck. "It's the ice, you see. I couldn't get control."

"Like trying to control the weather," he told her with a visible breath on his chapped lips. "It can't be done even in the best of circumstances." His attention was drawn from the damage to the woman underneath the scarf. "Kathleen?"

Kathleen, twenty years older, was stunning in her adulthood as she had been in her youth. She looked up from the bumper. A warm smile greeted him; so warm Thomas wondered if it could melt the snow. "Thomas Rothchild? The last time I saw you . . ."

"Was the night of the carnival, twenty years ago . . ." as he completed her thought, a set of toxic emotions coursed through him in remembering why he had stopped trailing her.

Despite his dithering, they shared more than insurance information that blisteringly cold day. They discussed similar religious and right-wing political interests over hot cider. During the spring they held one another at drive-in movies. There were days when Thomas would look out from his office window and think of her. He cultivated the love in his heart for her until, one day, when it was particularly sunny, and the sky was the bluest it had ever been, Thomas propped himself on a knee offering Kathleen his hand in marriage. As Thomas slid the diamond engagement ring up Kathleen's finger, a monarch butterfly skipped in for a closer look. They married in his estate's backyard and consummated their bond by making love in a patch of lavender lilacs under a waning moon.

Throughout the spring, and into the summer's heat, they sat on the porch of their house fanning themselves with patriotic cardboard paddles. On the weekends they drank sun tea with lemon. They made love every evening and shared dreams from the previous night. They played Chinese checkers while cicadas screeched and fireflies tickled the hedges beyond the porch banister.

There were times when she would ask Thomas what he had been running from the night of the carnival. Thomas would respond by saying "even though it may not have seemed it, I was running towards you and our future happiness."

When autumn arrived and the leaves began to crinkle, her stomach grew larger, like an inflated balloon testing its strengths. An ultrasound of Kathleen's midsection gave proof that, within the shadows of her belly, something precious stirred. Husband and wife would cuddle under the covers, she with her belly facing out, he spooning her fondly from behind. His heartbeat would coax hers to follow in its soothing rhythm. The baby inside her tummy was happy. It kicked. She smiled when this happened.

As Thomas climbed the economic ladder, scaling a steep mountain of employment to support his family, he forgot about his insecurities relating to the prophecies of the Dandelion Sisters. He dismissed the idea of magic and mythology from his youth while focusing on the practical adult world saturated in undeniable reason.

Jonas Rothchild was born on January 10th. He was a Capricorn like his father. Cradled in the crook of his mother's arm, Jonas' beady little eyes strained to make sense of his life. His tiny fingers tickled the fabric of his mother's hospital gown while his toes nestled tightly swaddled in a white cotton blanket.

"Isn't he beautiful?" Kathleen asked her husband who sat at the foot of the bed.

Thomas, staring out the window to the falling snow, was lost in thought perhaps pondering the perplexing prophecies from the Fates. It was only then that Thomas reconsidered his feelings. Though Jonas was his son, he couldn't help but to wonder what purpose Jonas would serve and how the dandelion key he had been given would factor. Shaking himself from such things, he smiled and held out a finger to his son's which was considerably smaller. As Jonas avoided his father's finger keeping close watch on the woman holding him, it was obvious who the child preferred.

"Are you going to hold him?" Kathleen offered their son to Thomas.

"He prefers you."

"Nonsense." Kathleen transferred Jonas to her husband who held him awkwardly while staring into the baby's wrinkled face.

Thomas was reflected in the bulbous steel gray eyes of his son. Jonas started to squirm. He handed Jonas to Kathleen who took him lovingly into her arms. Jonas was instantly calmed, enamored by his mother's eyes.

"Home," Kathleen sighed as the snowflakes thickened on the window's glass.

Four days passed. The Rothchilds strapped their newborn, and baby carrier, into the Mercedes. Kathleen was in the passenger seat, her face resting against the cool glass as she watched the snow descend. Thomas shuffled himself into the front seat clicking his seat-belt into place. He adjusted the heat which blew from the vents.

The prospect of going home far outweighed the journey they would have to endure to get there. The tires bumped and shook over the dunes of snow like a Jeep exploring jungle terrains. Jonas was tucked safely within his restraints dreaming of happier things. The profile of his chubby face puffed with involuntary intakes of breath. Though the windshield wipers swept the snow, heavier snow took its place.

Both Nathaniel and Annette knew that the trip home wasn't going to be a safe one. Nathaniel remembered standing out in the snow with Annette when she first came to the peg to provide the catalyst.

Annette, who had been witnessing this from the back seat as she had been sitting beside Jonas, darted her eyes out the front windshield where she spotted two figures standing at a distance in the blizzard: a past version of herself having been in a black hoodie and a past version of Nathaniel who accompanied her. Annette fled from the vehicle crunching through the snow in her wedding dress.

"Where are you going?" Nathaniel called to her.

"When we came to the inspiration, we saw two other figures, besides us, standing in the snow!" Annette called to Nathaniel over her shoulder.

"You're not going to find them, whoever they were!" Nathaniel called back to her.

She extracted the pistol, running through the snowstorm, as the accident concerning the semi-truck replayed.

From Nathaniel's perspective, Annette's white wedding gown made her transparent in the blizzard conditions. Disinterested in her current attempts, Nathaniel focused on the accident that had re-occurred between the Rothchild's Mercedes and the semi-truck. He watched as the past version of Miss Redmond had stumbled down a half-hidden ravine to help the victims. Nathaniel stood beside a past version of himself while witnessing the incident. Kathleen was dead. In the ditch, baby Jonas cried into the bleak landscape; a siren casting a plea that was torn apart by a ravaging wind that tossed malicious flurries. The entire landscape, to Nathaniel, resembled a field of fully matured, dying, dandelions.

*

Thomas Rothchild's story ended. Nathaniel was delivered to Annette's cathedral office and to the colored peg they had rotated counter-clockwise.

Annette was implanted in a far corner of her office. Realizing her chase proved futile, she relaxed, lowering her arms and pistol. She shook her head, incontestably whitewashed in her pursuit for evidence.

"I was certain I'd have the answers I was looking for when we turned that peg," Annette told Nathaniel. With the pistol returned to her holster, she crossed to the desk and opened one of the manila folders. She sifted through pictures. She held a picture to Nathaniel: a photograph of the dandelion key they had seen in Thomas' life. "On the day before my wedding, this picture came by way of unmarked post from an anonymous source. There was also an address of a residential home which was believed to have been the childhood home of the Thunderstorm Man."

She tacked the photo of the dandelion key on the dry erase board with the photos of Lyle, Doris and Sarah Milbourne. "I wonder what the key opens?"

"What we saw in Thomas' peg was him being the handed the key by the Sisters. Trinkets transfer hands over generations. Though the key was destined for Mr. Rothchild, it could have ended up in the hands of anyone!"

"No . . ." Annette stopped him. "During orientation, Fiona had stated that Jonas was wearing the dandelion key around his neck when he disappeared after his twenty-second violet envelope." She studied Nathaniel.

Nathaniel brushed his glasses to the bridge of his nose.

". . . Or at least I thought Fiona said that." Annette slumped into a swivel chair. "It's confusing, Mr. Cauliflower. I felt a sense of clarity when I regained my memories of being Annette Slocum, but now it's getting befuddled. I can't make sense of anything! I wish . . ." Annette silently studied the sprouted yellow tulips.

Nathaniel stepped forward. "You wish what, Mrs. Slocum?"

"I wish I could forget this business with Jonas," she explained with her back to him. "He's been my bully ever since I was a girl in my previous life. He was my enemy even through my adulthood before I was employed as a muse." She sighed. "And here he is, corrupting my second life!"

"He's corrupting your life because you're allowing him to," Nathaniel told her. "You're picturing him as this insurmountable opponent in a case he may not even be affiliated with! Yes, he was here as a Tenth Generation muse, and yes he neglected a violet envelope which brought you and nine other muses here to fix. But Mrs. Slocum," he took another step closer to her and said tenderly, "you're giving him too much power."

"So I return to my life and marry Adam. Then what? I'll still be working on a case that's already consumed my attention. Whether Jonas is responsible or not, the real 'Thunderstorm Man' is out there."

"Not necessarily," Nathaniel told her. "The life you're living as a missing person's detective can be changed."

"Changed?" Annette scoffed. "Like how Jonas stole that violet envelope?"

"Mrs. Slocum, Management has a way of rearranging things as long as it is on their terms. I've appealed with Management. They've re-positioned everything so that, after you blow out your candle on your personal pie, you won't be returning to your life as a missing person's detective. You'll be waking up, with your fiancé Adam, as a pie maker."

"What about the case?" Annette asked incredulously.

"I'll be handling it for you," Nathaniel told her.

"Why would you do that for me?" Annette asked, baffled by his generosity.

"That's what friends do," Nathaniel told her. "Despite our bickering and fighting, and despite your shortcomings and my temper, I think we would make fairly decent friends, don't you?"

"You talked to Management and rearranged everything?" Annette wanted to know.

Though he had told her many lies since she had been here, mostly in effort to keep her from harm, this was an honest moment. "Yes, Mrs. Slocum. It's arranged." He lifted a feathered white swan mask from her desk handing it to her. "We have enough time to visit the retirement masquerade . . ."

With that settled, Annette allowed herself to abandon her damaging fixation. She removed the pistol from the holster and emptied the magazine, contemplating her last moments as a missing person's detective. In the process, she mentally prepared herself for the life of a pie maker. She placed the pistol and magazine into the desk drawer, sealed it shut and whispered an almost inaudible goodbye to her past occupation. She faced Nathaniel free of the burdens that once tied her down to a dismal, outdated reality.

The masquerade ball Nathaniel mentioned commenced in the hallway which had been expanded into a large rectangular ballroom of polished floors and gothic windows with crimson drapes. Bronze candelabras with erect flame-tipped wicks lined the perimeter of the dance floor. A single Victrola record player was in a far corner playing a somber ballet. The muses, donned with their own masks and formal wear, waltzed fashionably. Paul Lawrence Dunbar danced with Anna Pavlova; Harriet unenthusiastically swayed with Mr. Andrews; Lucas and Icarus held one another as they moved in their own romantic tempo. A handful of clients danced on the floor with their own respective partners while others watched from the sidelines awaiting their turn.

Nathaniel stood to the side by Fiona observing the events. He hadn't worn a mask to the ball, believing the natural mask of his own harmless mendacity was sufficient enough. As a groundswell of evening gowns and tuxedos waved in front of him, Nathaniel couldn't help notice Annette who sat in a lone chair as the "odd man out" watching Lucas who wore a sleek, black shiny Pinocchio mask with small eye holes masking his face.

"You should dance with her," Fiona whispered to Nathaniel.

Nathaniel chortled. "And risk losing my ten toes under the misguided steps of her probable horrid dance moves? I think not."

The thought crossed his mind of taking Annette's waist. He rolled his eyes and stepped forward but someone beat him to it: the same black Pinocchio mask. Focused on Annette and her and her new dance partner, Nathaniel stealthily circled the perimeter listening in.

Annette held his shoulder and hand while he, with his own hands, touched her waist and wrapped his other hand around hers. She looked into the small eye-holes of the mask.

"I've missed you," she told him.

"I've missed you too," he responded.

"I'm sorry I've been so distant."

"I'm sorry we didn't do this sooner."

"I can't think of any place I'd rather be," Annette said to him.

He smiled at Annette, beaming. His eyes then shifted slightly to the side as if seeing someone, or something, distracted him.

Annette looked discouraged, knowing he was no doubt looking at Icarus wanting to be with him.

He frowned. "I have to go."

"I know," Annette sighed.

They stopped dancing but he still held her hand telling her, "This moment is something I'll forever treasure."

Annette wrapped her arms around him, holding him close. "I love you."

He smiled, leaving Annette on the dance floor.

Annette wasn't alone for long as Nathaniel tapped her shoulder. She turned and smiled at Nathaniel as he took her waist. She tilted her head back slightly and laughed as she took his hand in hers. They waltzed flawlessly, looking into each other's eyes. Her steps were pre-calculatingly precise. The music built to a crescendo and ended replaced by a slower piece that required less movement. Nathaniel stood awkwardly beside her. Annette intentionally guided Nathaniel's other hand to her waist and her arms went around and extended behind his neck. The distance between them shortened by a few inches as they swayed.

"You host a spectacular party, Mr. Cauliflower."

"Oh," Nathaniel told her. "There are few surprises yet to see." He batted his eyes to the right.

Annette followed his gaze where she noticed a pasty man with a prominent forehead and moustache. He had deep set eyes and black hair parted to the side. He wore a black suit and bow tie. He walked through the crowd, studying the details of the dance hall.

She turned her eyes back to Nathaniel. "Is that . . . ?"

"Edgar Allan Poe?" Nathaniel nodded. "Yeah."

She surveyed the room and surroundings. "He must be lost in a dream. From the looks of it, perhaps dreaming of something akin to the party in *Masque of the Red Death.*"

"Bingo," Nathaniel told her. "This section of the party was devoted entirely to our gothic horror writer for a spot of inspiration while he undergoes his own state of meditation or 'hypnogogia.' He's also our public speaker for this event."

"Edgar Allan Poe."

"Yes."

"Our public speaker!" Annette shook her head, smiling. "You've pieced everything perfectly. When I lived as Annette Slocum as a housewife to Lyle, I borrowed Poe's collected works from the local library. He was one of my favorites."

"I know."

"Do you?"

Nathaniel nodded. "I worked at the library, Mrs. Slocum." This comment took Annette by surprise. "In fact, I was there the day that you were hit by the blue Cadillac. I thanked you as you entered the library and deposited your library books that day. I don't expect you to remember. We were different people, living different lives."

"You remembered me? Me! A plain looking woman in a ratty house dress?"

"You had one of those hard-to-forget faces," Nathaniel told her. "Acting as the repairer of your library books, I kept tabs on you to make sure you were okay."

Annette looked at him with concern and asked "and why didn't you introduce yourself as my Library Book Rescuer?"

Nathaniel shrugged.

As the music played, she and Nathaniel danced oblivious to the undulations around them.

Meanwhile, a figure stood in the corner camouflaged by the contiguous crowd watching over the party. He wore a mask similar to that of a gray corpse. There were streaks of red paint marked from the eyes to the bottom of the mask. His closed floor-length cloak was a shade of deep crimson. He looked upon the party with a sharp derisive gaze. From this guest's perspective Icarus was at the concession table filling two cups of punch. Icarus turned, half expecting to find Lucas behind him, which his partner was not. The guest in the blood-red mask sneered and brought his eyes back to Nathaniel and Annette.

His apprentice, wearing the black Pinocchio mask, appeared beside him.

"Look at him," Jonas growled. "Our Prince Prospero; our Fortunato."

"I'm confused," his apprentice muttered.

"You've never read Poe? There are two short stories written by our public speaker," Jonas explained. At that time, Edgar Allan Poe crossed in front of and past them. "In Poe's words, Prince Prospero was a hero in a short story about a royal who locked his friends and family into a great fortress to avoid the plague that was destroying the globe. Prospero held parties in this fortress, content in his clever efforts to avoid the Red Death. But the Red Death attended his celebrations one night leaving behind a wake of dismal fatality. The character named Fortunato is from another short story written by Poe. In that story, Fortunato plays another form of antagonist: a drunkard who is unsuspectingly lured by his friend, Montressor, into an underground crypt in search of a cask of Amantillado wine. Unfortunately for Fortunato, Montressor leads him, not the wine, but to an untimely death. At the end of the brief story, Montressor walls Fortunato into a niche, burying him alive."

"Poor man."

"Ah, but Monstressor had his reasons," Jonas told his friend. "The beginning of the short story describes that Montressor had grievances although they weren't overtly addressed as to what Fortunato caused. We all have our own Fortunatos to deal with, our own Prince Prosperos to destroy. Look at this place. Nothing more than a crowded apartment with overused illusions! And look at her," Jonas sighed. "*Broccoli* has her so convinced that she's misinformed. She's received some of my numbered violet envelopes, I know she has! But from the blissful look on her face he's no doubt convinced her that what she thinks can't possibly be right."

"Broccoli?" his friend asked. "I thought his name was Cauliflower."

"It's a nickname I called him in his seventh life." Jonas shrugged his shoulders. "But it's ancient history. Or, at least, it will be." He lifted an arm and consulted a wristwatch. "In the next seven seconds."

The music stopped. The guests, except for Edgar Allan Poe, had already abandoned the party. Only the muses remained. Nathaniel faced Annette. Holding her, he knew he had to tell Annette the truth about everything, no matter the cost. His heart was fluttering, filled with a rush of adrenaline. He courageously opened his mouth and said "Annette . . ."

"Mr. Cauliflower?" she asked him.

"Annette, I . . . I have something I need to tell you."

Her eyes were locked indulgently on his. "Okay."

"Lots of 'somethings,' really." He took her hands, thinking of the right words to say. "It's about the last few pages of the manuscript. The ones concerning my seventh life? No doubt you've noticed they've gone missing. And also about the pegs that you had asked me to order from Management and review?"

Annette nodded.

A rumble of thunder erupted from the hallway ceiling followed by several more tremors shaking in sync with the chiming limited edition Steinway Grandfather Clock. There came shouts of horror from the crowd around them. A swarm of tuxedos and ball gowns twirled about. Nathaniel looked from side to side. Everyone was looking skyward. Nathaniel lifted his gaze to the ceiling to see waves of churning storm clouds above their heads. Within the rumbles of thunder, and between the flashes of lightning, were moments of history being re-written. There were moments of the car salesman Lyle, Doris the waitress, the violinist Jonathan, the bowling alley attendant Luanne, the glow-in-the-dark stars of a boy named Phillip and the assorted unknown adventures of a woman named Sarah Milbourne ripping like construction paper being shredded by a heated child in an uncontrollable tantrum.

Colored pegs began to fall.

Out of the corner of Nathaniel's eye he saw Lucas lift his Pinocchio mask from his face for a better look. As Lucas did this Nathaniel was suddenly aware of the red-masked vigilante who had been a stone's throw from him. Jonas, who lifted the mask from his face, waved to Nathaniel. As Jonas waved, Nathaniel could see the dandelion key hanging from his neck. Jonas then disappeared into the crowd as the muses scattered for shelter.

Nathaniel had never been a father, but he was a parent to the muses that had been housed inside the department. Like most parents Nathaniel believed that, despite all of the negative nuances that may have existed in Jonas, there had been goodness in him. It had been a hard lesson Nathaniel learned that day: that every "child" has evil within, but there are only a rare few that take it to extreme. And that Nathaniel, having felt like a father, had allowed Jonas' actions to flourish without immediate consequence. And so it was that with an immediate consequence, much to Nathaniel's misfortune, the retirement party, the walls, the floor, the muses and Edgar Allan Poe fissured into a cavern beneath him, resulting in a heart-stopping moment of the seemingly irreparable "Fall of the House of the Muses."

CHAPTER 15: WHAT REALLY HAPPENED WITH THE MAILBOX'S MISDIRECTED LETTER

Nathaniel's eyes refocused on the rotunda's oculus upon waking from a vivid dream. In the dream he had been an eighteen-year-old Russian immigrant during America's Roaring Twenties and a repairer of broken kerosene lamps. Recent recollections of his life as Yuri Abramovich greeted him in reverse order as he sat up: his second murder, the act of vengeance between him and the painter, the kerosene lamps of which had led him to the painter's doorstep and the broken promise pledged to Evangeline. Nathaniel, realizing that it wasn't a dream and that he had moments before been burned alive by his painter, presently assumed his actions disappointed Evangeline after she had waited over a century for him to resurface. This feeling troubled him. Nathaniel felt regrettably guilty for his actions which had precipitately separated them. How he wished he could see her again and to apologize that he had allowed his anger to cloud his judgment. But Nathaniel wasn't blessed in reuniting with Evangeline.

He sat in the rotunda alone surrounded by the leftover fragments of his second life. A column of sunlight traced the 2,307 kerosene lamps which were positioned as a collected reminder of his past indiscretion. They silently mocked him for his errors. There was also the sealed glass jar of six dandelions. As he lifted the jar to inspect the weeds, he palpably remembered his two encounters with the Dandelion Sisters; a sensation far stronger than hatred, an impressionable darkness that rushed like the rustling of raven wings.

A distorted reflection stared at him from the glass jar. He had been too busy trying to escape these offices the last time that Nathaniel did not take into effect that his appearance changed. Back in the afterlife, with a semi-reflective surface in hand, Nathaniel took stock of his apparent bald head and clean shaven face. He lifted his shirt and discovered that he no longer wore the youthful body as a painter in 1808, nor did he wear the slim body of a young man named Yuri in 1924. The look that Nathaniel had been given was alien leading him to believe that he was a different person on the whole. He wondered from which mold Management had pulled him.

A patch of white appeared on the other side of the jar's glass. Nathaniel lowered it to find Fiona.

"Hello, Nathaniel," Fiona told him.

"Who am I?" Nathaniel asked.

"That's a question that's been asked for centuries," Fiona told him "and will go unanswered for centuries to come. The real question should be, I suppose, 'Who am I in the eyes of Management?'"

"Fine," Nathaniel rephrased his question "Who am I in the eyes of Management?" There was a look in his weary eyes that projected his lack of faith in the system.

"You're a muse of the Second Generation," Fiona told him, "and our caretaker."

"Caretaker?"

"Would you follow me please?" Fiona offered an arm.

Nathaniel sat down the jar of dandelions, taking her arm. They crossed around the kerosene lamps past an alcove of framed painted portraits. Eventually they entered into the stretch of the agency's hallway.

"Since you've been absent, Nathaniel, Management has taken strides to ensure the everlasting integrity of our department." As Fiona said these words, they walked by several doorless offices that held their own unique postboxes from various continents. The whitewashed offices housed more people who had been employed in the interim of his absence. Nathaniel peered inside to see his comrades' faces.

"You'll find that we no longer require the use of Victrola record players or spinning discs with unique melodies to travel back and forth through time. As an alternative, Management has devised a more durable method."

Nathaniel was then introduced to a new arrangement: Lite-Brite boards, assorted colored pegs and envelopes.

"But I don't know anything about being a muse or a caretaker," he told her, inspecting a grid of inserted pegs.

"When Management puts His select few into these positions, the muses are given an exclusive perspective on their lives. Embrace the opportunity that Management has given. You may surprise yourself in learning what you're capable of." Fiona stopped by an office door. "And know, Nathaniel, Management is with you. You may occasionally find support from the others, but you must not forget to find the support in yourself. Believe that you're destined for magnitude and it will find you. With that being said I've procured a housewarming gift."

Fiona motioned into the office where there was a desk, inbox and Lite-Brite board. Standing behind the desk was an elderly woman with stringy ashen hair. A necklace with an opal stone was fastened across her pasty neck. The multicolored stone resembled a mass of forever fossilized tiny star clusters. She wore a white cotton lace dress with a floral pattern of colorless daisies. But it was the woman's face that Nathaniel instantly recognized.

"You're here," Nathaniel said to Evangeline.

"Bonjour, Monsieur Cauliflower."

"Yes, Nathaniel," Fiona told him. "Evangeline has been brought here as a Second Generation muse as well. There's no reason why you can't finish out your work, and solve the matter as to who you are in Management's eyes, in cooperation."

Nathaniel took to his muse work inspiring clients to the best of his ability. He gargled sips of water from the water cooler as Fiona had personally instructed. He provided nearly seven hundred catalysts to those in need. In the role of caretaker, Nathaniel was introduced to a sound studio where his narration was recorded for Management's instructional videos. Nathaniel transposed the music from the Victrola records onto staff paper; the notes were later translated into what would eventually become the Encyclopedia of Destinies. His office was the rotunda in which he had woken. He worked alongside the kerosene lamps and framed portraits of the muses and steadily developed into the centrically important component of Management's design. The tingling sensation in his fingers returned intermittently and Nathaniel, coming to terms that the tingling would never completely leave him as long as there were muses to paint, documented the faces of the newcomers.

While his work ethic flourished, Nathaniel's love affair with Evangeline deteriorated. The blatant actuality of his workload presented itself in an upsetting disenchantment. Though Nathaniel tried to apologize for his lack of attention, Evangeline's trust in him, based on his actions during his second life, was severely diminished. She was cold to his advances. She avoided eye contact with him as they passed one another in the hall or occupied the same conference room during staff meetings. The more he exhausted himself in keeping her near, the more Evangeline withdrew into her own reclusive despondency.

"Do you love me, Mademoiselle?" Nathaniel asked her one day after she returned from an inspiration.

For a brief second she hesitated. "You know I do."

"What can I do to make everything right?" Nathaniel begged. "What can I do to bring us to where we were?"

"We can't be what we were," Evangeline whispered.

"Why not?"

"Monsieur, *look* at me! I'm old. I'm tired. And with every colored peg, I pray to Management that I can finally shed this skin . . . this *cage*!"

"You're as beautiful as you were on the day that we were introduced!"

"In which life?" Evangeline asked, exasperated. "In which timeline?"

Nathaniel opened his mouth to answer but Evangeline went on with her statement.

"Monsieur, from your perspective, your life is a series of splashes in scattered puddles after a rainstorm! You've jumped from one life to another so effortlessly that you don't know what it's like to have *lived* a single life for as long as I have!"

"You're wrong," Nathaniel countered in a calm voice. "I don't see my life as a series of puddles. You may have lived one life, but I've lived a total of *two* lives with two sets of memories. I've twice encountered the Dandelion Sisters to be with you. It hasn't been as carefree as you think, Mademoiselle. But I've lived it and I don't regret a moment." He then ventured to ask, "Do you have any regrets?"

Evangeline propped herself against the edge of her desk for support with her hands gripping the edge. "Sometimes," she told him.

"You could live to be over a thousand and I'd still love you," Nathaniel earnestly told her with a soft and reassuring voice. "There's no one I've loved more than you. That will never change. I can't tell you enough how sorry I am for breaking my promise to you that night in your chateau. You deserve more than what I have to offer but, I can assure you, from this moment forward, I'll strive to show you how beautiful you are. Both in appearance and within. I don't mean by makeup or a Fountain of Youth. I'll transform this office into the most lavish atmosphere no one's ever thought possible. The transformations will be inspired by your beauty."

Nathaniel kept his word to Evangeline. The white-walled offices were replaced by improvised locales filled with splendor. He started with Evangeline's office in which he laid stones, erected walls and hoisted vaulted buttresses in her honor. What had once been a drab workplace with four walls was now a collection of stone cathedrals so cleverly created that its imposing implementation would have mystified the graphic artist M.C. Escher. In the same mode as a stone carver working a slab of marble with a chisel and hammer, Nathaniel constructed similarly unique breathtaking offices above and around them.

Nathaniel saved Fiona's office for last. As he stood creating an art gallery atmosphere with polished floors and bare walls with empty frames, Fiona stood beside him like a contractor's assistant. The details poured from his mind and manifesting so fluidly Nathaniel wondered if perhaps he was channeling Management's inventiveness in the initial moment of Creation. That perhaps he was tapping into the source like a rig finding oil beneath endless ocean depths.

As he hoped, Evangeline's spirits lifted when encountering these displays.

But his visions didn't stop there. Nathaniel reinvented the unexciting existing retirement parties with more pizzazz. Retirements which had once been a simple stroll across a stage, a handshake and the handing of discharge orders, grew into an array of awe-inspiring cherry blossoms and the passing of planets and stars. Public speakers shared their professions including, but not limited to: perfume makers, glassblowers and the earliest astronomers with their telescopes. Those who were brought to the office to entertain the muses were astute historians, exotic fire-eaters and prolific authors. They were visionaries, inventors and philosophers . . . and they moreover proved to be a distraction. Amidst Nathaniel's handling, he misplaced sight of whom he was building it all for and was too consumed in his own craftiness that he almost forgot about Evangeline entirely.

In his down time, Nathaniel busied himself trying to transpose a single unintelligible composition from a broken Victrola record. Where other records contained melodious masterpieces, this precise record held an immeasurably wrecked song. It looked as if it had been shattered and re-glued. Its surface had been scratched and worn which worsened the skipped notes of the already fractured melody. It dawned on Nathaniel that this record was the very same disc that he had shattered in his previous visit! To make matters worse, the lyrics thumped on a name, which repeated over and over:

"Evangeline . . . Evangeline . . . Evangeline . . ."

"Working hard?" Evangeline asked Nathaniel from his office doorway.

Nathaniel quickly forced the needle from the record which brought a screeching sound.

"Evangeline," Nathaniel said to her, standing from his chair. He crossed in front the Victrola. "Mademoiselle Evangeline. Hello."

"Bonjour, Monsieur Cauliflower. I've come to tell you that I'm one peg from retiring," She told him while stepping into his office. "And I . . . I have to ask where Management will send me?"

"Why are you asking me?" Nathaniel asked. The moment that it came out of his mouth, he considered the question too harsh. He politely rephrased. "What I mean to say is: 'why do you think I would know the answer?'"

"Because you're our caretaker," Evangeline asked, taking several steps closer to him and the Victrola. "You're our envelope aficionado. The one who receives the colored pegs from Management and assigns them to the muses. You're the one whom Management has given the task of transcribing Victrola records into encyclopedia entries. You, in short, have all the information." She studied him. "I've barely seen you. You're either creating another muse's office or you're in meetings with Fiona forming retirement parties, or you're buried in stacks of records as high as the domed ceiling. I figured that as our time together is expiring so I might at least sit with you. Perhaps listen to the records?" Her attention rested on the record behind him which Nathaniel tried to hide. "That one sounded as if it had a lovely melody."

"Did it?" Nathaniel asked. He lifted the record and fit it into its square sleeve. "You don't want to listen to these dusty things."

Evangeline flipped through the pages of the leather bound volume in which he had been writing.

"You listen to the records and transpose the notes into words which are entered then as the person's destiny?"

"That's right."

"It appears as if you've come across a rather complicated melody on that record."

"Yes, I suppose it is a complicated melody." He stored the record. "A melody that might complicate things if heard too many times."

"Complicate things?"

"Yes."

"For whom?"

"For whomever its message is referring."

"And to whom is its message referring?"

"No one," Nathaniel stammered. "No one important."

"Then you wouldn't mind if I listened to it with you?"

Nathaniel wasn't sure if she was being slyly snappish or if she earnestly wanted to spend time with him and share his experiences. Either way, he loved her too much to deny her anything. He turned and removed the record out of its sleeve setting it on the turntable.

They listened to the tune seven times. She sat beside him watching as Nathaniel scribbled the notes into the encyclopedia volume. When the page was scooted to her, she pensively read her destiny. Worry on her face blotted what shards of hope had remained. The record was switched off, extinguishing the lyrical message.

"Say something," Nathaniel begged. "Please."

Evangeline stood and left his office without speaking. As she left his office he closed the volume and stared at it with a blank expression.

A reassigned peg descended from the oculus to his inbox. Nathaniel inserted the green-colored peg and went to inspire his client, Lucas Richardson, by way of a guitar pick. As he stood in the World Trade Center cubicle, staring at a framed photograph of two young boys holding a guitar, he held the picture and stared at the image. He remembered the times that he and Evangeline had shared. Nathaniel recalled how innocent he and Evangeline had been. Nathaniel left the photograph and delivered the guitar pick to Lucas' classroom. Arriving back to his office, he found Fiona waiting for him looking quite concerned.

"What is it?" he asked. "What's happened?"

"She needs you."

He rotated Evangeline's final colored peg and found her standing at a mailbox holding a letter as storm clouds slithered like rapacious anacondas. He sensed her hesitation in this timeline and it sickened him.

"Mademoiselle Evangeline," Nathaniel whispered to her. He stood behind Evangeline affectionately. "Breathe, darling, it will all be over in a moment."

"You shouldn't have come here," Evangeline told him.

"I had too."

"You didn't think I could do it alone?" Evangeline accused.

Nathaniel frowned.

"Well, don't worry," she told him. "I've completed the assignments you've asked of me. Why would today be any different?"

"When you left my office, you had that look in your eyes."

"What look?"

"The look you get when you're thinking sinister thoughts."

"So you really did come because you believed I couldn't deliver the letter."

"I came for job security . . . and because I love you," he confessed. "I know you, Evangeline. And I know that if you had intentions of delivering the letter as instructed, you would have done so."

Evangeline's tears grew. Raindrops fell from the clouds. Choked for words, she said "I can't."

"Then let me help you." Nathaniel guided Evangeline's hand, and the envelope, to the mailbox. The process was agonizingly slow but Nathaniel remained patient.

"Please," Evangeline pleaded. "Please don't make me play the postman."

"If I could deliver the envelope myself, I would. But it has to be you, and only you. It's just an envelope," said Nathaniel. "That's all it is. One little envelope."

Evangeline shook her head.

"Yes, Mademoiselle, that's all it is. And when the envelope is in the mailbox, we can go home."

"Home," she sighed.

"Yes," Nathaniel told her. "Home: I'm picturing a quiet country house with an apple orchard. Doesn't that sound nice?"

"Tell me more about the apple orchard."

"The apples will be ripe when autumn comes. And we'll pick them together, you and me. The life that we can lead will be a simple one. No muses, no murderous painters, no dandelions and circus tents haunting our dreams."

Nathaniel's attention was then drawn to the sound of flapping heavy fabric. To his left he found a circus tent illuminated by a flash of lightning. Its exterior was made of mismatched Persian carpets and faded burlap. There was a posted sign which read as it had previously requiring three dandelions for admittance.

"Yes," Nathaniel told Evangeline. His voice cracked causing Evangeline's outstretched hand to falter. "All you have to do is put the envelope into the mailbox and we'll go away from here."

Evangeline looked to the left, seeing the circus tent for herself. She gasped.

"Yes, my love. I see it too." Raindrops poured heavily. Clouds twisted and tumbled in a thunderous roar. "We don't have much time. Ignore it. You have to put the envelope into the mailbox."

Evangeline parted from Nathaniel and pulled on the lid.

"That's it," Nathaniel said. "That's right . . . inside the mailbox."

Evangeline looked into the darkness of the space. Raindrops chased the wrinkles of her face cascading down the contours of her chin. And as she had stood there, contemplating what was to follow once the envelope was delivered, Evangeline closed the lid with envelope still in hand. She turned to Nathaniel.

"Evangeline," Nathaniel told her.

"I'm sorry," Evangeline told him. "I love you, but I'm sorry." She surrendered the envelope dropping it to the wet ground.

Nathaniel scrambled to save it from the flood.

As he did, Evangeline turned her back on him, the mailbox and the circus tent. With every step that she took, the cement splintered and cracked.

Nathaniel screamed above the din of the storm: "Evangeline!"

Evangeline turned to him. "I've wasted over one hundred years waiting for you. But it seems that every opportunity I spend with you things fall dramatically to pieces. I've missed so many opportunities, so many chances, so much happiness while waiting for you to come back to me. And yet, when you did, instead of feeling complete, I'm miserable. I love you, I do. But that love has proven a fatal toxin I can't shake."

"Evangeline . . ." Nathaniel began to plead.

"One hundred years, Monsieur Cauliflower! I've lived over one hundred years and not *once* did a muse come for me. Where was my muse when I needed him? Hmm? Where was he?" Evangeline shook her head: "I want you to forget about me. I want you to forget my face, forget my voice and forget about the memories you and I share. For my sake, please!"

"You don't know what you're asking!"

"If you love me, you have to release me from this curse you've put us under. Allow me to live my own life for me without you in it. You have to allow me a chance to find happiness elsewhere, because as much as I want to, I'll never find happiness with you."

These words were as painfully afflicting as a bullet to his heart. He wanted to provide her happiness but her words rang true nonetheless. Evangeline disappeared into the storm's gloomy sheet of rain. It was then that the colored pegs descended. The sky was torn to shreds as if it were an impressively deconstructed canvas. Nathaniel looked at the smudged letter in his hands. He looked at the mailbox and frowned. His expression was fierce.

Nathaniel pocketed the drenched envelope and shifted his stare from the mailbox to the circus tent which stood defiantly against the squall. Another flash of lightning ignited the sky. In that brief instant, the circus tent disappeared and Nathaniel was left alone with the storm. The increasingly fractured ground split further underfoot. Soon, the pop-up book flickered out like a defective attic light bulb. All that was left was Nathaniel, Evangeline's undelivered envelope and an endless cascade of colored pegs.

Evangeline's office returned to the bland four white walls as if her existence had been erased. Even the lingering smell of her lavender perfume had been vacuumed. Nathaniel found a discarded item on Evangeline's desk: the opal necklace she had worn. The stone caught the light. No doubt Evangeline had passed through the swirling white light at the end of the waiting room taking the memories they had shared. Though her sudden absence had caused the triggering of the numbness within, he granted her wish and freed her.

Fiona accompanied him for a walk along a real bustling creek in the living world's woods. The air was refreshing, balmy eighty degrees. There were birds twittering in overhead canopies. Stray twigs snapped beneath Nathaniel's weight as he sauntered.

"You could've told me that the record was hers," Nathaniel said to Fiona.

"Oh," Fiona said coyly. "Was that Evangeline's record?"

"You know it was." He stopped in front of the creek. He held in his hands the single volume in which Evangeline's destiny had been written. Questions trickled from his lips in the same fashion as the water washed over submerged stones. "What if I had never come to her chateau that afternoon in 1807 to paint her portrait? What if she and I had never met? What if I'd never held her or shown her the portraits of the ghostly faces? What if the painter had never found the paintings in the attic loft? What if we were able to live out our love story unhindered? What if the Dandelion Sisters had never bothered me? What if I was just a normal person? What if . . ."

"What if . . ." Fiona interjected. "It's a common question. The important thing to remember, Nathaniel, is that the words 'what if' are often wrongly placed in the past. 'What if' could also be placed when thinking about what's coming. But even then there's a conundrum. One should never focus too much on the 'what ifs' in either the past or the future. We must live for today."

"Please," Nathaniel told Fiona. "Call me 'Cauliflower.' If I can't be with her, it would be nice to hear the name that Evangeline so often used."

"It would be my pleasure, Mr. Cauliflower." Fiona smiled. "I'll give you a moment with your thoughts." With that, Fiona walked the path without him.

Nathaniel held the encyclopedia volume inspecting the spine where the letters "Sl" had been scribed. He frowned. There were other destines inside that book; additional lives that had been documented. But he knew that holding onto the volume would bring him additional pain. "What if . . ." he whispered to the book, and to the wind, hoping that it might carry his wish to the proper recipient ". . . what if Evangeline came back to me someday? Or perhaps . . . I may find someone else to love?" He tossed the volume into the creek. It was carried downriver. "Perhaps I may find someone else to love," he softly repeated.

"Mr. Cauliflower?" He turned to find Fiona waiting for him.

*

Nathaniel strained to open his eyes. There was a pain on the back of his head which had been slightly elevated.

"He's awake!" Fiona told the others. She was kneeling down beside him. "Mr. Cauliflower, are you alright? Are you with us?"

"I'm with you." He sat up, looking around.

Edgar Allan Poe and the Nine Greatest muses surrounded both Nathaniel and the Head Muse. Annette stood from the others in a corner. The muses still donned their ball gowns and tuxedos. Some held on to their masks from the Masquerade.

"Took a nasty spill, did we?" he asked Fiona.

"The department floor collapsed under the weight of the falling colored pegs," Fiona explained. "Most had the wind knocked out of them but you hit your head and went unconscious."

Nathaniel nodded. He discovered that his tie had been loosened and the top few buttons were undone. Evangeline's opal necklace could visibly be seen around his neck. He concealed it with the shirt fabric, straightening his tie.

Nathaniel could see the seventy-five degree steep incline of the tilted musing floor. At the base of the near-vertical slant was a junk pile of desks, postboxes and Lite-Brite boards. Included in the heap were torn sheaths of retirement party illusions, overturned culinary dishes and a fluttering of both white and violet envelopes. The energy efficient bulbs short-circuited and occasionally showed the showering colored pegs.

The contents of the glass combination cabinet had been haphazardly scattered. There were shards of broken kerosene lamps and punctured portraits. Annette shuffled her way through the exposed paperwork of Nathaniel's manuscript and, as she did, uncovered the final portion regarding his seventh life. She examined the last chapter he had kept from her and looked at Nathaniel with disappointment. Annette retreated a few steps into the awaiting crowd looking at him expectantly for instructions.

Nathaniel wasn't sure where to begin with his apologies.

"Well then," Nathaniel told them over the din of falling pegs, standing. "Until further notice, our retirement party has been postponed. Our recourse is to wait for the pegs to stop and assess the situation from there." Even though the caretaker had yet again failed to keep the integrity of his bureau, he advocated a sense of optimism sharing that confidence among his peers as a good muse, in Management's eyes, is expected to do.

CHAPTER 16: A WEATHER WIZARD'S INFLUENCE

In the same layered style of Nathaniel's strange personal adventures, so were there several unmapped layers to the hereafter. When the colored pegs of the severed six storylines had fallen, and when the department's floor had collapsed beneath the inspiration-offering coworkers, the debris had inevitably landed into a cavernous Purgatory where the resonance of the descending colored pegs echoed the vast bulwark of invisible crypts.

Six markedly dissimilar thunderheads dominated the gloom releasing a visual ongoing outpouring of fulsome minutiae. This image depicted how much damage had been inflicted on humankind due to Jonas' manipulations; a palpable reminder of history's fragility. These luminous cinematic flakes of Jonas' victims plunged amongst the actual pegs in a steady cascade of wrecked dreams and interrupted hopeful futures.

Though the other muses had sought immediate shelter from the tempest, Nathaniel maintained a close vigil over the storms hoping that the falls would ease. He barely noticed his glasses which had slid down his nose several centimeters. His arms were crossed before him almost in defiance of the pegs.

Fiona was beside Nathaniel, reverently watching the exhibit.

"When I was a boy in my seventh life," Nathaniel told her "my mom and I were alone. She worked double shifts and, due to that, asked me to visit my loving great aunt at our family farmhouse. She sent me with suitcases filled with handpicked library books. It was an undersized home complete with a tiny living room, cramped shotgun kitchen, a petite dining room of aged dark wood and two narrow bedrooms with four poster beds. The covered back porch held storage units and an ancient washing machine. The weather-beaten front porch was constructed of a green-painted wood which creaked underfoot. There was an old porch swing with groaning chains. Open windows were dressed in thin, white lace curtains. The lumpy beds were topped by handcrafted, white cotton quilts. In one of the corners of the largest bedroom was, and I remember this perfectly, a red wooden rocking horse on squeaky springs.

"There were all sorts of treasures in that house: a stereoscope from the turn of the century coupled with a box of black and white photographs, cabinets of sparkling china, frying pans with leftovers that were fed to the stray cats, a sapphire peacock-shaped perfume bottle resting on the green and yellow striped vanity, a wood burning stove, a chimney stack and a farmer's calendar hanging beside the outdated icebox and a Frigidaire. There was a tapered staircase to the right of the only television. The stairs led to a door and, through that door, there were rickety stairs which led to a confined attic that smelled of mothballs. On rainy days I used to go into the attic and examine the photo albums, studying the black and white memories. Though I loved the library books that I brought with me, there was something spooky about looking through those photos and wondering what their stories had been. I daydreamed about what their voices might have sounded like. It's like they were in the attic with me whispering blameworthy admissions.

"What I remember the most about the farm house," Nathaniel explained "was a miniature green Dutch cabin dubbed a 'Weather Wizard.' There was a thermometer on the front side of the little house. Flanking the thermometer were two rectangular doorways. In one of the doors were miniature twins. If the weather was pleasant, the twins moved out of the door. If the weather was stormy, or had the propensity to be bad, a witch arrived from the other door. My great aunt told me that the device was more accurate than any weather man could have predicted." Nathaniel sighed. "No matter how many memories are in my head after seven lifetimes, the image of that farmhouse, and the Weather Wizard, holds prominent. Whenever I hear the sound of rain or the rumbling of thunder, I'm reminded of the witch. I'm instantly brought to those days in the farm house and of the photographs. This was before the seventh visit to the Dandelion Sisters and rescuing Annette's library books, of course."

"While these memories of yours are nice, Mr. Cauliflower, you may want to be careful how much you recall." Fiona's warning was stressed. "We're in Purgatory. Memories and dreams aren't safe here."

"Yes, I know."

"We can't stay here, Mr. Cauliflower," Fiona said worryingly. "I've corralled the muses who are ready for the departure to a safer location. We're waiting on you and Mrs. Slocum."

"Mrs. Slocum?"

"She's refusing to comply with my wishes until she's spoken with you."

Nathaniel frowned and chided, "Imagine!"

"Mrs. Slocum's been trying to solve the case of the Thunderstorm Man, and you've been rushing her out the door without giving her an honest chance to try." She put a hand on Nathaniel's shoulder and said "At least talk to her."

"And say what?" Nathaniel asked. "Everything that's led to this moment from her previous life is inside that manuscript. What more is there to say?"

"She hasn't read it, Mr. Cauliflower," Fiona reassured him. "While you've been standing here, staring up at the broken lives of these clients, Mrs. Slocum's been waiting for you to tell her the story."

Nathaniel chortled.

Fiona stepped between Nathaniel and the falling pegs. "She read the first page and casually skimmed through the rest."

Nathaniel kept his eyes on the falling clients as if evading his Head Muse's statement.

She touched his hand. "Rescue this story, Mr. Cauliflower, as you have the bound library editions in her life . . . and say something to her."

Nathaniel moved his eyes from the storm to the smooth patch of limestone at his feet. The muses examined the colored pegs as if they were on a carefree grassy knoll watching a classic drive-in movie. Lucas was standing comfortably while leaning back into Icarus' arms. Harriet was solitarily rigid with her arms folded. Anna Pavlova danced to the drumming rainfall. Mr. Andrews and Mr. Dunbar whispered about the debacle. Prolonged guest and public speaker Edgar Allan Poe was not interested in the storm. His attention was on Annette who had reset her desk, Lite-Brite, swivel chair and dry erase board. The manuscript from Nathaniel's seventh life rested on the edge of her desk, untouched.

There were two women whom Nathaniel had loved. The first had been Evangeline. The second had been the socially outcast bookworm who he saw before him, whose wedding dress poofed like a melted campfire marshmallow.

The affair with the rescued library books had been merely a sliver of the anonymous tale that had encircled. Nathaniel was warily convinced it was a story, with its overly tattered binding and violent undercurrents, that he could rescue. It was far easier to be condemnatory of Annette's occasional uncompromising qualities than it was to love and accept, then promptly lose her.

He had about as much desire to go and talk to her as someone might detest walking into work on an early, busy Monday morning but he trudged to her anyhow.

"So . . ." Annette melodiously placated while turning a page of her case files.

"I don't want to fight," Nathaniel blurted.

"Who's fighting?"

Nathaniel, suddenly feeling his blood pressure rise, flared in defense. "There's that tone again."

"Tone?" Annette nonchalantly asked. "What tone?"

"*That* tone. The tone you often use . . . a sort of outwardly conciliatory sing-songy, condescending tone which hints to an assumed unspoken 'I'm right and you're wrong.'"

"There's no argument, Mr. Cauliflower. You admit that I'm right and you're wrong and we'll leave it at that."

"That's not what I was saying," Nathaniel countered.

"Oh?"

He removed his glasses and massaged the bridge of his nose. "Alright, fine. You were right. I was wrong. But I have a perfectly good reason, or perhaps *reasons,* for doing what I did." He opened his eyes to find that Annette was no longer there. Placing the glasses where they belonged on his face, he turned in search of her. "If you would give me a chance to explain . . ." Nathaniel found that Annette had circled behind the white dry erase board where he was handed three colored pegs. "What are these?"

"The pegs from the three initial violet envelopes: the ones corresponding to the transgendered woman Luanne, Phillip and his glow-in-the-dark stars and Jonas' father, Thomas Rothchild."

Nathaniel looked askance.

Annette clarified her request. "We rotated these pegs counter-clockwise. We didn't rotate them *clockwise.* We may gain insight as to where Jonas is or, perhaps, where he took them."

He held them in his hand without responding.

"What?" Annette asked. "I found them in my desk drawer where I've kept them."

"These colored pegs won't tell you what you need to know," Nathaniel somberly told her.

Annette poked an index finger to them. "We turn these pegs, we find out where in the timeline Jonas messed things up, and we'll have him. We'll return everyone home, close this case and conclude this charade." She pointed to the falling pegs. "What you see there is a result from six timelines being altered. If we fix those timelines, the colored pegs disappear. Isn't that how it works?"

"Yes, that's how it works."

"So let's hop to it, Mr. Cauliflower. Put 'em in the Lite-Brite and rotate them!"

But Nathaniel didn't "hop to it" as he had been instructed. Nor did he "put 'em in the Lite-Brite and rotate them." He dolefully looked at the colored pegs. "The stories that you're seeking are no longer in the pegs, I'm afraid."

"What do you mean?"

"What I 'mean' is that each of these individuals had a story. That story has been stolen. If we rotate these pegs, we'll see what once was and nothing more."

"So you're saying that to restore their colored pegs we have to re-write their story?"

"That's right."

"Then how do we do that?" Annette wanted to know. "The Encyclopedia of Destinies?" She focused on a mountain of overturned books mixed in the junk pile.

"No, the volumes specifically tell a person's destiny and a moment when a muse is supposed to intervene to make that outcome possible." Nathaniel picked up a lone volume to prove the information was invalid. "It doesn't have single moments of a client's life. It shows particular increments where a muse is able to be inserted. Especially after the initial inspiration – as a fail-safe if you will."

"A fail-safe?" Annette considered his words. "Inside every colored peg?"

"In case the initial inspiration didn't take effect like it should have," Nathaniel told Annette "a muse has a second, sometimes third or fourth, chance to provide the inspiration."

"So," Annette turned her eyes to the dry erase board "because Jonas shanghaied these fail-safes and manipulated the storyline, there's no reason to rotate the pegs. What good is a story without its client?"

Nathaniel frowned. "Precisely."

"If we were to find Jonas, rescue the victims, use the fail-safe to reinsert them . . ."

"Mrs. Slocum," Nathaniel started.

". . . It's achievable. We have to figure out where Jonas has taken them."

"Mrs. Slocum," he tried to explain but Annette wasn't paying him mind. "Listen to me, will you?"

Annette spun, enraged at his indecency.

"The afterlife is more than Lite-Brite boards and colored envelopes," he told her. "When the offices collapsed they landed into a level known as Purgatory, where we are currently."

Light bulbs flickered on the expansive Cimmerian shade like heated bursting popcorn kernels.

"Purgatory?" Annette caught sight of misplaced illuminated industrial barn lights hanging from the non-existent ceiling. "Those lights," she pointed upward.

Nathaniel looked at the lights with mounting concern.

"Were they here previously?" Annette asked.

He grabbed her hand and guided her from the hanging lights. She recoiled but Nathaniel was adamant. He called for the muses to gather round Annette's Lite-Brite board.

"Muses!" Nathaniel told them. "We need to find another hideout. Purgatory is creeping closer. The lights you see," he explained "will populate in number the longer we linger here."

"Why?" Lucas asked.

Icarus responded, "After being led through the double doors by the mechanical boatman, I was taken into the Underworld which lies below Purgatory. While I visited the Underworld, I encountered an irresistible woman named Persephone, who led me here to Purgatory for a brief tour. Purgatory," Icarus' face was ominous "is a warehouse where damned souls are forced to ship dreams to the living. In the process, their own identities are split until there's nothing left but a drained armor. It's a place where a soul's hopes, dreams and beloved memories are devoured. The longer we stay, more hanging lights will accumulate above our heads until we find ourselves immersed in its inescapable endless warehouse – eaten by its inhospitable void."

"Maybe some memories are better eaten," Lucas told him.

Icarus said nothing in response.

Nathaniel found a spare Lite-Brite and held it to his chest. He pocketed the three colored pegs he'd been given. When his hand reached into his pocket, he felt the ridges of the lone glow-in-the-dark star he had taken from Phillip's inspiration.

"I'm not going anywhere until Cauliflower here gives me answers," Annette told them.

"Mrs. Slocum," Nathaniel told Annette. "Remember those three violet envelopes I reassigned to you after orientation? I've reviewed them. Prior to you providing the catalysts, I knew how the stories were meant to wrap."

More barn lights erupted.

"I rotated them as if reading three cherished library books. I know why Luanne was destined for the Christmas ornament. I know why Phillip was preordained for the stars! I can tell these stories to you, verbatim. I can recite to you what I know in hopes that it'll gain us a better insight into the mind and actions of Mr. Rothchild. If it's what you really want, I'll help to repair this story for you."

Twenty vintage barn lights flickered to life from the ceiling.

"But not here. Not in Purgatory. Maybe Mr. Richardson was correct. Some decrepit memories are best devoured while other important memories, like mine and yours, may determine everyone's fate." Nathaniel added these words to his devotion: "I promise."

Annette, with pistol back in her thigh holster under the fabric of her wedding dress, tucked her case files, including the pictures and numbered violet envelopes, under an arm. She gradually accepted Nathaniel's hand.

Fiona seized a spare Lite-Brite board to take with them. She also held an uncapped mason jar labeled "In Case of Emergencies." The Head Muse explained to Nathaniel that the jar had toppled and emptied in the department's collapse. Though it was normally filled with multiple pegs fashioned for quick escapes, only one remained from the spill. In reaction to these words, Nathaniel gave her a questioning, mistrusting look.

The muses linked hands as if fashioning a group prayer. Nathaniel extracted the orange emergency peg. He inserted it into the face of Annette's Lite-Brite board rotating it.

Purgatory ignited with a thousand added barn lights.

He looked at his muses, one by one, and to the falling colored pegs beyond them. In the life of Luanne, Nathaniel noticed a shard in which Luanne had been Louis prior to her surgery. Louis studied the features of a small Dutch house with twins in one door and a witch in the other. Though it had been a trinket from Nathaniel's childhood, he and Luanne had shared memories of the same Weather Wizard.

Eventually, everything would be explained to Annette in due course as to how the barometer had passed from his and Jonas' hands to Luanne's.

The atmosphere folded and unfolded delivering them from Purgatory's endangerment.

They were delivered to a derelict moonlit sanctuary decked with overturned pews, shattered stained glass windows and scattered dried leaves.

"I know this place . . ." Annette told Nathaniel.

"Yes, Mrs. Slocum. It's the sanctuary where you were to have your wedding." Nathaniel brushed a finger along the edge of pew collecting a thin film of dust. "But it's also home to an added timeline. It was in this building in my seventh life, many, many years ago, when I had met a young boy named Jonas Rothchild."

*

Meanwhile, in the same living world, in a study studded with gothic furniture, heavy maroon drapes with gold stitching and an ornately crafted fireplace with flames in the grate, Jonas consulted a shadow-covered object on the mantle.

His hooded apprentice entered the study. "We're in the sanctuary of the church, like you predicted. What do we do now?"

"We wait for the events to transpire."

"We aren't collecting clients?"

"No." Jonas studied the object. "We need two more individuals to join our humble crowd, and they'll arrive on their own terms once they've uncovered the sanctuary's clues."

"What's the endgame?"

"The endgame?" Jonas looked toward his apprentice. "You want to spoil the surprise?"

"We've gone about an awful lot of trouble to ruin six lives. I don't see where this could lead. What good could come from this?"

The shifting illumination from the flames heightened Jonas' stern stare. "Ruin? We didn't ruin these lives. We saved them. Don't tell me you're having second thoughts; that I've plucked you from your own timeline by mistake. You begged me to be a part of this, remember?"

"I'm not having second thoughts," his apprentice stammered.

"Good," Jonas spat. "Keep it that way, for your sake. Go back to the sanctuary. Keep an eye on them. And keep your anonymity. Understand?"

The apprentice ducked out of the room leaving Jonas with his thoughts. On the mantle was the barometer from his childhood. He recalled Nathaniel, in the farm house, having showed him the twins and the witch. It had been the Weather Wizard that led Jonas to his occupation as a meteorologist. Parting from the barometer, Jonas touched a photo album from the farm house attic. As he flipped through the pages and surveyed the photos, Jonas mentally peeled personal layers of himself and Nathaniel remembering how they met as children and contemplating where those facts would lead them both in the superseding days.

CHAPTER 17: ASPHODEL

The church had gone into such a state of disrepair that it no longer looked like a dignified place of worship. Instead, it had taken on the role of an abandoned dwelling where the presence of Management had gone through a gnarled metamorphosis resulting in a dilapidated version akin to Heaven's infamous Rebellious Angel. As the dropping colored pegs rapped on the building's exterior, gentlemen loosened their bow ties and, in some cases, stripped from their jackets. The women removed their opera gloves and let down their hair, except for Harriet who kept hers in a tightly fastened hair-pinned bun. Some inspected the fractured stained glass windows while others casually perused dust-covered Bibles and hymnals. And then there were those visibly distracted by whispered conversations.

"It's a shame that this place had to change so significantly," Annette whispered to Nathaniel. They were sitting in a cushioned pew near the altar steps. Her eyes soaked in the poor condition of the Nave while Nathaniel focused on the rotted armrest next to him. "How many years in the future are we from my wedding day?"

"This is your wedding day," Nathaniel said matter-of-factly.

"No. My wedding day is filled with bouquet arrangements of yellow flowers. There were tasteful ribbons and finely-constructed wedding invitations. The carpets were vacuumed and the windows were washed and intact."

"Not anymore," Nathaniel sighed as the sound of drumming colored pegs continued. "As the six timelines were destroyed, this is your alternate wedding day. A day without roses. A day without a bride or a groom for that matter."

"Adam's not here."

"No, Mrs. Slocum. He wouldn't be. This is an alternate timeline. In the alternate timeline, the wedding day didn't happen."

"And yet here I am in my wedding dress."

"We're in the middle of a paradox, Mrs. Slocum. A limbo between what used to be your wedding day and today."

"Paradox?"

"This is a parallel universe to what should exist. In this particular universe, which was split from the previous, you and Adam aren't married. In this universe, billions upon billions of resulting people throughout history are uninspired because the six destroyed timelines. It's a ripple effect. Somehow, both universes are currently existing at the same time. Out there in time somewhere, you're wedding day still exists. But it won't for much longer. If we don't rescue the timelines, this universe will become our universe." He shifted in the pew. "It's difficult to explain."

Two letters had been etched into the wood which Annette assumed were a person's initials. "J and R. Did Jonas scratch those?"

"Yes," Nathaniel said flatly. "I was eight years old. And he was nine."

"And . . ." Annette coached.

Nathaniel sighed and began the story of his seventh life and his relationship with Jonas starting in his boyhood years. As he retold of his adventures, and as the morning sun rose, the crouching clues were exhumed making him incorrigibly vulnerable to a past he had tried to keep interred.

*

The year was 1987 when eight-year-old Nathaniel sat at his kitchen table in his white dress shirt, brown suspenders, corduroy pants and bow tie. His fine blonde hair had been wetted and parted to the side. Though his exact expression was unreadable due to the thick glasses that covered most of his face, his disinterest in the affairs of that night's dinner was obvious as he gave a sigh. His mother, Justine, had brought another potential male suitor to dinner. Nathaniel had seen many men come and go in his mother's romantic life. None of them had lasted long enough to make an emotional impact.

The Casanova was a prosecuting attorney who recently moved to town and fell in love with Justine, as all men tended to do. The attorney smelled of stale hairstyling product and an odious musk. Nathaniel wondered, as the serving bowl of spaghetti and the basket of half-burnt garlic bread was passed around the table, how much longer this fellow would be gracing their lives.

"I have a son about your age, Nate," his mother's date announced as he twirled a fork to scoop up a helping of slick, sauce-encrusted noodles.

Young Nathaniel had an immediate distaste for him. He shyly turned to his mother asking "May I please be excused?"

"But you haven't touched a bite of your spaghetti, Nathaniel. Here. Have some garlic bread that Thomas made for us."

Nathaniel stared at his plate of spaghetti. He looked at the piece of over-baked bread his mother tossed to his plate. He then looked at her paramour who fought with a few strands of noodles which wriggled like limp garden snakes. Nathaniel was irrevocably put off from his hungriness.

"Seven bites and you can scurry off," Justine told Nathaniel.

Justine was an unhealthily thin, middle-aged woman with fine, dirty-blonde hair. She wore a frilly, flowery blue dress with nearly invisible straps and low cleavage. She also wore faux jewelry which clinked as she moved her hand interestingly to her chin. Her overly-accessorized makeup was almost clown-like as she nodded at the date's poorly executed advances. She didn't parade in this attire normally. Justine was generally quite conservative. Seeing his mother like this disgusted Nathaniel but, because he had been taught polite respect from an early age, he didn't say anything.

Those seven bites of his dinner were excruciating. As Nathaniel lifted the noodles to his mouth seven times, he suffered through witnessing the deplorable mating ritual that materialized. There was witty banter between his mother and the date, who was as attentive as a male peacock displaying multi-colored plumage to attract her. Nathaniel mentally counted each bite until his sentence was terminated. Leaving the piece of garlic bread, Nathaniel scooped his plate, silverware and paper towel napkin and started to leave the table.

His mother asked Nathaniel to "Thank Thomas for the garlic bread" to which Nathaniel mumbled his unenthusiastic appreciation to his contributor.

Laughter and the occasional rise and fall of conversation could still be heard despite Nathaniel's bedroom door being closed. Nathaniel's room was filled wall to wall and floor to ceiling with crowded bookshelves. His desk and two nightstands were also topped with books transforming his room into a grotto of literature. He tried to bury his attention into the passages of the library book in his hands but the tête-à-tête was the annoying equivalent of a pesky hovering summertime mosquito. He required silence when he read. Only then did the music of the words offer to him their own rampant opus. When the noise of his mother's conversation died, and the sudden revving drone of the attorney's Mercedes eventually faded into the distance, Nathaniel was able to fully enjoy the book.

As he flipped the page preparing himself for the words there was a knock on his door. Justine stood in the frame with a hand to her forehead looking at her son. From his point of view, she looked slap-happily bewildered.

"Nathaniel," Justine said to him. "Nathaniel, there's something serious that I need to speak with you about."

Justine sported this look with every man that had come to call so it meant nothing to Nathaniel as she swooned. Justine sat on the side of his bed asking him to bookmark the page.

Nathaniel respectfully did this.

"Nathaniel," Justine told him. "As you know, Thomas and I have been dating for almost five weeks. And, in those five weeks, we've grown close. So close that you might say we're virtually inseparable." She put a loving hand on Nathaniel's. "I know that you spend more time at your great aunt's farm than you do here and I know that me working double shifts hasn't helped. But I think, with Thomas in our lives, that might change . . . for the better. He has a son from his previous marriage. I think it would be nice for you to have a friend. I think . . . I want to marry Thomas. What are your thoughts?"

Nathaniel stared at his mother through his thick lenses, not phased in the least. He had seen this state and it never lasted. Playing the deferential son, Nathaniel said to his mother "Whatever makes you happy."

Justine broke out into elated tears hugging her son who cleaved the library book. Little did Nathaniel know that, by giving her his misguided blessing, the silence he relied on was about to be broken – by way of an unpleasant step-brother.

It was on the day of the wedding when the two boys met. They had tried to meet previously but Nathaniel had either been too immersed in a book to care or the other boy had been experiencing his own exploits. As Justine and Thomas said their vows, Nathaniel sat in the pew with his new family member – a nine-year-old boy named Jonas who intentionally, out of sheer boredom of the ceremony, carved his initials into the pew with a pocketknife.

The house that Nathaniel once felt comfortable to roam became a battlefield of inarguable land mines. The physical attributes of the house changed bringing forth mounds of legal office paperwork which Nathaniel dared not touch for fear of being reprimanded. The furniture was replaced. The stern-faced pictures of the Rothchild ancestry on the walls and mantel accumulated in number. The only room that felt remotely recognizable was Nathaniel's room but even then he was watched and outwardly judged by his step brother if he consulted a library book. Nathaniel succumbed to a habit of asking permission to enter rooms that Jonas occupied.

There was no escape from these irregularities. The farm house in which Nathaniel had once felt safe became part of Thomas and Jonas' monthly routine as Justine invited them to meet, and share dinner with, Nathaniel's great aunt. The humble house that had been a refuge was appraised and undermined by Jonas. The stereoscope was considered "junk," the red rocking horse was dubbed "a prissy baby's toy," and the peacock perfume bottle that Nathaniel had admired was knighted "the gayest thing" Jonas had ever seen. There was one saving grace to the farm house interior: the Weather Wizard. Jonas dismissed it at first but then found himself staring back at it as if entranced. It was that look that led Nathaniel to believe in a side to Jonas that wasn't so uncompromising.

Lines were drawn in regards to territory when they moved into a larger house that same summer. It was a one-storey house with gray siding. While family activities (such as dinner, holiday gatherings and movie nights) happened in the upstairs living room, additional den and spacious kitchen, the medium-sized basement common room strictly acted as the boys' alternate recreational area. There were two bedrooms on the main floor and two in the finished basement which was also home to a storage room that housed a separate built-in washer and dryer. The two bedrooms in the basement were more than spatially accommodating and on opposite ends with a shared bathroom. The boys settled that each room was their own restricted territory. Nathaniel was able to increase his personal library while Jonas' room was decidedly decorated in sports paraphernalia. The common room was compromisingly neutral with an oversized subwoofer surround-sound entertainment system with an assortment of game consoles. Thomas spared no expense in adhering to the boys' needs and was pleased that, for a brief time, an unspoken peace came between them.

But the treaty didn't last.

Nathaniel was sleeping soundly while clutching a copy of Oscar Wilde's *The Portrait of Dorian Gray* when Jonas opened the bedroom door. He sneered at the sight of the book in his step-brother's arms and jolted him awake.

"Nate," Jonas whispered.

Nathaniel groaned, rolling to his left side.

Jonas tried to revive Nathaniel, shaking him harder. "Nate, wake up!"

Nathaniel sat up in bed with his eyes closed. His hair was sticking up on one side. Fumbling for his glasses on the bedside he put them on and stared at Jonas accusingly. "What are you doing in my room, Jonas? We agreed."

"Forget about that and shut it!" Jonas snapped.

The bedroom door inched slightly on its own. As it did this, Nathaniel and Jonas brought their attentions to the creaking hinges. The door stopped moving, stayed for a moment and forcefully slammed shut by itself. Both boys jumped. They sat in the bed wide-eyed to see if it would do it again which it did not.

"My door did that a minute ago too," Jonas whispered to Nathaniel.

"Nu-huh," Nathaniel shook his head. "You're lying. You're playing a trick on me to get me scared."

"I swear, Nate! I was lying in bed falling asleep when I heard my own door slam. I watched as it reopened on its own and slammed again. Happened three times or I'm a monkey's uncle!" Jonas grabbed Nathaniel's arm. "Say you believe me, you snot! Say it or I'll knock you into next Tuesday!"

"I don't believe you," Nathaniel said with as much courage as he could muster.

Jonas reached to strike Nathaniel but the sound of the bedroom door opening stopped him. Both boys watched as, yet again, the door opened slowly on its own. The gaping darkness from the hallway greeted them. Nathaniel switched on the bedside light which ushered a sense of relief. But that relief was soon transformed to dreadfulness as the door slammed shut on its own. Jonas carefully started for the door.

"Jonas!" Nathaniel squealed. "Don't go over there!"

"Shut up, Nate!" Jonas ordered through clinched teeth. He reached out to the knob. As he did so, the knob turned by itself. The door opened a crack. "Unbelievable. Are you seeing this?"

The boys heard a series of overlapping whispers from three ghostly young girls chanting a lullaby. "Are you hearing this?" Jonas added.

"You probably have the stereo on a loop or something playing a scene from a scary movie," Nathaniel alleged.

Jonas grabbed Nathaniel's arm pulling him out of bed. "Come on, chicken." As Nathaniel was dragged from bed Jonas sized his step-brother's pajama wardrobe which was blue plaid with tiny lighthouses scattered about on the fabric. "Well, the good news is, Nate, whatever it is they're talking about they'll be more afraid of your pajamas then we are of them. Let's go."

The boys ventured into the basement common room. They followed the voices into the storage room where they switched on the lights. Past the washer and dryer and into the far right corner's hallway which had been used to store Christmas decorations, the boys proceeded to an eerie blue glow that came from a single door which had not been there before. The blue glow shined from underneath.

Jonas tried the knob. "It's locked."

"Jonas . . ." Nathaniel clutched him as something appeared under the door. "Jonas! Something's crawling!"

But Jonas was more interested in the dandelion keyhole insignia. As Jonas examined the keyhole, wondering about the key it required, the voices fell silent.

He realized that Nathaniel had been clutching onto him and shook his step-brother off. They watched as the sliver of blackness scurried along the door's perimeter. The object forcefully crawled itself from beneath the door to the storage room floor. Nathaniel screeched, thinking it to be a bug of some sort. Alternatively it was all the more unusual – a white flower with six distinct petals. On the petals were individual reddish-brown lines in each segment.

"You were afraid of a flower," Jonas jeered.

Nathaniel pouted.

"A flower! Oh what a riot!" Jonas belted in hysterics. "You are never . . ." he tried to say, while laughing "ever . . . going to live this down!"

"Boys!" They jumped and reeled to find an agitated Thomas in his night robe. "What are two doing up so late slamming doors and making racket?"

"We . . . we found a door," Nathaniel was the first to speak.

"Door?" Thomas asked. "What door?"

"The door right . . ." but as Jonas turned to show him they only found a concrete wall. "There was a door here! I swear dad!"

"Enough. Boys should be in bed this late at night not wandering around making commotion." Thomas led the boys from the storage room and to the rest of the basement where there were no lingering signs of slamming doors or ghostly voices.

"Dad, I swear. Nate and I both saw it. The door was locked and had a brass dandelion-shaped keyhole!"

Thomas seemed startled by this. His face became pale. With trembling hands, Thomas closed the storage room door. "There's no such thing and the next one who speaks of it is grounded," he told them while whisking them to their own bedrooms. He hurriedly disappeared upstairs.

Later that night, as the house settled into a serene calmness, Nathaniel touched the flower with his fingertips. He felt foolish for having been afraid of such a thing and was likewise curious as to what type of flower it was. Nathaniel scoured the shelves for his gardening book. It took him nearly thirty minutes to match the flower to a picture.

"Asphodel," Nathaniel sighed into the pages. "I've heard of you, but from where? Where?" And then it struck him. He opened his book on Greek mythology and inspected the index finding the passage. While the asphodel was a common garden plant in the lily family the mythology of it brought more interest. In Greek mythology, Homer had once written of a meadow of asphodel flowers which had grown specifically in the Underworld. The grayish pallor had alluded to the dead in that subterranean level. Nathaniel looked at the flower, pondering its origins. "Where did you really come from?" Nathaniel asked.

In another part of the house, Thomas lifted the lid of a jewelry case in which he kept his cufflinks. Also in the case was a key with a dandelion symbol that the Sisters had given him. He thought a loaded question to himself while turning his eyes to the bedroom window: *"What had been on the other side of that phantom door?"*

*

"The storm's ended," Nathaniel told Annette. The absent sound of falling pegs left a reassuring stillness. The sun had risen exposing the sanctuary to daylight. A blue glass vase of asphodel flowers stared at them. "I see our meteorologist has taken on the role of florist." He stood from the pew and looked at Annette.

"Surely that's not the end of the story," Annette told him.

"No, hardly the end," he responded. "But we've been cooped in the department and in this dismal arena. Let's inspect the day."

Muses stirred as he crossed to the door. As he pulled the heavy church door, he was expecting to be greeted by clean morning air awash with the recognizable scent of dew. He expected birds to be chirping happily in nearby trees. He wanted there to be exposed clear-blue skies above the parting storm clouds. But as he stood on the stone patio overlooking the gravel parking lot, he discovered that the shredded sky was colored a stale sepia. Falling colored pegs had torn holes through the tree leaves and lawn shrubbery like bite-marks caused by gluttonous caterpillars. The weed-grown lawn was overwrought with piles of colored pegs in such a way that it looked like an aggressively arranged Easter egg hunt. Laughing ravens circumnavigated the landscape's wide-ranging malaise which flickered and scratched like a ruined projector film.

"Holy Management," Annette said.

Nathaniel told her, "I've frequently thought there's nothing as inspiring than the dawn of a new day. Now I'm not so sure."

Annette spotted a large 9 x 12 inch manila envelope zipped into a large plastic freezer bag. The package had weight alluding to its possible bulky contents. With her case files protectively under her arm, she reached inside the envelope to find a compass and a graffiti-etched folded map of the area. Annette extended the map to find that a hand-drawn path had been marked in a red permanent marker. The path led to an undisclosed spot which had been circled. Beside the spot was a single, scribed number "6."

"Mr. Cauliflower . . ." Annette began.

Nathaniel consulted the map. "Six."

"Yes, six," she nodded. "Sarah Milbourne, nine. Doris the waitress, eight. Lyle Slocum, seven. I think what we're looking at is a map to wherever he claimed his sixth victim."

"Where he claimed his sixth victim?"

"Where else is he going to lead us, Mr. Cauliflower? If he wanted me to find where he's currently keeping them, he wouldn't have played these games."

"He's even provided us a compass so that we won't argue over directions. Isn't that thoughtful?" Nathaniel said in a mockingly playful tone. "Well then, what are we waiting for? Lead the way, detective."

Annette kept a fast-paced clip as they trekked the condemned scenery. There were pointy branches, uneven trails and mischievously placed jagged rocks of varying size in the dense woodland.

"So tell me, Mr. Cauliflower. What happened after you found the asphodel in the storage room?"

"Well," Nathaniel started to say, but in keeping up with her, he felt winded. He had not had this much exercise in a while and it showed. "Every night we would find ourselves in the same storage room waiting for the door to reappear so that we could investigate it more and, perhaps, get a spot of irrefutable evidence."

"Did it?"

"No, it didn't. And we often got in trouble with Thomas for staying up so late. School was about to start in a few weeks and our sleep schedules were out of whack. One night at dinner Thomas set his foot down stating that we were 'Men, by God' and we should stop with this 'haunted house ridiculousness.' Jonas insisted that the door existed and showed his father the asphodel to prove it. Thomas insisted, 'You boys need to start focusing on other things like sports or making new friends or your upcoming schoolwork. You're scaring

Justine.' Thomas didn't want to hear another word about it. Back then, I considered myself a fairly well-behaved lad so I did what was expected of me. Jonas, on the other hand, turned to me. 'Tell them, Nate!' he ordered. 'Tell them what we saw!' I simply sat there eating the broccoli on my plate, biting my tongue. That's when Jonas called me a newfound nickname 'Broccoli.'"

Annette stopped. "Broccoli." She shook her head. "I'm sorry, Mr. Cauliflower. When we met, I pressured you about your name. I didn't know."

"Don't worry." But it was obvious from Annette's concerned gaze that she did. "Honestly, Mrs. Slocum, it's nothing. Let's keep walking, yes?"

A hill of purple wildflowers with a steep downward slope led to a grassy field. Past that field was a small, rundown motel with an empty parking lot and an indecisive vacancy sign. Annette consulted the map and the compass and devised that the motel was, most likely, their destination.

"Oh no . . ." Annette quickened her pace. "Not Jonathan. Not my violinist! I remember visiting him after his inspiration, Mr. Cauliflower. I visited him at the river walk where he played his instrument for gathering audiences. I remember the benefit concert where he met his future wife! I remember watching him grow progressively older! He called me his muse! Don't tell me that Jonas stole that storyline from me!"

Moments later, and with Nathaniel a bit worse for the wear as he collapsed in a lobby chair, Annette dinged the front desk's bell. She stood at the counter nervously tapping the surface of the desk. She spied a wall calendar that read March 25th. The bell was rung again.

The manager appeared. He was in his mid-sixties. His thinning, light colored hair initially led Annette to believe he was bald. There were bags under the manager's eyes as if he hadn't slept in days.

"Sorry for your wait," yawned the manager. He had a raspy voice and a smoker's cough. "I usually work nights but today I'm working a double. Must have dozed for a spell. What can I do you for?" He was a bit stymied by Annette's wedding dress but didn't question it.

"We're looking for someone who may have stayed here," Annette told him.

"Oh?" The manager raised his eyebrows.

"It would have been a man with a violin who went by the name of Jonathan."

Upon hearing the word 'violin,' the manager's face fell. "Oh. Him. You must be Annette Redmond?"

Annette nodded.

The manager gave a deep sigh and told her, "Wait here."

With that, Annette and Nathaniel were once again left by themselves in the lobby.

"This is the place," Annette told Nathaniel. Outside the lobby window, Annette could detect the ruined, colored-peg gnarled timeline. "He didn't seem upset about the sky, did he?"

"To him it's a typical quiet day," Nathaniel explained. "When an inspiration ends, we feel the rumbles of thunder and hear the flipping of pages. The same applies to the disarray out there. It's for our eyes only."

The manager stepped into the lobby with the shattered violin in hand. "I believe this is what you're looking for? He was here for a few nights until the stranger in the storm came for him. Jonathan's visitor wore a black suit and tie and a nasty disposition. Real piece of work. Handed me an envelope." The night manager transferred the violet envelope with the number "6" written on it to Annette. "He told me not to open it or he would know. He said you'd be by in three days time asking about him," the manager turned his eyes to the calendar then back at Annette. "And he was right." He scooted the violin closer to her. "Whatever business you have with this guy, I wish you the best. He doesn't seem to be the type to cross, if you know what I mean."

"Thank you," Annette smiled, taking the envelope and violin.

As Nathaniel stood from the chair the night manager had more to say.

"One more thing. On the night that your friend was taken into the storm . . . there was someone else in the lobby that left right after him joining them in the rain."

"Someone else?"

"Yeah, a little guy. Sat right there," the night manager pointed to one of the lobby chairs; specifically the chair Nathaniel had been sitting. "I didn't get a good look at the face or any of his features. But I do remember he was wearing a black hoodie over his head. Come to think of it, I'm not even sure it was a guy. It could have been a girl – not much to go on, I know."

"Any witnesses who may have seen him?" Annette asked.

"Me and the vacancy sign, that's it. No security cameras either."

"Thank you," Annette turned to Nathaniel who blanched at this statement.

They left the motel and crossed the parking lot to the hill. Annette walked slower while attempting to open the violet envelope. "I don't like what he said," Annette told Nathaniel. "I don't like it, not one iota."

From Nathaniel's view, there hadn't been dandelions when they had walked down the slope but there were certainly dandelions at present.

It was the last week of summer for both Jonas and Nathaniel. They went to church on Wednesday nights to involve themselves in youth group activities. Jonas made acquaintances who, to Nathaniel, were unfriendly. The friends learned of Nathaniel's nickname and referred to it without abandon. Jonas was playing with these friends while throwing a football in the church's front lawn. Nathaniel heard them from afar with *Dorian Gray* in hand; its pages were open and the words exposed to the afternoon light. Nathaniel wore fitted jeans and a blue, short-sleeved buttoned shirt. His back was propped against the church's concrete sign which had been erected near the lawn's edge.

The football the boys were playing with was jettisoned through the air and struck Nathaniel in the face. Nathaniel recovered, retrieving his glasses that fell to the grass. He reached the football. With the glasses over his eyes, Nathaniel stared at the boys in the yard who were overly amused by the bookworm's plight.

"Well, Broccoli?" Jonas called to him. "What are you waiting for? Throw it!"

Nathaniel frowned. Feeling a surge of rage, he tightly gripped the football with both hands and tossed it. The ball didn't land far from him which caused the boys to convulse in laughter. Nathaniel returned to his library book. There was a crunching on the dried grass. Nathaniel peered to find Jonas with football in hand standing over him. His friends accompanied.

"You know why you couldn't throw that football, don't you Broccoli?" Jonas asked. "It's because you're always reading those stupid books. Isn't that right boys?" To which the friends agreed nodding their heads condescendingly. "There are times I wonder what kind of step-brother you'd be without those damn books. I think that maybe, just maybe, you wouldn't be so much of a momma's boy! That you'd defend yourself. That you'd be a normal kid. That maybe you'd be able to throw a football!" He grabbed *Dorian Gray* hoisting it above Nathaniel's grasp.

"Give me my book, Jonas!"

"I'll tell you what," Jonas told him. "You can have your book as soon as I give you a free lesson on how to throw a football." He handed the football to one of his friends and said to Nathaniel, "The key to it is that you've got to have a good throwing arm, like me. You take the football," Jonas demonstrated with the book "and do as I do. Watch closely, Broccoli!" He made himself into the proper stance by slightly leaning his body with the arm positioned up over his head. He then took a step backwards and brought his arm forward sending the book through the air and onto the inaccessible roof of the church. "See?" Jonas smirked while taking the football from his friend. "That's how you throw a football."

Nathaniel was not amused. Wrath caused him to explode. He repeated the motions that Jonas had taught him but, instead of throwing a football, Nathaniel threw an angry fist into Jonas' right lip. Nathaniel took off running for his life. He hid around the side of the building feeling miserable. There was nowhere for him to run or hide! He was eight! No matter where he ran, it wouldn't change the fact that he had to live with Jonas and, more importantly, live with the consequences.

An hour later, the boys sat in the family kitchen of their house explaining to their parents why Jonas' lip was bleeding. The boys were scolded by both Thomas and Justine and forced to shake hands. Jonas grabbed Nathaniel's hand and gripped it hard. Nathaniel didn't wince. He too gripped his step-brother's hand showing Jonas that he wasn't afraid.

The boys then parted to recover. Nathaniel found himself rushing through the forest behind their new house. There was a bustling creek and a discarded miniature paper sailboat by the water's edge. He held the boat close to his glass-covered eyes checking to see if it was water-tight. He placed the sailboat on the water and sighed as it drifted downstream. He wished that he were small enough to sail with it.

Nathaniel's wish was granted, though not in the approach he was expecting. A damaged encyclopedia volume with faded letters on the spine also floated downstream. He caught it and shook it dry. The leather had been ruined and the words had faded. There was no saving it from its peril. A patch of dandelions appeared. Nathaniel's eyes then settled on a circus tent on the water's surface. The front flap was opened.

To make matters worse, Jonas also found his own refuge from his father's punishment: the branches of an apple tree across town. As he sat in the branches nursing his swollen lip, he heard the subtle sound of a page turning in a book. He looked down and saw a young girl reading. It reminded him of earlier that afternoon with Nathaniel and made him furious. In taking out his leftover aggression, Jonas plucked an apple from the tree. With the same arm and force in which he had chucked *Dorian Gray*, Jonas tossed the apple at the girl and, in-so-doing, changed Young Annette's course forever.

*

As she and Nathaniel continued their trek to the church, Annette opened her case files to show him the violet envelopes she had previously collected. "I ran a fiber analysis on these violet envelopes. I was hoping for some kind of helpful watermark, brand or discarded DNA. I had the lab run a spectrometer on them. There were no traces as to where the envelopes had come from or to the identity of the manufacturer. No DNA either. But do you know what they did find? On the inside of the envelopes, near the seams, were handwritten words."

She showed Nathaniel the three violet envelopes from her dry erase board. Three words stared at him from the three seams: the words "a", "for" and "me."

Nathaniel recognized Jonas' handwriting. "You couldn't have shown these words to me before?"

Annette scowled. "Coming from the muse who kept your memoir's seventh life section secretly locked in your library book cabinet?"

"Touché."

She asked Nathaniel to hold her case files as she opened Jonathan's violet envelope. Annette found three other envelopes. They were marked with numbers "5" through "3." The evidence was spoiled as she forced the envelopes apart to reveal the additional three words. She asked for the first three envelopes and flipped through the papers to arrange the words into a complete sentence. The additional words were "works" and "dishonest" and "ally."

As she did this, Nathaniel stood like a faithful Dr. Watson to her inner Sherlock Holmes.

The papers were then stacked and utilized as a medium-sized flip-book which she showed to him. There were six words in total which read the following statement in Jonas' hand:

A dishonest ally works for me.

"Well," Nathaniel sighed as he looked to the dislodged countryside. "It's like you said earlier. I don't like it. Not one iota."

CHAPTER 18: THE REPAIRED LIBRARY BOOK AFFAIR, RETOLD FROM ANOTHER POINT OF VIEW

Jonas' correspondence to Annette also included four colored pegs which she held in the exposed palm of her right hand. The green peg corresponded to the life of the violinist. The purple peg definitively belonged to her former ex-husband. The cream-colored peg with pink polka-dots had, she assured, belonged to Doris the waitress. Annette surmised, and outwardly concluded, that the blue peg once housed the story of the unknown client Sarah Milbourne. What the envelopes lacked was a reason why Jonas had been stealing his victims but Nathaniel supposed that "not knowing" was part of his hazardous amusement.

As they traversed to the church, Nathaniel felt inside his pocket and ran his fingers along the edges of another envelope. He took out the blue envelope and handed it to Annette saying "For you."

"Another envelope?" She opened the envelope and found index cards from Management's library. Frowning, Annette said to Nathaniel "When I was a little girl, I had this mysterious friend who rescued my library books. He would sneak into my room in the middle of the night and stitch the books as if they hadn't been damaged. I pictured him to be a confident person in my peripherals who protectively observed me. When I was a Ninth Generation muse, I even met that young boy in a root cellar and inspired him to fix my library books. He believed in himself. And I never lost faith in him. Whatever happened to that boy, Mr. Cauliflower?"

"The boy that you trusted may have believed in his talents but he never believed in himself, Mrs. Slocum. I was a purely normal boy who occasionally utilized an extraordinary talent. I was there during recess in 1989 when Jonas tossed your library book, *The Hobbit*, into the busy street. I watched as you dodged cars to retrieve it. It reminded me of how I felt when Jonas tossed my copy of *Dorian Gray* onto the roof of the church two years prior. When you disappeared downstairs for dinner that night, I ascended the trellis of climbing roses outside of your childhood window. I took the copy of *The Hobbit* to the root cellar and gingerly fixed it. I returned it to your pillow without you knowing it was missing. It was the same with *Dracula* in 1991 when you were twelve. I repaired the book right then and there under the moonlight at your bedroom's desk."

Nathaniel remembered having seen young Annette as she had slept in her bed that night. He recalled the exciting gush of hormones. It had been the first time that he had seen Annette in close proximity. Though Annette had been plain looking to anyone else, Nathaniel had guessed there had been more to her. Having been in her room Nathaniel had equated this moment to opening the plain front cover of one of his library books to examine the exemplary prose.

"You didn't wake me," Annette said to him thoughtfully. "And when I did stir you were out of the house running through the woods."

"There was a brief second when I considered staying there, presenting you with the book and introducing myself."

"So why didn't you?"

"You would've woken to find a boy in your room. Whether I was your rescuer of the library books or not, I didn't want to scare you."

Nathaniel recalled having heard Annette that night. He had jumped at the rustling of her bed covers. Young Nathaniel had applied the finishing touches with trembling hands. He had then adjusted the book perfectly on her desk and climbed down the trellis. Annette had switched on the light and, from her window, searched the woods where he had hidden. He had looked at her from behind a maple tree thinking, if he kept running away like this, they would never be friends.

Nathaniel hadn't been alone in the woods. As he had occupied Annette's bedroom rescuing *Dracula*, and as he descended the trellis, Nathaniel's own blood-sucking fiend, Jonas, had stalked from far afield. Though Jonas had not known what Nathaniel had been doing in her bedroom it was enough to dangerously pique his curiosity.

Nathaniel recited this to Annette adding:

"When Jonas saw you reading the repaired copy of *The Hobbit,* he came home furious. When our family visited the library on the weekends, I noticed that he paid more attention to the books you had borrowed and returned. He inspected *The Hobbit* and *Dracula,* trying to understand how the damaged books had been repaired so perfectly and in a short amount of time. It bothered me the way that he flipped through the books and it worried me that he might find one of my stray fingerprints which would have led him to me. The core of the issue was control. In our family, he had little control over our parents' relationship and little control over me. He asserted authority over someone that he could control and, by that same token, gained control of an uncertain situation regarding your rescued library books."

"Jonas never controlled me."

"He didn't share responsibility for you burning the copy of *Les Miserables* in a bucket at your driveway? You think he egged you on because he found books to be a ridiculous waste of time? No, Mrs. Slocum. Jonas wanted you to burn that book so that he might witness its reformation! To meet the person who rescued the others!" Nathaniel shook his head. There was a hint of disdain in his voice sodden with acidic jealousy. "Then . . . then you married the car salesman who introduced you to the champagne-colored VW Beetle on that rainy summer day after graduation."

"How do you know about the VW Beetle? Were you there?"

The church, with its condemned walls, hail-beaten roof and nearly-crumbling spires reminded them of the ruins, both physical and emotional, from their past.

"Yes, Mrs. Slocum, I was sitting in the Mercedes that parked in the lot on that rainy summer day in 1999. I was looking out the tinted windows into the rain as you selected the Beetle and as Jonas swooped in to make you feel miserable." Nathaniel sighed. "In retrospect, I wonder what would have happened if I had gotten out of our car and joined you in yours; if perhaps we would have explored the world! If I had the opportunity to fix that moment, I would be sorely tempted . . ."

"But you didn't introduce yourself."

"No, I didn't. It's because of my lack of actions that an unhappy set of circumstances unfolded. Some of those circumstances dealt with Jonas discovering, and attempting to maliciously extort, my talent. And all because I climbed a familiar church rooftop on that very same night in 1999 to find my library book that Jonas had chucked there twelve years prior." He turned his eyes to the roof of the church where Jonas had thrown his copy of *Dorian Gray*. There was another memory he wanted to share in which he had sought to retrieve the abandoned book but that story was for another time. He smiled wanly at Annette. "Shall we go inside, Mrs. Slocum? I'm sure you're anxious to unmask the hooded individual that the motel manager mentioned."

Annette said with some hesitancy, ". . . Yes. Yes, I suppose I am."

*

It disappointed Nathaniel to think that, after many years and well into Jonas' afterlife, his step-brother was capable of evoking the odious monsters within those he encountered. Whether it was a disparaging remark, a mere suggestion of a debilitating memory, or being in his presence for any length, Jonas poisoned those around him. Nathaniel considered Annette and how Jonas' involvement in her life had sensitively affected her. It wasn't until they reached the church that he understood the transformation's extent.

When she and Nathaniel entered the sanctuary, they found a discarded black hoodie on one of the pews. She lifted it and shifted her eyes to the muses wondering which serpent had shed its casing. Annette's interrogation skills as Detective Redmond were chilling. She was cold, emotionless and uncaring as she met with each muse privately in a run-down Sunday school room. They sat in flimsy plastic chairs. The black hoodie was on a dusty rectangular table. She required Nathaniel to sit with her as the questions and answers were bounced between her and the suspects.

He obliged but, as Annette dug into interrogation-mode, he was aware of how the case had rotted her spirit. Annette's core, based on Nathaniel's perspective, had been robbed of optimism. Though Jonas had not personally been a part of her life as Annette Redmond, his presence as an unresolved issue injected venom that coaxed Annette into a gruesome, devilishly-wrought version of her earlier self.

She mentally mapped the interrogations so that each piece of information received led to another which aided in narrowing the facts and the list of suspects. She listened to the muses as they told their stories. Annette unsympathetically familiarized herself with the sordid details of their lives and prodded for regrets, disappointments and moments of despair that Jonas may have used to his advantage. She made notes of downtime activities, what groupings they had formed and mentally clocked the person's use of the department's popular black hoodie.

She determined that every muse had worn the associated apparel at some point during their second stay. There was only a handful of muses who had encountered Jonas which may have advanced the implications of her closest, most trusted, peers. Alliances that she had once shaped between Harriet, Fiona, and Lucas, were spectacularly set to flames during this process with Annette standing pitilessly over the smoldering cinders.

"How dare you'd insinuate that I've been working with that devil?" Harriet spat. "If you recall, Annette, I was there with you in his apartment when we stole your obituary! If I was on anyone's side it would have been yours; more specifically, Management's. Jonas is a creep. I've shared that feeling multiple times but no one listened to me." Harriet stood. "You're no better than he is, Annette! If I ever come across you or that meteorologist again, the attention I'll be giving is a fist to the face!"

When Fiona was interrogated, she took a calm breath and shook her head. In regards to Harriet's actions, Fiona said: "Harriet has a lot to learn if she is going to be Head Muse. I'm sorry that she acted in such an emotional manner. I believe she has enough passion for the job; positively channeling it will be an issue." To the accusation of being the apprentice, Fiona commented: "I'm used to witch hunts. I was indicted for witchcraft during the Salem trials. Mr. Cauliflower can attest that, in the beginning, my motives for our office's evolution were perceived as questionable." She looked at Nathaniel as she said this. "Throughout the generations, I hope I've proven my loyalty. Though a client, or a muse, may not get the happy ending they think they deserve, I try to implant a happier ending than they ever imagined for themselves." To which Fiona added "if there is one thing I'm guilty of it's believing that, despite what's happened, Mr. Rothchild has integrity."

Lucas was last in the line of interrogations. He said nothing for a moment while staring at the hoodie, absorbing the blame. "No, I'm not working with Jonas," Lucas said truthfully to both Annette and Nathaniel. "As I told Icarus, I wouldn't change anything for fear of being any different than I am now." He looked into Annette's eyes. "Whenever I would visit your cathedral office, you were always on an inspiration or inundated in that mound of paperwork from your missing person's case. I've been waiting for you to talk to me so that we could build from the foundations of our friendship. Here we are face to face for the first time – but instead of a friend," he shook his head and sighed. "There's a stranger, you know?" Noticing Annette was still stoic, Lucas asked "So we're done?" He turned his eyes to Nathaniel.

Nathaniel whispered "Yes, Mr. Richardson. We're done."

Nathaniel noticed that Lucas, upon leaving the room, had purposefully discarded Gabriel's guitar pick on the tabletop.

Annette turned to Nathaniel. "There's one individual left to question."

Nathaniel blinked. There was no one left for Annette to interrogate but the department's caretaker.

"You said so yourself, Mr. Cauliflower. You have moments in your life that you would change if given the opportunity."

"I've been nothing but honest with you, Mrs. Slocum. Any questions that you've asked of me, I've answered. Given that you know about my turbulent relationship with Jonas, I can't imagine that you would find fault with me."

"How do I know if any of what you say is true? It could be an intensely sculpted lie to throw me from your scent."

Nathaniel deflated in his chair.

Annette added: "I mean no disrespect but I have to look at this from many angles, Mr. Cauliflower. The words written in the six envelopes state . . ."

"I know what the words state, Mrs. Slocum." Nathaniel nodded. "Perhaps I should be the one interrogating you."

"Me?"

"How many people have you told about the department when you were a Ninth Generation muse?"

"How many?" Annette quickly answered "No one."

"No one?" Nathaniel pressured her. "Think about it, Mrs. Slocum. Think about your clients in your last employment term. I can think of two to whom you aired your dirty laundry."

"I may have mentioned something to Patrick - the public speaker for Lucas' retirement party."

"And . . .?"

"And to my ex-husband, Lyle . . . to Adam Mansfield . . ." Saying these names, Annette's face grew pale. "But everyone hated Jonas, Mr. Cauliflower. Everyone! No one in their right mind would work with him on something this dubious. Besides, the only people in the sanctuary were the muses. If Patrick, Lyle or Adam were in the sanctuary, I would've known."

Nathaniel gave her a fixed stare. "I want to tell you a story," Nathaniel offered. He recalled his own moment of victory over Jonas in 1999. As he began Nathaniel could mentally hear the rain in the car lot on that summer day many years ago. "When Thomas drove us to the car lot on that May afternoon I expected him to buy Jonas a fancy luxury vehicle for graduation. Though I sat in the Mercedes looking out the window, I could read the body language between Lyle and Thomas. Jonas was tormenting you over your choice in the Beetle and Thomas wanted to humble his son by buying him the very same vehicle. But, because you were instantly attached to the Beetle, Jonas accumulated a rusted, horribly outdated 1957 Chevy two-door Sedan. I never forgot that look on Jonas' face: a look of defeat. I wanted to taste that victory."

As Nathaniel said the story out loud, visions of the passing incidents danced about him like vividly colorful Cancan dresses in a bordello.

"That night, after the rain had stopped and everyone had gone to bed, I filled a dark green backpack. To camouflage myself, I wore a black long-sleeved shirt and dark jeans. There was a thin coating of mist on my glasses as I rode my bicycle through the night-shadowed streets, down alleyways and past storefronts until I reached the parking lot of our church. I propped my bicycle near the bushes and searched for the kitchen door. It was there that I said a prayer and picked one of the locks. Once inside, I closed the door and found myself in near silence. The kitchen's countertops were barely noticeable from a nearby streetlamp shining through one of the windows. I knew the church well enough to orient properly. With the aid of a flashlight from my bag, I found the flight of stairs leading to the main hallway. The church was filled with silent, invisible angels. As I snuck up the flight of stairs, my flashlight glowed on various objects: the glass windowed heavy oak doors of the fellowship hall, the vending machine in the vestibule and the banister to another flight, which I grabbed on to while climbing farther and farther up the staircase to another small landing. Another flight of stairs winded in the opposite direction.

"The church had been a fairly expansive area even in the daytime; at night it was like scaling a medieval armory! Hallways were stretched. Side tables, cushioned chairs and couches lined the walls. I passed the parlor on my left and the church offices on my right. My flashlight shined on another flight of stairs at the far end of the hallway which led me to the level with the classrooms and gymnasium." Nathaniel crossed to one of the classroom windows while remembering his path. "On that night, I exited this exact classroom's window." Nathaniel could see the roof. It reminded him of that night and how he had opened the window and gained access to the roof. "The shingles were slick but I didn't care. I had a whiff of triumph in my nostrils that I couldn't shake. I looked to the same yard in which I had stood with Jonas twelve years prior when he had thrown my library book. I knew I was in the right place. Then," Nathaniel told Annette "after a few minutes of searching with my flashlight . . . and with the help of a newly approaching thunderstorm's lightning . . ."

*

In his mind's eye, lightning had revealed a portion of the roof that had recently been cloaked in shadows. With his heart racing, teenage Nathaniel crossed the roof with confident, sure footing and reached the niche. There were countless crinkled leaves from past autumns that were choked into the neglected alcove. Though he wasn't completely sure that *Dorian Gray* had been hidden there, he sifted through the leaves and trusted the instinctive tug on his heart strings. As he did so, rain fell and thunder crashed. Nathaniel's fingers touched a familiar leather spine. Accented by a bolt of nearby lightning, he held the unbearably spoiled copy of *Dorian Gray*.

Weather hadn't been kind to the book after twelve years. The pages had crinkled and bent in on themselves. The inked letters of the prose had been distorted. The blemished cover was unrecognizable. But the pocket in the back of the book was still there with the library's ledger that held his first and last name in cursive.

As Nathaniel stood on the rooftop with *Dorian Gray* in 1999, Jonas had awoken with a start in his own bedroom. Lightning flashed through his window onto his face. Upon seeing the lightning, Jonas abandoned his covers. Barefoot, he exited his bedroom and approached the downstairs common room from which there was access to the backyard. Jonas unlatched the lock on the backyard door and stepped out to investigate the oncoming storm. As he opened the door, a strong gust tickled the fabric of his white t-shirt and dark blue boxer shorts. Thunderheads churned and released electric feelers into the neighborhood's skyline.

Jonas' eyes settled on a chain dangling from a wind-chime that was forced into a clamor. The chain dangled low enough so that Jonas, who had grown considerably taller in the passing years, could easily grasp it. As Jonas held the chain, another flash of lightning brought illumination to the object attached to it: a key with the dandelion insignia. Though he wasn't sure where it had come from, Jonas knew to which lock it belonged.

Meanwhile, on the church's roof, Nathaniel crossed the roof's ridge. There was an explosion of lightning which brought with it manifestation of the Dandelion Sisters' circus tent. Nathaniel, upon seeing the tent again, stopped. The flap didn't open, nor were there dandelions at his feet. The only direction to safety was on the other side of the tent. Despite that, he felt honorable in his mission to successfully retrieve the library book. He had plans to take it home, repair it, and savor that victory over his step-brother even if it killed him. He thought he would be happy by repairing those library books. He felt it would make him better than Jonas. More evolved. More civilized. However, he didn't realize at what expenditure.

In his retelling, teenage Nathaniel circled around the tent he spied the open window to the classroom. But his foot slid on the shingles. Nathaniel stumbled from the rooftop and frantically grasped for the fabric of the circus tent for support. But it was too late. Clawing at the remaining shingles, Nathaniel fell into midair. As he dropped, Nathaniel noticed another face staring at him from the rooftop – a man in a three-piece suit, wolf-life eyes, brandishing a cane with a small pewter brain on its tip.

Nathaniel collided to the ground, landing into a thick ooze-like puddle of mud. Though the mud was pliant it wasn't cushiony. A jagged pain shot from his right leg. Nathaniel saw the exposed bone from his leg which led him to surmise that he'd broken it during the fall. White pain torn through his entire body as he shouted and cried. As the storm bellowed, and as the pain worsened with the slightest movement, Nathaniel noticed that the circus tent, and the mysterious man with the wolf-life eyes, had disappeared from the roof. The echo of his folly pulsated throughout. With each wave of pain, new memories of his past lives rushed to him like an invasion of enraged blood cells charging onto the battlefield of his torn skin and exposed fractured femur.

*

"I received three 'gifts' that night," Nathaniel told Annette. "The library book, a broken femur . . . and a head full of seven memories and lifetimes. Management had humbled me, you see. I found myself in a cast lying stationary in my bed with my foot elevated. Thomas and my mom wanted to know what I had been doing on the rooftop but I couldn't bring myself to tell them. The circumstances in that house changed, you see. I didn't see myself as a boy anymore. I knew who I was, and who I had been in the past six lives. Something else changed. Jonas stood at my bedside. He took a red sharpie marker and was the first to sign my cast. He didn't ask me why I was on the rooftop. I had a feeling he already knew. This gave him power over my imprudent measures."

He said to Annette, "I say this to hopefully humble you before you too are addicted. You have to let go of Jonas at some point, Mrs. Slocum. This isn't the life that Management meant for you. You were meant to be happy – happier than anyone I've ever come across. Can you honestly say that you're happy?"

"Yes . . ." Annette said with diffidence. Then she sighed, letting out a single word that countered it: ". . . No." She said earnestly. "I wanted to be a modest pie maker. I wanted to live each day to its fullest and to appreciate each moment that Management had given me. I don't know where it went wrong. Every day I look in a mirror and see a cynical reflection." She shook her head and added "I wish I could forget, Mr. Cauliflower. But I can't. I won't. At least not until I complete this case."

Nathaniel left Annette to her thoughts, escaping into the hallway. He closed the door and propped himself against the wall taking a few soothing breaths. He heard two male voices from around a far left corner.

Lucas and Icarus were in another room discussing the interrogation.

"I kept something from detective Redmond that I want to tell you, if you'll listen," Icarus told Lucas. "When I was brought through the double doors in the ramshackle Underworld amusement park, I was introduced to a young woman named Persephone, who had been a flower in a garden of pesky overgrown, thorn-infested weeds. She was owned by another creature – the chilling God of the Underworld. He took the form of a young boy with brass kaleidoscopes for eyes. Stupid me, I fell for Persephone's advances and the boy noticed how much she, in turn, lusted after me. As punishment, he gave me a task: he stated I would be brought back to life and, if I collected a single feather from every species of bird (living and dead) and if I was able to construct a second pair of wings with those feathers in three days, he would deliver me directly to Heaven and into the arms of an awaiting Persephone. If I failed, he promised that I would be doomed to spend the rest of eternity in an even darker, more foreboding place of anguish."

Nathaniel approached, keeping out of sight.

Lucas asked "And what happened?"

"I leapt at the opportunity, of course. I should've seen through his sincere façade to the true wretched trickery underneath. There's more to this story but I'm worried that if I tell you, you won't love me. The reason I'm explaining this to you, Lucas, is because I've been affiliated with evil. No matter how long I exist, I can't detach. Detective Redmond is looking for an affiliated monster. To receive penitence for my diabolical behavior, I have to confess."

"Confess to a crime that you didn't commit?"

"It's because of my past that we're here in this church waiting for more of the colored pegs to fall."

Nathaniel pressed against the door frame listening intently.

"Please tell me you're not working for Jonas," Lucas asked. "Please . . . please tell me."

"I can't promise anything, Lucas."

"What are you saying?" Lucas asked.

"You deserve better." The sound of a chair scraping against the floor signaled Icarus' departure.

"Icarus . . ." Lucas said. "Icarus, wait!"

But Icarus was already out the door leaving Lucas alone in the room. He nodded to Nathaniel as he walked by.

Nathaniel stood in the doorway of the Sunday school room looking down at Lucas who sat with his face buried in his hands. He silently approached the table and sat the guitar pick in front of Lucas who was not aware that he had company.

*

Annette had wandered from the interrogation room to a lounge where muted sunlight from an open window struck the yellow-colored walls and peach-colored carpet. A slight breeze brushed the curtains. A sad-looking Bradford pear tree could be seen outside. Much had changed since she had been in this room last. It had been in this lounge, and in this same wedding dress, that Annette had waited for her wedding. It had also been the same room where Fiona had entered and handed Annette an invitation back to the department as one of the Nine Greatest Muses.

Annette stood at a tarnished wardrobe mirror where she studied her current reflection. Her wedding dress in the limited light seemed to lose a bit of its magic. The hoodie was in her hands which she clutched to her chest. She reached into the pockets in hopes of finding a clue to the culprit's identity. There were three trinkets: a small cube of blue billiard chalk and two wedding rings that she didn't recognize from someone else's wedding. She looked up and noticed Adam standing behind her smiling in the frame of the mirror. Excited to be in his arms, she turned to find that she was the only one in the room and that Adam must have been a fabricated trick of her imagination.

*

Icarus found himself in the same classroom in which Annette had earlier interrogated. He was saddened that it was empty and hinted to a missed opportunity to plead guilty. He studied the faded children's storybooks. The blackboard in the room had begun to crack. Cobwebs hung from the unkempt ceiling. Feeling dejected, he sat in one of the seats. He contemplated his misadventures in the Underworld and how they had blackened his soul. He thought of Lucas and his love for him. He thought of Persephone and his love for her. Icarus wished that he didn't have a heart and that he was incapable of loving.

Icarus caught sight of a single white flower. He picked it up and studied the petals of the asphodel. Seeing this flower reminded him of Persephone.

He was too distracted by the flower's petals to notice that he was no longer alone. The apprentice's foreboding figure crept behind him and raised his arm with a candlestick from the sanctuary's altar.

He dealt a blow to Icarus' head disuniting his victim's vision and consciousness.

*

On the afternoon where Jonas was writing on Nathaniel's cast Jonas's eyes locked onto the retrieved copy of *Dorian Gray*. But Jonas didn't said anything to Nathaniel about the book. Jonas' personal threat was presented in the message he had written on Nathaniel's cast. When Jonas capped the red Sharpie marker and left the room Nathaniel reviewed the message. It stated the name of his painter who had murdered him back in 1808 and also in 1924. By the time Nathaniel looked up from the cast the insidious reincarnation of his painter had closed the door sealing Nathaniel into his book-riddled cell to recuperate in distressing immobility.

CHAPTER 19: SISYPHUS' SURVEILLANCE

The one-storey house with grey siding known as 252 Sisyphus Hill was appropriately named for the plodding gradient on which the dwelling, and the surrounding neighborhood, rested. Though the yard's patterned shrubbery had been upgraded throughout the shifting decades the house's exterior, with its single car garage and concrete driveway, had remained firm in the testament of its own structural history.

The residence had seen numerous visitors since its completion in the 1950's. It was first home to a custom door maker who, for twenty years, prided himself on his exquisite work on various richly-contrived ingresses. That is until one late evening, while working in his basement workshop, his eyes settled upon a singular door that had not previously been there. It was vertically propped atop a stack of other unhinged doors staring at him with conviction. He inspected it thoroughly wondering by whose mind the design had derived. The door was no different than any other door except for an inauspicious bronze dandelion keyhole. What made this keyhole so anomalous was a blue light shining from the other side which wouldn't have been so baffling if the door was attached to the wall. The detached door was standing upright atop other doors causing him to question his sanity. The door maker had lost his son years ago and, on seeing this door with its keyhole, he wondered if it was a doorway to the afterlife. He wondered if, by opening the door, they may be reunited. In an irritating rage, the door maker rattled the knob. He clawed at the keyhole with his tools and, eventually, his own fingertips until they bled. The door maker could hear his son's voice on the other side calling to him which raised his urgent efforts. When he took an axe to the wood of the door, the blade barely nicked the surface. The door maker eventually doused the door in gasoline and set it on fire. He laughed senselessly as the flames licked the lustrous wood. The flames stretched to the other doors in his workshop bringing the room to a radiating blaze. While the extra doors rotted, the door with the keyhole remained intact. As he sat on the floor collapsing into a state of inconsolable grief over his son's death and the door's reminder of it, the flames consumed the room around him.

    In his last few moments the door opened of its own volition. The blue light spread across his figure mixing with the orange, red and singing yellowed flames. In seeing the light, the door maker understood its mystery. There was a spared shard of wood from the wreckage of another door which he held in his burned hands. He extracted a pen from his pocket and scribbled a simple message onto the contours of the wood detailing the door's meaning. The door maker found his metal toolbox. He secured the piece of wood within and fastened the lock. As he held the toolbox an overflow of white asphodel petals respectfully ushered him through the door. The door closed again.

    Intermittent renovators were contracted to gut the ashen remains. They finished the basement, replaced damaged beams and installed new insulation and carpeting so that it covered any evidence of the door maker's demise. But even though the checkered past was enclosed, there was still the vague disappearance of the residence's tenant. Neighbors on the street believed the house to be polluted by its ambiguity.

An unsuspecting, family moved into the house in 1987: a prosecuting attorney named Thomas, his second wife Justine, and their two sons, Jonas and Nathaniel. Throughout their adolescent years, the house was there to shelter them. It watched as the boys grew harshly into young adults. It was intrigued as they developed their own separate hobbies of destroying, and repairing, library books. It cradled Nathaniel through weeks of recovery in which his broken femur slowly healed. From the house's perspective, Nathaniel often sat staring at the cast praying that he could heal his leg the same way that he was able to mend Annette's books. Despite Nathaniel's prayers, his leg healed in its own expansive time.

When Nathaniel was able to walk with the aid of crutches he fled to the root cellar of his great aunt's farm where he repaired the copy of *Dorian Gray*. Once the pages were reverted to a spotless state, Nathaniel found the stamina to repair another book that had been in worse condition – the burnt ashes that had once been *Les Misérables*. Between the months of May and November of 1999, Nathaniel worked indefatigably to repair her library book. In that time, his leg also healed giving more satisfaction.

Alas, Nathaniel wasn't lucky enough to hand the book to her. The hapless hero discovered that she had married Lyle. Luck was not on Nathaniel's side even after as Jonas exploited his step-brother's talent. Jonas intentionally damaged *Dorian Gray* over and over. He ruined it with grease stains, spilt wine, shears, wet cement, sharp tips of sewing needles, a paper shredder and lawn mower. Each time Nathaniel, who by then developed an intense obsessive compulsive disorder, repaired the library book without giving Jonas the benefit of showing him how his work was administered.

The boys drifted apart. Nathaniel received his education in Library Sciences at the local community college and lived in his childhood home during the first and second year. Jonas moved to another college out of state where he earned his own degree in Earth

Sciences. Though the boys rarely met in the two years that passed, they encountered one another during school holidays.

One spring break lead Jonas back to Sisyphus Hill. It was during this visit that Jonas rediscovered and held the copy of *Dorian Gray* that he had left in his room.

"Show me how you repaired it," Jonas ordered Nathaniel.

"Going on about that, are you?" Nathaniel sighed, consulting a textbook while staying ahead of the class work. "I'll show you if you bring Annette here."

"Come with me and we can show her together!" Jonas ordered.

"I'm not going back to the Slocum house," Nathaniel told him.

Jonas sneered, reaching for Nathaniel's textbook. Nathaniel shot him a look. Both knew that, no matter what Jonas intended to do with any book his actions would be thwarted by Nathaniel's ability to repair it. Nathaniel tried to be humble about his gift, but it were these moments that he relished the idea of his power. In attempt to gain control, Jonas visited Annette's residence in a last exertion to discover Nathaniel's secret, but was discarded by Lyle. Jonas knew upon returning to his childhood home empty-handed, and having heard Nathaniel say in a condescending tone "What, couldn't get her to follow you?" that his tactics for being in command needed to change.

For the remainder of the spring semester, Jonas was granted a medium that he, to a great extent, required. She was a noticeably beautiful young woman with luxurious brown hair and bright blue eyes. Jonas licked his lips and felt his pulse quicken. He approached her and smiled warmly. The woman, who looked no older than twenty, also smiled. It appeared that they had met before, with the look of recognition that had spread across their faces.

"Hello," he told her. "My name's Jonas."

"Hello," she told him. "My name's Roberta."

Her face was almost uncanny to that of Evangeline's back in 1808 and Jonas was instantly convinced it was her. He let out a genuine light-hearted laugh, keeping his devious agenda to himself. Roberta genuinely laughed in kind. It was on that day that he began to court the young woman believing her to be the reincarnation of Nathaniel's love. They formed a relationship and he proposed to her several months later. He wasn't sure if he loved her or not but the point was that Jonas had successfully stolen someone from Nathaniel's story. He thusly regaining the sense of control over his rival.

Jonas and Roberta were married in the backyard of Sisyphus Hill that summer. As Nathaniel looked at his step-brother's wife, it had been clear that he too, understood what Jonas had noticed. Nathaniel also believed her to be the reincarnation of Evangeline. As Roberta passed by Nathaniel along the aisle, they stared at one another for several seconds. There was a sudden look of recognition in her eyes which they both couldn't ignore. By then it was too late. Nathaniel turned his eyes to the ground and Roberta shifted her eyes to Jonas, realizing her inaccuracy.

The house, in witnessing this, brought a shadow over the congregation hinting to its surveillant nature.

Nathaniel moved out of the house shortly thereafter into his own apartment and dismissed the house and its memories. He visited it on remote holidays. It was on those visits that Jonas brought his two children: Ajax and Josiah. They were good kids and affectionate towards their uncle Nathaniel who had impersonally embraced them. On family visits Roberta stared at Nathaniel and initiated occasional conversation. But Nathaniel had grown cold, shying from her contact, physical or spoken.

As Nathaniel's nephews played in the backyard one spring afternoon, Jonas stood beside his step-brother. Jonas cracked a beer while stating casually to Nathaniel: "Kinda makes you wish you would've shown me how you repaired *Dorian Gray*, doesn't it, Broccoli?"

In the following months, Nathaniel's mother developed a malignant cancer and passed leaving Thomas to live in the empty house by himself. As he had never maintained meaningful relationships with either of his children, Jonas and Nathaniel hardly visited. Eventually, Thomas too passed and willed the estate to Jonas who, with his wife and two children, took residence. The "love" that Jonas and Roberta shared vanished. With the victory over Nathaniel having lost its allure, Jonas felt less compelled to make love to his wife and, therefore, busied himself with his work as the local meteorologist. His attention drifted to the days of his childhood with the unanswered questions regarding the repaired library books. He often talked about those years to Roberta and regularly referred to Annette and how he had tried to fix her. Roberta felt that she was living with another woman. Hearing Annette's name brought her blood to boil.

The house no longer cared about Jonas or Roberta. It focused on the children in whom the history of the house later flourished.

Josiah became the house's owner where he raised his own family. Josiah developed into a handsome man with short cropped hair and a fit body. His physique was evident during the night when he held his baby boy while soothingly rubbing the child's back in effort to coax the toddler to sleep. Josiah had a tattoo on his forearm, a series of stars, which implied his occupation as an astronomer. His young son, Phillip, traced them with his small fingers. The house watched respectfully as Josiah put his son to bed and switched on the mobile of spinning planets.

The house watched as during the Christmas holidays his brother Ajax, who had also developed in the same handsome fashion, would bring over his own family: his wife and newborn son Louis. The house was there as witness when Louis received his precursory Christmas ornament.

Without a doubt, the house had seen a myriad of visitors through the years. At length, the house received visitors even into its present day.

Jonas, playing the role of a "muse-gone-bad," stood at the study's fireplace staring at the Weather Wizard. The witch reigned supreme.

"Are you alright?" his apprentice asked. The hoodie was missing but his face was still obscured in the room's shadows.

"What's it to you?" Jonas scowled.

"I have the muse you were asking for," the apprentice offered. "He's restrained in the basement storage room, per your request." To which his cohort added "What you're doing to these people . . . it's cruel. You know that, don't you?"

Jonas nodded. On the desk was a toolbox which he opened. Under the light of the desk's lamp, Jonas took out a piece of old wood. He exited the study and passed the rooms of his victims. Each room was occupied by the clients he had stolen and who were currently tied to their own miseries. They were the least of his concern. Jonas stepped downstairs and opened the storage room. He flipped the lightswitch to reveal a squirming Icarus who had been bound to a chair and gagged. There was a bloody wound on Icarus' head.

"Muse," Jonas whispered. "I've brought you here for information. When I was a boy, I found a door in this storage room a few steps from where you're sitting. There was a dandelion insignia on this door which was unlocked by a particular key . . ." Jonas held the key to Icarus' eyes. ". . . Which I found hanging from a wind chime in my backyard. When I inserted it into the lock I opened the door. I expected to find the source of a mysterious blue light. Instead, I found a tiny room with a single wooden lectern. On that lectern was a fastened toolbox which I opened. And found this." Jonas held the piece of wood to Icarus' face. "See what it says? Can you read it? It says 'The answer to this door exists with Icarus.' You see it, don't you?"

Jonas tossed the wood aside. He removed the gag so that Icarus could answer. "Level with me, Muse. Tell me what you know about this door and about the asphodel flowers."

Icarus growled the following words: "If you think you're getting anything out of me about that door, you're an idiot."

Jonas grabbed Icarus' neck choking him. Icarus sputtered, kicking his legs.

"See here, you insipid adolescent. You will tell me about this door! It's because of that door that I remembered being who I was in a past life and it's the door that will help me understand for what purpose!" Jonas released Icarus but stayed close. "Tell me about the door or I'll go after your precious boyfriend Lucas. I'll bring him here and have him suffer in your place!"

"I'll tell you what you want to know," Icarus hacked.

On that night, both Jonas and 252 Sisyphus Hill leaned in close to hear the stories Icarus had to tell which exposed how the door had come to the door maker and what it meant to the house's history. The house listened as its moral foundational character in relation to the Dandelion Sisters, the Man with the Three Piece Suit, along with the unexplained Boy with the Kaleidoscope Eyes, was recanted; this information was in conjunction with Icarus' timeless epic story from Greek mythology and how he had been shockingly integrated. It was a baffling origin story that had spanned for centuries prior, and would continue to spread even through the unremitting lives of Jonas' grandchildren.

Icarus said these words to protect Lucas but also knew that, by telling the truth to Jonas, it would make Icarus more of the person that he personally despised.

Meanwhile, the apprentice walked the halls of the house checking in on the sufferers. He looked toward the closed attic door.

He reached and pulled on the string. He brought the wobbly stairs to the ground. While climbing, he considered the story of Sisyphus from mythology – an ancient king who had been punished by the earliest Gods due to his deceitfulness. The chastisement in the afterlife had been an eternity of rolling a gigantic boulder up a steep hill only to watch it roll in reverse. The act of repeating the same action had been the king's damnation through time immemorial. The apprentice considered its significance to the street name in which this house had been erected.

The attic was awash with yellow light as he clicked the string. In front of him was Annette's attempt at delivering a catalyst to Phillip: the displayed star-charts, the propped astronomy books, the dangling mobile and the message written in the glow-in-the-dark stars urging her client not to forget his past. The apprentice studied her work. He shook his head at her guile. He knew that he was trapped in this house with an enemy he never should have made alliances with, but it gave him a sense of hope in knowing that the muses were at work to make things right.

He stood at the attic's window and stared at the clamoring thunderstorm. Streetlamps shone like beacons against the murky darkness reminding him of a quote that he had once read by Tennessee Williams: "We all live in a house on fire, no fire department to call; no way out, just the upstairs window to look out of while the fire burns the house down with us trapped, locked in it."

There was no leaving this house, it seemed. Jonas had kept him on such a tight leash that even the smallest inkling of insubordination brought wrath. The apprentice left the display as he had found it and turned out the light. He descended the stairs.

The glow-in-the-dark stars picked up on the flashes of lightning that ignited from the small rectangular window which gave the hopeful insinuation of resounding authority.

CHAPTER 20: MADEMOISELLE EVANGELINE REMEMBERS

Light extended through the kitchen bringing the dusty countertops into view. It had been years since Nathaniel had set foot in this space and the memories of that distant night signaled his synapses. As he trailed his fingers over the countertops leaving streaks within the dust Nathaniel compared how he had seen the church kitchen back in 1999, before rescuing *Dorian Gray,* to how he saw it now. Seeing the kitchen in the present was like surveying cryptic cave paintings during excavations of uncharted subterranean cavities. There had been church dinners, chili cook-offs and bake drives in this kitchen which were removed from the deprived skeletal cookhouse.

A blue envelope awaited him by the stove. Nathaniel brushed his glasses to the bridge of his nose and lifted the envelope with both hands. Management, catering to the common starvation, had graciously supplied the ingredients to the muses' upcoming meal. Management also supplied cleaning products which humored Nathaniel's need for sanitation during preparation. Nathaniel set to work cleaning the kitchen counters. He scrubbed the sinks, de-clogged the drains, polished the excess metal countertops, made the glass windows spotless of grime, mopped the floors, changed out the light bulbs and even scraped the minutest of particles from the tiniest nooks and crannies. When he was satisfied that the church's kitchen was suitable for his chef work, Nathaniel consulted the ingredients.

Management had placed the fixings for Puttanesca – a pasta dish including garlic cloves, ripe tomatoes, pickled capers, Greek olives, red pepper flakes, tomato paste, freshly-washed anchovy filets, copious amounts of olive oil and several boxes of spaghetti noodles. There were also loaves of crunchy Ciabatta bread. Copper cookware had been supplied to the mix alongside a series of cooking utensils. Nathaniel possessed the elements to succeed in his culinary endeavors. He took full advantage by filling one of the pots with water and turning on the stove's heat.

"You're cooking?" came a voice behind him. Nathaniel looked over his shoulder to find Annette who had snuck into the kitchen with inaudible footsteps.

He turned his eyes to the boiling water and said nonchalantly: "Muses have to eat, Mrs. Slocum."

Annette came behind him and peered into the pot.

Nathaniel quickly repositioned himself between her and the view.

Annette didn't care. She propped herself against the counter facing him and touching two garlic cloves with unwashed hands.

Nathaniel looked over the frame of his glasses to the garlic cloves that Annette held. In a non-verbal command to surrender the cloves, he held out an open palm.

She placed the cloves into his hand and stood attentively beside him. "What are we making?"

"Puttanesca," Nathaniel said dryly, placing the cloves on the counter.

"Gesundheit," Annette said quickly.

"No," Nathaniel shook his head. "Not a sneeze, Mrs. Slocum. A spaghetti. Spaghetti ala Puttanesca. Its exact origins are unknown but there are those who believe that it was created by an unnamed shop owner who didn't have enough ingredients to make a dish for his hungry patrons. He threw various odd food elements together from his kitchen and thusly created, by sheer happenstance, a legendary, tangy sauce. And then there's the association of it being linked with female prostitutes in the sixteenth century. The word 'Puttana' in Italian translates to 'whore.' The recipe of the pasta dish was considered simple and quick to make between their risqué clientele's visits. It was a pasta dish that essentially could have anything put into it furthering the connotation of it being associated with the ladies of the evening."

A brief silence came over him as Nathaniel stared into the pot of water. It reminding him of the puddles that had accumulated on the day that Jonas' wife had come to Nathaniel during an afternoon rainstorm.

"You think of Evangeline a lot, don't you?" Annette wanted to know.

"She crosses my mind more than I'd like," Nathaniel reached for the ingredients. "She's everywhere I go and in everything I do, whether I want her to be or not." He sighed, taking a garlic clove and crushing it with the flat edge of a wide knife. "But it's my burden to bear."

As Nathaniel removed the skin of the garlic and grounded salt onto the cutting board to soak up the garlic juices, Annette asked "Whatever became of Evangeline, Mr. Cauliflower?"

While roughly chopping the garlic, Nathaniel began the account of Evangeline's occurrences. He told Annette, from his perspective, how Jonas had found the reincarnation of Evangeline during college.

*

Evangeline had taken the guise of a young woman named Roberta who looked, and sounded, almost identical to how Evangeline had appeared in 1808. Though Nathaniel couldn't understand how Evangeline had fallen in love with the reincarnation of the murderous painter, he ascertained that Evangeline alleged Jonas to have been the reincarnation of Nathaniel. The disheartening disillusionment was realized as she saw Nathaniel in the crowd on her wedding day. It further broke Nathaniel's heart as Evangeline birthed two children with Jonas.

Due to these circumstances, Nathaniel took a secluded position at the state archives in the preservation department during the week and worked part-time at the circulation desk of his local library on the weekends. His life was enveloped by books and articles which provided him a faithful substitute to Jonas' deplorable romantic relationship. Nathaniel tried, and failed, to think less of her every day. Though he shied from his unreturned thoughts for her, Jonas' wife found her way back to Nathaniel.

She came to his apartment unannounced one afternoon in 2009, while Nathaniel was thumbing through an anthology of short stories and making a lunch of spiced tofu, cooked Brussel sprouts and steamed butternut squash. She carried a checkered-cloth draped wicker basket of banana nut muffins which, she assured him, was a gesture of peace. He accepted her muffins and opened the front door. They sat with the muffins at his kitchen table for several moments unsure what to say. Conditions had changed drastically since the mailbox on her last inspiration. He didn't announce this, of course, as he was a gentleman and didn't want to upset her. She seemed upset enough as it was and tearfully aired her personal business. According to her, Jonas was emotionally distant and, because of that, Jonas had not touched her in over a year. She was starved for affection and needed to be touched. She needed to be held. Nathaniel politely inquired why she didn't seek the attention from her two sons, Ajax and Josiah. She diverted from his question by telling Nathaniel that she had habitually thought about the night that they had made love in 1808. She anxiously yearned to revisit it.

"You shouldn't be saying these things to me." Nathaniel pushed the untouched basket of muffins back to her. "You're married and I'm not a home-wrecker." He started for the kitchen door to show her out. She carefully touched his hand. To Nathaniel, it felt as though a shot of electricity had passed from her fingertips.

"Please, Monsieur Cauliflower," she whispered.

He closed his eyes and sighed longingly. "Why are you doing this to me, Mademoiselle?" He asked her.

She crossed in front of him.

She unbuttoned his white cotton shirt one button at a time and opened it to reveal his chest. She hesitantly traced the outline of his chest with her eager fingertips. He shuddered at her touch and was angry at himself for feeling it. But then he gave in. He wrapped his arms around her middle and drew her to him. The lavender perfume she wore was the same that she had worn in 1808. Her hair swayed and tumbled the same way it had back in Paris on that fateful night. She fumbled for his belt buckle as he lost control and tore at her blouse. He spun and laid her on the kitchen table where they both shook off the rest of their clothing. As they made love, the basket of muffins spilled to the linoleum floor.

*

As Nathaniel was telling Annette this information, he kept his hands busy with the rest of the sauce. He added in the capers and anchovies, bringing it to simmer. He unsealed the boxes of pasta, emptying them into the boiling water.

*

After exhausting themselves from their lovemaking, together she and Nathaniel lay naked and motionless in bed. He felt the warmth of her sinewy skin. He relished in the idea of having Evangeline in his arms again and, though he knew it wouldn't last, he soaked in this moment. It had nothing to do with a victory over Jonas – no. It was more the idea that Evangeline loved him. It was the satisfaction in knowing that all of his pining and searching for her over the course of seven lifetimes had been for not.

And then she opened her mouth to speak: "You must have loved that Evangeline woman very much."

Nathaniel tilted his head to look at her, confused. Roberta looked slightly different. Roberta told him that Jonas had talked about Nathaniel's unrequited love for Evangeline and Jonas had further explained to his wife that she had looked like her. Roberta was not Evangeline, she thoroughly explained. She had gathered as much information as she could from her husband to abuse Nathaniel's need to be with Evangeline.

She looked at him and said, "When I saw you on the day of the wedding, you were attractive and I knew that I had to have you at any cost. So when Jonas grew distant, and I grew more desperate for attention, I played the role of Evangeline. Don't you think I played it well, Nate?"

He jumped out of bed and reached for his boxer shorts, piecing himself together. He stared at her, unsure of how to feel. Roberta ruffled the covers and nakedly approached him.

"Nothing has to change, Nate. You and I can still be lovers. I need someone with your stamina and zeal. You need someone who looks like Evangeline to love and worship. It's a win-win situation." She reached out to touch him but Nathaniel withdrew.

"Get out of my house," Nathaniel whispered. "Please leave."

Roberta's stance of power deflated and she rolled her eyes. As Roberta dressed and left the house with her basket of uneaten muffins she looked at Nathaniel and said "You're never going to find the real Evangeline, Nate. You know that, don't you?"

*

With the sauce simmering in its own pan and the pasta boiling, Nathaniel paused for effect. He stirred the sauce and dipped a spoon into the contents bringing a taste to Annette's lips with his hand underneath.

Annette tasted the sauce and moaned slightly at its deliciousness.

"What does it need?" he asked. "More crushed red pepper flakes?"

Annette shook her head. "It's perfect."

Nathaniel nodded and washed the spoon under the faucet from one of the nearby sinks.

Annette said to Nathaniel, "You know what Roberta told you wasn't true?" She looked into Nathaniel's eyes. "You'll find Evangeline, Mr. Cauliflower."

"Oh," he sighed. "I know. Believe me, I know." Nathaniel placed the lid on the sauce to let it simmer a little longer. "After that day, I found myself at the library thinking about Evangeline. Though I worked with books and was acquainted with the library's collection, there was one book that hadn't yet been presented . . . until one afternoon. As I was shelving books in the fiction section under the 'Cs' I touched a leather-bound book in circulation. It was an aged copy of Geoffrey Chaucer's *Canterbury Tales* with its damaged spine facing me. I pulled it from the shelf and held it in my hands. As I did, I was instantly reminded of being the Russian immigrant Yuri Abramovich in the 1920s. I recalled how, on that fateful night, when Evangeline had warned me not to seek out the painter, she also told me that she read Chaucer every fall in remembrance of our love affair in Paris. I flipped through the pages. It had the same weight, look and feel from when I had seen it in my second life. Evangeline had bent the corners of several pages where she stopped reading for the night. It was as if she was a phantom reader right along with me leaving traces of her own reading habits. I didn't check the log. I wanted to savor this moment and treasure the idea that perhaps this book had been handled by Evangeline's reincarnation. I wanted to know what she had read during each autumn as she remembered our love affair. I read the stories and absorbed the characters, the themes and the plots, connecting to the past in the only tangible way I could. Turning the pages, I felt my hopes rise. Each time I found a bent upper corner of the page, I envisioned Evangeline and how she would have closed the book while retiring for the evening in the past. We were on a journey together reading the same book in two separate timelines. The feeling indescribable, Mrs. Slocum! Can you imagine?"

"I suppose I can . . ." Annette said breathlessly.

"When I read the last sentence I closed the back cover and slept with it at my side. The following day I went to work at the library and took the book with me. I researched the call number and checked the log for who had borrowed the book. Evangeline had read it every fall when she had been alive. I figured that, if her reincarnation had been out there, perhaps that person unknowingly borrowed it. My hunch was verified."

He looked seriously at Annette. "There was one other person who touched that book in all the years that the library had kept it in the collection."

Annette spun with her back facing Nathaniel, unable to breathe. "Stop it," she gasped. "Please stop."

"You know who this other person is, don't you?" Nathaniel asked.

With her back still to him, Annette stammered. "Please, Mr. Cauliflower, I don't want to hear!"

313

"I found that it was checked out, every fall, by a housewife to a new-and-used car salesman. It was checked out . . . by you – Annette Slocum."

"That's a coincidence!" Annette told him, gripping onto the countertop. "Anyone could have picked up that book during the fall and read it!"

He circled around to face her but Annette spun facing the opposite direction. "Why did you check that book out every fall, Mrs. Slocum? Out of the entire collection, why did you choose that book to borrow over and over?"

"I . . . I . . . I don't know . . ." There were tears in her eyes.

"It's because you, Mrs. Slocum, are the reincarnation of Evangeline."

"But I don't remember being her, Mr. Cauliflower! I remember being detective Redmond and Mrs. Slocum. Before that, there's nothing! I'm not . . . I'm not . . ." but the more Annette tried to convince herself of the fact the more her memories changed. As she stared into the kitchen, Nathaniel undid his tie and top collar to show the opal necklace that he had worn since Evangeline had disappeared. Annette turned to him and saw the opal necklace. She looked at the stone, then at Nathaniel's eyes, then back at the stone. She shook her head slightly, quivering. A look of concentrated consideration of the truth passed over her face as she looked into Nathaniel's eyes. Annette opened her mouth to speak and closed it again. Still, the words came out nonetheless and this time with an unanticipated subtle French accent. "Monsieur Cauliflower?"

"Yes, Mademoiselle Evangeline . . ."

CHAPTER 21: RHAPSODY REEXAMINED

The rain hit the quiet house like wooden sticks repeatedly striking a snare drum. Deep rolls of thunder boomed like wielded timpani mallets pounding skin-stretched copper bowls. It was a steady battery that eluded to Jonas' percussive, yet disruptive, frontline ensemble. Though he had been trapped within Jonas' scheme, the apprentice had also been orchestrating his own plan to reverse the hateful discourager's disturbed arrangement.

With the hood around his head and the jacket zipped around his figure, the apprentice inched to Jonas' open study door. He found that his overlord wasn't occupying the space. Tiptoeing across the threshold, he was careful to avoid any loose creaking floorboards that may have given away his position. Blackened fireplace logs struggled to keep the dwindling ashen embers aglow and a brass banker's lamp, with a green glass shade, had been earlier switched on atop the study's desk. They supplied the apprentice ample light to sort through the collected paperwork. He discovered the Weather Wizard on the fireplace mantle but paid it little mind. It was another device he was after: the Lite-Brite board Jonas had been using to capture his mistreated victims.

As he was sifting through the desk's violet envelopes, he spotted it resting against the study's fainting couch. Its typical papered grid stared at him in such an innocent way that it was hard to believe such calamity could arise from a singularly childish toy. But it wasn't a "childish toy" in Jonas' world. The apprentice knew good and well that it was a means of transportation. Jonas had taken his cohort on many two-way trips through the pegs that had been inserted.

He lifted the Lite-Brite and studied it. There was one cream-colored peg with pink polka dots in the grid. The apprentice wondered who the peg belonged to and how Jonas had intended to destroy that particular client's timeline.

"What are you doing?" asked a female voice behind him.

The apprentice spun to find Doris, the woman whom Jonas had handed a Valentine in the graveyard, standing at the door. She was a slender middle-aged woman with coke-bottle thick glasses that magnified her brutally judgmental eyes.

"You know you're not supposed to be in here." Doris folded her arms. "Jonas gave you strict instructions never to enter his study without him being inside it." She looked at the Lite-Brite board in his hands. "Drop it," she ordered.

The apprentice hesitated, considering any possible alternatives.

"Don't be stupid," Doris squinted menacingly. "If you don't put it back on the couch, I'll scream bloody murder."

The apprentice looked at the Lite-Brite board and considered the reasons why he decided to retaliate against his captor. He thought about the lives that Jonas had forced him to ruin by way of this device. He thought about the rainy days and the lies that had been told during them. He thought about his own ruined timeline and how it had turned him into a person that he didn't want to be. Complying with this misplaced woman's misunderstandings wasn't worth the prolonged aggravation. Something had to be done and, to the apprentice, the time had finally come for him to step to the plate. He may not have known how the exact physics of the muse world worked but he knew there was a kidnapped muse bound in the basement who, once freed from captivity, would know how to utilize the Lite-Brite to get them to safety.

He bolted for the door with the Lite-Brite in hand.

Doris, turning her back to him and focusing on the hallway, screamed Jonas' name in such a shrill banshee-like roar that it could have shattered the windows. The apprentice, without thinking of a more logical solution, seized the banker's lamp. Its chord was snapped from the wall. Like the candlestick in the church, he drew it over Doris' head bringing an end to her shouting. As Doris' body fell and the apprentice heard Jonas' footsteps approaching, he looked at the blunt object. He dropped it with an audible clang. As the fireplace cinders fizzled into thin trails of smoke casting the study into blackness, he considered the demonic acts he had performed in this whole ordeal. He hoped that this act would help to reclaim him his worthiness.

*

Annette's physical features didn't change even though the past life memories of Evangeline resurfaced in a surge of extravagant imagery. She was outwardly disorientated, scrambling to collect as many recollections as she could to construct a complete depiction. Nathaniel aided the piecing fragments, keeping a stream of informative prattle.

"I knew that the only way to know for sure if you were Evangeline's reincarnation was if I looked into your eyes and witnessed the truth first-hand. You were an antisocial bookish housewife and to even get close enough to you, let alone look into your eyes, was going to be an impossible feat. The only time we were in close proximity was when you regularly dropped your books through the return slot at the circulation desk. One afternoon the sliding glass door opened. There you were. You stuffed the library books into the return slot and whisked past so speedily I didn't get a chance to look into your eyes for confirmation. All I could say to you that day was 'thank you.' Off you went in search of more library books. I followed you that day but you were agitated by a woman in a cream-colored pants suit, our Head Muse Fiona, who was also trailing after you. I watched as you crouched by the magazine rack by the front sliding doors in an attempt to escape her. I watched as you rushed outside, car keys in hand, to avoid interaction with your pursuer. I didn't want to implicate myself by accosting another married woman for my own justified happiness. I held your returned library books and considered your life with Lyle and wondered if you were happy. Then there came a screeching of tires and the shouting of pedestrians. I fought my way through the growing crowd of people at the street. You had been struck, and killed, by a blue Cadillac. Your eyes were open giving me verification. A single orange Lite-Brite peg rolled out from a violet envelope and landed by your left ear. Fiona, who had dropped the envelope, stared at me. I remembered her from my previous visits to the afterlife department. She nodded at me as if to say 'Yes, Mr. Cauliflower. She's Evangeline, and she's in my care again.' Then Fiona, the orange peg and the violet envelope were gone. There was an increasing wail of approaching ambulance sirens as your lifeless body faced Heaven.

"Thomas was the prosecuting attorney in your trial. I was there in the courtroom as the judge declared the imprisonment sentence of vehicular manslaughter on an amateur violinist, named Jonathan. Life post-trial was like a broken music box with a flat-toned melody. I visited your grave and placed asphodel petals on your tombstone every Memorial Day. Jonas took your death harder than I did. He clung to your obituary with an unhealthy obsession keeping it tucked inside the cover of *Dorian Gray*. Perhaps he believed your death to be the end of an era – an epoch of sunlit summers, puzzlingly repaired library books and compelled power over those seemingly weaker than him. His obsession with your death led Roberta to file for divorce and take custody of his kids. She remained in the house while Jonas rented an apartment closer to the weather station. He became crueler than he had been in our youth which incontrovertibly showed when you resurfaced in his life in 2012. As you were there inspiring the bookseller Adam Mansfield, he watched you hoping to understand how after three years you had resurrected. Jonas pretended that he was out for your best interest but I was convinced that he had resumed his work of asserting control. When he blackmailed you with your obituary, Jonas wasn't expecting you to retaliate. You stole your obituary from him in a spinning, victorious battle!

"He told me this one afternoon right before our last thunderstorm together. I had a suspicion that you'd returned as a muse and that he had seen you in a client's life. But I kept this from him. By telling Jonas this information it would have given him the power he had dreadfully desired. When it was obvious that Jonas wasn't getting anywhere he switched tactics. As the atmosphere grew increasingly dark with the storm on the horizon, Jonas looked through the front door's window. He wore a black suit, matching tie and a light gray shirt. His eyes were filled with lethal acrimony. Jonas' hair had turned gray over the years and crows feet had formed around his eyes. I, on the other hand, was completely bald, and sported the same brown glasses, tie and suspenders, looking as I do at present.

"'You know, Broccoli,' Jonas told me on that day 'I know about your affair with Roberta.'

"To which I asked apprehensively, 'Do you?'

"Jonas nodded, turning his face slightly to mine. 'It's been a common thread for us, eh, Broccoli? In your seven lives, we've seen and suffered one another in many forms; you as my apprentice in 1808, then you again in the twenties as a Russian immigrant and the subsequent four lives in between. We've met many times and, near the close, we conclude with me murdering you.'

"I could sense that there was a part of Jonas that wished it didn't have to be so. No one is ever truly evil, Mrs. Slocum. No matter how bad a person is, there's still a side that harbors honor, even if short-lived.

"Jonas went on in saying 'Why must we endlessly orbit this destructive path throughout time?'

"To which I responded, 'Perhaps, you can pray about it. Management may give you the answer.'

"'Because you won't tell me. Will you Broccoli?' Jonas sneered. 'You know the answers, and yet you deliberately act ignorant.' He turned to me and approached slowly. 'Tell me the answers, Broccoli.' Lightning flashed outside the window followed by a distant roll of thunder. We were nose to nose. I instinctively retreated a few steps but stopped and stood my ground. 'Well, Broccoli? What's it going to be? Are you going to tell me what I want to know or aren't you?'"

Nathaniel took a breath.

Annette was speechless while listening to her storyteller.

"I took the answers to the grave," Nathaniel went on. "My seventh life ended with me being murdered by the painter. Only instead of being thrown from the attic loft of his French chateau, or being mercilessly choked and burned by the flames from an overturned kerosene lamp, our pertinacious dueling ended in amateur swordplay. I died on freshly mowed grass stabbed by a serrated garden trowel on the rain-dappled backyard lawn. As the grown Pampas grass in my garden shifted in the wind, and as Jonas stood over me lit by lightning, my eyes remained on the blackened storm-filled sky. All I could think about was you and how, once I allowed my life to slip, we would be reunited."

*

A spark of sunlight pierced the storm clouds in the last waking moments of Nathaniel's seventh life. Though he remained on his back for several moments absorbing his lofty internal surroundings while staring at the domed ceiling's oculus, Nathaniel knew he was securely delivered to his branded afterlife office. His old acquaintances from the past seven lives were there to greet him: the ghostly paintings, the shining kerosene lamps, a collection of fountain pens, various polished globes, volumes of destiny-filled encyclopedias, along with a hefty soaring compilation of repaired library books. It was methodically organized into a private gallery of memorials referencing bygone days.

"I hope it pleases you how I've arranged everything," Fiona told him, entering the open doorway of his office. "Seven lifetimes is a long time to go searching for someone," Fiona said with a sigh. "But I suppose in my mind the story of you and Evangeline is almost as common as a modern day muse filling a Lite-Brite board."

"I won't be reincarnating again," he told her while standing. "I found her."

"Have you?" Fiona bore a look of confusion.

"Didn't you take her with you?" Nathaniel asked with his head tilted questioningly. "Evangeline, Annette Slocum rather, died in front of the local library after being struck by a Cadillac."

It was clear that Fiona had no recollection of the accident to which he referred.

Having sat through the orientation video in which he familiarized himself with his work, he passed by each office of the current muses. Nathaniel realized that time worked differently in the department. Even though he may have seen Annette's passing, that didn't mean it had necessarily happened yet in the agency's timeline. Nathaniel watched as a mistrusting Harriet had, moments before, been brought to the afterlife as an Eighth Generation muse. Nathaniel took a distant interest in a Seventh Generation muse, Lucas Richardson, who had barely dotted his own Lite-Brite board with designated colored pegs.

Nathaniel, as the caretaker, reassigned colored pegs to his fellow muses. He delivered white and violet envelopes to the various postboxes. He revisited the pleasure of cooking for his peers. But no matter how many colored pegs fell into his inbox, or how many envelopes he delivered, or the countless hours he spent in the kitchen practicing his stylishly alluring gastronomies, Nathaniel relentlessly thought of Annette and pondered as to when their timelines would eventually coincide. Nathaniel scripted his memoirs and locked the secrets into a glass cabinet secured by a ten-digit combination lock. In so doing, Nathaniel healthily compartmentalized his feelings ridding his mind from the fixation.

When Annette arrived as a Ninth Generation muse, Nathaniel was busy clearing the plates from his recent dish of chicken Marsala. The dishes were virtually empty except for a spot of vegetable oil in one, a lone mushroom in another and a bowl that housed a single piece of discarded lettuce. Though he would have normally bussed these used China plates, glass goblets, and silverware, Nathaniel's attention was elsewhere as Fiona said behind him "She's here." Hearing these words he abandoned the plates and joined Fiona by the waiting room door.

Fiona looked at Nathaniel and said "Are you ready to see your friend again face to face?"

Nathaniel whispered "Yes."

But when Fiona turned the doorknob and held the door wearing a managerial smile for Annette, Nathaniel suddenly felt ill and closed himself in the bathroom locking the door. Though he felt foolish for behaving out of involuntary reflex, Nathaniel remained in the bathroom until he heard the instructional video replay. And, as the video replayed in the conference room, Nathaniel entered Annette's office where he poured out swarming emotions. The passion for her that he had kept was projected in the minute details that he swiftly manifested as Annette's private empty library.

Nathaniel kept his distance while waiting for the perfect moment for introductions – a moment which, to his chagrin, never came. Annette attached herself to one of her favorite clients: a living bookseller named Adam Mansfield who worked in an underground shop called *The Muse's Corner*. Annette had feelings for this client and often visited him by rotating his peg clockwise. The more visits that she paid the bookseller, the more Nathaniel felt a beating to his pride. Nathaniel was consumed with juvenile jealousy and was disappointed that he had not gotten the courage to say or do anything to attract her. As Annette neared her retirement, and as she rotated the colored peg to spend her final evening in the loving arms of Adam Mansfield, Nathaniel administered his revenge. In her absence, he stuffed sixty-eight violet envelopes into her postbox. Nathaniel knew that his anger should have been directed at himself but he felt a sense of vindication nevertheless. The love that he had for her was poisoned by the fact that she hadn't known who Nathaniel had been to her, therefore did not reciprocate.

It was during the last of those sixty-eight violet envelopes that Annette traveled back in time to inspire a young version of Nathaniel in the root cellar. Annette's sudden realization of Nathaniel's involvement in her life led Management to request that he set up a table of the repaired library books during her upcoming retirement party. Not to disappoint Management's wishes, even though his respect for their demands was low as of late, Nathaniel obliged. He stood at a table as the sun rose on the morning of Annette's retirement party. He listened as the cherry blossoms from nearby trees shifted. The hope of meeting Annette and showing her how he repaired her library books seemed empty. Nathaniel believed that, even if he showed his trick, she would have thanked him and parted company with another man on her mind. That thought sickened him.

*

"'Something came up,'" Annette interjected at this point. Her stare was unwavering. As he had been telling her this information, Nathaniel served bowls of the Puttanesca, placing them on the church kitchen's rectangular countertop. "That's what Fiona told me during my retirement party when I stopped by your table to find that you weren't there."

"Yes, something did come up," Nathaniel nodded. "I realized that, no matter what I did, we were never destined to connect. So I left the table and walled myself into my office where I sat out the remainder of the party cleaning kerosene lamps."

"Why?" she asked.

"I wanted you to be happy," Nathaniel explained. "Meeting you would have complicated things. Though you retired and reincarnated into a woman named Annette Redmond I knew that you would be happy. I made it a conscious effort to work with Management in putting you in a life where your joy would be guaranteed. Adam Mansfield reincarnated into a man named Adam Eustace McCloud. You two met under the light of a solitary street lamp on Christmas Eve as he carved a muse out of ice. I watched as you two started a normal life. It was the best gift I think I could have given my dear Mademoiselle Evangeline: a gift that you once asked me for – a life without me and of the misadventures that tended to accompany. The first, and last, time we saw each other before this debacle was on that same snowy Christmas Eve in the graveyard. I waved at you. And you waved at me. I knew that I could find you and look in on you whenever I wanted and, though it hurt, I knew you were safe with Adam McCloud. Safe and satisfied."

Nathaniel fell silent. There were mere centimeters between them but they didn't touch. Annette's wedding dress was a reminder of her pending vows. Nathaniel, being the hopeless gentleman, politely respected that boundary.

A faint rumble of distant thunder brought Nathaniel to business. "Ah, I see this inspiration will be coming to an end soon," he said while turning to a chilled bottle of Zinfandel. "We'll have plenty of time to enjoy our meal before that happens, thankfully."

"Inspiration?" Annette was jolted.

"Yes, Mrs. Slocum, we're in an inspiration." Nathaniel uncorked the wine and poured several stemmed glasses which Management had also provided. He seized one of the glasses and swirled the wine a few times. He sipped and added, "Every colored peg contains a client that needs our special touch, as you know. This peg is no different."

"I'm confused." Annette studied Nathaniel. "Who's the client in this drawn-out inspiration? Was it the motel lobby manager that we met?"

"It was not." Nathaniel positioned the plates in a perfect row. They were measured apart by the same distinct increment. He folded the nine cobalt cloth napkins into floppy fleurs-de-lis.

Annette watched with awe as his confident fingers flew and the napkin fabric whirled. "Then who?"

Nathaniel looked from his work to suggest the kitchen.

"The kitchen's the client?" Annette asked dryly.

"This whole church! No client is too great or too small. Buildings aren't meant to stand vacant. Sometimes by residing in a place and utilizing it the way it used to be is considered a type of inspiration."

"I can understand how a person would benefit from a catalyst but a building?" Annette asked, not fully grasping Nathaniel's point.

Nathaniel was more interested in the sound of the dinging oven timer. With both hands covered in navy blue mitts, he opened the oven door and extracted the tray of baked Ciabatta garlic bread.

"Mr. Cauliflower?" Annette asked from behind him.

Nathaniel was too distracted by examining the toasted pieces of bread on the tray for imperfections. He pursed his lips, stacking the bread onto a separate plate.

Annette said from behind him: "Monsieur Cauliflower . . ."

The truth was that Nathaniel was too embarrassed for rendering his heart on his sleeve. To cope from such an imprudent exchange Nathaniel impulsively, and attentively, focused on the compulsive desire for order in his parade of foods.

"Nathaniel will you please turn around and look at me!" Annette demanded.

Nathaniel stopped stacking the garlic bread and looked at the white tiled kitchen wall before him. He slowly turned to Annette. They stood for several seconds looking at one another neither sure of what to say. This moment did not last long as the door to the kitchen opened and Fiona stepped through.

"Well," their Head Muse took in a whiff of the meal's aroma. "Something smells nice. Oh, I hope I'm not interrupting . . ." she started to the door.

"Not interrupting," Nathaniel said, taking the plate of bread in his hands. "In fact, Mrs. Slocum and I were finishing the Puttanesca and garlic bread. We were on our way to fetch you and the rest of –" his words were cut short as Fiona was followed by the group who entered the kitchen after catching the wafting smell of the noodles and sauce. ". . . The rest of the muses," Nathaniel finished saying as they stared hungrily at the spaghetti-filled bowls. "Muses, the meal was cooked by none other than Annette Slocum as an apology for her brutal interrogations. Isn't that right, Mrs. Slocum?" To which he handed her the plate of bread.

Her eyes went wide as she took the plate. She sheepishly nodded. "Yes, that's correct," Annette told them earnestly. She looked at Nathaniel. "I'm sorry."

Each muse procured a bowl of Puttanesca and a glass of wine. They approached Annette's bread plate held in offering. Fiona winked as she took her piece. Harriet looked suspicious as she took hers. One by one the muses took a slice of Annette's bread and, thusly, accepted her apology along with it. Edgar Allan Poe was next to last and graciously accepted the snack. When Lucas approached the plate she looked at him and frowned. "Forgive me?"

"Hey," Lucas shrugged "what can I say? A friendship isn't a friendship until it's been christened by a fight, you know?" He smiled.

Annette smiled.

He took a piece of bread and smiled even more at Annette showing his attractive dimpled cheeks.

"We're missing someone," Annette told Nathaniel as the muses dispersed with their plates. Counting heads she was one short. "Where's Icarus?"

The kitchen's side double doors leading into the fellowship hall opened dramatically with the same panache as a cowboy passing through the swinging doors of an Old West saloon. Icarus stood in the center, entering on cue. His clothing had been tousled. His tanned skin was pelted with sweat and signs of physical assault. His expression was one of distinctive apocalyptic somberness.

"What happened?" Nathaniel offered him a stool to sit.

Icarus explained how he was abducted by Jonas.

He told Nathaniel that he had failed as a muse. That all that he had ever wanted to do was fly through the sky as sprightly lighthearted as a bird with the wind in his face. But now he had been as beached as he had ever felt. Regardless, he was determined to rebuild what had been damaged. He started with reciting Jonas' demands.

"He wants detective Redmond," Icarus' words were focused in Annette's direction. "He's aware that you're the reincarnation of Evangeline. He knows about the destiny on the broken record. The one you didn't want. The one that caused you to neglect your inspiration at the mailbox. And it's due to that destiny that he's requested you join his collection."

"His collection?" Annette asked.

"He said that you might be inclined not to submit. In which case he told me to tell you that he currently has someone dear to you that he's stolen from another timeline. A man who you once loved and who's also one of your favorite clients."

"Adam!" Annette shot a look to Nathaniel. "He has Adam!"

"He mentioned that if you don't come to his residence at 252 Sisyphus Hill and join his collection he's going to kill this person and then start eradicating the victims he's abducted. He said to tell you that he's serious in this threat." Icarus turned to Nathaniel. "And he also mentioned that if Mrs. Slocum has any lingering doubts about what he's capable of, she's to review how many times he's murdered you, Mr. Cauliflower."

"We have no choice," Nathaniel told Annette.

Fiona closed her eyes and bowed her head. This was the moment that Fiona had referred to in the beginning – what it might have meant by bringing Annette back to the department as one of the Nine Greatest Muses. This was the moment that Nathaniel had tried to protect her from as the recent retirement party had neared.

"There's one more thing he wanted me to mention," Icarus said with the clearing of his throat. "He asked me, on behalf of him, to thank you for your assistance in playing his apprentice, Mr. Cauliflower. But your association is no longer required."

Annette's eyes widened.

Nathaniel retreated a step.

Another roll of thunder shook the walls of the church.

Nathaniel whispered to Icarus, "That's a lie!" He turned to Annette who drew the pistol from her thigh holster with both hands and aimed it at Nathaniel. Nathaniel's own hands shot up in surrender.

"It's a lie. A downright lie, Mademoiselle Evangeline! I'm telling you!"

All Annette could say was "Sanctuary. Chat."

With the pistol aimed at his back, Nathaniel started for the kitchen stairs.

"Icarus, you know I'm not working with Jonas," Nathaniel told him. "You know I'm not capable of that kind of behavior! Why are you lying? Who are you trying to protect?"

Icarus quickly shifted his eyes to Lucas then back to Nathaniel. Nathaniel nodded.

Annette looked at Fiona, motioning with her head for the Head Muse to follow.

Fiona obliged and calmly asked the others to finish their meals while everything got sorted.

As the three of them walked up the several flights of stairs and through the hallways of the church toward the dilapidated sanctuary, Nathaniel tried to explain: "He's lying to you, Evangeline."

"Detective Redmond, Mr. Cauliflower, please."

"Fiona can attest that I've been there for the department. Everything that I've done as the caretaker has been for the betterment of the workplace . . . and humanity!"

"You're a storyteller," Annette said coldly. "A good storyteller but a deceitful wordsmith just the same."

"You know I'm not lying. You felt it. You know in your heart that you are Evangeline!"

"I'm not Evangeline, Mr. Cauliflower. This story of yours has most likely been a manipulation from the beginning. You thought Roberta was Evangeline but she wasn't. You wanted me to be Evangeline but I'm not."

"But there was a look in your eye."

"I got that look in my eye whenever I read any romance smut. It doesn't prove anything."

"And you borrowed Chaucer's *Canterbury Tales* every fall."

"Again, you're basing that on what you want so badly to believe. It isn't real. It was an impressively constructed cover, Mr. Cauliflower. Sadly, it's the ones that we least suspect, the ones who have been the most influential, the ones with imaginatively crafted stories, who are the culprit."

They approached the closed sanctuary door.

Nathaniel turned to Annette. "I'm not the culprit, Evangeline. You have to listen to me!"

"Detective Redmond, Mr. Cauliflower. Detective Redmond! I've listened to you weave your way through your stories only to realize that everything has been just a big imaginative tale."

"That's not true."

"That's why you didn't want to help me turn my pegs, isn't it? You were afraid of me uncovering your secret? That's why you tried to rush me to my wedding and take the case into your own hands. It makes sense. You wanted the inspirations to yourself and I was getting in the way. I was getting too close, wasn't I?"

She rambled on these questions without allowing him to respond.

"Tell me, Mr. Cauliflower, if you didn't want me interfering with yours and Jonas' plan, why did you have Fiona hand me an invitation? Why did you give me my memories of being Annette Slocum when you wanted me out of the picture?"

"Management chose the invitation recipients, Mrs. Slocum. Not me. I had to give you your memories if we were to get out from under this mess."

"In," Annette ordered.

Within seconds Nathaniel was sitting in the pew with the carved initials. The yellowed afternoon sunlight shined through one of the stained glass windows coloring the vase of asphodels. His attention wasn't on the asphodels though. Nor was it on Jonas' carved initials. His eyes settled on the splintered violin and bow that they had been handed at the motel. Annette tossed it into his lap and barked to Nathaniel, "Fix it."

Nathaniel sighed. "It's not a library book."

Annette aimed the pistol toward Nathaniel making a clear motion of removing the safety. "Repair the violin, Mr. Cauliflower."

"Mrs. Slocum honestly," Fiona started. "Is this necessary?"

"Yes, it's necessary. If he repaired my library books in my youth he can repair the violin. He needed motivation when he was a kid in his root cellar. I'm giving him a second round."

"Then be a muse to him, Mrs. Slocum," Fiona preached, "not a gun toting detective."

Annette had no intention of placating him as a muse. "Repair it, Mr. Cauliflower."

With Annette's pistol aimed at his head and the other muses peering through the opened sanctuary door, Nathaniel touched the violin and bow. He handled it with the same care that he had Annette's library books.

The thunder rumbled several times, growing in sound and intensity. The inspiration was approaching its end but Nathaniel didn't mind. He worked as his fingers brushed over the wood and strings. The talent that had been given to him by the Dandelion Sisters was slow but, as he focused his energy, the violin reconstructed itself piece by piece. Nathaniel had waited for this moment – to show Annette what he could do. And he wished, as he did so, that it was under better circumstances.

The repaired violin and bow were handed to her. Even though she tried to suppress her awe at seeing his handiwork, Annette still admired the phenomenon.

"There's no guarantee that it's tuned properly or that it'll play," Nathaniel told her.

"The colored pegs in your pocket, if you will." Annette held open her right palm.

Nathaniel dug through his pocket. He felt the glow-in-the-dark star and closed his eyes. He stroked its shape and recalled Annette's first inspirations. He wished he could go back in time to those innocent moments and work harder to avoid this incident. Nathaniel opened his eyes and took out the colored pegs he had carried with him. He poured them from his hand to hers.

Annette held the red-colored peg associated with Phillip. "I've been to 252 Sisyphus Hill," she told him. "I followed a lead to the residence but I didn't find Jonas. I found Roberta and her two boys. Per Roberta, Jonas had been dead for at least four years which puzzled me at the time." She brought the single red peg in front of Nathaniel's eyes. "Is this how you've been traveling to him, Mr. Cauliflower? If I turn this peg clockwise will it take me to that house and to the timeline where he, and the other victims, reside?"

Nathaniel frowned but didn't respond.

"Tell me, Mr. Cauliflower. Will it send me –"

"Yes!" Nathaniel shouted. "Yes, detective, it will."

Annette ordered Nathaniel to stand which he did. She then asked for the Lite-Brite board Fiona had taken with them from Purgatory, which sat at the other end of the pew.

Fiona handed Annette the spare Lite-Brite board.

Annette took the Lite-Brite and placing it on the altar beside the potted asphodels.

Nathaniel watched as Annette inserted the red-colored peg into the Lite-Brite board rotating it clockwise. With the pistol in one hand, the colored pegs clinched in the other and the violin tucked under her left arm, Annette stood like a solitary warrior poised for battle. And then she was gone at the helm of Phillip's unfolding clockwise ruminations.

"Why are you sitting there?" Fiona told him. "You have to go after her!"

He had gone after her many times and it exhausted him. He had spent so much time and energy trying to find her in the past seven lives, and protecting her from Jonas in the afterlife, that he felt following her was futile.

A figure appeared from behind the altar emerging from the choir loft and organ. Partially hidden behind the ray of afternoon sunlight, Fiona and Nathaniel adjusted their eyes to discern the identity of the person. Whoever it was donned a black hoodie with the hood over their head. Nathaniel, recognizing the black hoodie, stepped from the front pew to address the owner.

Thunder shook the sanctuary and the floor beneath his feet. The walls and windows broke apart.

The apprentice stepped into the light inspecting the Lite-Brite board with the red-colored peg in its grid. He too had another Lite-Brite under his arm. The stranger turned to Nathaniel and unzipping the hoodie to reveal a worn and rumpled tuxedo. The hood was peeled away exposing the malefactor's true identity: Adam Eustace McCloud. He quickly asked about his fiancé's whereabouts.

Nathaniel and Fiona shared a look of substantial distress.

CHAPTER 22: AN APPRENTICE'S ACCOUNT

Without Annette there with him, Nathaniel experienced his standard accustomed terrain. He had been so inured to the strident racket of her company that the muteness from Annette's ardent departure appeared almost a reprieve. But the feeling that he presently sensed was unlike what it had been before. Loving Annette and existing with the unexpressed, unreturned feelings was one thing. It was quite another with Annette being out in the world knowing full well of Nathaniel's emotional plight. It tore within him thinking that she had blatantly rejected him. Even if he had been granted the chance to be with her, Nathaniel didn't know what he would have done with such an opportunity. Having wasted seven lifetimes chasing after her Nathaniel didn't even stop to consider how he would suitably hold or care for her.

The church's group inspiration was rotated clockwise to provide temporary safety from the erupting luminary Purgatorial barn lights.

Annette's fiancé sat in one of the sanctuary pews. In trilling the account to the muses, he fidgeted with the eroded cube of blue billiard chalk from his hoodie pocket. Adam was a fairly good-looking young man of Russian decent. He had an athletic build. His toned cheeks, which hadn't been shaved in a week, showed prominent laugh lines. His full head of hair, which had been stylized with gel and brushed to the side, was indolently askew. His eyes were blue and projected boyish innocence. His mannerisms were subdued and polite as he spoke in a soothing lower-pitched voice while describing, in detail, how he had come to be and how he escaped from being, Jonas' apprentice.

*

It began on the evening before Annette and Adam's wedding day during the bachelor party in the downtown billiard hall. There was roughly a half-dozen men in Adam's entourage. The group was divided into two pool tables in the far right corner underneath glowing neon signs advertising the beers on tap. It was a typical last night of bachelorhood for any groom filled with male camaraderie and a convoy of alcoholic refreshments. The hall was active with striking pool balls, sprightly country music over the speakers and a symposium of rowdy crowds. Adam stood amidst all of it grinding the cube of blue chalk against the tip of his cue. He thought to himself how lucky he was to have such great friends and how grateful he was to have earned the love of his adored fiancé who, at this time, would have been busy in the affairs of her own bachelorette party. The church had been decorated top to bottom in yellow tulips and similarly-colored assorted flowers. The reception hall had been booked well in advance and the plane tickets for their honeymoon had been safely tucked inside the pockets of their pre-packed suitcases. His tux had been rented and pressed. The invitations had already been mailed out and presents from their gift registry had trickled in by post. The wedding day had the predisposition to run like clockwork somewhat in part to Adam's eager assistance in helping Annette-the-orchestrator during the planning.

But it was on the night of the bachelor party, before all of the hard work had come to completion, when the unwelcomed ill-favored thunderstorm arrived to dismantle the entire execution.

Adam leaned over the pool table focusing on his cue stick and the scratch ball in an attempt to knock the last yellow-striped "nine" ball into a corner pocket. As he drew his arm and pool cue back to gain force for the impact, the lights in the billiard hall extinguished. There was a flash of lightning and a rumble of thunder which successfully managed to capture everyone's attention bringing a short-lived stillness to the room.

In the glass window of the billiard hall was the outline of a man in a suit and tie who casually slipped in with a closing black umbrella. Adam, who had since stood from his previous position at the pool table, looked at the dark silhouette with an understated suggestion of familiarity. When the lights and music restarted Adam was able to see the stranger in more detail. The person had white hair, cold gray eyes and a stern frown that hinted to the newcomer's current unhappiness. The feeling of familiarity that Adam felt before was doused in a certain feeling that they had never met.

Actually, Adam McCloud and Jonas Rothchild had not yet encountered one another in this present life. Adam had no previous memories beyond those of his current childhood or early toddler years. This updated version of Adam wasn't aware of Jonas' previous involvement in Annette's and the bookseller's affairs. Adam didn't remember Annette's prior heroic attempt in having rescued her own obituary from Jonas in 2012. He didn't remember tumbling angrily with Jonas over the rain-spattered pavement of their shared apartment complex. He didn't recall Jonas having been struck and killed by lightning and therefore was not aware that Jonas had transformed into the intentionally neglectful Tenth Generation muse. Instead, Adam was simply Adam Eustace McCloud: talented ice sculptor by trade and devoted fiancé to detective Annette Redmond.

Unfortunately for this reincarnation of Adam, the suited man from the storm had come to use this fact to his advantage; Jonas had set out to act upon a glorious, yet mischievous, sleight of hand. But Jonas' initial tricks were not executed without a methodically manipulative plan. The diverse implementation of his preparation had to be calculated precisely to the minutest degree. And so, instead of charging forward, Jonas simply stood. He mentally moved his metaphorical pawns across imaginary checkered black and white squares.

Unbeknownst to the stranger's true agenda, Adam didn't feel threatened. He unsurprisingly assumed the stranger had come in for respite out of the rain and happened to catch eyes with Adam while doing so.

Adam's best man, a middle-aged athletic fellow in a dark green polo and baggy pants, wrapped an arm around the groom in a side-crippling bear hug jostling Adam's attention. His laughing buddy was caught in a conversation in which Adam wasn't involved.

"Where are you, McCloud?" asked his best man. "I go through this trouble to plan party for you and you're a million miles away."

"I suppose it's the thunderstorm," Adam told his friend while fishing for his cell phone in his jeans pants pocket. He lifted the phone to answer a call from Annette.

"What's her deal, brosky?" his friend asked. "Whenever a thunderstorm comes into town, you'd think it's the end of the world for her."

"We have an agreement," Adam told him. "When there's a thunderstorm brewing, and we're not in the same room, I'm supposed to check in."

"That's an odd agreement," he said with a laugh. "What does she have against thunderstorms?"

"'It's more about *who* might be in the thunderstorms that she's concerned about." As the words had come out of his mouth, he wanted to retract the statement. Annette asked Adam never to discuss her missing person's case, or her neurosis concerning it, to anyone. Adam bit his lip and laughed it off, blaming his babbling nonsense on the alcohol he consumed.

He answered the phone and felt reassured by the sound of Annette's voice. He believed that the days of checking in, while they were far apart, were soon at an end. Eventually there would be no need to verify his unknown status with her as their marriage would fuse their proximities.

Or so that had been the plan if Jonas, in his calculating wisdom, had not entered the billiard hall on that tempestuous evening.

In the hour that transpired, as the thunderstorm ebbed and the alcoholic accumulation intensified, the bachelor party was brought to a lofty level of inebriated masculine playfulness. All the while, Jonas sat in the corner with an untouched bottle of beer in front of him staring at Adam. He didn't wave or acknowledge Adam with any gestures; it was the steady sinister stare in Jonas' eyes that locked on to him. Adam wasn't a brawny physical bar-room brawl type. Instead of rolling the sleeves of his navy blue button-up shirt to prepare for a few punches, Adam took it upon himself to keep from consuming any alcohol. He feared that it might hinder reflexes he might need in case the stranger decided to approach with malintent.

Compared to Jonas' grand entrance during a flash of lightning, his exit was as notable – he vanished from the table. One moment he was there. The next he wasn't. It was as if he stepped out of the current timeline.

Relief passed through Adam and, as it did, he found himself exhausted from the instinctual tensing of muscles. Adam inspected the table from afar noticing that the stranger hadn't offered the waitress a tip for the beer. He approached and removed his billfold taking out a few dollars to set down on the un-bussed table. A violet envelope had been addressed to him with the name "McCloud" scribbled on the front. Adam flipped the envelope over. The number "4" had also been added. Annette had mentioned the significance of the numbered envelopes in conjunction with the Thunderstorm Man and it caused his hands to shake slightly as he lifted the flap.

Inside the envelope was their wedding invitation. On the reverse side was another message:

> Detective Annette Redmond will be abducted on your wedding date by the person around whom her missing person case revolves. If you want to save her in time, you'll meet me alone on the rooftop of *The Muse's Corner* tomorrow at noon.

It was signed "A friend who is on your side."

The rising noise that accumulated in the billiard hall receded bringing about a daunting, unnerving stillness. Despite the calling voice of his best man, Adam dropped the dollar bills on the table and, with the violet envelope and wedding invitation in hand, fled the billiard hall.

Stars poked through patches of lingering clouds. Street lamps buzzed an orange glow as Adam's eyes caught sight of a deserted neighboring storefront. There was a 'For Lease' sign in the window. Cupping his eyes on either side with his hands, Adam stared into the vacant building. Several years ago, before the proprietor named Gwendolyn Mansfield had liquidated her stock, it had been a used bookstore called *The Muse's Corner*. It had sat empty ever since. It would also prove to be the spot where Jonas cold-heartedly planned to abduct him.

*

Adam fiddled with the piece of billiard chalk while taking a few moments to recall the rest of that evening. He went on to further explain that, "Several weeks prior to my bachelor party, I decided to change my wedding ring selection I'd picked out to something less befitting a missing person's detective and more a pie maker. I also put down a loan deposit on that empty building for her. I was going to give her the best wedding present any groom could give his bride: I was going to give Annette the long-awaited fantasy pie shop she had frequently mentioned."

Nathaniel turned to Annette's fiancé with a look of incredulity. That pie shop had been Nathaniel's initial idea and that snake fiancé of hers had stolen it! Hearing this crushed Nathaniel's soul. He had watched Annette and Adam from a distance for years. He had grown somewhat comfortable with the theory of their upcoming marriage and the safety it presented. But as he listened to Adam's recanting of old memories, Nathaniel was too close to the relationship. Even though he couldn't hold Annette the way that Adam had held her or spend meaningless minutes and hours with her throughout a lifetime as Adam had been privileged and even though Nathaniel had visualized being a loving husband to Annette and having children – the fact of the matter was Nathaniel could never have that life with her. It was an exclusive club where he had been denied membership. It was a relationship that survived healthily without Nathaniel's involvement proving him to be obsolete in its collectiveness.

With this thought, Nathaniel decidedly stepped away from Adam's stories.

The narthex of the church was a narrow lobby in the back of the sanctuary with beveled glass windows. Though the structure of the narthex was the same, the aesthetics had depleted over the years resulting in a shadier temperament. Discarded dust-covered offertory plates were stacked by an aged, yellowed guest book and dried up ink pen. Seeing the guest book reminded Nathaniel of the ledger in the tent of the Dandelion Sisters. He recalled each of his seven visits to the Fates and how, on his last visit after he had scrawled his name with the quill, Nathaniel had intentionally scratched two lines through his last entry to break his bonds.

The plates also brought about another distinct set of memories. During his childhood years, while having suffered the pangs of being Jonas' younger step-brother, young Nathaniel waited in line as a miniature usher during the offertory. As he had stood by the open side doors waiting for the anthem to begin Nathaniel remembered watching, Sunday after Sunday, as Jonas had been misbehaving with his friends in the back pews.

"You're missing an interesting account in the sanctuary," Fiona said from the nearest open door.

"What does it matter how Adam became, or escaped from being, Jonas' apprentice?" Nathaniel said with a hint of disdain.

"It matters a great deal how Mr. Rothchild manipulated Mr. McCloud at the beginning," Fiona offered. She slipped the rest of the way into the door. "While initially meeting with Mr. McCloud on the rooftop of *The Muse's Corner*, Mr. Rothchild pretended to be you. He also had Mr. McCloud convinced that you were Miss Redmond's missing persons culprit; that you had somehow stolen her the same way that the victims from her case files had been taken. Of course, it wasn't long after falling into the trap that Mr. McCloud realized the lies. By the time the violin had been extracted from Jonathan's fingertips in the motel, it was too late . . . He wanted to reach out to her. But Mr. Rothchild forced him to watch us under strict orders not to expose his identity. He threatened to do harm to Miss Redmond if her fiancé didn't adhere."

Nathaniel's focus was then on the beveled glass where he could make out the dark blotted shape of Adam in the front pews. "A play-by-play isn't needed, thank you," he said flatly.

Veritably, Nathaniel didn't need a play-by-play. What he needed was to hibernate. He wanted so badly to disappear from this state of affairs by burying himself in his work and, in the process, cram the memories of Annette into the crevice from which they had surfaced. Sadly, returning to his private sanctuary was no longer an opposite alternative. The fragmented pieces of his office rested in Purgatory like cracked shards of an unwanted porcelain. The emotionally fortified rotunda walls, which had been built to keep out Evangeline and her invading reincarnations, had been fragmented beyond repair.

"Please talk to me, Mr. Cauliflower," Fiona said sympathetically.

"What else is there to say?" Nathaniel looked at Fiona. Though his words were sharp, his tone of voice was composed. "You held Annette and Lyle's honeymoon flight in 2009 so that Adam Mansfield could board the plane at the last minute. You gave Annette Adam's blue-colored peg when she was a Ninth Generation muse. I watched as you stitched their stories into a romance. You even brought Adam here to Annette's first retirement party so that, if she had reincarnated, he could reincarnate with her. You caused Annette Redmond and Adam McCloud to meet under a street lamp on Christmas Eve in their new lives and I had to watch them as they developed the relationship that you, yourself, set into motion. And you have the nerve to stand here giving me a rundown on his deceitful actions as Jonas' apprentice as if you're still on his side, rooting for him!" Nathaniel stared at her intently. "You knew how many lives I'd suffered to find Evangeline. You knew how much I'd yearned to be with her over the decades and throughout various reincarnations to evoke that one secluded evening we had in 1808. You knew how I felt about Annette and yet you were uninterruptedly an advocate for their union!"

The acidity in his voice deflated. He physically buckled under the weight of this stress and leaned his forehead against the window's glass melting into an overwhelming defeat. Nathaniel closed his eyes. "I'm at the lowest I've ever felt. I can't do this anymore, Fiona. There's no sense in trying to cling to something that I know Management doesn't want for me." He gave a long sigh and spoke in a volume no louder than a whisper. "I give up."

"Words that no muse should hear from anyone," Fiona quietly responded.

Nathaniel was too inflexible with hopelessness to move.

"My intentions to bring Mr. Mansfield into Mrs. Slocum's life were in your best interest," Fiona started to explain. She paused for a brief moment to allow a response from Nathaniel but he was too wrapped up in his misery to answer. She went on. "When Mrs. Slocum was indoctrinated as a modern day Ninth Generation muse I felt confident that, after you had waited a healthy length of time for her official arrival, you would introduce yourself properly to your childhood friend; that you would perhaps put an end to the avoidant silent silliness. Instead, you ducked into the restroom and kept yourself apart from her furthering the circumvention. As you and I both know, you ducked out of sight whenever she entered a room. You made more of an effort to sidestep her than you did to be a part of her life. I knew that you loved her but I also knew that you didn't appreciate the effort that Management went through to return the reincarnation of Evangeline. So I took steps to implement an alternate love affair for Mrs. Slocum. Not out of nastiness but to vicariously spur you into action. I figured that if you noticed she was with someone else you would fight to tell her how you felt.

"To my surprise, you did nothing. You allowed their relationship to flourish and, as a result, you were broken-hearted. You punished her with sixty-eight violet envelopes at the end of her musing term. I thought you would be inspired to act upon your feelings in a constructive way then, but no. You avoided her at her retirement party. You were so close in meeting her, Mr. Cauliflower. All you had to do was stay at the table with library books. If Mrs. Slocum would have stayed, met you, and taken the role as my replacement . . ." Fiona shook her head. "But Mrs. Slocum didn't stay. She reincarnated. You let her walk out that door as if she was just another muse when I knew she meant more to you!"

Fiona kept on with her story. "Management and I gave you another chance, you see. It was Christmas Eve and the snow was falling heavily upon a graveyard. As you and I meandered through the field of gravestones, I knew that Miss Redmond was watching us closely. You had the opportunity then to intervene. You could have introduced yourself to her on that night and been a part of her life but you didn't. She waved at you, you waved at her, and that was it. Management and I gave you every occasion to reconnect with her but you intentionally neglected the favors. I've never understood why."

His eyes opened at this but his forehead remained stuck to the glass.

"I suppose that's one of humanity's most basic follies: letting feelings go unspoken. Take a look at Harriet, for instance: she died of a torn aorta before she could tell her friend Harold her true feelings. And Mr. Richardson: he lost Gabriel during the terrorist attacks on the World Trade Center before they were able to express their emotions. I suppose take my story as well . . ."

Fiona grew complacent. "There was a young man during the Salem Witch Trials, Alexander Thibodaux, whom I loved dearly. I never expressed my adoration. I want to say we were in love, but we only batted eyes at one another a few times prior. It was nothing that you could constitute as a shared appreciation. I, like you, was given talents that were considered the work of the Devil. When Alexander's father accused me of witchcraft I stood trial and was ultimately sentenced to death by burning. In the end, because of my neglectfulness, Alexander was brutally attacked while defending me in the trials. He didn't know of my unspoken affections and I wonder if he would be alive if I had expressed my feelings. I wonder if we would have blissfully lived the rest of our lives apart from the colonists. But my words went unspoken. Alexander's father forced his son to light the pyre. And as the fire cooked the straw beneath my feet I watched as Alexander was promptly murdered for his supposed conspiracy to save me. As snow fell on the ground that day, also collecting on the blank expression on Alexander's lifeless face, I died. After three thousand pegs I was given one that sent me back to Alexander. But I couldn't hold him. I couldn't speak to him. I watched his life race through the years that he had been alive each time ending in the fateful moment between him and the angry Salem Puritan mob. I gave the colored peg to you for safekeeping and haven't reviewed his life since. My thoughts went to him as they often do but no amount of wishful thinking could bring him to me the way that he was.

"What I have left of him is a portrait on my office wall and an old faded parchment that contained a love letter I meant to give to him three days before the trial. Mrs. Slocum graciously brought Alexander back to me for her Ninth Generation retirement party but it wasn't the same. You see, though he was present at the party it was a mirage. It was as if revisiting the yellow-colored peg. We couldn't touch. When he opened his mouth to speak he didn't have a voice. He couldn't hear or understand me due to his ghost being deaf and dumb. I couldn't communicate how much I loved him. And then he was gone. He faded with the other retirement illusions.

"You at least told Mrs. Slocum how you felt about her. Expressing those feelings gets it out there into the open. Imagine how painful it feels, Mr. Cauliflower, to love someone and to know that, no matter how much you want to, you can never tell them. And what's worse that you can never, like me, save them when they needed rescuing the most."

"Annette doesn't need my help," Nathaniel told Fiona. His gaze was toward the window looking past Adam and the muses to the visually distorted Lite-Brite.

"Of course she does, Mr. Cauliflower." She turned to him. "The majority of the Nine Greatest Muses, including the two of us, are already dead. There are a small fraction of them that are alive – Mrs. Slocum being one. She's fragile, Mr. Cauliflower. If something goes wrong at the slightest misstep Mrs. Slocum could die again. I can't make any guarantee that she'll return to us or that you'll ever find her. No matter how many times you reincarnate."

Fiona placed a comforting hand on Nathaniel's back. As she did, Nathaniel flinched slightly with a brief intake of breath.

"You've lived seven lifetimes with regrets, Mr. Cauliflower. I'd hate to see that trend persist. The past gives us a firm foundation to build upon. We must not be so concerned with the roots that we forget to ride on the growing, winding branches that rise above."

Nathaniel considered Fiona's words. He stood upright. "What needs to be done once I get there?"

"Mr. Rothchild has taken several inspirations from us," Fiona said matter-of-factly. "For this to end, we need to steal them back and return everyone, including Mrs. Slocum, home safe and sound."

The grand exodus had already been set into motion. All Nathaniel needed was to gather his strength and fearlessly assist. Even though he may not be the ultimate victor by winning her heart at least Nathaniel could live without an added regret.

"The individual who takes over your role of Head Muse is going to have large shoes to fill, Fiona."

"They'll be who they'll be," Fiona said with her own smile. "They'll bring their own wisdom, backgrounds and agendas. We must have faith that, no matter who we invite into our offices, that person has righteousness; even if it may take seven lifetimes, or even three-thousand colored pegs, to find it."

Nathaniel left Fiona in the narthex and passed by the pews on his way to the altar. Adam was involved in telling about his escape from Sisyphus Hill. His story was put on hold.

"Hey! Hey Nate!" Those were the words called out as Nathaniel went by. He didn't stop as his childhood name was called by Annette's fiancé.

Adam caught up with him and said "Nate, wait up!"

"Yes, Mr. McCloud?" Nathaniel asked with pursed lips. His fingers were on Phillip's red-colored peg ready to rotate it clockwise.

"You can't go to that house. There's no getting out. Icarus and I barely escaped."

Nathaniel started to rotate the colored peg clockwise.

"Trust me, bro. Annette's marooned. You don't know the house like I know it."

Nathaniel raised an eyebrow and said blandly, "You'd be surprised."

Adam reached for the colored peg but Nathaniel gave him a pointed look. He said to Nathaniel, "Fine. If you're going I'm going with you."

With this proposition, Nathaniel looked over his shoulder at the dilapidated church and the muses who gathered at the front pews. From his standpoint Lucas was trying to converse with Icarus but was greeted by depressing avoidance. Nathaniel looked at Edgar Allen Poe who casually sat on the side gathering ideas for his future writings. He looked to Fiona who stood at the narthex door with her arms folded. She nodded to Nathaniel as if accepting Adam's terms on the contender's behalf. Nathaniel knew that if he succeeded with this commission he would be returning back to the same building in the original timeline. He knew that, in the correct timeline, this building would be immaculately littered with yellow flowers. The pews would be occupied by family and friends. Nathaniel knew that he would have to allow Annette to go. Though this saddened him, and though he would have to live without Annette in the long run, Nathaniel took satisfaction that his personal send-off would be spectacular.

CHAPTER 23: A BITTERSWEET ACT OF MERCY

On the kitchen counter sat a carton containing a dozen large eggs, a half-gallon jug of skim milk, an unopened bag of all-purpose flour, a stone jar filled with sugar, a box of baking soda, a decanter of vegetable oil, a closed cardboard cylinder of salt, a flask of vanilla and a sealed plastic bag of powdered sugar. These ingredients encircled an empty glass bowl which Doris stared at with a blank expression. She was positioned in the halo of a yellow light from a single bulb above her head. It was a slimy color akin to the mucus-like pastels of a putrid, fly-infested swamp. Her thick coke-bottle lenses, in their unflattering black frames, accentuated her profound absentmindedness.

Doris hoped that, by instinctively reaching for an egg, the recipe would come to her. As her fingers touched the cold hard shell of the first egg, Doris felt a wave of concentrated confusion. The egg, or what the egg represented, wasn't familiar. She left the egg alone and reached for the bag of flour. But she second-guessed herself on that, too. Her eyes shifted to the half-gallon of milk. No matter where she started, Doris frowned upon strange objects that didn't seem to add up.

"What are we making?" said a male's voice. Jonas' hand was wrapped affectionately around her middle from behind. Her lover's chin rested on Doris' left shoulder with his lips, and soothing voice, centimeters from her ear.

"I . . . I don't know," Doris tried to explain as she fell into him. "I don't know."

"You don't know how to cook," Jonas told her. "Why don't you leave dinner to me?" As he nibbled on her ear lobe, Doris closed her eyes.

"Yes . . ." Doris sighed happily. Then her eyes opened. "No. No, I set out to make something here, baby." She pulled from him and reached for the egg again. She was too busy with the ingredients to notice Jonas' look turn sour. Doris went on in saying, "When I was a girl, my parents took me to the county fair. They would buy me funnel cakes. I know how to make a funnel cake or at least I think I do. I need to remember how." Confusion swept over her. "I know the dry ingredients need to be separate from the wet –" Her words were cut short as Jonas playfully turned Doris around to face him. She wore a frilly black-and-white 1950's house dress complete with a white apron which rippled as he twirled her toward him.

Jonas pelted her with heated kisses and Doris fainted into them. His hand went up her skirt and Doris giggled.

"Baby, we have guests!" As soon as Doris said these words she was sober and serious. She turned to the ingredients. "And I want to make a good impression on our newest tenant. What was her name? Annette? She's pretty. Almost too pretty," Doris said these three words in a whisper with a hint of insecurity.

He turned her around slower this time and looked through Doris' lenses to her magnified eyes. "Doris," Jonas cooed. "I love *you*. You're more beautiful, more exquisite, than any woman I've met." Jonas shrugged his shoulders. "That's not to say that Annette isn't important. As I've told you, Annette is the reason that we're here. But she's not you. Nor does she compare." It was evident that his flattering words, even though they were a lie, affected his personal audience as distinctly as he had intended. "You love me too, don't you?" He kissed her fingertips.

"Yes," Doris blushed.

"There isn't anyone I could love more than you," Jonas sang. "And there's no one else out there who could love you any more than I ever could. No other man could possibly see in you what I do.

It's us, baby. You and me. I'll take care of you. I'll be chef enough for both of us." The enamored look in Doris' eyes told Jonas he had her where he wanted her. "Now, why don't you check on our guest? See if she's tried on that dress that you picked out for her. Meanwhile, I'll clean everything here in the kitchen."

Doris surrendered her task work, smiled and flitted out of the kitchen. The superficial head wound suffered from Adam's blow in the study had settled. She seemed as much herself as she had been. While most lovers would be pleased to see that an injury like this had healed, Jonas' paramour façade crumbled leaving the monstrous look that was true to his soul.

He found the ingredients and frowned. He opened the cabinet underneath the sink where he discovered the trashcan. Furiously dumping in the ingredients, and the glass bowl, into the black garbage bag with forceful punches, Jonas cursed the items. He ripped the bag from the trashcan and sealed it with the plastic straps, double-knotting the entrance to assure no one could gain access. He replaced the old bag with an empty one. He promptly fit the trashcan under the sink and closed the cabinet drawer. With the sealed trash bag in hand, Jonas switched out the light.

Passing by the living room on the way to the garage, Jonas spotted the bereft Lyle Slocum sitting in a tufted brown Chesterfield chair in the upstairs den hypnotized by re-run episodes of *My Three Sons.* Jonas grinned at his cleverness in keeping Doris from recreating the funnel cake recipe. If Doris had been successful in baking a funnel cake, performing the act would have run the risk of precipitately ending his long-standing agenda. Jonas had Doris and Lyle right where he wanted them. He was fiercely determined to do whatever it took to keep them, and the others, in his totalitarian control.

*

It wasn't long after the incident in the kitchen that Jonas stopped by the open study door. His newest guest was standing in the space amid the clutter. A sleek, floor-length black satin cocktail dress clung to Annette's figure as she stood in front of the fireplace mantle inspecting the pervasive petite witch of the Weather Wizard. Jonas wondered if she was trying to picture the farm house in which it had been taken. He wondered if Annette imagined the farm house to be the same quaint abode that he often did, which had served its purpose in the humble beginnings of he and Nathaniel. Dusty photo albums and other memorabilia from Jonas and Nathaniel's past littered nearly every inch and crevice of the space scaling the interior's confined perimeter. These clusters of physical evidence, which stemmed from Nathaniel and Jonas' initial collision as children, served as a stilled shockwave that once emanated from the Weather Wizard's epicenter.

The house had been empty when Jonas had disrupted Phillip's timeline. This "crap", as Jonas so often eloquently put it, had accumulated shortly after. It had cropped up in every room like misshapen fungus. Aged furniture from previous lives led, moth-eaten curtains and fragile photo albums had sprung up so often Jonas would enter a room to find something else had appeared. Whether it was another item or trinket, like a blood-stained canvas or a kerosene lamp, or a hand-knitted handkerchief with cryptic messages in red thread, these objects would compellingly conjure memories that Jonas would rather choose to forget. When he had been a Tenth Generation muse in the department, the real judgment for his actions had come from within. Here in the living world, the longer he resided at 252

Sisyphus Hill the objects themselves, and their representations, physically appeared instead.

Nothing tangible in the room spoke more of Annette's involvement than the unorganized pile of unmarked violet envelopes which were scattered about the study's desk underneath the illuminated antique brass banker's lamp that Adam had used to bludgeon Doris. Atop the pile were three violet envelopes that were numbered "4" and "2" and "1."

Though her back was to him, Jonas watched as Annette lifted both envelopes and opened the flaps. Pictures alluding to Jonas' latest additions were taken from the envelopes. He could hear her muffled anguish as she opened the "4" envelope to find a picture of her fiancé in a billiard hall accompanied by their wedding invitation.

In the envelope marked "2" she uncovered a photograph of Nathaniel in his youth on Justine's wedding day. In the photograph, Nathaniel was eight years old and dressed in a miniature tuxedo. Beside him was another boy, nine-year-old Jonas, who was also dressed to the nines. Behind both of the boys was the waist of Justine's white wedding dress along with Thomas' pant legs.

Three photographs were found in the envelope marked with a "1." Through a progression of time periods, they told the story of Evangeline and her reincarnations. The first image was a daguerreotype of a middle-aged Evangeline as she sat in a wing-back chair amidst the foliage of her château solarium. The second was a torn wedding photograph of Annette when she married Lyle Slocum in 1999. Lyle's portion of the picture had been removed during the third abduction in 2009 after Jonas, and his apprentice, had forcefully broken the front doorknob with an electric drill. Lastly, Annette found the third picture in the group: a recent photograph of her as Detective Redmond which had been taken as she had exited her bridal dress shop after a fitting.

Annette spotted another advantageously placed object amidst the desk's disorder: A Christmas ornament constructed of a crushed soda can with the face of Santa Claus painted on it. Annette approached the ornament and, looking slightly over her shoulder and missing Jonas who stood outside of her peripheral, hooked her index finger through the attached loop of red string. She lifted the ornament several inches bringing it to the palm of her left hand.

"There you are," Annette said to the Christmas ornament.

"Settling in?" Jonas asked.

Annette gave a slight gasp and turned round to face him with the Christmas ornament clinched in her hand keeping it out of sight behind her back. Jonas didn't mind that Annette held the ornament. He knew that once she touched that ornament Annette would be exactly where he wanted her.

"How do you like your room?" Jonas inquired.

Annette nodded, inspecting the study. There was a brown-leather fainting couch that served as Annette's bed which wasn't accommodating due to the precarious stacks of photo albums that rested on the cushion. "It's nice," she told him. "Vintage. Chic."

"Tour," Jonas stated with a forced smile which promptly sank as swift as it had surfaced. "And be sure to bring that Christmas ornament with you."

He nonchalantly guided his less than enthusiastic detective around a house encased in its own foul gloom.

She was introduced to the master bedroom where Doris sat at the vanity staring at her down-hearted reflection. Lyle was discovered in the upstairs den lodging in the Chesterfield chair with his glazed eyes glued to the flickering black-and-white images on an outdated 1960's tube television. A woman, whom Annette recognized as Sarah Milbourne, slept soundly in a sedate ruddiness of the pink-shaded living room lamp. A book, specifically pertaining to the scholarship and properties of storms, lay on Sarah Milbourne's waist as she dreamed. On a nearby coffee table, Annette spied a hefty stack of other college textbooks from his academic years as an Earth Sciences major. Jonas explained to Annette that Sarah Milbourne was an undiagnosed narcoleptic whom he had been assigned to inspire.

"I felt in my heart that I was brought to her to inspire her to wake and seek medical attention for her disease. To grasp what the world had to offer," Jonas told Annette in a full voice. There was no need to whisper as Sarah Milbourne was intensely deadened by paralysis. "But how could I, in good conscience, introduce her to a world that I, myself, hated? I knew that if she was going to wake, or if anyone in this world had to successfully survive, I had to pick things apart to make it adequate."

Also asleep in the living room on a separate couch was another one of Jonas' victims: the man from whom the violin had been taken. Jonathan slept in the same troubled position which Jonas had found him. From Jonas' perspective, Annette carried an authentically saddened expression on seeing the impecunious violinist.

It was a look that she sported as a door to the upstairs guest bedroom was opened a crack and Annette peered in. This had been Phillip's room during his glow-in-the-dark-starred childhood when the red peg had been turned counter-clockwise. The room was void of prior cosmic accoutrements. In the space were intentionally torn canvases of ruined paintings from Jonas' Romanticism period as a painter; the discarded artwork was propped against the room's four walls as a deliberate aide-mémoire of how it had originated in 1808. A wooden chair was positioned by the room's only window. It had been the same window that Phillip had looked out in his teens when he found his mother making a bonfire of his father's belongings. Sitting in the chair, with his back turned to Annette, was Phillip as he stared out the glass to the billowing thunderclouds. The clouds blotted the stars that may have inspired Jonas' grandchild, further establishing Jonas as an empowered regulator.

"This could have been avoided," Jonas told Annette as they approached the stairs leading to the finished basement. "There was a broken record with a scratched melody that both you and Broccoli listened to. It was the 'singing destiny' on that vinyl that brought us here. If you hadn't been so impetuous to hear the record that Broccoli was playing then you wouldn't have known the destiny that awaited. If you hadn't known that destiny, you would have, in all likelihood, put the envelope into that mailbox as instructed."

They stopped at the closed basement door. It had been kicked in at some point from the looks of things but had been rehung. Jonas did not enter. Instead, he yakked directly to Annette. "If you had put the misdirected letter in the mailbox, you wouldn't have escaped and reincarnated through seven lifetimes. And Broccoli wouldn't have chased you. He and I wouldn't have reincarnated into this life and become step-brothers. History would have been different, Annette. So, in essence, the person you have to blame for this mess . . . is the same red-headed detective who's been obsessing over this case. Irony is a depraved thing, isn't it?"

Annette looked at Jonas and scrunched her face into a righteous scowl. "If you're trying to discourage me from rescuing these people, it's not going to work."

"Annette, Annette, Annette . . ." Jonas shook his head with a smile. He took hold of the handle and turned it, opening the door wide. "I'm not trying to discourage you to do anything, honest," he said with a warm, inviting smile. He showed her through the door. Annette gave him a distrusting look but went in regardless. Jonas entered the room and closed the door behind them. The single kerosene lamp-lit common room was as he had left it but with a slightly irritating festive excess in its formerly tasteless decor.

Similarly, as the funnel cake ingredients had appeared for Doris in the kitchen, uncapped plastic totes topped with Christmas decorations had appeared as blistering cankers. There were wreaths and garlands of timeless replica foliage, crinkled oversized red ribbon bows, faded piano sheet music, a tatty snow sled from Thomas' youth and, finally, several tangled balls of burnt-out Christmas tree lights which Luanne feverishly tried to disentangle. A fake tree stood resolute in the center of the room which Luanne had intended to embellish once the lights were in working order. Thankfully for Jonas, the Christmas decorations lacked the very enhancement that it so desperately required: an assemblage of dangling ornaments.

"Oh, Jonas, thank goodness you're here," Luanne said as she turned to find him watching. She looked at Annette. "Oh, hello."

"Luanne, this is Annette. Annette, this is Luanne," Jonas cordially made introductions even though he knew that Annette was aware of Luanne's transgendered, bowling-alley worker origins.

Luanne asked Jonas, "Would you mind giving me a hand with these lights? If I can get the physical kinks out, I'll go through bulb by bulb and find the ones that are causing the rest to go dark." She turned her attention to the totes and then the tree. "Not to mention that I can't find a single ornament, not one! I know I had a collection of them around here somewhere but it seems to have grown legs . . ."

"Luanne," Jonas took the mass of jumbled lights into his own hands. "Christmas isn't for a few months yet. There's no use stressing over the lights, or the ornaments, at this point in time. You look exhausted. Why don't you rest in your room? I'll work on each strand until they're exactly where they need to be."

Exhausted confusion crossed over Luanne's face as she surrendered her work. Luanne disappeared into a doorway to the downstairs bedroom that had once belonged to Jonas in his youth leaving him and Annette in the common-room.

With the ball of Christmas lights still in hand, Jonas stepped closer to Annette and frowned. The room's lit kerosene lamp accentuated his stern facial features as he stared with his emotionless eyes.

"You want to give her the Christmas ornament, don't you?" Jonas gave a chortle and said "Fine. If you're so inclined to give her the ornament, I'm not going to stop you." He stepped aside to let Annette pass.

For a moment, Annette had a look of distrust and didn't move.

"What is that piece of junk anyway?" Jonas sneered. "It's not worth two cents to the person who dreamed it."

"It's a symbol alluding to the connection between her and her children," Annette explained. "If you had taken the time to review your granddaughter's storyline, you would've noticed the importance of the Christmas ornaments in her life. There's nothing greater than the bond between a loving parent and their child. Though I didn't rotate her peg clockwise, I would imagine that's what this ornament was supposed to teach her."

"The bond between a loving parent and their child," Jonas said in a whisper. "Excellent point, Annette." He took a breath and said to her in a friendly voice, "You know I wonder, before you give Luanne her Christmas ornament, if you might want to finish the tour? There's one guest whom you haven't met."

Annette's eyes squinted questioningly. "Where are you keeping Adam?"

"Adam?" Jonas turned his head quizzically to the side, "Oh, that dupe fiancé of yours?" He grimaced. "He escaped through my Lite-Brite board. I tried to keep a tight leash on him as my apprentice. He whacked Doris over the head with the study's lamp. Some man you've got there, Annette. A real lady-killer."

"Adam . . . Adam was the apprentice?" Annette gave a confused stare. "You told Icarus that it was Mr. Cauliflower."

"If I told Icarus that Adam was the apprentice, you wouldn't have come running. They escaped together to the church through Broccoli's clockwise-turned blue-colored peg. You remember that peg, don't you? You rotated it and inspired him as a boy to repair *The*

Hobbit. I used the asphodel door to visit Management's library. I found Broccoli's, and your previous clients' peg, in the system. I stole them and brought them here. When I turned Broccoli's peg clockwise I was able to visit the department to review the newest colored pegs when you and Broccoli weren't looking. That's how I was able to access Phillip's peg. And Luanne's. And my father's. It was also how Adam escaped from the house. It took him to Broccoli's future. It took him to the church where, I suppose, he is currently. With Adam having escaped to your arms, I had to take steps. Before he and Icarus disappeared into the folding and unfolding, I threatened Icarus for Lucas' safety and gave him orders." Jonas gave a slight smile. "To tell you that the apprentice was Broccoli. I knew it would make you doubt him and cause you to inevitably travel here. It's sort of a game he and I have played since boyhood. Seeing him suffer is like sucking fresh air for me."

"So Adam isn't in the house?"

"He isn't here in the house."

"Who's my favorite client you're holding captive?"

He tossed the ball of Christmas ornaments to one of the totes and motioned for Annette to follow him to the room opposite of Luanne's: the bedroom that belonged to his bookish step-brother.

The personal library that Nathaniel kept in his bedroom had sprouted in the same mildew-type infestation. A man was sitting on the edge of the bed that faced the far wall so that the identity of the occupant remained elusive. Jonas watched from the open doorway as Annette quietly approached the person and stopped far enough away so as not to startle him. From Jonas' vantage point, the man held in his hands a gardening book which had been opened to reveal the page on asphodel flowers.

"Hello?" Annette asked the figure.

The man turned around and, seeing Annette, jumped from the bed hugging her warmly.

"Daddy?" Annette's eyes widened as her father from her life as Annette Slocum greeted her with affection.

This was the same influential man from Annette's previous life who had encouraged imaginative thinking; her father who had taken her to her first violin concert when she had been eight years old and said as the lights had dimmed in the auditorium: "Allow the violin to paint a portrait in your head, then tell me all about what you imagined when we go out for ice cream." This was the same father who had once preached to Annette that, "The next time they pick on you, speak as a main character in a book would speak, with strength and confidence. Annette, reasoning is better than fist-fights and, in ten years, everything will have changed. As you grow older, think to yourself how you want to be remembered." This was the very same man who had bought Annette her first car after graduation, a weathered 1979 VW Beetle, so that she could explore the world. It was the same inspiring man who, moments before Annette had married Lyle in 1999, as the bridesmaids, flower girl, five-year-old ring bearer, congregation and Lyle had all been awaiting her arrival, had said to his immobile antisocial daughter: "Don't let your marriage to Lyle define you. He's a good man, yes, and he'll make you very happy, no doubt about it. He'll be able to support your family. Annette, if you ever listened to your old man about anything," her father had taken a breath, smiled. "Don't forget to find things in your future that inspire *you*."

"Annette . . . ?" her father told her at present, choked with tears. "I thought you were on your honeymoon in Vegas with Lyle. What are you doing here?"

It was true, Jonas had managed to reconnect Annette with her father by way of interrupting an important timeline. But the reunion he had formulated, though heartfelt, also carried with it a price.

"Annette . . ." Jonas said, clearing his throat. "A word?"

Annette looked at her father and smiled. He smiled back. She squeezed his hand and, turning to Jonas, sported her scowl. Seconds later, she and Jonas were in the common room. Jonas closed the door, distinguishing a barrier between Annette and her father.

"As you know, during your Vegas honeymoon with Lyle in 1999, your father encountered heart issues which brought him to the hospital. He died from complications in a last-minute late-night surgery bringing about his untimely death. I've brought him back for you before all that as a welcome gift."

"That's generous," Annette wiped a stray tear from her cheek.

"I have to wonder, though. Did your father have any issues with his heart prior to that night?" Jonas wanted to know.

"Not that I know of. Why?"

"You're absolutely certain?" Jonas asked. When Annette nodded, Jonas nodded. "Have you ever heard of potassium chloride?" The gratifying look of a chilling defeat on Annette's face brought Jonas' heart to race. "It's what's commonly used during a prison inmate lethal injection. The individual is placed under an immediate anesthetic followed by a calming paralytic agent. Then, the potassium chloride is injected which slows the heart rate causing an imbalance in the electrolytes. It results in ventricular contractions . . . therefore inducing a heart attack.

"We come to the point in our conversation where a decision needs to be made, Annette. You can give the Christmas ornament to Luanne. You can save your victims, if you desire. If you do, however, I'll be sure to inject your father with the potassium chloride. And don't think you'll get away with inserting him into his cream-colored pink-polkadotted timeline where I wouldn't get my hands on him. I know where I can find him at any time and, when I do, I'll kill him.

"Imagine though, if he lived. Think of how many people would have been inspired by him! Imagine how many lives your mother would have touched had she not been consumed by suicidal depression from your father's death? I'm offering you a second chance with them. A second chance to make things right."

Annette was visibly shaken.

Jonas slinked around her and said smoothly, "Before you go around talking about what a brute I am, I want you to remember that I'm following in your footsteps."

"I've never threatened the life of your parents," Annette argued.

"I see it differently," Jonas countered. "It was a cold, snowy morning during January in 1979 when you and Broccoli stood in the middle of a highway road. My father and mother were driving through the blizzard in their Mercedes. I had just been born, you see. Only a few days old when you and Broccoli caused a devastating accident. An accident, interestingly enough, which caused my mother to die because you had to play the perfect muse! I wonder if Broccoli and I would have even met if my mother hadn't been killed in that accident. My dad and I wouldn't have been introduced to Justine. We wouldn't have moved to another state. You and I would've never met under that apple. So it comes full circle, Annette. It's your fault."

He put an arm around Annette, crushing her. "All you have to do is to go with me and stop the car accident from happening. You can do that, can't you?"

"Stop it yourself," Annette spat while trying to pry herself from Jonas' snare.

"Oh, if I could, I would. I've tried, Annette. Out of the colored pegs my dad's is the one I can't rotate. Almost as if it doesn't want to be rotated . . ."

"That should be a clue you shouldn't be messing with it."

"Inaccessible no matter what I do!" Jonas went on, ignoring Annette's words. "But you, Annette, are the one who owned the peg when it was assigned. Part of me believes that Broccoli hoodwinked it so that it couldn't be rotated by anyone else . . ."

Annette sighed. "I see where you're going with this."

"If you stop the accident from happening, your father will go free."

"What do you hope to accomplish?" Annette wanted to know. "If we spare your mother, you won't meet Nathaniel and therefore won't end up being who you are. Your work in stealing Luanne, Phillip, Lyle and the others would be for nothing. We'd be encountering another paradox."

He shook his head. "That's not how I see it." His grip around Annette's arms tightened. "Once that change happens, everything else will fall into place. The Dandelion Sisters have promised me that, in my new timeline, I'll be in charge. A sovereign leader in an alternate world where everything is to my liking! You see, Annette? I'm not trying to discourage you from giving Luanne her Christmas ornament. You should consider weighing your choices appropriately.

"In my new world, we'll be happy. I'll have my mom. You'll have your father and everything else will disappear like it never happened. Think of it. You can make different choices. You already know where to find Adam Mansfield in that *Muse's Corner* bookstore of his. If you play our cards right you can have that pie shop."

There was more that Jonas had to say in regards to the mysterious door and the toolbox, but he kept this information to himself.

Jonas was surprised at how quickly Annette measured, and accepted, his proposal with four straightforward words: "Alright, I'll do it." Jonas expected Annette to fight with the same dynamism that she had employed when stealing her obituary from him during her Ninth Generation term. This was no longer about procuring a wrinkled clipping from a local newspaper. There were higher stakes for everyone involved leading Jonas to question if Annette had accepted defeat on purpose.

Jonas positioned a spare Lite-Brite from the study's closet. As Jonas had hoped, Annette was able to rotate Thomas' peg counterclockwise. Together they watched as Thomas' youth and his love for Kathleen unfolded. It recited Thomas' visit to the Dandelion Sisters and developed, passage by passage, eventually delving into the details of Jonas' birth. At last, the blizzard appeared and time slowed. From a distance, past the wall of falling flakes, Jonas and Annette watched as the past versions of Nathaniel and the red-headed detective Redmond stood in the snow-wrapped landscape. Jonas could hear the past version of detective Redmond's voice as she called "Hello!" followed by an additional comment: "Hello, out there in the snow!"

The past version of detective Redmond waved at them.

"We're the people standing in the snow," Annette said to Jonas. "I remember that from the inspiration. I remember waving to two dark strangers thinking that they were my clients. But we're those strangers."

"How does it feel, Annette?" Jonas stepped forward as the current Annette Slocum shivered in the black cocktail dress. "Knowing that we're looking at a past version of ourselves and that, at any moment, we'll both have the lives we've wanted . . . deserved?"

When his question went unanswered, Jonas spun to find that he was alone in the snow. He looked to his left, then to his right. He squinted his eyes while attempting to cut a ribbon of vision through the blizzard. Though Annette had left him, Jonas was mildly satisfied that he wasn't expelled from this event by her absence. Perhaps all that he really needed was Annette to rotate the peg and he didn't need her to stay! He turned to the accident as the cars approached on the icy road. Even if Annette wasn't going to be there to help him, Jonas felt confident that, as he had been able to control the lives of the other victims, this particular instance would bow to his will. He clinched his fists and stomped through the snow wincing at the iced lashes of the whipping sleet. A warming thought akin to the fires in the fall of

Rome burned on his mind: once he changed this timeline, the Dandelion Sisters would have no use for Annette. She would be irretrievably dispensable.

*

Nathaniel entered his childhood room where three filled syringes were laid on his nightstand. They had been numbered as to suggest a particular injection's order. There was also an open medical kit that included a clean towel, sterile adhesive bandages, gauze pads, alcohol wipes and latex gloves.

He and Adam stood over Annette's sleeping father studying his face. It reminded Nathaniel of the lifeless faces of Justine and Thomas in their caskets.

"Listen, Nate," Adam told Nathaniel. "I would appreciate it if you wouldn't tell her that I was Jonas' apprentice."

"What would you suggest that I tell her?" Nathaniel wanted to know.

There came a knock at the bedroom door. He and Adam scrambled to various shadow-draped corners of the room. Nathaniel watched from behind a bookcase as Annette stepped into the room and approached her father's bed, kneeling. Nathaniel and Adam shared a look of recognition. From Nathaniel's perspective, Annette's eyes darted to the three syringes on the nightstand. He could see tears on her cheeks as she leaned in close.

"Daddy?" she whispered. "Are you awake?"

For a split second, her father didn't stir. His eyes opened and he smiled at his daughter.

"Daddy, I don't know what to do."

"Annette . . ." her father smiled. "I was listening at the door to what Jonas was saying."

"I want to make you proud," Annette whispered.

"Oh Annette . . ." he said, "You've made me proud! I've heard the things that Jonas said about you when he thought I wasn't listening. How you inspired these people and how you might, one day, come to save them. I've heard him whispering to his apprentice about how you had been a Ninth Generation muse in the afterlife. He talked of the future and who you had grown to be. He discussed the lives you changed in the years after you married Lyle. You're an important muse, my darling. Think of what you've learned and encountered. Think of the lives you've changed for the better. I don't want to see any of that go to waste. You can't give in to his demands. Sometimes we have to make sacrifices in our own lives so that others may flourish."

"No . . ." Annette shook her head. There were tears in her eyes.

He looked at his daughter and smiled. "You and I both know what has to be done." He handed the syringes to her. Annette groaned and shook her head. "I'd rather you be in charge of administering the injections than Jonas."

"No." Annette looked into his eyes. "There has to be something else we can do."

"Jonas has stolen these people from their timelines. From the bright futures that God has preordained. They have to be returned, honey. And I refuse to live if it means that even one individual goes uninspired." He reached out and touched Annette on her cheek. "I remember you, Annette. I remember that you were my muse on my wedding day with your mother. You shined so brightly those many years ago and I would hate to see anyone, even yourself, take that light." Annette reached for her father's cupped hands with her own. "Do what needs to be done. And tell your mother I love her, won't you?"

Her father gave one final nod to Annette.

Nathaniel watched out of respect for her father's wishes as Annette administered the lethal injection and kissed her ailing dad lovingly on his forehead. Though he wanted to be there with her, Nathaniel knew it was right that she do this by herself.

A rift in space opened from Adam's stolen Lite-Brite board. There had been a single peg in the Lite-Brite's grid when Adam had seized it. And her fiancé turned that specific cream-colored polka-dotted peg now, which tragically belonged to Annette's father. Living home movies displayed before them which told the story of Annette's growing relationship with her father from her birth through to her wedding day and settling to this exact moment.

Nathaniel watched as Annette delivered her father to the moment he had been taken from so that he might seek medical treatment. But Nathaniel knew that Annette Slocum's father would not be revived and he said a prayer for his soul. As Annette cried, Nathaniel nodded to Adam. Adam stepped forward to receive Annette into his arms. Seeing her fiancé, Annette rushed into his embrace desperate to be held. With Annette's back to Nathaniel as she was cradled by her fiancé, he stepped out of his own respective shadow. Because he loved Annette and didn't want to see her hurt more than she already was, Nathaniel refrained from exposing Adam's truth.

Nathaniel quietly left the bedroom and revisited a familiar blizzard. From his perspective, Jonas overlooked the untouched wreckage of the motor vehicle accident in the ravine. He stood reverently beside Jonas as the instant replay of Thomas' life reached its bookmarked half-way point.

"I couldn't change it, Broccoli."

"It isn't supposed to be changed, Jonas . . ." Nathaniel sighed. "None of these timelines were supposed to change."

Jonas stared into the debris. "I had hoped that you would see my logic eventually, Broccoli. But I see you're more deluded from Management's Kool-Aid than I thought. I was trying to build an empire here. One where everyone would be free from the Pharaoh's decree of slavery. Everyone that Management touches is a blinded bondservant for someone else's will."

"You have it wrong, Jonas. The pharaoh in this story isn't Management. It's you who's the tyrant. And I've come to take them all home."

"Here we are," Jonas sighed. "At odds with one another." He circled around Nathaniel, giving his step-brother a sly smile. "You and I both know how this is going to end, Broccoli." He approached Nathaniel who reflexively retreated several steps. "Once things are changed in my way, there'll be no need for Annette as a muse. Because the destiny on that long ago broken vinyl record will be redirected to me. And when I'm in charge, I'll find Annette in one timeline or another when she's most vulnerable. I'm going to rip her away from you for good, just as you stole my mother!"

Nathaniel reached the edge of the ravine and stumbled into the steep slope of the ravine.

Jonas grabbed him by the scruff of his dress shirt. He dragged Nathaniel to his feet and shoved Nathaniel into the side of the Mercedes where, through the glass of the passenger window, Kathleen's lifeless face could be seen.

Nathaniel spied Kathleen and looked at Jonas. Nathaniel's left glasses lens was cracked.

"Perhaps, Broccoli, I'll take Annette when she's reading a book at the local library. Or when she's standing over a pie pouring in the filling. Yes, I think that's more fitting: allowing her a head start on happiness, don't you?"

There came a piercing sound that sang through the falling flakes.

Jonas' eyes squinted. "That sound . . ." Jonas whispered, thrashing his head to hear it better. It was a solid high-pitched note on the broken wind. "That sound!"

The pop-up book of Thomas Rothchild violently broke apart beneath them. They were in 252 Sisyphus Hill where the note rose in crescendo. Nathaniel surmised that Jonathan had gained possession of his violin again and had taken a bow to the strings.

With Jonas' grip still on his step-brother's shirt, Nathaniel reached into his pants pocket and took out a repaired, unwound string of Christmas lights from the downstairs family room. He wrapped them around Jonas' wrists securing the string into a tight, inescapable knot. Jonas looked at the knot. His eyes were furious. Jonas screamed as he tried, and failed, to flee from his bondage. He charged toward Nathaniel, accidentally crashing into the side table with the kerosene lamp. It wobbled as Jonas stumbled but the lamp remained upright. Nathaniel dodged Jonas' advance and seized the excess string of lights. Jonas lost control of his balance giving Nathaniel the opportunity to guide Jonas toward the center of the room where Jonas collided with the tree. It toppled on top of him. Nathaniel took the seconds to secure Jonas' feet with a string of lights making him entirely inert. It was Nathaniel's turn to stand victoriously over Jonas. Instead of looking smug, Nathaniel was more interested in the colored pegs that had been kicked up into the air, suspended like dust mites.

The fallen colored pegs were rising again, signaling the repairs to Jonathan's timeline.

Rumbles of thunder in correlation to the repaired timeline shook beneath his feet. Nathaniel looked down at Jonas who wrestled the knotted Christmas lights. He then found Annette, who stood across the room. Nathaniel wasn't sure what was going through her head but he hoped that she noticed Jonas' current vaulted condition. He hoped she carefully considered what this could mean for their severed friendship.

The violin music played on. Though the first few notes that came from Jonathan's repaired instrument were questionable, the memories of his violin experience reignited. What had started as a simple series of notes transformed into a brilliant violin partita by Johann Sebastian Bach.

The direct results from the music were instantaneous. As the solo was played, Luanne was in the presence of her Christmas ornament. Phillip stood from his chair to spy a single star in a patch of night time sky beyond the parting clouds. Doris looked from her vanity. Lyle stirred from his Chesterfield chair. Sarah Milbourne's eyes opened slightly. With this awareness, more colored pegs rose into mid-air.

But this small victory was nothing compared to the deadly warfare that lay ahead.

As Nathaniel and Annette bridged the spatial gap between them, Jonas excitedly spied a pair of polished sharpened shears in one of the overturned holiday totes. Out of the fungal enhancements of his physical memories that had sprung since he'd been here, Jonas found one he could utilize to his advantage and he promptly put it to use.

CHAPTER 24: THE MIRACLES THAT BROKE FORTH

Nathaniel was unaware that Jonas had covertly obtained the scissors and therefore he did not invest in a mad dash as he ascended to the upstairs. While Jonathan's violin music rang throughout the house, Nathaniel found the Weather Wizard on the mantle. He frowned and shook his head slightly at the eye-catching reminiscences it invoked. He recalled, in colorful detail, the farm house from where it had been taken and the lazy summer days young Nathaniel had spent in the company of his great aunt. He recalled the cracked dining room floor as it had buckled from the weight of the heavy table and chairs. He remembered the sweet frozen milk his great aunt had stashed away in the freezer. Nathaniel recollected the afternoon that she had showed him, first-hand, that "by cutting off the butt of a wasp with a kitchen knife does not mean the wasp would instantly die." These memories of the farm house, and the additional fragments of those slothful childhood days, blinded Nathaniel as he stared at the Weather Wizard's miniature witch.

To make matters more problematic, the stack of photo albums on the fainting couch were disturbed in the ruckus and they collided to the floor. One opened on its own to reveal pictures from Nathaniel's childhood which showed him as an infant being held aloft by the arms of his smiling mother. Flipping the pages, Nathaniel found images of his great aunt. Memories snowballed on Nathaniel: hallucinations of countless bedtime stories that his great aunt had read to him. It had been her active involvement in Nathaniel's early tot years that ignited his intellectual pursuit of reading any book that he could get his outstretched hands on (children's, classic or otherwise).

After his great aunt had died many years later, Nathaniel had collected scores of favorite books in his adult life because some of them, when held, brought a sense of safety. When Nathaniel had been alive, he hunted through extensive book drives at the library. He had picked through other people's collections at short-lived garage sales and frequented off-the-cuff used bookstores, like *The Muse's Corner,* to track missing manuscripts for his personal museum. He had never ordered online, nor had he gone to larger chain bookstores to obtain his copies. Half of the fun of acquiring the titles he coveted was procuring the used copies himself.

By happenstance, he had much success procuring most of the compulsory titles except for one: an illustrated children's book entitled *The Talking Eggs* written by Robert D. San Souci. The illustrations were drawn by Jerry Pinkney. Out of all of the books, that one had the most impact. It had been the first book that Nathaniel had remembered his great aunt having read to him.

*

A comforting autumn breeze brushed through the farmhouse curtains as she read aloud to Nathaniel from the children's book. He would forever remember the varying vocal inflections his great aunt adopted in telling the Creole folktale of a sweet girl named Blanche, who lived with her mean older sister Rose and an overbearing mother. While Blanche obediently did the chores around their dilapidated farmhouse, Rose and her mother sat lazily and talked about a fantasized life of riches. They were cruel and downright cross to Blanche ordering her to do duties without lifting a finger themselves.

One day, as Blanche fetched water from a nearby well, she kindly aided a mystical old hag in obtaining a cool sip from the liquid deep underground. The water dampened the woman's cracked lips.

In the story, upon the main character visiting the old woman's farm as a reward, Blanche found oddities including misshapen cattle with corkscrews instead of horns and whistling multicolored chickens. Blanche watched in awe as the beldam removed her own head and sat it on her lap to braid her hair properly. Blanche, being an obedient and respectful child, did not laugh or gawk and stare at the crone who put her head back on appropriately. The harridan had been nothing but kind to her so Blanche continued to be a well-behaved young lady. She courteously fetched kindling for the woman's crazily concocted feast and was genuinely overjoyed by the after-dinner festivities as rabbits in dapper frock coats and colorful trail-train dresses danced on their hind legs to the playing of a banjo. Blanche's exciting adventures in the magical house commenced the following day as she dutifully helped the benefactress with the morning chores of her own volition.

Blanche was told she had to return to her own home but, before she did, the woman gave her an unexpected incentive for her good behavior. Blanche was told to go to the henhouse on her way out of the farm and to abide specific instructions: Blanche was allowed to take the eggs that said "Take me" and leave the ones that stated otherwise. Per the request, once Blanche retrieved the "Take me" eggs, she was counseled to toss them over her shoulder while on the road home. She found two types of eggs in the henhouse – plain eggs that sang "Take me" and bejeweled sparkling eggs that screamed "Don't take me" just as the woman had explained. She implicitly observed the directives given to her, even though Blanche so desperately wanted to take at least one gold one! With the basket of eggs in hand, Blanche waved goodbye to her elderly hostess who, in turn, waved back. And so, at this point in the story, Blanche had the first of many plain eggs she collected and tossed it. She was pleasantly reassured and overly ecstatic with what had poured out from the broken shell.

*

"Monsieur Cauliflower, where are you?" Nathaniel waved his interrupted childhood memory to find Annette standing beside him and the open photo album looking concerned. Jonathan's violin music could be heard from the upstairs living room.

Nathaniel was suddenly very cognizant of his memories.

"It's this house," he explained while consulting the photo album. "These things are too much of a trigger. I don't know what's worse, really. Being present in Purgatory where the memories that define you are ripped apart or standing in a place like this: where there are too many memories to conceivably manage." He moved his cracked drooping glasses frames to the bridge of his nose. "I've spent the majority of my lives remembering when I should have been living." He said earnestly, "I don't want to remember so much anymore that I forget to live in these current moments."

Annette nodded slowly.

It was one thing to be told about a personal vice by someone else; it was another to be aware of it for oneself. Nathaniel wanted to believe that he could shed the memories and make a life for himself in the future but he wasn't sure how to fathom an expedition of that magnitude. The truth was, in anyone's case, not all memories were meant to be disregarded. The memory of his great aunt's reading of San Souci's fable was the model for how Nathaniel would live the rest of his life, assembling himself into the paradigm of a male protagonist.

*

"See what's happening here, Nathaniel?" his great aunt whispered to him at the turn of the page. "As a reward for Blanche's pleasant behavior, all sorts of things spilled out of those plain broken eggs. An assortment of treasures: diamonds, rubies, coins, beautiful dresses and satin shoes. Even a proud pony and a big old carriage!" She went on to say, "If you live your life as a sweet soul like Blanche, you'll be as content. Remember, Blanche wasn't expecting payback for her kindness. Promise me that you'll live your life as selflessly, and meekly, as Blanche."

Young Nathaniel looked to his great aunt and said, with as much belief as his young lungs could muster, "I will, Auntie . . . I will."

*

The current Nathaniel closed the photo album and placed it, and the others from the floor, on the cushion of the fainting couch, thereby actively conceding his domineering recollections.

Annette opened her clinched fist to show the storyless colored pegs.

He held each colored peg up to his ear to discern the owners. Within several seconds, he matched the singing destinies of the storyless colored pegs to the uninspired clients.

The victims of Jonas' actions, while listening to the serenade, watched as Jonathan's bow glided along the strings. Nathaniel watched as Annette approached her violinist who immediately acknowledged her. The violinist composed a melody that mimicked the feelings that seeing his muse ignited. The bereaved bachelor Lyle, seeing the face of his ex-wife at the head of the group, approached her with tearful recognition. Even Doris accepted Annette by whispering two words of recognition: "Jiminy Cricket . . ."

Nathaniel took a deep breath and rotated Jonathan's peg clockwise signaling the mass departure.

In the same manner as Blanche's plain eggs had broken apart to expose her newfound assets, Jonathan's life filled the space as an appropriate indoor cocktail party of living illustrations from the violinist's "pop-up book."

There were moonlit nights on a pier as the reverberating music from Jonathan's bow and violin inspired passersby. The pier fit snug into the confines of Jonas and Nathaniel's childhood home like an impressively constructed hall of mirrors which gave a sense of excessive liveliness to the concomitant, music-filled nightfall. Nearby was the tinkling sound of dropping coins and shuffling creased dollar bills as they were tossed into an open blue-velvet instrument case at Jonathan's feet. When Jonathan touched the bow to the violin the notes of his improvised compositions were all his own and delivered a message of hope. Even the stars and moon above Jonathan's head looked down on his hopeful wishes which rested in the underlay of his unrehearsed opuses.

Another aspect of Jonathan's life was piled on top of the pier and his nighttime string-induced melodies so that both existed on the same level: visions of a sprawling indoor restaurant where Jonathan bussed and waited tables, rebuilding his self-esteem and making enough money to pay rent for a small one bedroom flat. His flat was another defined visual that promptly added itself to the already chaotic mounting mixture. Still, there was more added: a live well-delivered solo violin recital in a brilliant Siamese Byzantine decorated concert hall. It was followed by thunderous applause of approval during a celebratory banquet of his playing achievements. It ultimately resulted in Jonathan meeting his Juilliard-educated second wife and starting a family with their own respective mismatched beloved instruments.

In Nathaniel's experiences as peg and envelope auditor it wasn't uncommon for him to see a client's storyline rush with supremacy. What troubled Nathaniel was that Jonathan's life had expanded in such a violent way and that the plot did not adhere to common chronological order; it built on itself with each of Jonathan's experiences and, furthermore, did not come to any fixed conclusion. Its intense particulars sustained magnification while paralleling the escalating dexterity of the violinist with each note played.

With Jonathan's inspiration already re-established, Annette looked to Nathaniel in a silent appeal to rotate another.

Nathaniel hoped that, by rotating another peg clockwise, it would indicate the direct closure to Jonathan's business. In actuality, Jonathan's life remained as Doris' story collided on top of it in a horrid combination akin to stripes against plaids. The waitress found herself in a familiar kitchen where Annette supervised the successful creation of funnel cakes. The funnel cakes erupted in multiple precarious sugar-specked columns that rose into the air as Doris' flourishing attempts at baking the flaky batter were praised. From Nathaniel's perspective, Annette's work with the heart-broken waitress was not complete.

"But Jonas wouldn't love me anymore if I left him," Doris sighed. "He's already told me that no one is going to love me like he does. I can't abandon what he and I have going, Jiminy Cricket."

"There is someone who will love you," Annette reassured her. "See that man?" She turned Doris to Lyle who stared in awe at Doris' culinary deliciousness. "Recognize him? He was the Man with the Eggs in the diner. I dropped the donut that you'd handed to me with the tongs so that he could catch it. So that you and he could begin a dialogue."

"But I don't even know how to begin a dialogue!"

"You already have, Doris," Annette urged. "These funnel cakes are your dialogue. These funnel cakes are your opening statement that will propel you two together. You've seen what miracles have happened with the violinist, yes? You have to have faith that the same thing will happen to you. Believe me, I've seen what Management has in store. Have a bit of faith in the process, however silly. Take this," Annette took a funnel cake from the mix and handed it to Doris on a spare paper plate. "Go to his house. Ring the doorbell and, for the love of Management, wait for him to answer . . ."

Doris looked questioningly at Annette. "Jiminy Cricket, are you sure?"

Though Nathaniel couldn't hear Annette's last words to Doris over the roar of approaching thunder, he surmised that they were at least sufficient in the completion of the rescue. Within seconds Doris was puffed with certainty as she brandished the paper plate with the funnel cake of powdered sugar. She found the tumbleweed-type bush that haunted the mailbox at the side of Lyle's road.

Nathaniel rotated Lyle's colored peg clockwise as Annette promptly approached her ex-husband. As with Jonathan's diagramed data and Doris' aromatic aesthetics, Lyle's decrepit details descended in the jumble. It was a house fallen into disarray that had shown itself – dishes piled in the sink, dusty furniture and piles of dirty laundry. Annette rode her own wave through the house ushering Lyle from his depression so that he could move on from her death in 2009 that had initially separated them from their marriage obligations. A backyard appeared where Annette hung the laundry to dry. It was here that she gave Lyle the encouraging words needed:

"So you see," Annette told her former husband "answering the doorbell is top priority."

"But I've never been a fan of funnel cakes."

"It doesn't matter, Lyle. Eat the funnel cakes. Don't eat the funnel cakes. The point is it's time to get over my death and move on."

"I have to tell you, Annette . . . It took you leaving for me to realize how much I needed you. At your funeral I actually begged you to come back so that we could talk about Tolstoy's *War and Peace* and John Steinbeck's *Grapes of Wrath*, and for a chance to change history, to keep you safe instead of visiting the library on that day."

"But there's really no way to change history, Lyle. Management orders events for a reason. You must understand that."

"I swore I'd change if you only came back for one more day."

"You can still change, Lyle. You can live your life. You can be happy again."

"But you're dead, Annette. I can't live my life without you."

"No, but you can live your life with Doris."

"Doris?"

"All you have to do is answer the door when she rings and take her to dinner. Try a new restaurant; someplace you've both never been. Explore as much as possible. Time to let go of all the memories and propel yourself forward."

"I'm too old to propel forward, Annette."

To which Annette responded, "Believe me when I say that you are not too old to propel forward, Lyle. I know a man who has lived for seven lifetimes. He outranks you by many years and experiences. Even he is propelling forward . . . the best he can."

Doris rang Lyle's doorbell in her own visible timeline. It was the ringing of the doorbell that Lyle heard as he looked at, and listened to, Annette.

Hearing the ringing of the doorbell, Annette told her ex-husband: "It's a new opportunity, Lyle. Take it, and be happy."

That is exactly what Lyle did. His and Doris' timelines merged together into a splendid fast forward in which several uncomfortable dates roared. Lyle and Doris ate at new places that were far from the beaten path, they shared movie popcorn and played miniature golf. Soon their dates became spontaneous and unpredictable. Each outing was an escapade. As time progressed, Lyle fell in love with Doris, and Doris fell in love with Lyle. They had a baby girl who they decided to name after the muse who had changed everything.

Though it was hard for Nathaniel to watch Lyle get his happy ending he accepted it with as much possible heart.

Sleepy Sarah Milbourne watched these timelines unfold. There were no further words needed in order to describe how important it was for her to seek medical treatment for her narcolepsy. She was privileged to see the wonders that Management had provided and was spurred into action due to them. Nathaniel rotated her colored peg clockwise bringing forth an extra canopy.

These images of Sarah Milbourne's, Jonathan's, Doris' and Lyle's lives were at often times boisterous adventures saturated in music and laughter. They forcefully brought the once drab abode of 252 Sisyphus Hill into the state of a melodious, yet equally dangerous, enclosed rain forest of rising multicolored Lite-Brite pegs. It was dangerous in so far as to the figure that Nathaniel noticed standing beyond a wave of inspirations: Jonas, unbound, and with the broad scissors in hand.

"There are more inspirations," Annette said behind Nathaniel. "Adam's found the ceiling door to the attic." Her words were hushed when she, Nathaniel assumed, noticed Jonas approaching with the scissors.

Nathaniel's ears were filled with the voice of his great aunt as she had once said to him "Never forget what happens in the story of *The Talking Eggs,* little one, and the lessons that must be learned." He watched as his step-brother slowly approached. His great aunt's voice had said, "When Blanche returned home with her treasures her sister Rose was extremely jealous and sought out the old crone. Rose was disrespectful to the hag and was overtly dismissive of the magic and wonders at the farm house. Rose made fun of, and laughed at, the old woman demanding she be given the same presents that Blanche received. In return for the older daughter's wickedness the woman gave the same instructions about the eggs. However, Rose was anxiously covetous of the alternative jeweled eggs that screamed 'Don't Take Me!'"

Remembering these words, Nathaniel held tight to the Lite-Brite as Jonas clawed an infuriated path through the virtually tightly-packed impressions left behind by the rescued timelines. As Jonas approached closer with the scissors poised for attack, Nathaniel finished his great aunt's words out loud.

"When the jeweled eggs were thrown over Rose's shoulder on the road out came vapors of venomous snakes, speckled slimy toads, stinging yellow-jackets with other vicious insects and even a ravenous gray wolf – which chased her . . ."

"Mr. Cauliflower, we have to move!" Annette shouted at him over the din of the surrounding repaired timelines.

He felt a firm tug on his right arm. They dashed into the dense pulsating pictures and siren-wailing sounds. Thunder roared above and below them causing the images to quiver and shake. Nathaniel could hear Jonas' shouts of protests and the swiping sound as his scissors caught, and madly sliced through, the agitated backdrops. He could see Phillip and Luanne running several feet ahead. He could hear as they so desperately tried to catch their breaths while jogging to the attic door. Jonathan's violin music was crazed in its attempts to musically narrate the insanity and tumultuous motions. During this, the rising colored pegs jettisoned upward like multicolored hail in reverse.

The rickety ladder from the attic door appeared. From Nathaniel's perspective, Adam was in the process of climbing the rungs and urging Phillip then Luanne to hoist themselves. Annette gained a second boost of energy and ran faster to the ladder to join her two clients in a maddened desire to reclaim ownership. He watched as everyone, including Annette, climbed inside. She poked her head out and yelled for Nathaniel.

Nathaniel fell behind. He turned to look over his shoulder. Jonas was only a few steps away and gaining speed, seemingly not winded by this chase. Fortunately for Nathaniel the collection of pop-up books began to refold causing the ground to break. The ground-level jetted into a dramatic slant bringing Nathaniel to the attic's ladder and to the eagerly reaching hands of Annette. Before he could touch her fingertips, the ground dipped. Nathaniel grabbed hold of the ladder's middle looking up at Annette with a worried gaze.

A sharp pain tore through Nathaniel's right shoulder bringing him to collapse against the ladder. He loosely held on to the remaining rungs. As he tried to climb he felt a searing pain that alluded to the obvious: Jonas' scissors had pierced Nathaniel's flesh. Jonas grasped at Nathaniel's legs and torso, impatient to climb over Nathaniel to the attic's opening. Below, the pop-up books from the previous inspirations tore apart leaving an empty chasm of churning storm clouds ignited by flashes of lightning. Both Jonas and Nathaniel looked at the storm bringing about a cohesive fervor to climb upward.

"See, Broccoli?" Jonas growled in Nathaniel's ear as he scraped behind his step-brother. "Even after your efforts to save the day, I'm going to win. The scissors were meant to slow you for a brief time. I'm really saving them for her. I have a feeling that the scissors will be more fatal, don't you?"

Nathaniel looked at Annette who reached to him. With a spare hand, Jonas grasped the pair of scissors and jammed them deeper.

"Are you listening, brother? Think of it as me doing you a favor, Broccoli. Take a good long look at her. It's the last time you'll see your precious Evangeline, I can assure you."

Nathaniel closed his eyes. Though he wasn't one to admit it, the current white pain that he felt did offer Nathaniel an unexpected luxury. The intense aching offered him a few moments completely free of memories. It seemed a bestial deal.

Then came the gunshot.

Nathaniel felt a weight leave his body. He thought for a moment that he had been shot and that he was falling into the abyss with an indescribable weightlessness. When he opened his eyes Nathaniel found that the bullet had not been intended for him, but for Jonas, who tumbled down the remaining ladder rungs like the plummeting of a rolled-up carpet. Nathaniel looked at Annette who stood at the entrance with her smoking pistol. Nathaniel slowly found his footing and climbed up two rungs before being dragged into the attic by Adam and Phillip.

The attic door was sealed bringing stillness to the madness that had transpired. As the scissors were extracted and Nathaniel's wounds began to heal, he turned to Annette. She aimed the pistol to the closed attic door. When she was satisfied that Jonas wasn't following them, she put the pistol into the thigh holster which was covered by the black cocktail dress.

In the moonlight pouring from the window, Nathaniel could see that Annette's appearance had reverted from Mrs. Slocum to Detective Redmond. The plain visage was replaced with the fiery red hair and tanned skin that she first sported when she arrived as one of the Nine Greatest Muses. He wasn't sure how to feel about it but Nathaniel was pleased that the scissors had not pierced Annette's skin during the climb. Even though they as a group were secure it didn't change the sobering fact that the Lite Brite had dropped from Nathaniel's grasp during the process. Without the Lite Brite there was nowhere for them to go but where they were. Nathaniel considered *The Talking Eggs* and the treasures that erupted once the shells were tossed over a shoulder. What if there was no one to crack open the eggs? If that was the case, the treasures remained encapsulated without being exposed to the daylight. They were like those incubating treasures – stuck inside eggs that pleaded for someone to either "take them" or "not to take them." Unfortunately, no one was in the figurative hen house to hear them.

CHAPTER 25: DARK MATTER

"It feels like an eternity since we were in this attic," Annette told Nathaniel who sat with his arms outstretched on his upward-arched knees in the corner of the room. Nathaniel, who had presented himself as "put together," was atomizing into a rarely untailored aspect. His dress shirt was unbuttoned and untucked with the sleeves casually rolled to his elbows. A v-neck undershirt could be seen beneath with slightly discolored from sweat stains. In the mild darkness that pervaded the garret, Evangeline's opal necklace could be seen around his neck. Moreover, Nathaniel had taken off his glasses and kept them folded at his side which made him unrecognizable.

Annette, from Nathaniel's line of sight, was standing beside him with her back propped against the wall. Though her eyes moved across the room, she held the physical stance of a sentinel watching the attic door for intruders.

Annette went on, "Everything is the same as when we left it: the mobile, the empty picture frames affixed with the unrolled star charts, the flimsy solar system mobile . . ." She made the outward observation that even the accumulation of dust on the well-worn trunks, raised female bust, and black sewing machine was the same. When she didn't get a response she turned her eyes to the bright beams of moonlight as they settled on the glow-in-the-dark message.

Phillip had not yet seen the message as he was engrossed in the encircling expansion of the improvised cosmos. As he flipped through the books, he bore a look of slow-acting scrutiny.

"But we've changed. Haven't we, Mr. Cauliflower? It's hard to believe how much we've had to go through to get here," Annette's words were directed to the room. "You know," She turned to Nathaniel. "I've been going over everything in my head – imagine that, right? Me over-analyzing. I can't wrap my mind around why you would be Jonas' apprentice and it got me thinking. You and Jonas never played nice which leads me to believe that maybe what Icarus said in the church, about you being Jonas' assistant, was hogwash." She paused, allowing Nathaniel to respond. When her pause was met with silence, Annette pushed the issue. "Every noticeable action that you've taken has been for my safety, the progression of your muses and your clients. You said so yourself in that instructional video 'Butterfly wings and earthquakes, dear muse . . . butterfly wings and earthquakes.' Why would someone preach adamantly about one thing and then overtly do something counteracting it? Am I right?"

Nathaniel did not respond, keeping a near-sighted vigil over the room.

"I'm not an idiot, Mr. Cauliflower."

"I never said that you were," Nathaniel replied softly.

"I saw those two wedding rings, and the cube of billiard chalk, in the pocket of the black hoodie. I know where that chalk came from. And I have a suspicion that you do too."

Nathaniel looked from Annette toward Adam, who stared meditatively out the window viewing the moon. It vexed Nathaniel to think that Adam, who no doubt overheard this conversation, wouldn't take ownership of his conduct.

"Don't you tire of the interrogations?" Nathaniel sighed defensively.

"Please answer my question, Mr. Cauliflower."

"Yes, fine. You're right. Miss Redmond is always right, let's give her a prize!"

"Don't placate me, Mr. Cauliflower . . ."

"If you're already certain of your answer, then why do you need me to validate it?" Nathaniel asked. "It won't make a hill of beans difference if I do."

"Yes, it will."

"No, it won't."

"Yes, it *will*."

"*No*, it *won't!* And do you know why? I'll tell you why. Suppose I unmask the apprentice, what then? We'll be closed up in this attic, without a Lite-Brite board, and restricted in our pains to move ahead with this cockamamie arrangement." Nathaniel went on, clearly in a huff. "Even if we manage to rescue these remaining clients, which I don't see how without rotating their pegs, you'll return to your life as a missing person's detective, a pie maker or *what have you* . . . I'll go back into my little hole of an office in the afterlife, spinning colored pegs this way and that for the rest of eternity, in an exertion to keep peace in this fragile universe for as long as there's a Management out there to watch over it."

"Are you that presumptuous and self-absorbed to think that you know what Management has planned before it happens?" Annette asked, her full attention now on Nathaniel.

Nathaniel stood to meet her level. He put his glasses on and stared at her furiously. "You think I'm self-absorbed?"

"Oh, Management. I don't think you're self-absorbed, I can give you a million reasons that will prove that you're self-absorbed."

"Oh, can you?" Nathaniel smirked.

Annette counted the reasons with her fingers while saying, "Writing your own exhaustingly extensive memoirs from your past seven lives, for starters; building an office of seven obsessions from those said lives to safeguard yourself inside; relating to the other muses with your, frankly, over-the-top office decorations and, I'll admit, mouth-watering dishes, and how it consistently connects to serve your inflated ego . . . ."

"Is that all?" Nathaniel scoffed.

"Nope. I can go on until the sun comes up," Annette teasingly chided. "Would you like me to? I can!"

"You know, I liked you a lot better after your face, and attitude, had reverted to humble Annette Slocum. One gunshot from that pistol and here you are in full militaristic dispute – the inconsiderate, ill-tempered colleague, consumed with debilitating indignation that it's categorically calamitous!"

"If I hadn't have fired that pistol, Jonas would have climbed over you. Management knows what would have happened!"

"Well . . . I'm glad that you fired that pistol, then!" Nathaniel shouted. "Aim a little bit better because I could have sworn that the bullet abraded my ear in the trajectory!"

Annette was unmistakably amused. "I've missed this – our sparring. Haven't you?"

Both were suddenly aware that their bickering had turned into a performance watched by a small audience. The spectators included Adam, who took a few steps from the window, while Luanne stared at the verbal brawl from the closed green trunk labeled "Phillip." Mercifully, Phillip's concentration was not focused on the mud-slinging. His eyes were on the glow-in-the-dark stars on the attic ceiling which plummeted to his feet as if he were amidst an up-close and personal meteor shower. Nathaniel had been too inconvenienced with the quarrel to notice but was directly attentive. They didn't need a red-colored peg to inspire Phillip. He was already right where he needed to be, in the presence of his catalyst.

Phillip's life moved forward, retelling the subsequent biography from the accurate standpoint as if Jonas had not interceded.

The life of Nathaniel's step-grandchild, which had initially preluded with tiny inked stars on his father's forearm, continued with the same tattooed stars as grown Phillip marked on his own arm in honor of the father who had abandoned him. Phillip rekindled his discarded love for astronomy thereby sparking a prevailing desire to find his missing parent.

Phillip, who was two months shy of his thirty-ninth birthday, impulsively quit his poorly paying warehouse job and procured another unprofitable position as a custodian at the astronomical observatory. Phillip kept his head lowered as he swept and mopped the tiled lobby floors. He kept his attention focused on the dry-erase boards as his rag brushed unwanted notes after the professors completed nightly classes in the study rooms. He leaned in the doorframe of the building's modest theatre projection hall where he observed one of the facilitators test out planetarium shows. In these moments, as the universe expanded on the domed ceiling, Phillip embraced the cosmos. While closing the building for the night, Phillip would empty the trash cans in the offices of graveyard-shift employees. His ears were perked for indications as to where his formerly-employed father had vanished.

Though his meager income did not allow him to obtain financial loans for his graduate degree in the field, Phillip did not concede. He educated himself in astrophysics literature. Phillip's genius-like comprehension of its complexities enhanced exponentially with the fervor he had excelled in during his childhood. His cosmic mastermind projected Phillip as a misunderstood mad-scientist who preferred the company of his own rented telescopes over friendships except for his mother whom he rarely visited.

His mother, who had grown senescent during her residency at the retirement community, snatched Phillip's wrist during one of his visits as he was unpacking the last of three paper grocery bags. It was a look of absolute consternation upon seeing the small tattooed stars on his forearm.

"Don't do this to us," his mother glared. It was evident, based on her doddery beleaguered stare, she was uncertain if she was speaking to Phillip or to his father.

"Please, tell me where he went, Ma," Phillip pleaded with her, but to no avail. Time and emotional distance on her end had wedged the clues farther from any pending investigations.

Phillip, eventually accepting that his mother no longer held answers to his father's whereabouts, kissed her on the forehead, folded the paper grocery sacks and left her with an impassive blank stare she often wore.

On a not-so-special evening, as Phillip mopped the floor tiles of the observatory's offices, his eyes glanced to an open door. Inside was a room of electronic gadgetry associated with the observatory's high-powered telescope. The equatorial room, as Phillip came to understand, was similarly domed akin to the planetarium to protect the equipment from the elements. Tonight, however, the dome was ajar; its largest telescope stretched into the star-sequined skies.

Positioned in a swivel chair was an older gentleman in a pale yellow dress shirt, jeans and aged tennis shoes. From behind, the observer looked no different than the other astronomy college professors Phillip had seen in the hallways. The difference that struck Phillip's emotions so brashly was the collection of inked stars on the observer's forearm. Phillip swallowed. He looked at his own tattoo coming to terms that his father, whom he had been searching for, was there!

Time raced forward showing a working friendship concerning Phillip and the tattooed observer named "Mel." It wasn't explained why Phillip didn't ask if the man was his father. Nathaniel surmised that Phillip didn't want to be wrong in assuming. After all, it had been over twenty years since he had seen his father. Without pictures to remind him of his father's face, and the way that the observer's face had aged making his identity indistinguishable, it was natural for Phillip to be delayed. Through a series of moments, the relationship between Phillip and the astronomer grew. The man named "Mel" came to understand how brilliant of a mind Phillip possessed and, through the course of time, he took Phillip under his wing. They would sit and study cosmic wonders. Phillip would attend lectures in night classes, or participate in the lab activities and report to Mel what he gained from the application.

 Night after night, after Phillip finished his janitorial duties, he and Mel would discuss the complexities of the universe and focus on the loftiness of space than their individual lives. When Mel handed Phillip an envelope with a heftily numbered check, their conversation turned delicate.

 "This is what's left from my life savings," Mel told Phillip. "It's my gift to you."

 Phillip looked at the draft which was sizable enough to put him through his desired continuing education. He shook his head, handing the check to Mel.

 "This is too generous," Phillip told him. "I can't accept it."

 "What am I going to do with it?" Mel asked. "I've used enough in the account to make sure I'm well taken care of at the time of my death. I want you to have the rest."

 When Phillip declined the gift a second time, Mel referenced their tattoos. There was a long pause before Mel said "Phillip, I had a wife, and a kid, but I didn't value them as much as I appreciated the stars. And they were taken from me because I wasn't there as much as I probably should've been. As a result she divorced me and gained full custody of my son. She even went so far as to bar me from seeing him."

 There was an intake of breath from Phillip's lips.

"I fought for him, my son. Believe me, Phillip, I did! But no matter how many steps I took, my ex-wife was there forcing me to retreat. Eventually I gave up trying. My son was little when I saw him last and I knew that, even if we did reconnect, he wouldn't remember me. He wouldn't love me . . . ."

"That's not true . . ." Phillip shook his head.

Mel studied Phillip, considering his friend's words. "I wish I could tell you that I'm your father, Phillip, but I can't. There was another astronomer, your dad, who worked here as well, years ago. He, too, had a similar story. He too had a jealous wife. And an astute son, whom he had adored, and lost, in a divorce due to the stars. He and I were roommates in college in our younger years. Our friendship was accurately a meeting of the minds, like yours and mine. We went through four years earning our bachelor degrees and together suffered our collegiate graduate years. After we earned our doctorates, we got matching tattoos on our forearms so that we'd remember the shared brotherhood during our postdocs. We kept in close contact by regular mail and e-mail as we cultivated our own research and taught at separate universities. We wrote about our families. He wrote about how special you were to him. He acknowledged your propensity for astronomy and the sciences surrounding it. He loved you very much, Phillip, and told me how proud he was of you . . . ."

"Loved?" Phillip asked. "Where is he?"

"I don't know," Mel sighed. "I applied for a research position here at his observatory but by the time I got here, he was gone. I found a letter on my desk one afternoon. It was his final letter. I wrote to him several times and received notifications of 'return to sender.' There was no forwarding address. No observatories in the United States, or around the world, had information. He simply disappeared. After a while I naturally assumed that, like a dying star, he flickered out from existence."

Mel looked at Phillip who had tears in his eyes.

"Though I'm not your father, Phillip, I consider the friendship that we share to be closely akin to that kind of paternal relationship. Though you aren't my son by blood, you're the closest that I have. That's why I'm giving you this check. Though some stars occasionally blink out of the night sky it doesn't mean that others can't be born in their absence. I've always believed that everyone has a story to tell. That we're connected to one another in small ways that may present themselves later. Though each of us may be considered 'separate stars' in the macrocosm, we collectively construct a figure in a constellation. I've considered life, and all of its sometimes unhappy moments, to be the dark matter sandwiched between those glowing stars. Holding us in a glorious outline that could only make sense through someone else's eyes."

Time propelled forward as Phillip, in the coming year, lived those moments of "dark matter" that was his life. He forgave his mother, not necessarily by condoning her reaction to his father's absence, but by accepting it. He released the bitterness that had accumulated in his heart due to these circumstances. Phillip and Mel built the relationship that they had so desperately craved. Phillip found a surrogate father within Mel; Mel was filled with happiness in knowing that Phillip was the son he had never cultured. Five years later Mel died peacefully in his sleep and Phillip, every Memorial Day evening, sat by Mel's grave with a telescope and star charts.

The story of Phillip's life integrated with Luanne's timeline as Phillip babysat, and put to bed, his second cousins: the twin girls that Luanne, herself, had abandoned and currently sought to reconnect with.

Luanne, who had been sitting on Phillip's green trunk in the attic watching this exchange, stood and tightly clutched the Christmas ornament.

One of the girls traced the stars of Phillip's tattoo with her fingers and asked him, "Phil, tell us a story?"

Phillip had told his second cousins many stories in the past but mostly of made-up things. Tonight was different. Tonight Phillip looked to the bedroom wall where a message appeared that seemed to come forward from another time – a message that read "Phillip, Don't Forget." He smiled, looked down at the girls and told them a story.

"Well," Phillip started his retelling, "I suppose . . . it began with stars."

As Phillip said these words, he looked up from the twins to find someone standing in the bedroom door frame. Phillip invitingly nodded to the stranger, initiating that the story-time include this additional person.

Luanne, at present in the attic, caught sight of the smiling figure in the light of the twin's bedroom doorway. It was a figure that she recognized as her own. Tears streamed down Luanne's eyes as she foresaw the future: in which she, and her daughters, were happily reconnected.

These images from Phillip's life, like the images from the previous rescues, built upon themselves simultaneously spinning in place like busy hamsters on a wheel.

"Like a Zoopraxiscope," Nathaniel told Annette without looking at her. When he didn't hear a response, he sighed at her silence and explained "The Zoopraxiscope was invented by Eadweard Muybridge in 1879. He would paint single images on the outer edges of glass discs and shine them through a projector. The individual stop-motion silhouettes differed slightly and, once spinning, would give the impression of movement. Watching Phillip's life like this reminds me of Muybridge's invention, for some reason."

It pleased him to think that he and Annette had rescued Phillip and changed his life. Nathaniel couldn't help but to be proud that he and Annette, in a way, were a part of Phillip's "constellation." Watching the clamor of Phillip's life, Nathaniel felt in his pocket for the glow-in-the-dark star collected from the initial inspiration.

Running his fingers along the edges, Nathaniel thought about the constellation that he and Annette shared.

Nathaniel turned to Annette. He wanted to say, "Yes, I did enjoy our verbal sparring to some degree." And he also wanted to tell her, "Regardless of Adam acting as Jonas' apprentice, or whatever arguments we find ourselves, or whatever becomes of us, I hope you know I'm glad we had the opportunity to change Phillip's life." Oh how he badly wanted to say these things.

But when Nathaniel faced Annette he found Jonas. A string of Christmas lights had been strung into a fitted noose around Annette's neck who aggressively, but mutely, fought for freedom. Before Nathaniel could reach out to Annette, Jonas began to rise. His step-brother was at the rudder of a soaring evergreen that had taken root underfoot. In Jonas' hand, and peeking from the branches, Nathaniel could see the Lite-Brite with Luanne's peg shining on the board. He could also see Luanne desperately grasping at the bark with the smashed soda can Christmas ornament in her hand.

An object fell from the tree's altitude and landed on the ground with an audible gunshot. Nathaniel looked at Annette's firearm which lay without its owner to wield it.

From Nathaniel's point of view, Adam also watched as Annette was lifted into the air by Jonas' impermanent chariot.

Nathaniel turned to the attic door which was covered in a sickening pile of rotted dandelions. He envisioned how this could have happened. Perhaps Jonas had landed onto solid ground; following that, he could have climbed up the ladder to the attic. Phillip's life had provided the perfect distraction which had given Jonas the perfect chance to slip in undetected. Regardless of how Jonas had arrived in the attic, or how he had obtained the Lite-Brite board, it didn't matter. Nathaniel looked to the evergreen, which was spotted with thousands of shiny glass Christmas ornaments, as it took on a more defined shape in comparison to its other surroundings.

The inexorable darkness within Nathaniel was paralleled by the contiguous geode of blue-tinted razor-edged icicles that formed in a tight hollow cavity shaped like an underground well beyond the winding pine tree's stalk.

Even if Jonas did let Annette go before her last breath, the fall through the creaking ever-belligerent mangling tree trunk would be penetratingly terminal. It was also foreseeable that, if Nathaniel didn't climb up to save Annette or her fiancé or even the last remaining client Luanne, he would be the remaining star in their collected illuminant assemblage. So, as Phillip's story quivered with thunder, Nathaniel ascended hoping that his own personal inner star, or contribution to Management's design, might not befittingly dwindle as an unknowable consequence.

CHAPTER 26: TANNENBAUM

Thick tree sap suctioned to his grasping fingertips like avaricious leeches. His clothes snagged on the contorted branches which heatedly beat down upon him. Nathaniel removed his suspenders and dress shirt, which had been his greatest drawbacks. As he ascended, Nathaniel's skin was threadbare from prickly pine needles which drew blood from his arms and face. He winced, gritted his teeth and kept climbing regardless.

Epic remixes of Christmas carols, some with vocals and some without, assailed Nathaniel as he tore up the tree's rasping cortex. The twinkling ornaments, as if they were alive, sang with the voices of holiday choruses belting musical bridges that hinted to Luanne's life. Nathaniel ascertained the following: After Luanne received the crushed soda can Santa Christmas ornament, she moonlighted a part time occupation working in a year-round Holiday atmosphere. She made mass-produced ornaments on a do-it-yourself assembly line and ultimately was employed as a side-kick elf in a shopping mall winter wonderland. Luanne met a kindred spirit on this interchange: a fellow lover of Christmas and collected ornaments who had also gone through his own familial perils resulting from a female to male transgender operation. Though the friend's name was never stated, Nathaniel gleaned that Luanne's co-worker had happily reconciled with his family.

"There's hope for you, Luanne," her friend told her. His voice was heard in an ornament as he explained, "The evergreen is meant to signify the eternal human spirit. We put lights, and sometimes candles, on the tree to remind us of Christ's light and love in the world. There are dark patches in the tree so we put the ornaments to fill those additional dark spaces. The ornaments signify those closest to us, be they family or friends, who unite us and fill our soul. It's time to find new ornaments and new connections that make your life worth experiencing."

The friend's words were interrupted as Nathaniel grasped a branch and accidentally dug the palm of his hand into a hook. He shouted a curse word, inspected the abrasion, and continued to climb. There was a shattering below that brought Nathaniel to stop. The ornaments were disintegrating as if snuffing out the hymns of Luanne's life. He surmised that Jonas was at the top of the tree telling Luanne Management-knows-what to keep her discouraged. He was thereby forcing the lights and music to waver.

Nathaniel growled, shimmying up the tree. The ornaments above him, which were presently gleaming, told how Luanne's hope to reconnect with her children was restored even though she harbored doubts.

"I don't want to hurt my children more than I already have," Luanne told her friend in another ornament.

"How happy do you think they are without you in their lives?" her friend asked in a neighboring ornament.

This conversation between Luanne and her friend went on as Nathaniel clambered. The fracturing ornaments below gained speed underfoot, devouring the light. Nathaniel climbed quicker and more rapidly, ducking and dodging insistent swinging branches. Hand over hand and foot over foot, Nathaniel struggled to reach the top to save Luanne's storyline, along with Annette and Adam, from Jonas' grip. Through Luanne's maddened remaining canticles, Nathaniel learned that the bowling alley attendant's life, for all practical purposes, was about change. Luanne's former wife, Halia, had been given a different work schedule. Halia had asked the twin's favorite older second cousin, Phillip, to watch over the kids. Nathaniel learned that the unsuspecting Phillip, upon bringing the twin children to the winter wonderland to meet the mall-appointed Santa Claus, recognized Luanne. And that, through a series of untold circumstances including Halia's eventual small-dosed tolerance, Luanne was able to openly face her children as her updated female self which brought Luanne's story and Phillip's story to a penultimate intersection . . .

The tree engulfed in shadow. Nathaniel paused, for fear of a gaffe in movement.

Conditions had radically distorted resulting in the blue-tinted surrounding icicles to progress inward and bite at the trunk like a thousand axes bent on dismantling the tree. Adam could be seen near the top but, like Nathaniel, was temporarily immobilized by the shifted gravity of the hardwood as the icicles chopped the husk.

Holding on to the branches, Nathaniel looked out through the summit of pine needles. The foliage was thinning and showed the tree top.

Jonas stood at the tip like a perched gargoyle clenching the squirming Annette in his claws. A thunderstorm was approaching above the tree top crown.

"He wants me to come and save her," Nathaniel thought to himself. *"He does! Jonas wants me to join him up there to reclaim her as my own as I've always done."* Why else would Jonas go to such trouble to construct an abnormally high tree to keep her from Nathaniel's immediate reach? If he wanted Annette dead, she'd be dead. Nathaniel knew that, if he had played into Jonas' hand, their insane cycle would travel the same destructive trail. Nathaniel needed to rescue Annette out of his common modus operandi in such a way that Jonas wouldn't expect.

Luanne, who looked to be in shock, was between Nathaniel and Adam. She wasn't considering the Christmas ornament that gamely dangled from her finger by the red strap. She was noticeably paralyzed due to an observable vertigo that kept her movements in check. The tree was in a critical status because Luanne's spirit was on the brink of collapse. Her insecurities were causing the promising sapling to crumble into ligneous twigs.

If Nathaniel was going to rescue Annette from the falling woody perennial he needed to save Luanne first. It was the best, if not only opportunity. With determinative gumption, in spite of the retrogressive tree, Nathaniel turned his eyes from Annette's plight and mounted several branches toward Luanne.

He met her gaze and took her shaky hands in his. Nathaniel kept Luanne's stare focused on him as he asked, "What do you have there in your hand?" Luanne's eyes reflexively looked at the ornament and darted to Nathaniel. She was visibly more concerned about falling than focusing on the ornament. But Nathaniel was determined to corral her apprehensions and transform them.

He went on in saying to her, "Can I let you in on a little secret, Luanne? I'm not much for heights either. Especially large pine trees that erupt without notice. I know you rode this branch as this tree jutted from the ground so you didn't have the opportunity to witness the ornaments. However, I know that you saw something in Phillip's story: a moment with your children. As I climbed this tree, I listened to the ornaments. They sang about the astonishing things that'll happen to you in the future. They attested that what you saw, what you've been hoping for, will happen!"

Luanne shook her head disbelievingly.

"I know," Nathaniel nodded. "How can you have blind faith in a promising future if you don't see for yourself how it'll play out in advance?" He kept his gaze and said earnestly, "The future isn't as bleak as we fear it'll be, Luanne. Yes, it feels as if we've run through our own ordeals that, frankly, appear to be punishments. I get that. Completely. My life, or the past seven of them total, has been nothing but trial after trial after trial. I've recently considered that maybe it'll mean something. Even if I may not believe it's right for me. Do you understand?"

Though the pop-up book was coming to an end, Nathaniel allowed time for Luanne to respond.

"I think so," Luanne answered.

"I'm going to make a pact with you, Luanne. From here on out, I'm going to believe that positive things can, and will, happen! Even if I have to make them happen myself when everything else is falling apart, even when the darkest days come and it feels like there's no hope, I'm going to find something, anything, to keep me moving forward. Let's both do it. Let's both promise, right here in these thorny needles, to let go of the past and think of the amazing things that can happen to us if we at least try?"

He lifted Luanne's hands bringing the ornament to her eyes.

"Let this ornament signify the future . . . a positive future with more ornaments signifying hope."

Luanne looked askance at Nathaniel for a moment. And then her sorrowful eyes were clear with recognition.

"Do you really think I can be happy?" she said. As she held the ornament closer to her, Luanne could feel Nathaniel affectionately patting the top of her hands.

Nathaniel had been too intent to inspire Luanne that he had neglected to realize that his hands were sticky with drying tree sap. Thankfully, this didn't deter Nathaniel's speech from taking perfect aim like an arrow through a bull's eye.

The tree righted, ablaze with lights and carols as if a fuse box had been tripped to restart. The encircling icicles melted into an arctic membrane of harmless snowflakes which overlay the branches. Luanne, all smiles, released Nathaniel and receded into the lights and sounds with her ornament, intentionally immersing into her timeline. Luanne quickly aged before him until she became an older woman with a Christmas tree sweater. Luanne, Nathaniel realized, ultimately renovated into the ornament vendor that he and Annette had initially taken the ornament from.

Nathaniel thought about the pact that he made to Luanne and felt optimistically liberated.

Nathaniel raised his eyes to the tree top. He didn't save Annette. He gave Adam the chance to save his fiancé. It wasn't that Nathaniel felt that he was incapable. It wasn't that he felt hopeless about this situation as he had in the church. In a point of fact, Nathaniel knew that he would never be happy if he followed the same hazardous routine. Clutching onto the branches, he felt it passable about delegating the responsibility and forgoing his tediously ensconced pursuit.

He did not present them with a silver tea set for their pending nuptials. He did not gift them with China dishes or a pre-paid card to a high-end home furnishing store. Alternatively, Nathaniel supplied them with the solid ground on which their success could be planted in these final chaotic moments of evacuation.

His donation was presented by the following: Multiple helical-turned pop-up books spiraled into closure. The details of the previous rescues filled the snow-covered well, which held Luanne's supercilious tree, as if it were a clogged drain. Distinct violin music erupted from the attic's crevices and bounced on hovering solar systems to distant star clusters within an expanding universe. Wafting through the music was the aroma of freshly-baked funnel cakes and the new-car smell of rubbed-down leather car seats. Colorful client images created a living patchwork quilt of pasts, presents and futures which collectively eddied with multilayered insights.

Rising colored pegs acted as hands at a revolving potter's wheel in molding the detonations into a single, clumped form. The worlds coalesced in reversed acceleration collapsing into a spiraling singularity. In this process of increased density the plane reformed to a spiraling disc.

In this gravitational disorder, Adam was able to free Annette from the string of Christmas lights. Jonas launched himself at Adam but was restricted by a falling stained-glass window which banned admittance as it landed to the ground. More stained-glass windows appeared and were accompanied by wooden church pews and bellowing organ pipes. When the Greatest Muses in History appeared in this setting, it was obvious that the sanctuary's pop-up book was also shutting. Nathaniel was relieved as the men banded together to bind Jonas.

He could see Annette and Adam. She urged him to stay in the church and wait for her while she sorted everything out in the afterlife. Her fiancé protested but surrendered.

The department was reconstructed. The hallway walls, doorless offices, desks, postboxes along with piles of white and violet envelopes, all trotted the repairing slope of the agency's floor. Energy-efficient light bulbs burned brightly. Nathaniel's luscious feasts from the botched retirement party returned. The painted portraits of the muses, the kerosene lamps, repaired library books and the encyclopedia of destinies realigned in the rotunda of Nathaniel's seven obsessions. Steady crashing waves from Icarus' private Grecian beach could be heard as well as the rumbling approaching gales in Lucas' Hall of Thunderstorms.

When the department mended, bringing an end to the reversals, a well-known tranquility that Nathaniel had needed was presented. Everything that the department stood for, and had achieved by way of its inspirations, returned to its former splendor with the muses, their detainee Jonas Rothchild, and public speaker Edgar Allen Poe, to inspect the wonders.

Fiona smiled and said, "We're home."

Indeed, they were home. It was a feeling that Nathaniel equated with revisiting the boarded, vacant farm house in his adult years. Though the department didn't have the same musty smell as the farm house, Nathaniel couldn't help but to think of it at present. This hallway and its offices was his home and, while it was meant to give him a sense of safekeeping, Nathaniel knew that it wasn't Annette's. With the timelines corrected and Jonas apprehended he knew it was a short matter of time before she was to leave this "vacation house" and discard Nathaniel, who was one of the visited cottage's bygone antiquities.

CHAPTER 27: WHAT WAS SALVAGED

A blue and white Copeland Spode pitcher and wash basin was used as Nathaniel dipped his cupped hands into the cold purified spring water. He splashed his face. Looking at himself in an antique tri-fold vanity mirror with distressed glass, he found that the cuts, scrapes and bruises had healed without scarring.

Fiona was waiting patiently in the reflection.

Taking a white cotton face towel from a pewter hook, he carefully wiped his face dry. He reached for his cracked glasses and fit them on. Nathaniel turned to face Fiona with the towel which he used to finish drying his hands. He wore the untucked, sweat-stained v-neck undershirt with Evangeline's opal necklace around his neck.

They stood in Nathaniel's private office washroom which was decidedly colorless with its white marble countertops, pallid cabinets and pasty honeycomb floor tiles. Hints of cerulean came from the wash basin, the tinted glass of the shower doors and Fiona's baby-blue pants suit.

"You've not said a word to anyone since we've arrived. It's been a relatively protracted interval. Can you help me understand?" Fiona agreeably asked. When Nathaniel didn't answer, she said "This has to conclude, Mr. Cauliflower. The Nine Greatest Muses in History no longer serve a purpose. They're anxious to return home to their own lives and their own timelines."

"You know where the ivory boxes are as well as I do," Nathaniel presented. He placed the used towel on the hook and met Fiona in the doorway. "You don't need me to officiate the farewell ceremonies, do you? Have them put their objects inside the ivory boxes. Seal the chests in the vault behind the mural in the conference room. Have them retire. If they're insistent on a warm meal, the retirement party food is still set. The victuals are roasting."

He brushed past the Head Muse to the main rotunda of his office where a mainstay of daylight transferred through the oculus to his desk, water cooler, inbox, three Lite-Brite boards and the nearest ring of visible kerosene lamps.

"Some would like to say goodbye to their caretaker," were Fiona's words as she heedlessly followed. "A certain red-headed missing person's detective turned pie maker, for instance."

"There's nothing that I have to say to her," Nathaniel announced as he busied himself with executing minor maintenance to the kerosene lamps.

He refilled the kerosene in those that had been absorbed. He replaced the used wicks and greased the knobs so that, when revolved, the soundless process of igniting each lamp produced an equally noiseless afterglow. With the outer band of kerosene lamps burning, the circumference of Nathaniel's office expanded to show the alcoves that held the encyclopedia of destinies, collection of writing pens, portraits of muses and glass-faced library book cabinet. He walked the office making sure that everything was in its place. One of the portrait frames was off by a centimeter and, with scrupulous eyes, he tilted it into place. In his typical obsessive compulsive behavior, Nathaniel assured that his pens were laid pristinely parallel to their ink-filled companions.

Nathaniel asked, "What are you going to do with Jonas?"

"When the retirement party ends, we'll do what we always do. Mr. Rothchild will pass through the waiting room, at which point he'll walk through the far door and reincarnate into a new life, a better life, where his soul can eventually learn from mistakes that he's made."

Nathaniel shook his head.

The exit, to which all muses walked through, regardless if their destination was Heaven or reincarnation, had been the same "asphodel door" that tormented the door maker at Sisyphus Hill. When the original muses had retired, the waiting room door had been commissioned as a muse's specific departure gate at the retirement of their term. It was its divergent ability to transform a soul, transitioning it from "dead" to "alive" and vice versa. It had been obvious early on how safe-guarded it was to be kept, considering its secure location at the end of a soundly fortressed waiting room. While the door was depended on by the department, Nathaniel didn't trust what it had to offer. In his experience, it was a temperamental fixture both erring on the side of good or bad and cloaked in ambiguity.

"And where would you send him, Mr. Cauliflower, if given a choice to decide Mr. Rothchild's fate?"

"To the warehouse in Purgatory where his memories will be wiped. But also where his soul will be deconstructed completely. It's been proven, after multiple reincarnations already, that no matter where you send him he'll return to the same devilish core. Releasing him into the wilds of an added unsystematic life for the innovation of his soul is sending him on another fool's errand." Nathaniel looked at Fiona and added, "But that's who you are, isn't it Fiona? Giving everyone a second chance? Believing that they'll find the goodness that you see in them? Why do you believe in his potential?"

Fiona gave a questioning look. "Oh, I don't know. Perhaps it's for the reason that I've seen too many miracles in my day demonstrating otherwise."

"And he's currently residing where, pray tell?"

"With Harriet who's keeping watch."

Nathaniel said gravely, "Oh no . . ."

*

Strictly, Harriet and Jonas sat in the Hall of Thunderstorms listening to the differentiating clouds and dissimilar tempests as they rumbled through the nine archways. Some breezes were warm while others brought Harriet, who was sitting alert in a swivel chair, to shiver slightly and squeeze her already intentionally strapped-tight blouse.

Jonas, who sat in his own swivel chair, restrained by a set of pinched handcuffs behind his back, didn't seem bothered by the chill. He opened his mouth to speak but Harriet cut him off before words were spoken.

"Don't start, scumbag," she interjected.

*

The more Nathaniel thought about Fiona's choice in having no-nonsense Harriet watch Jonas, he understood why.

Nathaniel circled the office and was satisfied with the placement of his things. He sat at the desk with both hands on the surface.

"I knew who I was before this happened," Nathaniel explained. "My life was heading in a direction. Admittedly, this was a direction that dissociated me from everyone. Including Annette. Though it wasn't a perfect existence, it was comfortable. The dust has settled and here we are starting afresh in a daring domain. I don't know how to live in this new-fangled situation, Fiona. I'm mindful of how I'm expected to feel: excited and grateful for opportunities and needing to embrace the chance to make my soul mean something. I've helped rescue multiple timelines and also brought Annette back safe and sound, as you've asked. I know that, if I really wanted to, I could tell Annette how I feel about her. I could say the words 'I love you' instead of wishing I could."

Both hands were then swept apart exploring the nearly empty tabletop. There they stayed near the desk's side edges with palms faced down. He looked over the top of the glasses rims to Fiona.

"But I can't, Fiona. Everything that's inside me screams against it. Perhaps it's the small part of the old Nathaniel or maybe it's a piece of me that's unknown and restructured. From my gut to my soul, I feel that telling Annette how much I love her is unwise. You tell me that regrets are unsavory but something in the pit of my stomach tells me that if I tell Annette, it'll be another regret. I have to release her. I have to feel how I feel in my own way, in my own time, regardless of how Management believes."

"So you've chosen to discharge Miss Redmond, the reincarnation of your beloved Evangeline whom you've lived and died in search of during seven lifetimes, without even talking to her?"

Nathaniel tossed his hands up in capitulation. "Yes, Fiona. At this time, I choose to sit here unobtrusively at my desk. I choose to paint portraits of upcoming muses and wait for the ensuing healthy colored pegs to drop."

Fiona looked at him and said "There's more to it than that, isn't there, Mr. Cauliflower? Of what are you really scared stiff, my friend?"

Another woman appeared in the doorframe, rapping her knuckles against the wood. Fiona and Nathaniel turned to see Annette Redmond in her strapless Chiffon wedding dress. Annette looked to Nathaniel then to Fiona. It was obvious that she had interrupted a serious conversation.

"I'll come back," Annette started to duck out of the doorway.

"Nonsense, Miss Redmond." Fiona's words and tone of voice were friendly as she stepped aside so that Annette could enter.

Pleasantly, as an aside to Nathaniel, Fiona added: "We'll talk about this later?" Without further ado, Fiona left them alone in the room.

Upon seeing her in her wedding dress, Nathaniel pursed his lips.

"The main door to your office was open, so I . . ."

From where Nathaniel sat, he could see a reddened loop around Annette's neck; a keepsake from the cord of Christmas lights that Jonas had shaped into a lariat during their rescue. She had attempted to cover it with foundation but parts were partially noticeable. His visage, though he tried to disguise it, was emphatically saturnine.

Fretful, or possibly self-conscious, Annette brought a hand up to her throat. "What?"

"Nothing," he lied. "I see you've found your wedding dress."

"When I stepped into my cathedral office, I found it had been dry-cleaned and placed into a hanging wardrobe bag." As she looked at her dress and spun to make sure there weren't any imperfections she may have missed, Nathaniel noticed that the circlet ran the back of her neck as well creating a reddish-purple necklace of skin discoloration.

Nathaniel stood quickly and returned to the collection of encyclopedias on the back wall. He asked to the books, "Did you need me, Miss Redmond?"

"I have a parting gift for you."

He shook his head. "No. No gifts."

"Why not?"

"Not necessary."

"What do you mean 'not necessary'? Of course it's necessary."

Nathaniel shook his head, circled around the desk and led her to the door.

"Look," Annette sighed as they approached the cabinet with the repaired library books on the way to the office's door. "It's not like I picked some crappy bagatelle from a twenty-four hour convenience store."

"Whatever it is, I'm not interested." He opened the door to the hallway.

Annette, who was pushed slightly out the door, stopped, turned and asked "Why not?"

"Still stuck on those same two words, are we?" He started to close the door an inch or two, hoping that she would take the hint to leave. Annette didn't take the hint and acted the role of an immovable doorstop. "See here, Miss Redmond. I appreciate that you want to revisit this, this, this . . ." evidently at a loss for the accurate word, he waved his hand as if shooing a fruit fly from his ear. ". . . This, whatever you call it."

". . . Bickering?"

"Thank you. Bickering."

"I didn't come here to bicker."

"Didn't you?" Nathaniel said dryly.

"I came here to say goodbye to a friend, Mr. Cauliflower. I wanted to give you a gift to show my appreciation for your hospitality." She added a brief addendum: "Unless . . ."

Nathaniel took his glasses off and massaged the bridge of his nose. "Unless, Miss Redmond?"

"Unless you'd prefer me to stay."

Nathaniel fitted his glasses back on his face and repeated, "Stay?"

"Would you like it if I stayed here, Monsieur Cauliflower?"

A part of him wanted Annette to stay. He wanted her to choose him over Adam and to remain in the afterlife where they would continue their bantering, which he thoroughly enjoyed despite what he had claimed. Nathaniel imagined, for a brief moment, a life where he and Annette would lose themselves in witty, perhaps borderline imprudently romantic repartee like leads in a screwball comedy. But the bruising around Annette's neck brought Nathaniel to the unforgiving actuality that congested his constructive excitement.

He looked Annette squarely in the eyes and said, "No. I don't want you to stay here."

"Then close your eyes," Annette ordered "and hold out your hands."

He closed his eyes and listened to suggestive acoustic sonances that might give him a clue as to the type of gift he was about to receive. He heard the scuffling of her footsteps. When he received the tenor of a cabinet's latch being unhooked, Nathaniel started to peek. He thought better of it when he heard the fabric of Annette's dress as she walked to him. Though Nathaniel guessed that Annette had opened the cabinet of repaired library books, he was stunned that the object was not the weight of a book but something lighter. With his eyes closed, he could determine that Annette took steps to her original position.

"May I open them?" he asked.

"Yes."

In his hands was a recognizable rain-blotted misdirected envelope that Annette, during her years as Evangeline, had neglected to deliver.

"Found it in a pile of items from your office when the department plummeted into Purgatory. It was sticking out of my copy of *Canterbury Tales*." They looked at the envelope then to each other. Annette smiled and said to Nathaniel, "I was hoping that, as a last field trip, and because we're in a habit of repairing damaged timelines, we might reexamine that off-course moment. And as I'm subsequently retired, you'll need to reassign my corresponding destiny from the broken record into someone else's capable hands."

Nathaniel felt a swell of outworn sentiments. All he could do was repeat Annette's words, "'one last field trip . . .'"

He looked at Annette and nodded. "Absolutely, Miss Redmond. Have no worries. From the moment we return you to your wedding with Mr. McCloud, your fortune will be someone else's problem. There's nothing that I can think of that will deter Management, or myself, to find a suitable replacement for the commission."

*

"Do you know why you can smell the rain before it arrives?" Jonas asked Harriet.

"What makes you think I'd care?" she said with a heaving, angry sigh.

"The zing in your nostrils as a storm approaches is the scent of ozone." As he said this, his grey eyes turned to one of the open archways. "The electrical charge of lightning as it splits atoms in our sky and also the smell of ozone as it's carried to higher altitudes by downdrafts. When rain arrives, the water repositions molecules on all manner of dry objects including vegetation or a paved street of concrete or asphalt. Some things, when struck by the rain, reveal a pleasant smell of the given surface while other odors can be foul. I love the smells right before a thunderstorm. They're idiosyncratic."

He turned his eyes from the archway to Harriet.

"It sort of reminds me of the aroma that I sense the longer I sit here with you."

Harriet, hearing this, glared at him. "I don't smell, thank you."

"Oh, Harriet."

She crossed to him with a balled fist. Jonas didn't blink. "Go on, say my name again. I dare you."

"You wouldn't stoop to the same level as your abusive father and ex-husband, would you? You remember those days of your father's red pick-up truck outside of your childhood home and how that stirred such hostility within. And those mornings, afternoons and evenings, covering up your bruises with your face cream and foundation and how you would, so often, stare at your reflection thinking 'I've become my mother.'"

There was a look of fury in Harriet's eyes. She raised her fist for a right-hook blow to Jonas' jaw line but, the longer she poised for attack, the more Jonas' words sunk in. The separate skies in the archways grew darker as the dense clouds formed. There were consecutive blazes of lightning and rolls of thunder as she righted herself and stared at him.

"You smell different because you're not like the muses here. You may act like the Head Muse protégé. You might play with your Lite-Brite pegs and eagerly await envelopes in your postbox. You might drink your water from the water coolers like everyone else. But you're not like them. There's something unique about you, isn't there? Something that you've been keeping from them that not even Annette, Lucas, Nathaniel or Fiona know. Something that runs deeper than your past abusive relationships but is ineradicably tied. Maybe you've been lying to yourself for the reason that, if they discovered what you really are, you wouldn't belong here. Am I right, Harriet?"

"How . . ." Harriet looked frightened. ". . . There's nothing different about me," she said defiantly. "I belong here! I. Belong. Here." Harriet grabbed the scuff of Jonas' shirt and screamed "Say it! Say 'There's nothing different about you. You belong here!'" Rain poured through the porches flooding the dark-stained wood. When Jonas didn't say it fast enough, she held him tighter. She shook him hard and said "Say it, you animal!"

"How can I say it if isn't true, Harriet?"

She felt hands on her shoulders and, in a fit of rage, spun to find Lucas offering a comforting embrace. Harriet's fury turned to severe melancholy. As Lucas consoled her, urging Harriet not to look at him, Jonas talked with his eyes out to one of the storms.

"Like the smell of an oncoming storm, you should've known I'd poke at you, Harriet. I mean, come on, with a battered woman like you who keeps lethal life-altering secrets from her co-workers so she can stay where she is, it's too easy! However, my beef isn't with you, or your blithering fairy friend. It resides with a definite cheeky ginger and her four-eyed friend to whom I must return."

There was a burst of lightning that set the floor on fire. A crash of thunder shook one of the boards loose from a porch banister. Howling wind ripped through the room bringing a sheet of rain to spatter their faces. Lucas and Harriet found the chair empty. The handcuffs, which had bound Jonas, swayed from side to side in the wind. They were latched but without a prisoner.

"Where did he go?" Harriet wanted to know. "Where did that bastard run to?"

Lucas searched the corners of his office and poked his head out to inspect the hallway. His face, and his clothes, were dripping wet. He turned to Harriet who looked both parts water-logged and emotionally wracked.

Lucas told Harriet while looking provoked, "He pulled a Harry Houdini, you know?"

*

A blue umbrella was opened by Annette as Nathaniel's office folded and unfolded into the same suburb street that had been abandoned during Evangeline's term. Strong wind gusts, pointed white strands of lightning, resounding thunder and sheets of rain shot from the billowing deep indigo cumulonimbus mass above. Here they were, standing in the same rain-soaked downdraft, about to put an end to a longstanding appointment.

Sadly, joining them was a surly Jonas who propped himself against the mailbox.

"This thundershower reminds me of the afternoon that you came to inspire me as a Ninth Generation muse, Annette," Jonas sneered. "That was the day that you told me about your work as an inspirer. It was the day that I challenged Management to show me the kind of procedure they had included you in so that perhaps I could fix everything to my liking. That same storm, once I died, latched on to me during my journeys. It's appropriate that you called me the Thunderstorm Man in your reports. I suppose you could say that the storm isn't a part of me. It is me. I intend to take that misdirected envelope and that destiny from your fingers. And I'm going to do so with your consent or not."

The wind became gradually tornadic bringing several microbursts in their circling periphery. Tree lines flattened, shingles shook and windows on the neighboring cul-de-sacs shattered. Lightning struck power lines bringing death to the lingering streetlights. Annette, with Nathaniel beside her, hurtled through golf-ball sized hailstones which punctured holes in neighborhood cars. Each draft of blustery weather acted as a series of punches similar to a thousand battering rams with the ferocity of fired cannon balls which tore at Annette as she landed at the foot of the mailbox. As she reached to open the latch, a flash flood engulfed the neighborhood submerging the street, cars and mailboxes. Though she and Nathaniel held tight to the mailbox the surging water's current was too strong. She was running out of air and losing consciousness. Nathaniel glanced at the envelope in Annette's hand, looking bereft.

His glasses were taken by the current which slightly blinded him. He could see streaks of igniting lightning beyond the water's surface. Debris weaved through the current. The mailbox slipped from the waterlogged sediment. Nathaniel tried, and failed, to keep the mailbox and Annette who clung to it. He was horrified as the mailbox, and its female lodger, were separated from him. Nathaniel had never learned how to swim. In the most placid of waters, he could barely tread or practice a decent backstroke. Despite this setback, Nathaniel dizzily pawed at the fuzzy, gurgling water bubbles. He felt powerless. He felt doomed to failure.

The inspiration folded and unfolded bringing with it a dispersing tributary. Leaving the thick river of water and the maelstrom in the pop-up book, Nathaniel collapsed to his knees gasping for air. A collision of wood and glass was heard. He could see the floorboards of his office but that was as far as his near-sighted vision would allow. He padded on his hands and knees until his fingers touched broken glass. He traced the glass to an overturned bookcase. Beneath the bookcase was Annette's outstretched arm and motionless hand which held the misdirected envelope.

"No . . ." Nathaniel gasped, checking Annette's wrist for a pulse. "No. No! Annette! Mademoiselle . . . Mademoiselle Evangeline?"

It wasn't Annette that answered. "You know, Broccoli . . ."

Nathaniel set his clammy forehead against Annette's cold skin.

". . . If you stop and think about it, history is filled with many ways to die. Being pushed off an attic loft, burned alive by an overturned kerosene lamp . . . or several lamps depending on how many you have in your collection . . ." There came another breakdown of glass and a wave of fire that ate the floorboards. Nathaniel could tell, from the sound and temperature, that Jonas had smashed several of the kerosene lamps forcing his office to a conflagration. "Stabbed to death by garden shears, choked by a string of Christmas lights. But there's something about seeing your beloved bookworm crushed under the weight of your library books that adds certain flavor to this verse."

There was a crunching of his glasses that announced Jonas' shoes as they stepped closer. Nathaniel opened his unfocused eyes to see Jonas' hand as it snatched the envelope.

"I gave her a chance to live, Broccoli. And she chose wrong. I also gave you time to conform but you wouldn't. You brought this upon yourself, step-brother. Remember that, in what little time we have left in Management's afterlife. The Sisters are prepared to change everything."

Jonas' hand, and the envelope, disappeared from sight. His footsteps became faint.

Fire reflected in the shards of glass at Nathaniel's fingertips. There were explosions as the remaining kerosene lamps tipped and added size to the blaze. He could smell the scent of burning leather and ashen paper as the encyclopedias caught fire. He could smell the melting acrylics on the canvases. Though he couldn't see it, Nathaniel knew that his office was destroyed. It mirrored the state of his heart upon looking at Annette.

He stood and turned to the door of his office. With a limp in his step, Nathaniel found the blurred image of Jonas who walked the hallway to the waiting room door. Gathering as much energy as he could, Nathaniel stumbled toward Jonas. He shoved himself into his step-brother who came into plain view. A struggle ensued in the waiting room. The nine identical chairs were overturned. The single black and white clock on the wall collapsed to the floor.

Nathaniel snapped the dandelion key free from Jonas' chain. Without a candle, Nathaniel made his own optimistic wish. Nathaniel grabbed the knob of the asphodel door at the far corner of the waiting room. He inserted and twisted the key clockwise. The door swung open. Nathaniel elbowed Jonas inside. Where there would have typically been a swirling white light, there was a vaulted crypt. Though he couldn't see where he'd taken Jonas, Nathaniel could only ascertain from its smell of rot and decay that the sealed tomb was made of profoundly dense dry stone and packed sand. He ripped the misdirected envelope from Jonas' hand and shoved him into the blackness. Nathaniel heard the overturning of stone jars as Jonas fell to the floor.

"Where have you and that door taken me?" Jonas wanted to know as he scraped at the floor to regain a comfortable stance.

Nathaniel didn't have anything more to say to his step-brother. He headed to the open door and the waiting room's yellow rectangle of light.

"Broccoli, where are we?" Jonas tried to stand but tripped over unseen objects.

By now, Nathaniel had stopped at the door and considered the set of ancient Egyptian hieroglyphs in the nearest stone. The markings were made visible by the hallway light. Nathaniel stepped from the threshold of the ancient Egyptian crypt and closed the door sealing Jonas within.

From Jonas' perspective, when he found his footing he ambled through the shadows expecting to find the door. What he felt was the cold inescapable stone of his imperishable, pitch-black cage which was void of helpful Lite-Brite boards and transitory thunderstorms.

In the waiting room, Nathaniel turned the key in the dandelion keyhole and locked the Thunderstorm Man inside his own burial place where the grating discouragements could no longer be heard. Nathaniel pressed his forehead against the wood. He pocketed the key and found a fistful of asphodels at his feet. To Nathaniel, the flowers trumpeted the conclusion of Jonas' period of influence.

Icarus' fuzzy shape, which sat in one of the waiting room chairs, spoke to Nathaniel with a shaky voice. "That door, Mr. Cauliflower," the wingless mythological hero looked at the asphodel entrance. "That's the one that my father, Daedalus the door maker, found in his workshop, isn't it?"

Nathaniel didn't want to talk about the door or its origins. As confirmation, he respectfully handed Icarus the asphodels and walked through the smoke to the fire-picked bones that was his office.

*

In his private bathroom, as the fire raged only in his private office, Nathaniel cradled Annette. She had suffered from massive internal bleeding and outwardly noticeable cuts from the shards of glass. She lay motionless in his arms and was without breath. Emotionless, he dipped a spare, clean hand towel into the water basin. Carefully and slowly he brought the moistened towel to Annette's lacerated skin and dragged the plush fabric from her unmoving shoulders to her static elbows. He cleaned her forearms and non-trembling fingertips. Nathaniel closed his eyes and, for the last time, thought of the culminated moments that had brought him here. The towel was rinsed of her blood. It was moistened and reapplied. He patiently washed the cuts and removed the glass from her broken neck. As Nathaniel washed her face he reflected on Annette and the lives that she had touched. Nathaniel remembered their bickering. He recalled her smiles when she had laughed at something Nathaniel had said. He deliberated on the visions of her frowns, her scowls, and the expressions of her pent-up frustrations.

"I love you," he whispered to Annette. "That's why I didn't want you to stay. I couldn't imagine seeing you vulnerable in this kind of environment."

He placed the crimson-stained towel into the basin.

Though Annette was stock-still, Nathaniel held her. "You asked me once, Annette, what my favorite story was. I never gave you a real answer. I've read many books in the lifetimes that I've lived but there's been one story that I've loved. That story, Annette, is yours." He looked to the white tiles of his bathroom. Nathaniel gave a sigh and closed his eyes giving a confession: "You were the greatest library book that I've ever checked out from Management's collection."

For at least ten minutes, Nathaniel held her and warmly remembered their story from start to finish. Despite remembering what there was to recollect, Nathaniel felt starved for more. But he knew that there wasn't more.

Feeling a hand on his cheek, Nathaniel found Annette was awake. Her raised right hand was placed on his cheek. She looked at him attentively. In the same miraculous manner that he had repaired the library books in his life, Annette had been stitched! There were no signs of cuts or bruises or markings on her of any kind. As she smiled at him, and he gazed at her, Nathaniel couldn't help but to live in this perfect moment – those exceptional seconds that resounded following his most unanticipated considerable salvages.

*

A hammering of a post into the ground could be heard in the early morning air. The skies were clear. A single sparrow flew from one downed tree branch to another. The resulting damage of the recent suburban flood was overwhelming to witness. But there was a sliver of hope that presented itself: a lone, brand new mailbox which had been erected by Annette and Nathaniel. To anyone who noticed the mailbox it was a sign that promised, amidst chaos in any capacity throughout history, there will be a point in time charged with a serene hope to rebuild.

CHAPTER 28: CONCLUDING DEPARTURES

Directly after public speaker Edgar Allan Poe's speech, he was taken to his own time believing what he'd seen in the department to have been a fleeting dream. He had been brought to the muses after his brother, Henry, had died due to an illness partially related to alcoholism in 1831. He was returned on the same day where he fervently resurrected his prolific writing and publishing career thusly creating the well-known works that exist in anthologies at present.

As the group retirement party was exhausted of its mirages, the Nine Greatest Muses huddled at the end of the hallway. There were six candlelit pies on an office desk. Beside the pies were the respective ivory boxes labeled "Know Thyself" in Greek. While Nathaniel held the boxes open for the retiring muse he was dressed in a spare outfit of a white dress shirt, brown corduroy pants with matching suspenders and loosened necktie. He wore a second pair of glasses which granted him vision of the muses as they assembled. Fiona, wearing her baby blue pants suit, held the candle-topped pies.

Anna Pavlova placed her object of memory, a pair of ballet shoes, inside the box. She made a wish and blew out the candle activating the swirling light from the waiting room's asphodel door. As she walked to her respective timeline, Paul Lawrence Dunbar unhurriedly discarded his object. Forfeiting his memories, Mr.

Andrews blew out the candle on his own apple pie and strode into Heaven which, for a brief instance, smelled of a clean sea breeze.

Icarus stepped forward. He didn't break his stare as he placed the feather inside the ivory box of knowledge. He stopped in front of Fiona and thought about his wish. He blew the flame out with a single puff.

"Are you absolutely sure that's what you want, Icarus?" Fiona asked him.

He turned his eyes to Lucas who was in line. Icarus' look of longing was short. While looking at Lucas, Icarus nodded. He turned to Fiona. The dazzling illumination was replaced by familiar Purgatorial warehouse lights.

"What are you doing?" Lucas shouted. He rushed to Icarus and held him. "Whatever horrible things you've done, Icarus, whatever awful things have brought you here – you don't deserve Purgatory. You don't deserve to have your soul eaten like that, you know? You, Icarus, are whole. Gabriel once told me 'You're here to live in the happiness of which we all lose track. You are here; here is a start. Because no matter where you go, or come from, you can start where you are!'" Lucas turned to Fiona and Nathaniel in tears. "Am I right? Please tell me I'm right!"

"This door was meant for me, Lucas," Icarus told him. When Lucas turned to him, Icarus went on in saying, "My destiny isn't in Heaven. Nor is it through reincarnation."

"Your destiny shouldn't be a punishment!"

"Who said it's a punishment?" Icarus asked with a furrowed brow. "If anything, it's an adventure. An unwritten epic poem that needs a hero to challenge its dragons."

Lucas shook his head. "I don't see it as such . . ."

Icarus took Lucas' hands in his. He kissed him on the right cheek and whispered, "I'm not expecting you to."

Icarus released his friend's hands and slowly walked into the warehouse of Purgatory. Icarus turned to see Lucas and eventually disappeared into the shadows of forgetfulness.

When the light from the asphodel door returned, Nathaniel opened the lid of Lucas' ivory memory box.

Lucas scrutinized the box and felt for the guitar pick in his pocket. The grip on the pick was so strong that it left a tear-shaped indentation in Lucas' palm.

"I refuse to accept this curse of loneliness that Management's put me under. They took Gabriel from me and now Icarus? No. I'm not going to forget," Lucas told both his caretaker and Head Muse. The flickering candle on his personal cherry pie was then snuffed. "I'm going to find him and bring him back."

Hearing these words, Nathaniel wanted to stop him. He wanted to warn Lucas of the perils that came from journeying to find someone who didn't want to be found. At this moment, as he looked into Lucas' eyes, he could see himself as Fiona had seen Nathaniel while in hot pursuit of his reincarnated female companion. Like Nathaniel, there were lessons regarding the heart and jaunts that had to be explored, which Lucas needed to experience for firsthand.

With the pick still in hand, Lucas gave a nod to Nathaniel and Fiona. He looked at Harriet and Annette who stood waiting. Lucas waved at his best friend in her wedding dress and also to his own client, Harriet, whom he had inspired during his former term. The warehouse of barn lights returned. He exhaled deeply. With the music swelling within his spirit and the guitar pick in hand, Lucas began his expedition to dynamically reclaim what had gone missing from his heart.

"I suppose that leaves me," Annette said quietly as she stood in her recently re-stitched wedding gown. "I don't have an object to put into my memory box, do I? You had originally intended those sixty-eight violet envelopes to do the trick but it was your words that caused me to recall being the Ninth Generation muse."

Nathaniel spoke up first. "The three violet envelopes gave you back your memories. Not my words. However, due to those unforeseen circumstances, Fiona and I have something special that will take your memories. I'll give you the time-sensitive trinket when we return to your wedding day."

She approached Fiona and the flame-topped candle it held in the latticed strawberry rhubarb pie. Fiona asked Annette, "Are you ready to go home?"

Annette looked at Nathaniel who nodded slightly while looking at the candle atop her pastry.

Harriet was in Annette's line of sight who nervously bit her lip as the bride gave a goodbye.

Annette blew out the candle. The light from the waiting room door shone once more. With it came the sound of chirping birds in nearby branches, the sweet scent of fresh-picked yellow tulips and the tread of the church's parlor carpet underfoot. Prior to reinserting herself back into her own timeline, Annette surveyed the hallway of the department. She looked from floor to ceiling as if recalling what she had come to learn as a person and muse . . . and then crossed the drape of white. It was laced with the smell of honeysuckle as she crossed into the shining daylight of her mid-afternoon marriage.

*

Nathaniel soaked in Annette's reflection as she nervously ran her hands along the front fabric of her wedding dress. Her red hair had been put up into a solid bun of hair-sprayed curls. Her sculpted bangs had been positioned to the left. Her lips had been polished with a nude gloss. She wore a moss-based eye shadow to match the natural green in her eyes which were accentuated with thin black eyeliner.

Though to Nathaniel she looked exquisite, Annette sighed. "Something's missing," she said into the mirror. "I can't put my finger on it."

"Allow me," Nathaniel interposed. He approached her from behind and, with steady hands, took the opal necklace from around his neck and fastened it around hers. The stone fit perfectly. As Annette opened her mouth to object, Nathaniel captioned his gift in explaining, "Something old." He reached into his pocket and took out the two wedding rings from the black hoodie pocket. He dropped them into her open right hand. To this exchange, he added: "Something new." From another pocket, he extracted a small navy blue jewelry box. Nathaniel circled round and met Annette's gaze and opened the lid. Inside were Fiona's pearl earrings. "Something borrowed" He held a blue-colored Lite-Brite peg and placed it into the petals of her bouquet of yellow roses. "And the peg of Sarah Milbourne which started this whole mess that brought you to me. This makes your 'Something blue.'"

Annette hesitated. "I don't know what to say."

"It's the least we could do, considering what you've done for us. For Management."

"I could do more . . ." Annette told Nathaniel.

For a brief moment, a tongue-tied silence existed.

He took the pearl earrings out of the box. "You've done more than enough."

"Have I, Mr. Cauliflower?" When it was obvious that Nathaniel didn't have anything else to say on the matter, Annette took the pearl earrings and fit them in her ears. She looked at herself in the mirror and was openly satisfied with her up-to-the-minute appearance. "And what of the object that's going to take my memory?"

"The rings," Nathaniel spoke softly.

Annette studied the rings in the daylight.

"When Adam puts the ring on your finger, you'll forget being one of the Nine Greatest Muses and prior memories. When you put the ring on Adam's finger, he too will forget what's transpired."

There came a gentle knock at the closed parlor door. Annette and Nathaniel broke eye contact. Annette turned to the door as she heard Adam's voice.

"Annette," Adam timidly called, "Are you in there?"

"Yes, Adam, I'm here," Annette answered.

"I'm glad, you have no idea. When you left me I wasn't sure if you were coming. That is to say, I hoped you would. I know that I've done unspeakable things but I wanted to reassure you that everything I did was so that we could be reunited." He paused and, when Annette didn't respond, Adam went on. "I didn't tell the other muses this, but I did remember our past life together."

As Adam said the word memories, Annette looked down at the rings.

"The memories didn't come at once. In fact, the only memory that I had at the beginning came after I brushed my finger along one of the dusty empty bookshelves on the wall at the store. Memories resurfaced later but that initial memory was of the day you and I met in our first lives. I was reorganizing the history section when I found you, or at least the past version of yourself as a muse named Annette Slocum. I remembered how beautiful you looked that day standing there in *The Muse's Corner*. And how, even at that short-lived moment, I knew we were destined for one another. After everything, I believe that. Don't you?"

Annette didn't answer.

"Say 'yes,'" Nathaniel whispered.

She gave Nathaniel a sharp look for butting in. "Yes," Annette blurted loud enough for Adam to hear. "Yes, Adam, I do."

"If there's any way we could forget it happened and move forward, oh man. I would jump at the opportunity to get it right a second time."

Annette shot a look to Nathaniel who raised his eyebrows and cupped her fingers around the rings.

*

Pachelbel's Canon played as the wedding party processed down the aisle. Nathaniel, who stood beyond the sanctuary's rear doors, watched with finality as the ring bearer, a stocky young fellow of nine years, paraded with his pillow held high so the congregation could see. He was followed by the flower girl who Nathaniel roughly guessed to be about the same age. She tossed tulip petals to the ground as she approached the groomsmen, bridesmaids, priest and Annette's groom-to-be.

Annette was in the back of the church with, who Nathaniel guessed, was her father in her second life. Her full attention was focused on the procession. As the wedding march erupted from the church organ pipes, Annette took her first steps to her future and, justly so, her last steps from Nathaniel and the world of the muses. As she entered the sanctuary, heads turned. The congregation rose to their feet and gasped in admiration of her beauty.

The remaining three muses stood at the doors as Annette reached the front altar where the two lovers met with joyful smiles. The march ended and the priest, after a brief pause, requested that the congregation "Please be seated."

Nathaniel sullenly dug his hands into his pockets as Annette's father handed her to Adam's care. The preacher began the service.

"Dearly beloved, we are gathered here today in the sight of God to join this man, Adam Eustace McCloud, and this woman, Annette Liliana Redmond, in holy matrimony . . ."

The priest's reading spoke of marriage being a union of "two hearts" but his words were garbled as Fiona, in an audible aside to Harriet, said "And think, Harriet, once we return to the department, you have one peg before you so aptly take on the role of Head Muse, which I know you've been eager to obtain."

"Yes," Harriet's voice cracked a bit as she said to Fiona. "I suppose I am . . ."

Nathaniel, suffering from his misophonia and annoyance to certain sounds, which in this case was the sound of the two women talking over the ceremony, stepped forward to hear better the tail end of the priest's speech.

"Do you, Adam Eustace McCloud," the priest asked the groom, "take Annette Liliana Redmond to be your lawfully wedded wife, promising to love and cherish, through joy and sorrow, sickness and health, and whatever challenges you may face, for as long as you both shall live?"

Adam seized the ring from the boy and took Annette's hand. "I do . . ."

Not wanting to see any more, Nathaniel turned his back on the wedding. He started to go but Fiona stopped him.

"Will you be alright on your own, Mr. Cauliflower? Honestly and truly?"

Without turning to see Annette's blissful proclamation, Nathaniel nodded and said to his Head Muse, "Aren't I always?"

When he arrived to the department in the afterlife, Nathaniel's obsessive mind worked industriously as it had earlier. With the illusions of the retirement party having faded, leaving the plainness of the inspirational hallway and offices, Nathaniel secured the ivory memory boxes behind the mural of the original muses in the conference room. Nathaniel took the broom to the hallway tiled floors. He buffed and waxed the tiled floor until it sparkled under the newly installed replacement energy-efficient bulbs of the ceiling, which he also installed for safe measure. The post boxes were repositioned by the doorless offices and awaited envelopes. Not yet knowing who would be arriving in the wave of Generations, Nathaniel replaced the old decorations of the recently retired muses and draped rooms with four uniform barren egg-shell walls.

He started with the office of thunderstorms. Taking an axe to the wooden glass cabinet with the ten-digit combination lock, he splintered it into brushwood and tossed the fragments through one of the hall's nine different archways. He kept the framed photographs of the Nine Greatest Muses and discarded everything else. The blowing wind carried the pages of his manuscript and divided the passages until all that was left were miniscule pages flapping at a distance in the approaching storm's perspective. Along with his manuscript, he unscrewed the jars that contained both the twenty-one dead dandelions and the single torn ledger page. Nathaniel soberly permitted the wind to carry these portions. He reached into his pockets and emptied them of items. He took a special moment to toss the glow-in-the-dark star into the tempestuous chasm as if flipping a coin into the expanse. As the illusions disappeared, taking Nathaniel's prized memorials with them, he stood in the center of the office with the nine picture frames in hand. He considered the disinfected office for a short time. He then headed to the adjoining offices to further fumigate.

The living Grecian beach with its waves crashing upon sandy shores was stripped. The Russian cityscape and a brilliantly sculpted ballet studio complete with elegant mirrors and hardwood floors were torn down in seconds without a single dust mote left as a reminder. The Titanic in its gleaming majesty set sail and was replaced with nothing more than an empty cabin of plaster and dry-mold. Evangeline's obsolete office of sculpted ribbed vaults and elaborately constructed columns crumbled silently into a sinkhole until it was rid of anything equally as spectacular. Office after office, the department was peeled of its preceding miracles until it looked no different than any other empty organization that one might find on any given quiet weekend.

In his space, which held its unsightly façade from the extinguished fire, Nathaniel gave it his own special touch. The dandelion key was hung on a hook by his office door. He repaired encyclopedias of destinies that had been turned to dust and ash in the blaze. A broom and dustpan were utilized as the broken kerosene lamps were swept into a pile. Instead of repairing them Nathaniel purged the office of those that had been damaged and, more importantly, those that had not. With the same axe that he had used to break apart the cabinet in the Hall of Thunderstorms, Nathaniel took it to the wooden bookcase that held the repaired library books. He didn't second-guess himself as he tossed the library books in with the kerosene lamps. In short, Nathaniel took leaps to rid his division of anything excess that tenuously referred to his affairs with Evangeline or any of her reincarnations.

He did, however, restore the paintings of the muses that had been burned. The canvases were kept to serve as an archive for the muses that had inspired within Management's afterlife asylum. Annette's picture was intentionally displayed farther back than the others. It was completely hidden by repulsive unremitting occultation. He also kept the kitchen in the firm belief of his skills to feed his hungry employees with the memorized recipes.

Instinctively, Nathaniel set seven empty canvases on independent easels. They faced inward toward his reception desk. He produced a carved wooden box from within a desk drawer. He removed five tubes of acrylic paint: the three primary colors, white and black. Nathaniel removed a set of brushes: round, flat, bright, filbert, angle, mop, fan and rigger bristles, each in various sizes. The tools were set on the surface of his desk and placed perfectly side by side. He set out a square pallet in knowing that, at any moment, his hand would tingle with the approach of the forthcoming unfamiliar muse candidates.

He stared at the framed photographs of the Nine Greatest Muses. Suddenly motionless, Nathaniel could feel his emotions. He turned his eyes to Annette Slocum's snapshot and placed it face-down on his desk. To distract himself, Nathaniel seized the framed developed image of Fiona. But holding her picture reminded him of the Christmas Eve in the snow when he had waved to Annette Redmond. He also set Fiona's picture face-down.

He spotted the corner of a used white envelope peeking out from the back of Fiona's frame. He unfastened the back and took out the envelope which held something weightless inside. Nathaniel opened the flap to find a lone black screw which appeared to have been tossed into a fire at some point in history. When he turned the envelope over to see if it had been addressed, Nathaniel's hands trembled. There was an image drawn on the front of the envelope: the sketch of a cane's tip topped with a small pewter brain. Handwritten atop the drawing were two initials: M.J.

Nathaniel looked with recognition and said the name to whom he believed it belonged: "Mr. Jolly . . ."

He then focused on an extra easel that he hadn't placed amidst the group of his studio. On it was the painting that he had created in the attic loft in 1807; the acrylic visage of the Dandelion Sisters' circus tent. Where the painting had shown three young girls looking at him, he found the front flap was painted closed. There, in the icon, he noticed the sign announcing the cost of admission for fortunes told. Planted beside the sign was an identifiable cane similar to the one Mr. Jolly had brandished on his visits. It was identical to the etched walking stick on the screw's envelope. He wasn't sure what it meant, or how it pertained to things related to his Head Muse, but apart from its significance the painting was another slap in the face to remind

431

Nathaniel of his loss. To make matters worse, he wished Annette was there with him to help him find the answers.

As the normal colored pegs, including Harriet's final assignment, fell into his inbox, Nathaniel looked away. He tried to ignore the thoughts in his head. Try as hard as he might, Nathaniel couldn't stop the emotions. He suddenly felt consumed by them entirely. Nathaniel, who until this point had shed one tear in the sum of his employment, began to weep uncontrollably. As his body jerked in constant convulsions, he buried his face in his palms and bawled.

Yes, history is hectic with haunting mysteries eventually resolved. It is filled with long-forgotten secrets that, over the years, are spoken in due course. It is perverse with poorly-lit backstairs and catacombs of warriors, malefactors, unreciprocated tales of staunch adulation and wrenching anguish, ancient ledgers of ill-meaning agendas and disheartened reverie. It is overrun with the badlands of battles, of inactive hankerings, of unstable first steps and wayfarers in the hunt for ghosts of their explorations to revisit.

However, anyone can become so sidetracked by these details to notice the most imperative, time-honored inquest that history can educate. It's a subject that the original muse of times past, Clio, so often invited in her day. It was a three word message of hope that Nathaniel, in his current misery, learned in the following way:

Looking from his tears, he found Annette standing in front of him in her wedding dress. She regarded him with full recognition, love and devotion which was authenticated as she tossed him the wedding ring smiling playfully.

Nathaniel fumbled for the wedding ring and held it in his hands. He looked at the wedding band. He turned his eyes to Annette, speechless. His heart pumped heavily, not fully believing that she was standing there. The emotional brick wall of his heart tumbled. For the first time since 1807, Nathaniel sanctioned himself to smile. Much to his amazement, his joy was presented wider with each passing second than he had ever thought it possible.

And so, it came to pass that with a shrug of her shoulders and explicitly openly perplexed hands, Annette proposed history's chief captivating enigma in asking Nathaniel, "What happens next?"

ACKNOWLEDGEMENTS

Thank you to my editors: Debbie Toalson Jacobs, Susan Hayden and JD Nichols who helped to bring Nathaniel's words to maturity. A huge amount of gratitude to my "sounding board" officiates: Gary Coffman, Peter Miller, Floyd Burton, Samantha Lee Wallace, Eva Justice, Drew Scholl, Susan Summers, Ashley Hanley and JoAnna Wilkerson. Thank you to Don and Angela Ovens, Susan Baker, Chris Hays, Leslie and Mark Stock, DeeDee Folkerts, Earl Coleman, Erin Kolks, Meg Phillips, Bev Pfeffer, Robin Morrison, Martha Bollinger, Julia Chappelle-Thomas, Jessica Biddle, Brianna McGuire, Damita Kynard, Jaime Cravens, Edie Diel, Adam Espey, Linda Ferris, Van Hawxby, Mila Jam, Alex Kirby, the Knipe family, Lester Parkerson, Mike Morgan, Brian Miller, Kelley Shriner, Tom Skinner, Becky Sterling, Joanie Sorrels, Ashley Stephens, Tracy McCray, Daphne Sias, Jordan Powell and so many others I could name who have always supplied guiding positivity when I needed it the most.

Love and admiration goes out to both sides of my family for being there to help inspire me through each and every day. I'm also thankful for my church family at First Baptist Church in Columbia, Missouri. Thank you also to the members of the writer's group circle who still keep in touch: Erika Woehlk and Aaron Young. My love and appreciation goes out to my friends and co-workers at State Farm both in Columbia, Missouri and Richardson, Texas. Also a shout out the managers and crews at both the Barnes and Nobles in Columbus, Georgia and also Columbia, Missouri. Thank you to all of my friends and comrades, both onstage and off, involved with Columbia Entertainment Company. Thank you to all of the friends, family, other random individuals, and coffee houses with outlet plugs in Plano, Texas and Columbia, Missouri and Columbus, Georgia who have helped to make this book a success.

A personal thanks goes to the random stranger who played the violin to his friends outside of my apartment that long ago night. Thank you to Hasbro for inventing the Lite-Brite along with all the colored pegs that go along with it. Thank you to Mother Nature for all of the inspiring thunderstorms that came my way. I'd like to send gratitude out to my own unrequited "Evangeline" (who shall remain nameless). Finally, in closing, an unconventional "thank you" to those who have passed away during the making of this book: Lisbeth Yasuda, Renee Kite, David Kent Toalson, Barbara Toalson, Everett "Jake" Jacobs and Norene Wood.

About the Author

This is David's second novel.

When David is not writing, he enjoys ghost hunting and can often be found acting and entertaining audiences on the community stage. He also loves to draw and paint, finding comfort in anything creative.

David lives in Columbia, Missouri.

Contact the Author

https://www.facebook.com/DavidPJacobsAuthor/

Twitter:
@DPJMuseAuthor

www.davidpjacobs.com

Made in the USA
Lexington, KY
16 February 2017